TIME TUNNEL:

THE TWIN TOWERS

RICHARD TODD

Time Tunnel: The Twin Towers

By Richard Todd

ISBN: 978-0-578-52240-1

Library of Congress Control Number:2019907460

Dedicated to the heroes of 9/11

-- TOP SECRET --

DEPARTMENT OF THE ARMY
DREAMLAND RESEARCH FACILITY

MEMORANDUM THRU **28 OCT 2008**
TIMELINE 001

GENERAL AARON CRAIG
COMMANDING GENERAL
DREAMLAND RESEARCH FACILITY

FOR FILE

SUBJECT: [redacted] Mission, 27 October 2008

The purpose of this memo is to acknowledge the mishap that occurred on 27 October, 2008 in the course of the first [redacted] mission, as well as to outline preliminary contingency steps. The cause of the accident is unknown at this time. Due to compromised security at the [redacted] Complex that occurred as a direct result of the accident, a thorough review of the cause is problematic in the short term. It is unknown whether the cause of the problem lies in the [redacted] displacement technology or is the fault of human error or lapses in judgment.

The first priority of this office is to secure the facility. Once this is accomplished, senior staff will be directed to execute a comprehensive evaluation of system and personnel in order to determine the proximate cause of the accident. Once the cause is identified and resolved, recommendations will be solicited from senior staff regarding options to correct the damage caused as a result of the accident.

At this time, the status of Lieutenant Colonel [redacted] is MIA. It is not known at this time whether Lieutenant Colonel [redacted] has knowledge of the Colonel's location or present status.

The events that transpired yesterday are a direct result of my orders. I assume full responsibility.

Respectfully,

Aaron T. Craig
FG, USA
Commanding General
Dreamland Research Facility

-- TOP SECRET --

Soho Grand Hotel

New York, NY
September 10, 2001
09:12 hours

Kyle Mason opened his eyes. Next to him was the cavity of a vacant white pillow. The head that had rested there was gone. In its place, a strand of long black hair lay tucked into the pillow's ample folds.

He heard shuffling and looked up. At the foot of his bed, a tall young woman with brown skin and near waist-length black hair was pulling a maroon blouse around her braless torso. She buttoned up only halfway, allowing the tails to fall over her jeans.

"I didn't want to wake you," the beautiful woman said with a loving smile.

Kyle sat up in bed, returning her smile, rubbing sleep and sandy hair from his eyes. The sheet fell away from his chest.

Padma's eyes lit up. She thought Kyle looked like a god.

While the Army had buffed him, Special Forces had chiseled his six-foot-plus frame into an angled physique that his skinny former self had not thought possible.

Padma sat down on the end of the bed to pull on her boots.

"Where are you going?" asked Kyle.

"Out for coffee," replied Padma.

"We can get room service," said Kyle, pretending he didn't know what she was really up to.

"I prefer Starbucks," replied Padma, looking at him over her shoulder.

"You prefer American Spirits," Kyle said, referring to her favorite cigarettes.

Padma shot him a look, then got up and walked around to his side of the bed. Behind her was an overcast south-facing view of New York City. The colossal Twin Towers of the World Trade Center filled the window's landscape view.

Padma placed her hands against Kyle's cheeks and leaned in to kiss him. A fresh diamond sparkled on her ring finger.

"I like married women," Kyle said between kisses.

"I like being a married woman," smiled Padma.

She stroked a fresh tattoo on the inside of Kyle's right forearm. The crisp, black character was the feminine form of "Padma" in Sanskrit. The tattoo, less than a day old, was outlined with Kyle's inflamed red skin.

पद्मा

Padma reached for the dog tags hanging around Kyle's neck.

"I'm married to Major Kyle Mason," she said. "My parents are going to be so pissed."

"Pissed because you eloped or pissed because you married beneath you?" Kyle asked.

"Yes," she replied.

Padma stroked Kyle's chest with her fingers.

"It's not you," Padma explained. "You know they like you. They're just old-fashioned. "They wanted me to marry a doctor or a lawyer in a traditional ceremony."

"What's it called?" asked Kyle. "Viv…viva…"

"*Vivaah sanskar*," Padma replied. "I wear henna. You ride in on a white horse."

"I'd look good on a white horse," Kyle said.

"No doubt," affirmed Padma.

"So, you wear henna. Do you wear anything else?"

Padma leaned in to kiss Kyle.

"Nothing else for you, love," she said.

Their kisses heated up. Kyle reached into Padma's blouse. After permitting him to fondle her for a few moments, she took his hand and kissed it.

"Hold that thought. I'll be back in 20 with coffee."

Kyle glanced at the lump under the covers. "If you're not back in 20, it's not my thoughts I'll be holding."

Padma laughed and grabbed her black duffle coat on the way out of the hotel room.

"I'll be back soon, love," she said.

Kyle beamed in her wake. He couldn't believe his good fortune. He was newly wed to the most beautiful woman on the planet, and he was at the zenith of his career.

Against the wishes of Padma's traditional East Indian parents, she and Kyle had eloped the day before in a private civil ceremony at City Hall. New York's City Hall was, at once, the world's most and least romantic place to get hitched. With its long lines and numbered queuing system, it had all the allure of a traffic ticket processing center. Still, there was something exhilarating about the act of elopement—ignoring parents' commands like bad children.

Kyle jumped out of bed and picked up the phone to order room service. While on hold, he stood naked in front of the window, gazing at the metropolis. He hoped breakfast would be waiting for his bride when she returned. He knew she didn't normally eat much at the beginning of the day—he ordered wheat toast, fruit, and coffee. He wanted everything to be perfect during their short honeymoon in NYC. His generosity had already brought her to tears. She knew he had spent every last cent of his savings on her ring and their Soho Grand suite. Kyle's largess was not driven by pride—Padma's compensation was over ten times his military pay, and he had no illusions about who the breadwinner of the family was going to be. His Magi's gift was motivated by nothing more than a genuine desire to make his bride happy. Before she met Kyle, money had been little more than a number to Padma. With this gesture, he had made it meaningful to her.

What Kyle lacked in cash, he made up for in raw heroic talent. After graduating at the top of his class from West Point, he had become one of the youngest soldiers to receive a Silver Star for gallantry when his Humvee platoon came under fire from an Iraqi tank platoon in Operation Desert Storm. Though severely outnumbered and outgunned, a combination of quick thinking and guile translated certain defeat into a stunning victory for the freshly minted lieutenant. Kyle knew he had been very lucky. He also knew that luck mattered.

With this tailwind from his Desert Storm experience, Kyle applied to the Army's parachutist course, aka "Airborne School," then to the Ranger Assessment and Selection Program. After a tour as an Army Ranger, he applied to become a member of the 1st Special Forces Operational Detachment—Delta, more commonly known as Delta Force.

Padma was drawn to the danger of Kyle's job. Her world could not have been more different from his. She was a vice president at a Wall Street investment bank called Cantor Fitzgerald. Her life was consumed by numbers—numbers that translated into money.

At 35, she was a couple years older than Kyle. Padma had completed her undergraduate work at Columbia and then received her MBA from Stanford, graduating summa cum laude. Suitors from marquee firms like Goldman Sachs, Morgan Stanley, and JPMorgan pursued the gorgeous prodigy with lucrative job offers.

Padma found that she was very good at what she did, more than a match for the guys in the old boys' club, but she felt something was missing in her artificial world of numbers.

Padma had tried to explain her job to Kyle, but the convolutions of exotic derivatives made his eyes glaze over in half the time required to boil an egg. Padma loved their strangely conversed naivetés—Kyle was one of the world's preeminent masters of real life and death, yet he was so innocent about her cutthroat world of big money. She smiled knowingly when the guys in her shop beat their chests about their latest "kill." Padma knew better. She thought about her man with enormous pride, knowing the billionaire banker boys didn't have the first clue what they were talking about. Kyle was her lightning rod to the real world—the physical world, where decisions were truly permanent. She loved him completely, and though she knew how much she would worry when he was away, the thought of what he did for a living sent an electric thrill up her spine. Though the tempo of her work was a burnout pace, and the dialect was machismo, no one had ever died at the World Trade Center in the line of duty of investment banking.

Kyle walked to the bathroom to cleanup, wrapping a towel around his waist. The bathroom was beautiful—a black-on-white toile at chest level, with polished black bricks below. It was large by New York hotel standards, with his-and-her sinks. Her toiletries and toothbrush were next to the right-hand sink—his toiletries faced hers on the left. His bathroom toiletries would never be lonely again. He loved everything about being married to her.

Kyle rubbed the beard on his angular jaw, which framed an easy smile. Green eyes stared back at him from the mirror. He brushed back his sandy hair, which he had let grow well beyond a standard military buzz. In order to blend, many Delta operators let their hair and beards grow, depending on their assignment.

Kyle brushed his teeth, and then lathered up to shave. He heard the chirp of the electronic door latch.

"What'd you forget, hon?" he shouted from the bathroom.

He lowered his head in the sink to splash water on his face, then reached for a towel. He looked in the mirror. Someone was standing behind him.

"FUCK!" he yelled.

In the mirror's reflection, there was not one Kyle Mason, but two.

Corona, NM

July 6, 1947
02:40 hours

A tentacle of blue-white lightning cracked the pitch desert sky, silhouetting nine soldiers. Thunder pounded the men, rattling the ground. The soldiers were draped in drab olive-colored rubber ponchos to protect them from the pouring rain. The dark terrain was illuminated only by the soldiers' crookneck flashlights and the flashes of lightning.

A lightning bolt struck the ground. Its powerful thunderclap was instant.

"Jesus, Sarge!" shouted Corporal Rooney over the echoes of thunder rolling across the desert. "If that one had been any closer, we woulda been gonners!"

"We've been out here in this storm for hours," complained Private Beckworth. "Whatever the heck we're lookin' for ain't worth dyin' for."

"Buck up soldiers!" shouted Sergeant James Pal. "We have our orders. If HQ thinks finding a downed aircraft is worth our lives, then we're damn well going to die trying to find it."

"What the heck was anyone doin' flyin' in this soup anyway?" asked Corporal Rooney. "If you ask me, they got what was comin'."

"No one asked you!" shouted Sergeant Pal.

The soldiers grumbled as they returned to sweeping the desert ground with their flashlights, looking for some trace of the wreckage the radar operators at Roswell Army Air Field had tracked as it had fallen from the sky hours earlier.

The men trudged forward, their rain-soaked boots splatting in puddles. Corporal Rooney pointed to steam rising from an arroyo rift in the desert floor.

"Sarge, over there."

The soldiers approached and descended into the gap in the earth. The arroyo trickled with rainwater. Scrub oak and chaparral protruded from the earth. Private Beckworth reached for a branch as he carefully climbed down the bank. The scrub bush pulled out of the mud and the private slid into the arroyo, landing face first in the desert stream.

"Nuts!" he shouted, pulling himself out of the muck and wiping his face.

In a modest rock escarpment bordering the stream, the soldiers' flashlights congregated on a large, charcoal-colored object protruding from the rock. The object, 20 feet wide and deep and 15 feet in height, hissed with steam as it was pelted by rainwater. Through the haze, the soldiers could make out that the object's smooth disc-like contours were interrupted by sharply angled fractures where the rest of the craft had sheared off.

"It looks a little like the nose of a B-36 bomber," observed Sergeant Pal. "Fan out. Look for survivors."

The soldiers surveyed the site. Like the primary wreckage,

portions of the craft's hull that had broken away had smoothly curved, featureless surfaces, interrupted by sharp angles where they had fractured away from the parent.

"Sarge," said Private Beckworth. "This don't look like no bomber."

Corporal Rooney's flashlight beam swept upon something that was incongruous with the curved and cracked fragments—it was a boot!

"Sarge! I found one of the crew."

As the men gathered, Rooney's flashlight beam moved up the broken body. The crewmember was small—less than five feet tall. Its uniform was odd—a silvery-gray one-piece made from a material that seemed more metal than cloth.

A bolt of lightning flashed, illuminating the corpse's face.

"Jesus!" Mackey shouted as the light hit the crewmember's face. "Jesus fucking Christ!"

The soldiers cursed and scattered, terrified. "Take cover!" yelled Sergeant Pal belatedly as he scrambled to bring up the rear of his unit. Though most were battle-hardened World War II veterans, nothing could have prepared them for the sight. The soldiers hit the deck behind sparse cover, rocks and brush in the arroyo bed. They unslung their carbines and aimed their rifles and flashlights at the motionless body lying in the rain, spying for movement.

Corporal Mackey felt the cold rainwater pouring into his trousers from the arroyo stream.

"What do we do, Sarge?" he asked.

"Chuck a rock at it," ordered Sergeant Pal.

"I don't want to make it angry, Sarge!" protested Mackey.

"Do it!" shouted the sergeant.

Corporal Mackey patted his hand against the sandy ground, grasping in the darkness for a rock. He picked one up and threw it at the body. The rock bounced off its chest. No movement.

"Let's go," ordered Sergeant Pal, rising from his hiding place holding his Colt 45 pistol.

The soldiers cautiously approached the lifeless body. Corporal Mackey's flashlight beam shone upon the crewmember's face.

The face that stared back from the arroyo floor belonged to a head with an oversized cranium. It had large almond-shaped black eyes, a tiny nose and ears, and a creepy gray pallor. The creature's small mouth was wide open, and its small hands were pressed against its ears like a Munch "Scream."

"Lord Almighty!" said Sergeant Pal.

J.B. Foster Ranch

Corona, NM

July 6, 1947

06:30 hours

William Ware "Mac" Brazel threw a faded Navajo blanket onto his 14-year-old quarter horse, Tony, as the horse finished munching on his breakfast. The two stood on a patch of weeded ground next to Brazel's simple wooden shack on the vast J.B. Foster Ranch, where the 48-year-old cowboy spent his days tending sheep.

Brazel looked east, squinting at the early morning sun, already blazing as it cleared the horizon over a sandy plain of sparse dry grass patches and occasional juniper shrubs. The sky was completely clear, a stark contrast to the night before, when Brazel rode out a fierce storm in his primitive one-room house without electricity, telephone, or running water.

Brazel threw a saddle on Tony. The old bay, named for Tom Mix's wonder horse, paid no attention to the tack as he munched on the last straws of his hay breakfast. The seasoned horse was expert at his ranch job, though better suited for working cattle than sheep.

Brazel lifted Tony's head from his food, placed the bit in the horse's mouth, and pulled the worn leather bridle over his ears. He slung the split reins over the saddle and climbed onboard. Brazel adjusted his tan felt cowboy hat, and the pair jogged into the sunrise to find the herd and survey the effects of the storm.

Brazel sweated in the desert air, muggy from evaporating rain.

A mile east of the shack, Tony suddenly raised his head and snorted, his ears pivoted forward.

"What do you see, boy?" asked Brazel.

Brazel scanned the landscape. In the distance, he spotted the herd, 200 sheep. He instantly understood why his horse had been on alert. Normally, the sheep's heads would be low to the ground, grazing on the sparse dry grass. Instead, the animals were standing at attention, their heads up. All were facing the same direction.

As Brazel approached, he saw what had alerted the sheep. Hundreds of solid charcoal-gray fragments lay strewn over 200 square yards of charred earth. The fragments ranged in size from a few inches to several feet in length, width, and depth. Brazel's normally bombproof horse snorted at the strange sight. Brazel dismounted to take a closer look. He reached down and picked up one of the smaller fragments. It was several inches wide and light as a feather. One side of the solid dark gray object had a featureless, smoothly curved surface. The opposite site was cragged with sharp angles, as though it had fractured away from the parent body. Brazel took out his pocketknife and tried to cut into the smooth side of the object. His knife couldn't scratch the surface. He pushed the point of his knife hard into the fragment, trying to puncture it. His pocketknife blade snapped off.

"Damn!" he said.

Brazel collected several of the smaller fragments and stuffed them into a saddlebag. He rode back to his shack, where he found an old brown Dutch Masters cigar box to store the objects.

Brazel took the cigar box and climbed aboard his faded red 1937 Ford pickup truck, placing the box on the threadbare bench seat. After a couple of failed attempts to start the truck, the engine turned over, belching thick smoke from its tailpipe. Brazel put the truck in gear and sped off down a dirt road toward Roswell, New Mexico.

Chaves County Sheriff's Office

Roswell, NM
July 6, 1947
10:27 hours

Brazel parked his truck on the curb in front of the office of the Chaves County Sheriff, a small red brick building with a tin awning. Painted in gold on the front door's glass window was,

OFFICE OF CHAVES COUNTY SHERIFF
GEORGE WILCOX, SHERIFF

Sheriff George Wilcox looked up from his desk as Brazel entered his modest office, a single room with two desks, file cabinets, and a corkboard with tacked-on notices and wanted flyers. A wooden Philco radio sat on his desk. Brazel heard the final notes of "Boogie Woogie Bugle Boy" as he entered the office.

Wilcox was in his fifties, a portly man with short coarsely cropped salt-and-pepper hair and wire-rim glasses. The normally quiet town of Roswell considered him a steady man, serious about his peacekeeping job though kind and fair. He was a popular sheriff, a shoo-in for reelection.

Wilcox recognized Brazel. Though he didn't know him well, he had seen him in town from time to time. Brazel removed his cowboy hat. A few strands of combed-over straw-colored hair lay on his otherwise bald head.

"Those were the Andrews Sisters, singing 'Boogie Woogie Bugle Boy' here on KFGL Radio, with your host, Frank Joyce. The time is 10:28. Next up is a classic, the lovely Kitty Kallen with the Harry James Band singing 'It's Been a Long, Long Time.'"

Sheriff Wilcox turned down the volume on the radio.

"Mornin', Mac," said Wilcox.

"Mornin', Sheriff."

"What brings you to town?"

"Well," Brazel started. "I found somethin' peculiar on the ranch this mornin'. Thought I'd better have you take a look at it."

Brazel set the Dutch Masters box on the sheriff's desk and opened it. Wilcox took one of the fragments out of the box.

"There was a whole field of them things," said Brazel. "The field was burnt black. Some was a little like these. Some was a couple feet big-around."

Brazel lifted one fragment out of the box. "I tried cuttin' this one with my pocket knife. Busted my knife. There ain't a scratch on it."

The sheriff peered over his glasses at the fragment.

"What do you make of it, Sheriff?"

"I don't have any idea what to make of it, Mac," the sheriff said. "I've never seen anything like this before. You say there's a whole field of these objects?"

"Yessir," said Brazel. "A whole field chock full of 'em."

"Well I'll be," said Wilcox.

"I'd better phone the Army base," said Wilcox. "Maybe they'll be able to get to the bottom of this."

Wilcox dialed his rotary telephone. The heavy phone dial clicked down the numbers as it rolled back.

"Hello, this is Sheriff Wilcox. One of our local ranchers has brought in some strange objects he found on his ranch this morning. I've never seen anything like this before. I thought one of you fellas might want to take a look at it."

Wilcox held his hand to the receiver. "They're connecting me to some fella," he said to Brazel.

"Yes," Wilcox said into the phone. "Yes, Major Marcel, this is Sheriff Wilcox. I telephoned because one of our local ranchers has brought in some odd objects he found on his ranch...What do they look like? Why, they look a little something like pieces of a giant, broken, charcoal-colored eggshell. They're light as a feather, yet you can't scratch them with a knife. It's the darndest..."

Sheriff Wilcox's brow furrowed as he listened to the voice on the other end of the phone.

"I see. Yes, I understand. Thank you very much, Major. We'll be waiting for you."

The sheriff hung up. "That was Major Marcel at the Roswell Army Air Field. He said to sit tight. He's coming over to investigate. You might as well pull up a seat. There's a fresh pot of coffee on that hot plate over there if you want some."

The phone rang. The sheriff picked up the receiver.

"Sheriff Wilcox speaking...Good morning, Frank...Why, yes, I believe I do have something of interest for your listeners. One of our neighbors found something peculiar on the Foster Ranch. He's here in my office now. I'll let you speak with him."

Sheriff Wilcox put his hand over the receiver. "This is Frank Joyce on the telephone."

"The radio jockey?" asked Brazel.

"Yes. He calls each day to ask if there's news to report to his listeners. Would you like to speak with him?"

"Well, sure, I guess so," said Brazel, feeling a rush of excitement about speaking with a radio celebrity.

Sheriff Wilcox handed Brazel the phone.

"Hello? This is Mac Brazel. Well, yes sir, I found something unusual this morning on the ranch and brought it to the sheriff for a look. There's a whole field of these charcoal-colored things. The field was burned black. The pieces are indestructible, but light as a feather. I broke my darn knife on one, but it didn't make a scratch."

As Brazel listened to Frank Joyce, the office door swung open and two uniformed Air Force officers entered, removing their caps.

"Where did they come from? Honestly, I think they came from out of this world...You heard me. I think this is a genuine UFO!"

"Who is he speaking with?" asked one of the officers.

"He's on the phone with Frank Joyce from KFGL Radio," whispered the sheriff.

The officers looked at each other.

"Hang up the phone," ordered one of the officers.

Brazel looked up, confused.

"Mister, hang up the phone this instant."

Brazel handed the receiver to Sheriff Wilcox.

"Frank, I'm sorry, but there are some gentlemen from the air base here to investigate the debris and..."

One of the officers walked to the sheriff's desk, snatched the phone out of his hand and hung it up. The sheriff looked at the officer, astonished at the man's rudeness.

"Now, there was no call for that," said the sheriff as he stood up from his desk.

The officer, a lanky major with dark brown eyes, extended his hand.

"I'm very sorry, Sheriff. This is a matter of national security. I'm Major Marcel from Army Intelligence. This is Captain Cavitt. May we please see the objects Mr. Brazel found?"

Brazel stood up and handed the major the Dutch Masters box. Marcel opened it, picked up one of the fragments and showed it to Cavitt. Their eyes met. Marcel returned the object to the box and snapped it shut.

They heard Frank Joyce's faint voice on the sheriff's radio. Marcel reached and turned up the volume.

"...I repeat: This is a news flash. Roswell's Sheriff Wilcox reports that he is in possession of debris from a crashed UFO, found on the Foster Ranch by Mac Brazel. Officers from Roswell Army Air Field are investigating. Stay tuned to KFGL Radio for the latest developments."

Marcel switched off the radio and looked at Cavitt. Cavitt shook his head.

Marcel turned to Brazel. "Mr. Brazel, where did you find these?"

"On the Foster Ranch, near the southeast corner. There's hundreds of them."

"Has anyone else seen the objects of the debris field?"

"No sir. Just the sheriff and you fellas."

"Sheriff, do you have a map of the area?" asked Marcel.

"Why, yes," the sheriff said. He slid open a desk drawer and pulled out a folded pamphlet map.

Marcel picked a pencil off the sheriff's desk and handed it to Brazel. "Mr. Brazel, would you please point out where the debris field is."

"I could just take you fellas to it."

"That won't be necessary. Just mark it on the map."

As Brazel marked an 'X' on the map, Sheriff Wilcox's phone rang. He answered it.

"Sheriff Wilcox…Yessir. Where did you say you were calling from? KABQ Radio in Albuquerque? How did you hear about the UFO so darn fast?"

"Hang up," ordered Marcel.

The sheriff hung up the phone.

"That was a reporter from the KABQ Radio in Albuquerque. Frank Joyce put the story out on the United Press International wire service."

"Jesus!" said Cavitt.

"Major, what in the Sam Hill is going on?" asked the sheriff.

"Mr. Brazel, please wait for me outside with Captain Cavitt. I need to speak with the sheriff, then I will join you both."

The sheriff's phone rang again.

"Don't answer that," said Major Marcel.

After the office door closed behind the two men, Marcel turned to the sheriff.

"Sheriff Wilcox, the objects Mr. Brazel found are the remains of a weather balloon."

The phone rang again.

Sheriff Wilcox's jaw dropped. Military weather balloons were common in the Roswell area. He had seen dozens of them, as had Mac Brazel.

"Now, Major, you know as well as I do that those objects didn't come from a weather balloon."

The phone rang again. Marcel took a step toward the sheriff and looked him dead in the eye.

"Sheriff Wilcox, you are mistaken. Those objects came from a weather balloon. There is no UFO. There are no such things as UFOs. The Army considers people who spin wild rumors like that to be unstable, even dangerous. Are you dangerous, Sheriff? Is your family dangerous?"

Sheriff Wilcox blanched. He got the message. His life and the lives of his family were being threatened.

"No sir," the sheriff replied, "we're not dangerous."

"I didn't think so," said Marcel, smiling.

The phone rang again.

"It looks like you've got a call," said Marcel, turning toward the door. "I'll leave you to it."

Sheriff Wilcox slowly sat down in his chair, staring at the ringing phone.

Marcel calmly folded the map and slid it into his inside coat pocket. He picked the cigar box off the desk, turned, and left the office.

• • •

Marcel closed the door to Sheriff Wilcox's office behind him. Brazel and Cavitt stood on the sidewalk outside the office.

"Mr. Brazel, we need you to come with us to the airbase," said Marcel.

"What for?"

"We need to ask you some more questions about what you found on the ranch."

"How long will this take?" asked Brazel. "I need to get back to feed and water my horse."

"It won't take long," said Marcel. "We appreciate the help of a patriot like yourself."

Brazel felt pride welling within him. "Well, all right."

Brazel turned toward his truck.

"Don't worry about your truck. We'll give you a lift," said Cavitt, opening the back door to their olive Army Plymouth with a white star on the door. Cavitt gestured Brazel inside.

Roswell Army Airfield

Roswell, NM
July 6, 1947
11:34 hours

Cavitt's Plymouth approached the guard shack to Roswell Army Air Field, a small sand-colored cinderblock building with a sign reading,

RAAF
Home of the
509th Bomb Group

Cavitt stopped the car at a green and white striped boom barricade that blocked the entrance to the base.

"Is this here where the *Enola Gay* is?" asked Brazel from the backseat.

"Yes, it is," said Marcel. "After she dropped the bomb on Hiroshima, she came back home. We'll drive by her hangar."

"Boy howdy!" exclaimed Brazel.

"We sure showed them Japs, didn't we?" said Brazel, welling with pride. "That was the biggest bomb in the world. What was that bomb called?"

"'Little Boy,'" said Marcel.

"That's right. Little Boy. Whew, that was somethin'!"

Marcel was silent. He knew that, only a few hundred miles northwest in Los Alamos, scientists were developing the latest generation of multi-megaton hydrogen fusion bombs, with yields of 1,000 times that of the relatively puny Little Boy fission bomb the B-29 Superfortress named *Enola Gay* had dropped on Hiroshima only two years earlier. Still, with a yield of only 15 kilotons, Little Boy was more than sufficient to flatten a city and create a 6,000 degree fireball 1,200 feet in diameter. One victim of the Hiroshima fireball was known only by the shadow he left on the steps of Sumitomo Bank. The bank patron sat, patiently waiting for the bank to open when the bomb vaporized everything about him except his shadow. It was left, memorialized in the bank's concrete steps.

A guard emerged from the shack, wearing his olive uniform with a black "MP" military police armband and a Sam Browne dark leather belt across his chest. Marcel got out of the car and met the guard, who saluted the major. Marcel returned the salute and spoke with the guard while motioning toward him. The guard looked directly at Mack Brazel. Brazel felt uneasy. He wondered whether he had made a mistake showing the fragments to the sheriff. The guard retreated into his shack to make a phone call. When he reemerged, he opened the boom barricade and saluted the officers as they drove into the base.

Marcel parked his Plymouth at a sand-colored two-story brick building. A group of six MPs with side arms stood outside the building. As Brazel got out, the MPs approached him.

"Sir, you'll need to come with us," said one of the MPs.

Brazel, surprised, began to protest.

"I need to get back to the ranch," he said. "I need to feed and water my horse."

"This is just a precaution," said Marcel, smiling. "For your protection, as well as the security of the country."

Brazel was escorted into the building. The MP guided Brazel along a hallway, past a series of doors. They passed medical staff—nurses in white uniforms and caps, as well as doctors and technicians.

Brazel was gestured into a medical examination room with a green vinyl-padded exam table covered with white paper and an assortment of stainless-steel instruments on an adjacent tray. A glass jar of cotton balls sat on a nearby shelf, alongside a bottle labeled "alcohol." The MP escorting Brazel ordered him to strip. Brazel's jaw dropped. He stared at the MP, speechless.

"Take your clothes off—***now***!" repeated the MP.

Brazel removed his clothes—blue jeans, blue and white checkered shirt, boots and underwear—and stood, naked, for minutes in front of the MP, waiting, covering his genitals with his hands. Brazel's body had a farmer's tan. His face, neck, arms, and hands were weathered and brown from years working in the sun. The rest of his body, normally covered by jeans and work shirts, was a pasty color. A few strands of combed-over straw-colored hair lay on his otherwise bald head. Brazel's embarrassment at his nudity was magnified by his awareness of the contrast between his middle-aged body and that of the young, fit, fully clothed MP.

The door opened, and a man and woman entered. The man, a doctor, had receding black hair and wore black rim glasses, a lab coat, and a surgical mask. The nurse had wavy dark hair beneath her nurse's cap. She too wore a mask. Brazel felt embarrassed and vulnerable standing naked in front of these fully clothed people.

The doctor strapped on a head mirror and ordered Brazel to sit on the papered exam table. He performed a routine examination of his ears, nose, and throat, and then checked Brazel's reflexes by rapping his knee with a rubber reflex hammer. Brazel's leg bounced up in response. The doctor then asked Brazel to stand up. Brazel began to cover himself with his hands again. The doctor slapped his hands away, then turned to the nurse, who helped him pull on a pair of squeaky rubber gloves. The doctor reached for Brazel's testicles, checking for a hernia by pressing the inguinal canal while instructing Brazel to turn his head to the side and cough.

Brazel noticed anxiously that both the nurse and the MP were staring at his genitals as the doctor performed the exam. Finally, the doctor instructed Brazel to turn to face the table and bend over, resting his elbows on the table. The nurse applied Vaseline to the doctor's index finger.

Brazel, outraged, fought back tears as he felt the painful pressure of the doctor's finger forced into his rectum. The MP snickered as Brazel let out a grunt. When the doctor was finished, he pulled off his rubber gloves with a snap and handed them to the nurse. He then instructed Brazel to sit on the table again.

The doctor picked up a large metal-framed glass syringe from the table. The nurse strapped a rubber tourniquet on Brazel's left arm and swabbed the inside of his elbow with an alcohol-doused cotton ball.

"Make a fist," instructed the doctor.

The doctor slapped the inside of Brazel's elbow lightly. A vein swelled beneath the skin.

Brazel hated needles, and this one seemed very big. The doctor inserted it into Brazel's arm, missing the vein completely.

"Hold still!" the doctor said, trying to cover his mistake.

After two tries, the doctor punctured the vein, filling the syringe. He then handed the gorged syringe to the nurse, who squirted Brazel's blood into a test tube with an anticoagulant, then capped the tube with a rubber stopper.

"You can get dressed," the doctor told Brazel.

The doctor and nurse exited. Brazel, humiliated to his bones, picked up his underwear and stepped into them, furious with the people who had violated him. He was also angry with himself for not having the courage to resist. The only bright ray mitigating the ordeal was Brazel's belief that it was over. Brazel assumed he could return to the ranch and put this horrible episode behind him.

Brazel finished dressing in front of the MP. The soldier then escorted him out of the examination room and down a series of hallways. To Brazel's surprise, instead of escorting him to the exit, the MP took him to a tiny cinderblock brig cell, with a cot, forest green military blanket, and stainless-steel toilet and sink.

Brazel turned to the guard before he locked the door, asking him when he could leave.

"My orders are to confine you here until further orders," replied the MP.

The MP closed the cell door. Brazel heard the jangle of the keys and a clack as the door lock shut. Alone in his cell, the old cowboy sat on his cot, his head buried in his hands, as he shook with rage and fear. His life, so simple only days before, had transformed into a terrifying nightmare. All he wanted was to ride the range on his horse again, away from this madness.

Roswell Army Air Field

Roswell, NM

July 7, 1947

07:41 hours

A dozen black rotary phones rang at once in a large conference room. Twelve army officers in khaki uniforms reached for the phones placed in front of them on the polished wood conference table. They pressed the blinking extension light on their phones and listened.

A man in his thirties sitting at the head of the table was the first to speak. "Colonel Blanchard speaking."

"Is your team assembled and present?" asked a man's voice on the other end of the call.

"Yes," replied Colonel Blanchard, "we are present."

"Hold for the president."

Colonel Blanchard scanned the room as he heard a series of clicks on the line. His brown eyes met the worried eyes of the officers under his command.

"Colonel Blanchard?" asked a man's tinny voice through the phone.

"Yes, Mr. President."

"Colonel, I have FBI director Hoover and General Marshall with me."

"Yes sir."

"Colonel, we'd like you to start with a report of the current situation."

"Yes sir," Colonel Blanchard said. "As we reported earlier, the remains of an extraterrestrial craft were discovered the morning of July 6th. Four bodies were discovered with the wreckage. The bodies have been recovered, and we are in the process of collecting the craft wreckage.

"Today, we learned of a second crash site. A local rancher discovered the wreckage this morning and brought some of it to the local sheriff.

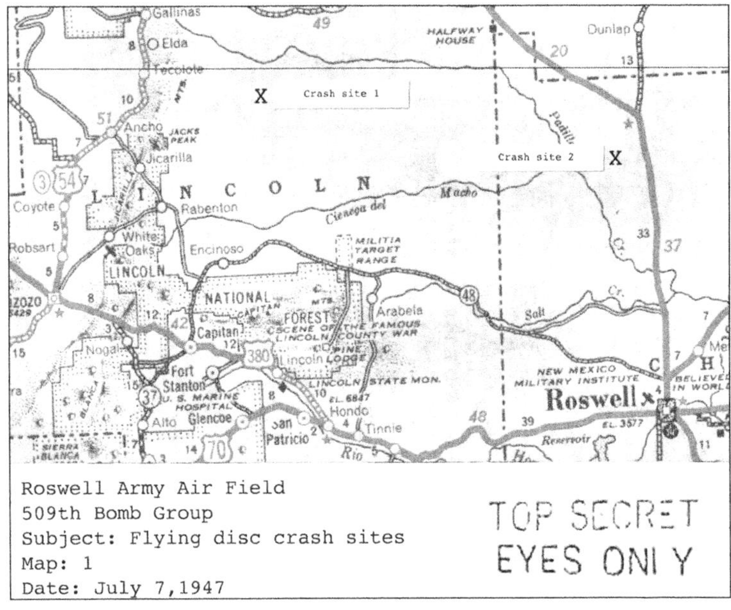

"There has been a complication. The rancher spoke to a local radio disk jockey yesterday and told him that the objects he found were from a UFO."

"Jesus!" exclaimed President Truman.

"Yes sir. The disk jockey proceeded to report the story on the United Press International wire service. The story is spreading across the country. It won't be long before reporters start swarming."

"Jesus Christ!"

"Colonel, this is General Marshall."

"Yes sir."

"How long do you estimate it will be until you are able to collect all the debris from the two sites?"

"Two days at a minimum," answered Colonel Blanchard. "The wreckage at crash site one is extensive. Some of the objects are very large and will require heavy equipment to collect and transport. Regarding crash site two, we are only now assessing it."

"Mr. President," said FBI Director Edgar Hoover, "we don't have two days. Reporters will be swarming Roswell in no time."

"We can cordon off the crash sites with armed guards," replied Colonel Blanchard.

"That's no good," said Hoover. "You boys post soldiers at those sites and you'll just chum the waters. We need something to take those reporters off the scent while Colonel Blanchard's men get rid of every trace of that craft and its crew. We need a misdirection."

"Do you have any ideas, Edgar?" asked Truman.

There was silence.

"Mr. President," began Hoover, "I have an idea. It's risky, but at present, I am unable to come up with a better plan."

KGFL Radio

Roswell, NM
July 8, 1947
08:25 hours

Lieutenant Walter Haut parked his Army jeep in front of a small pale-yellow stucco storefront office. Above an awning was a red sign reading "Radio Station KGFL" in neon letters.

The 25-year-old blond-haired first lieutenant climbed out of his jeep. He pulled his khaki garrison cap from beneath his shoulder epaulet, completing his fatigue uniform. The Roswell Army Air Field's Press Information Officer held an envelope containing the strangest press release he had ever written. Half an hour earlier, the base commander, Colonel William Blanchard, had dictated it to him for immediate release.

The press release's headline read, "RAAF Takes Possession of Flying Saucer."

When the young lieutenant had finished scribbling the colonel's dictation, he looked up at the colonel, his eyebrows raised.

"May I see it, sir?" asked Lieutenant Haut, referring to the flying saucer.

"No," replied Colonel Blanchard as he turned to leave.

United States Army
8th Army Air Force
509th Bomb Group
Roswell Army Air Field
Roswell, NM

Contact: Lt. Walter Haut,
Public Information Officer
Roswell Army Airfield
Phone: 101

N E W S   R E L E A S E

For Immediate Release
July 8, 1947

RAAF Takes Possession of Flying Saucer

509th Bombardment group at Roswell Army Air Field has taken possession of a flying saucer. The flying disk was recovered by RAAF personnel on a ranch in the Roswell vicinity after an unidentified rancher notified Sheriff George Wilcox that the instrument had been found on his premises.

Major J. A. Marcel, intelligence officer at RAAF and a detail from his department went to the ranch and recovered the disk. After the instrument was inspected by Major Marcel, it was flown to higher headquarters at Fort Worth Army Air Field.

###

Haut pulled open one of the glass double doors and entered the office. Inside was a room within a room—a cramped studio with a window enabling outsiders to peer in on the workings of the radio announcer. A sign reading "On the Air" was illuminated next to the window. Haut peered in. Inside the studio, a man in his thirties with wavy dark hair sat in front of a console with a microphone emblazoned with the KGFL logo. A vinyl 45 RPM record spun on a turntable to the man's left.

Frank Joyce looked up from his console. Seeing Haut in the window, he waved him into the studio.

When Haut entered, Joyce put a finger to his lips signaling that he should be quiet.

"That was 'Golden Earrings' by Peggy Lee. This is your host, Frank Joyce, at KGFL Radio. Next up is Frank Sinatra with 'Mam'selle.'"

Frank place the needle on the record and flipped a switch on the console.

"Mornin', Wally," said Frank.

"Mornin', Frank. I've got something for you. This is hot," Haut said, handing the envelope to Joyce. Joyce opened it up and read the press release.

"Wow!" exclaimed Joyce.

"So, Mac Brazel's story is on the level after all?" asked Joyce.

"That's what it says."

Joyce read on. "They flew the flying saucer to Fort Worth? There's gonna be a press conference this afternoon?"

"Yup," said Haut.

"Jeepers!" exclaimed Joyce. "If that don't beat all."

"Gotta run, Frank," said Haut. "Next stop is the *Daily Record*."

• • •

Haut's press release landed just in time to make the *Roswell Daily Record's* afternoon edition. Within minutes, the release had saturated the news wires.

Leased Wire
Associated Press

Roswell Daily Record

RECORD PHONES
Business Office 2288
News Department
2287

RAAF Captures Flying Saucer On Ranch in Roswell Region

Claims Army Is Stacking Courts Martial

Indiana Senator Lays Protest Before Patterson

House Passes Tax Slash by Large Margin

Defeat Amendment By Demos to Remove Many From Rolls

Security Council Paves Way to Talks On Arms Reductions

No Details of Flying Disk Are Revealed

Roswell Hardware Man and Wife Report Disk Seen

Movies as Usual

Ex-King Carol Weds Mme. Lupescu

Some of Soviet Satellites May Attend Paris Meeting

Roswellians Have Differing Opinions On Flying Saucers

American League Wins All-Star Game

Miners and Operators Sign Highest Wage Pact in History

Roswell Army Air Field

Roswell, NM
July 8, 1947
06:48 hours

An MP pounded on Mac Brazel's metal brig door with a wooden baton. The guards had beaten the door at the top of the hour throughout the night, waking Brazel as he began to drift off to sleep.

The guard unlocked the door and swung it open. Brazel lay on his cot with an arm over his eyes to shield them from the bright overhead lamp that was kept on all night.

Two uniformed MPs stepped into Brazel's cell, each grabbing him by the arm to pull him off his cot. They shackled his wrists and ankles, then escorted him as he shuffled down the hallway to a darkened room.

In the center of the room was a single Steelcase table and two metal chairs on opposing sides. A metal rod ran across the length of the table. One of the MPs instructed Brazel to sit in the chair, then shackled his handcuffs to the rod. A single-bulb light fixture with a green metal shade hung over the table. Minutes later, Captain Cavitt, the counter-intelligence officer, entered the room and sat in the chair opposite Brazel. He dropped a manila folder on the table and opened it.

"I need to get back to the ranch," said Brazel in a raspy voice. "I need to feed and water my horse."

Cavitt ignored him, looking at notes and photographs in the folder. "Mr. Brazel, I would like you to tell me about the objects you found on the Foster Ranch."

"I told you, I found the objects when I was riding my horse on the ranch."

"What objects?"

"The objects I showed you. Them charcoal things."

"You mean the remains of the weather balloon that came down on the ranch."

Brazel was surprised. "Them things didn't come from no weather balloon! I'm not stupid. I know what a weather balloon looks like!"

Cavitt scribbled on a note page.

"Mr. Brazel, I would like you to tell me about the objects you found on the Foster Ranch," he repeated.

"Fella, I don't get it. I just told you."

"Mr. Brazel, I would like you to tell me about the objects you found on the Foster Ranch," Cavitt repeated.

Cavitt recycled the same question for hours. Each time, Brazel repeated his story. Each time, Cavitt corrected him.

"Goddammit!" yelled Brazel. "I've done answered your questions! I want to go home! I need to take care of my horse! I want to get the hell out of here!"

Cavitt motioned to one of the MPs. He left and returned a minute later pushing a dolly into the room. The dolly was hauling a car battery with jumper cables.

Cavitt sighed. "Mr. Brazel, you are confused about what you saw on the ranch. I'm trying to help you with your confusion, but you are being uncooperative."

"I'm telling you everything I know!" cried Brazel.

"The problem is, what you are telling me is wrong. I'm just trying to help you."

"I'm not a liar," said Brazel.

"Then why do you keep lying to me?"

Cavitt motioned again to the MP, who rolled up Brazel's shirt sleeves and clamped each of the jumper cable clamps on each of Brazel's forearms. The clamp prongs dug into Brazel's skin.

"What the hell are you doing?" asked Brazel.

The MP attached one of the opposing clamps on one of the car battery terminals. The MP held the other clamp in his hand, kneeling beside the battery.

"Mr. Brazel, I would like you to tell me about the objects you found on the Foster Ranch," Cavitt repeated.

"I told you, I found the objects when I was riding my horse on the ranch."

"What objects?"

"The objects I showed you. Them charcoal things."

Cavitt nodded to the MP. He touched the jumper cable clamp to the battery terminal. A spark cracked from the terminal, releasing a puff of smoke.

Brazel shook violently, screaming in pain. The MP removed the clamp.

Brazel gasped. “God damn you!” he screamed. “God damn you!”

“Mr. Brazel, I would like you to tell me about the objects you found on the Foster Ranch,” Cavitt repeated.

Brazel began to sob. “Please, let me go!”

“Mr. Brazel, I would like you to tell me about the objects you found on the Foster Ranch,” Cavitt repeated. “Mr. Brazel, do you need another shock to help you remember?”

“No, no, please!”

“Mr. Brazel, I would like you to tell me about the objects you found on the Foster Ranch,” Cavitt repeated.

“I found the objects when I was riding my horse on the ranch.”

“What objects?”

“What objects, Mr. Brazel?”

“I found the remains of a weather balloon.”

KGFL Radio

Roswell, NM
July 9, 1947
09:00 hours

"This is Frank Joyce at KGFL Radio. In just a few minutes, we're going to have Mac Brazel in our studio. His story about the flying saucer debris he found on the Foster Ranch has caused quite a stir. He's going to tell our listeners his story. Coming right up. Stay tuned."

Joyce placed the needle on a record and waved his visitors into the studio. Three men entered the cramped studio: William Haut, Mac Brazel, and the MP who had aided Brazel's interrogation. Joyce gestured for Brazel to take a seat. Haut and the MP stood, watching Brazel. Brazel held his cowboy hat on his lap. He did not lift his eyes from the floor.

Joyce moved the microphone between the two men.

"Are you ready, Mac?" Joyce asked.

Brazel nodded, looking down.

Joyce flipped a switch on his console and picked up the record needle. "That was 'Chi-Baba Chi-Baba' by Perry Como. This is your host at KGFL Radio, Frank Joyce. We have Mac Brazel here in the studio today. As you've heard, Mr. Brazel found the remains of a UFO crash on the Foster Ranch earlier this week. He's here to tell our listeners his story. Thank you very much for being with us here today, Mr. Brazel."

"Yessir," Brazel replied. His voice trembled.

"Mr. Brazel, can you tell us about what you found on the Foster Ranch the morning of July the 6th?"

"I found the remains of a weather balloon," said Brazel, looking at the floor.

Joyce was shocked. He looked at Haut. Haut returned his stare.

"Mr. Brazel, that is not what you told me two days ago. You told me you found the remains of a UFO."

Brazel continued to look down. "I made a mistake. I found a weather balloon. I made a mistake. I am very sorry."

"Ladies and gentlemen, we're going to take a break. This is Frank Joyce, your host at KGFL Radio."

Joyce slapped a record on the turntable, then swiveled his chair to face Haut.

"Wally, what the hell is going on?" asked Joyce.

"Sorry, Frank. The interview is over," replied Haut as he turned to leave.

As Haut opened the studio door, Brazel leaned to whisper to Joyce, "Look, son. You keep this to yourself. They told me to come in here and tell you this story or it would go awfully hard on me and you."

"Let's go," said the MP.

Roswell, NM

July 10, 1947
06:00 hours

Captain Robert Shirkey gazed upon the black silhouettes of three C-54 Skymaster cargo planes queued up for takeoff on the Roswell Army Air Field's sole runway. Dawn had broken minutes before, and the brilliant yellow-orange desert sun burst through gaps between the planes, transforming the black night sky into an ascendant midnight blue. The planes' prop engines rumbled unevenly as they awaited clearance for takeoff. Though it was only 06:00, it was already nearly 80 degrees on the tarmac. Shirkey knew it was going to be a lot hotter at these planes' final destination. A fourth plane, a B-29 Superfortress bomber, taxied to queue up behind the Skymasters. The B-29's shiny chrome fuselage contrasted with the dull matte finishes of the cargo planes.

Resting inside the cargo bays of the four planes was the most secret consignment on Earth—something that held the potential to transform the world and terrify its citizens.

The planes contained smoking gun proof of two truths. The first was that humans were not alone in the universe. The second was that humans were not the smartest creatures in the cosmos. Someone out there was much smarter.

Edgar Hoover's misdirection had worked brilliantly. The arc of the Roswell story shadowed the trajectory of a B-29 bomber, carrying faked crash wreckage from Roswell to Fort Worth, where it was displayed on the floor of Brigadier General Roger Ramey's office on the afternoon of July 8. Ramey was commanding general of the 8th Army Air Force, and Colonel Blanchard's commanding officer. In a matter of hours, the spectacular announcement of the crash of an alien spacecraft had been carefully deflated into nothing more than a simple fallen weather balloon.

While reporters were snapping pictures of Major Marcel holding weather balloon wreckage in Fort Worth that afternoon, Mac Brazel was put to work recanting his UFO story for the local Roswell press.

On July 9, newspaper headlines parroted the Army's story.

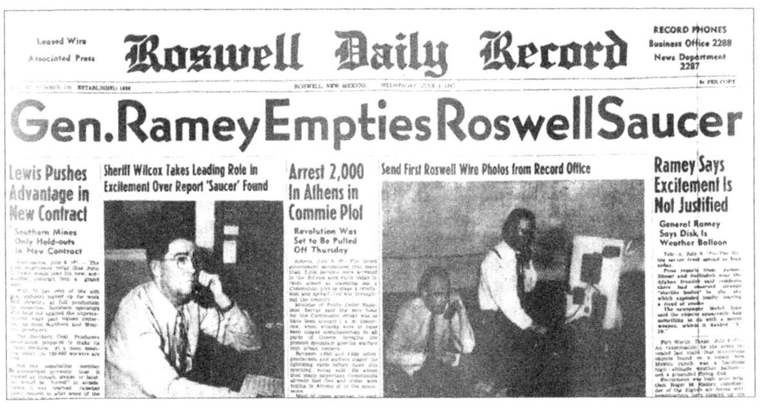

Leased Wire
Associated Press

Roswell Daily Record

RECORD PHONES
Business Office 2288
News Department
2287

ESTABLISHED 1888 — ROSWELL, NEW MEXICO — 6c PER COPY

Gen. Ramey Empties Roswell Saucer

Lewis Pushes Advantage in New Contract

Southern Mines Only Hold-outs in New Contract

Sheriff Wilcox Takes Leading Role in Excitement Over Report 'Saucer' Found

Arrest 2,000 In Athens in Commie Plot

Revolution Was Set to Be Pulled Off Thursday

Send First Roswell Wire Photos from Record Office

Ramey Says Excitement Is Not Justified

General Ramey Says Disk Is Weather Balloon

Mac Brazel was disgraced in the press for instigating the hoax. Satisfied that Brazel would stick to the official version of events, the Army released him after a week in custody. In the years that followed, until the day he died, when asked about what had really happened at Foster Ranch on the 6th of July, 1947, Brazel refused to say a word.

Harassed Rancher who Located 'Saucer' Sorry He Told About It

W. W. Brazel, 48, Lincoln county rancher living 30 miles south east of Corona, today told his story of finding what the army at first described as a flying disk, but the publicity which attended his find caused him to add that if he ever found anything else short of a bomb he sure wasn't going to say anything about it.

Brazel was brought here late yesterday by W. E. Whitmore, of radio station KGFL, had his picture taken and gave an interview to the Record and Jason Kellahin, sent here from the Albuquerque bureau of the Associated Press to cover the story. The picture he posed for was sent out over AP telephoto wire sending machine specially set up in the Record office by R. D. Adair, AP wire chief sent here from Albuquerque for the sole purpose of getting out his picture and that of sheriff George Wilcox, to whom Brazel originally gave the information of his find.

Brazel related that on June 14 he and an 8-year old son, Vernon were about 7 or 8 miles from the ranch house of the J. B. Foster ranch, which he operates, when they came upon a large area of bright wreckage made up on rubber strips, tinfoil, a rather tough paper and sticks.

At the time Brazel was in a hurry to get his round made and he did not pay much attention to it. But he did remark about what he had seen and on July 4 he, his wife, Vernon and a daughter Betty, age 14, went back to the spot and gathered up quite a bit of the debris.

The next day he first heard about the flying disks, and he wondered if what he had found might be the remnants of one of these.

Monday he came to town to sell some wool and while here he went to see sheriff George Wilcox and "whispered kinda confidential like" that he might have found a flying disk.

Wilcox got in touch with the Roswell Army Air Field and Maj. Jesse A. Marcel and a man in plain clothes accompanied him home, where they picked up the rest of the pieces of the "disk" and went to his home to try to reconstruct it.

According to Brazel they simply could not reconstruct it at all. They tried to make a kite out of it, but could not do that and could not find any way to put it back together so that it would fit.

Then Major Marcel brought it to Roswell and that was the last he heard of it until the story broke that he had found a flying disc.

Brazel said that he did not see it fall from the sky and did not see it before it was torn up, so he did not know the size or shape it might have been, but he thought it might have been about as large as a table top. The balloon which held it up, if that was how it worked, must have been about 12 feet long, he felt, measuring the distance by the size of the room in which he sat. The rubber was smoky gray in color and scattered over an area about 200 yards in diameter.

When the debris was gathered up the tinfoil, paper, tape, and sticks made a bundle about three feet long and 7 or 8 inches thick, while the rubber made a bundle about 18 or 20 inches long and about 8 inches thick. In all, he estimated, the entire lot would have weighed maybe five pounds.

There was no sign of any metal in the area which might have been used for an engine and no sign of any propellers of any kind, although at least one paper fin had been glued onto some of the tinfoil.

There were no words to be found anywhere on the instrument, although there were letters on some of the parts. Considerable scotch tape and some tape with flowers printed upon it had been used in the construction.

No strings or wire were to be found but there were some eyelets in the paper to indicate that some sort of attachment may have been used.

Brazel said that he had previously found two weather observation balloons on the ranch, but that what he found this time did not in any way resemble either of these.

"I am sure what I found was not any weather observation balloon," he said. "But if I find anything else, besides a bomb they are going to have a hard time getting me to say anything about it."

With press attention diverted to Fort Worth, the misdirection bought the Army the time needed to collect every remaining scrap of wreckage. The product of those efforts now lay packed into three cargo planes queued on Roswell's runway on the morning of July 10, 1947. Captain Bob Shirkey's orders were to ensure that the spacecraft remains were relocated, safely and discreetly, to their new home. The fourth plane, the B-29, contained the refrigerated remains of the four aliens.

Shirkey watched as a soldier, dressed in battle fatigues with his rifle slung, approached from the planes. When he reached Shirkey, he saluted. Shirkey saw the anxiety in the young soldier's face. Shirkey returned the salute.

"The planes are loaded and AOK," reported the soldier. "Awaiting your orders, sir."

Shirkey glanced at his watch. "Get onboard. We're taking off," he said.

The two men walked to the lead Skymaster and boarded through the forward hatch. Onboard, Shirkey glanced toward the rear cargo hold of the plane, which was packed with a mix of large wooden crates, as well as large curved sections of the alien ship that were too large to crate. Four soldiers were wedged into the cargo bay with the alien cargo.

Shirkey turned to the cockpit. The pilot and co-pilot, wearing leather bomber jackets, were strapped into their seats. The pilot turned to Shirkey.

"Orders, sir?" the pilot asked.

"Takeoff. Climb to 15,000 feet. Heading 330. Speed 190 knots. Maintain radio silence," replied Shirkey.

"Roger that, sir. Fifteen thousand feet, heading 330, 190 knots," acknowledged the pilot.

Shirkey strapped himself into a folding seat behind the co-pilot. The pilot and co-pilot glanced at each other and exchanged a nod in unison. Then the pilot placed his hand on the throttle levers and pushed them forward. The Skymaster's prop engines roared in response, and the plane began to move forward down the runway, picking up speed. The nose lifted off the ground and they were airborne, ascending into a stunningly beautiful clear desert morning. The brilliant sun was above the horizon, slightly to the plane's port side. Several hundred feet below on the starboard side of the plane at two o'clock, Shirkey could see the sun's blinding reflection off the B-29's chrome skin as it headed northeast.

The other two Skymasters under Shirkey's command had followed his plane into the air and assumed wing positions on either side of the lead plane. The only orders the pilots of those planes had been given prior to departure was "follow the leader." They did not need to know where they were going.

Though the planes did not have an official flight plan, it had been leaked that they were headed for Los Alamos, New Mexico. This was the heading Shirkey had given his pilot. Shirkey glanced at his watch periodically. Thirty minutes into the flight, he got out of his seat and tapped the pilot on the shoulder.

"Sir?" the pilot asked.

"New heading. Turn to 291. Maintain altitude and speed," Shirkey shouted over the roar of the engines.

"Heading 291. Maintain altitude and speed. Roger that," replied the pilot.

The pilot glanced at his co-pilot, who acknowledged the heading change with a nod. They banked the plane to port while Shirkey looked out the windows to make sure the other two planes were still in tow. He then turned to face the soldiers in the cargo bay.

"It's going to be a while, gentlemen," Shirkey said.

"Yes sir," the soldiers replied.

Shirkey kept a periodic lookout over the next few hours as his tiny fleet of Skymasters hummed through the clear western desert sky. The cargo windows of the Skymasters had been hastily painted over in an attempt to prevent the soldiers from knowing their destination. Only seven people in the fleet, the pilots and Captain Shirkey, would know the alien ship's final destination. Shirkey watched as the brilliant oranges and reds of Arizona's painted desert splashed the landscape beneath him. The landscape began to change from passion colors to duller browns and grays, with alternating rocky mountains and flat valleys.

Shirkey glanced at his watch. It was 09:00. They were close. He unstrapped from his seat and straddled his arms across the pilot's and co-pilot's seats, staring forward out the cockpit window. In the distance, he spotted a craggy brown mountain. At its left base was a white spot—something that seemed completely out of place with the rest of the scenery. It was as though someone had transplanted a circular patch of desert next to the mountain.

"See that white patch?" Shirkey asked the pilot.

"Yes sir," replied the pilot.

"That's your destination," said Shirkey. "Begin your descent. You'll be landing from the southeast."

"Yes sir, roger that," replied the pilot.

The white spot grew as they approached it, mellowing into a cream color. It was an enormous desert lakebed. As they got closer, they began to make out features—two parallel landing strips scraped out of the lakebed. They could also see vehicles and shelters pocking the surface. There were dozens of heavy earth-moving machines, as well as other vehicles strewn about the desert patch. They were concentrated on the southern side. A flaccid windsock signaled wind conditions to the pilots.

Shirkey's plane banked to port away from the lakebed, then to starboard to line up with the dirt runway. The pilot reduced speed, extended flaps and landing gear, and dropped his plane gracefully onto the desert runway. The yelp of the tires touching down signaled a textbook landing. As the plane slowed on the runway, Shirkey directed the pilot to taxi off the runway onto the lakebed toward the concentration of activity they had witnessed from the air. Behind them, the two trailing planes spaced themselves to land in succession. Shirkey ordered the pilot to kill the engines and stay in the plane, while he lowered the hatch stairs.

By the time Shirkey exited the plane, a collection of men and machines had already assembled to meet the Skymaster. Some of the men were wearing military khakis, and others were clad in civilian attire. The civilians included workmen, as well as a handful of men dressed in suit pants, white shirts, G-man sunglasses, and ties. Despite the fact that they had removed their suit coats, their dress was still comically inappropriate for the 90-degree heat.

Shirkey stepped onto the cream-colored sand lakebed. A colonel in khakis and Ray-Ban Aviator sunglasses stepped forward to greet him. Shirkey saluted. The colonel returned Shirkey's salute and extended a hand. Shirkey shook it.

"Welcome to Groom Lake, Captain," said the colonel, who did not disclose his name.

"Thank you, sir," replied Shirkey.

"You've accomplished your mission. Good work," continued the colonel. "We'll take it from here. We'll have your plane unloaded within the hour and send you on your way with some refreshments for the trip home."

As the colonel spoke, Shirkey watched the port doors on the cargo bay swing open. An olive military transport truck backed into the bay. Men rushed onto the plane and began hauling wreckage onto the truck. The workers were surprised at the lightness of the large pieces. Indeed, the wooden crates holding the smaller items were the heaviest articles in the manifest.

"Captain," the colonel continued, "I assume I do not need to remind you of the need for absolute secrecy?"

The men in suits, expressionless, trained their sunglass-covered eyes on the captain.

"No sir, I understand completely," Shirkey replied convincingly.

"I thought so," said the colonel, flashing a Hollywood smile. "Well then, why don't you make yourself comfortable in your ship, and we'll have you ready for the trip home in a jiffy."

Shirkey understood that he was not going to get the grand tour. A bolt of panic flashed through his mind. Given the extraordinary secrecy, would he and his crew even leave this place alive?

He climbed back aboard the Skymaster. The cockpit crew looked at him inquisitively.

"All's well. Good work, men," he said, with an easy confidence that masked his anxious desire to get the hell out of this strange place. "We'll be here for another half hour or so, and then we'll head home. How's our fuel?"

"Plenty for the return to Roswell," replied the pilot, "assuming that's where we're going."

"That's the last stop for today," said Shirkey.

Within 30 minutes, the last of the alien wreckage had been

removed from the cargo bay. In its place, the workers had deposited onto the Skymaster a feast of fried chicken, sandwiches, chips, cookies, fruit, and bottles of Pepsi Cola in a tin tub filled with ice. Shirkey didn't wait for his men to finish eating before instructing the pilots to take off. Within an hour of landing, the fleet had departed for Roswell in a cloud of desert dust.

In the hot, dusty wake of the planes' prop wash, the anonymous colonel returned to his construction project. The corrugated metal hangar and barracks being erected at the site were nothing more than temporary housing for the interstellar spacecraft and the people who would protect and study it. As the shelters were going up, the big earth movers were going down, burrowing deep into the ground to carve out the spaceship's permanent home.

Groom Lake, NV

June 15, 1955
11:47 hours

Twelve men sweltered under the summer sun on the Groom Lake desert lakebed, watching a bulldozer grade sand on a runway under construction. Two hundred feet behind them, a crane hung a corrugated aluminum panel, hoisting it into place on the side of a new airplane hangar. Half of the men wore matching black suits, with white shirts and black ties. Some wore black fedora hats. The rest of the men wore the dark blue uniforms of air force generals.

One of the suits, Arthur Green, led the tour.

"Gentlemen," Green said, extending his hand exultantly toward the bulldozer, "on this spot, we are building the most secret facility in the entire world. Here is where our boys will test the country's most advanced aircraft, beginning with the U2 spy plane."

The other men looked at each other and nodded.

Two hundred yards northeast of the runway, a small patch of sand shifted. A little periscope visor popped out of the sand, rotating to scan the landscape. The periscope missed the attention of the touring CIA and Air Force VIPs.

A hundred feet below the visor, an Army lieutenant peered intently through the periscope, leaning on the handles that bookended the scope's barrel. The subterranean control room could have been transplanted from a submariner cousin, with consoles with lights, dials, switches, and phosphorescent green cathode ray tube displays.

The lieutenant slowly pivoted the scope, examining the landscape. He stopped, focusing on the 12 men on the surface.

Lieutenant Houk snapped up the periscope handles. The periscope barrel sank to the floor.

"Well?" asked the lieutenant's commanding officer, General Leslie Groves.

"Some agency fellas and Air Force generals are up there," replied Houk. "They're building a runway and a hangar. Looks like the frames are going up for a second hangar and some crew quarters."

The general nodded at the periscope. "I don't suppose we have torpedoes on this thing, do we?"

"No sir. That's the Navy, sir," deadpanned Houk.

In the eight years that had passed since the Roswell incident, Dreamland had moved underground, leaving no trace on the Groom lakebed. The subterranean facility had expanded to over 100,000 square feet, with space for research labs, utilities, and quarters for 500 people. After spearheading the Manhattan Project, which produced the Little Boy and Fat Man atomic bombs, General Groves had been assigned to the underground archipelago to lead the team tasked with reverse-engineering the Roswell spacecraft and its pilots.

Dreamland's secrecy exceeded even that of the U2 spy plane's Project Aquatone. The handfuls of people in Washington with knowledge of Aquatone had no knowledge of Dreamland. Nor did the denizens of Dreamland know of Aquatone until heavy equipment began building its topside facility.

General Groves shook his head. "Well, this is an A-1 cluster fuck."

"Yes sir," replied Houk.

The general was silent for a minute.

"Lieutenant, assemble Major Thomson at the southwest freight elevator. I'll want you there as well."

"Yes sir," said Houk.

Houk turned to leave.

"Oh, Lieutenant. One more thing."

"Sir?"

"Better bring two MPs along."

"Yes sir."

Minutes later, the five men assembled in a 50-by-50-foot freight elevator on the southwest corner of the facility. Major Lawrence Thomson, General Groves' right-hand man, turned to the general.

"Do you know what you're going to tell them?" he asked.

"Not precisely," replied the general, "though I plan to figure that out sometime between now and when we reach the surface."

The general nodded at Lieutenant Houk. The lieutenant pulled a lever. A powerful electric motor whined as the elevator lurched toward the surface.

One hundred feet above, one of the Air Force generals, Robert McAdams, spoke. "Mr. Green, can you please elaborate on the precautions the CIA has taken to secure this facility."

"Absolutely. Groom Lake is 200 miles of rough terrain away

from the closest town. There are no roads to the facility. It can only be reached by airplane or helicopter. There are also armed guards and machine gun nests posted on the perimeter."

Green added, "This is the world's most secure facility. Absolutely no one can get in undetected."

At that moment, the sand shifted 25 feet away in the men's line of sight. The ground shuddered, then a giant cube-shaped mound of sand rose from the ground directly in front the men, startling them. The sound of an electric motor accompanied the desert erection.

"Mr. Green!" shouted General McAdams. "What is this?"

"I, I don't know," stammered Green.

Sand fell away as the object rose from the ground, revealing an enormous olive-green metal crate. The crate ground to a halt. The desert was quiet.

The side of the crate facing the men slid down, revealing General Groves and his men.

Arthur Green and his party stared at the soldiers, gobsmacked.

"Mr. Green, I believe you were saying something about how no one could get into this facility undetected," said General McAdams.

Experimental Science Building

Room 213
University of Texas
Austin, TX
August 1, 1966
11:25 hours

Lara Meredith's professor unceremoniously dumped a denim three-ring binder on Lara's desk, then continued passing out binders to other students. Lara tossed her long blond hair over thin shoulders and whipped open the binder as though she were tearing the wrapping paper off a present on Christmas morning.

The binder cover revealed the title page of a 200-page typewritten paper:

Contribution of Dr. Rosalind Franklin's
X-Ray Diffraction Images to the Discovery
of the DNA Double Helix

Lara Meredith

July 28, 1966

Over the title page, a single letter was scrawled in red:

Lara gasped.

"Professor Garfield, this is a mistake. This is the wrong grade," said Lara.

Professor Garfield plopped his stack of binders on another student's desk and turned around.

"What seems to be the problem, Miss Meredith?"

"This grade on my paper, Professor. It's the wrong grade."

Professor Garfield reached down in front of Lara to grab the binder from her desk, turning it to face him. He leaned in uncomfortably close to Lara to see the paper, pushing his horn-rim glasses up to a perch upon a beaklike nose. Lara could smell the professor's Old Spice aftershave rising from the collar of his short-sleeved white dress shirt, bound with a thin black tie. She noticed a cherry angioma she had never seen before on the top of his bald head.

"No, Miss Meredith, this does indeed appear to be the correct grade. You earned an F for your paper."

Professor Garfield slapped the binder shut and turned it back to face Lara, whose own face was blushing red. A room full of young men snickered at the class' sole female student. The professor turned to collect the remaining binders for distribution.

Lara was stunned. "Professor, I've never received anything but an A grade at the University of Texas. I've never received anything but an A in high school, junior high, or elementary school. I skipped three grades. I'm the youngest senior in UT history."

After collecting the stack of remaining binders, the professor plopped them back on a student's desk and turned to face Lara.

"Tell me, Miss Meredith, from what high school did you graduate so prematurely?"

"Waxahachie."

The young men in the classroom erupted in laughter.

"Well, Miss Meredith, while I have little doubt that you were able to dazzle the stone knife- and bearskin-wielding savages of Waxahachie, we hold our students at the University of Texas to a higher standard. Perhaps you might find Texas A&M more fitting to the academic capabilities of a young woman such as yourself."

The male students roared at the insult.

Lara decided to push her bad luck.

"Professor, may I ask why I got an F?"

"You received an F Miss Meredith, because you had the temerity to claim that two Nobel laureates, Francis Crick and James Watson, did not in fact discover the double-helix structure of the DNA molecule, but instead stole the discovery from some unknown woman."

"Her name is Rosalind Franklin," said Lara. "And the reason why she is unknown is because Crick and Watson stole her research."

Lara stood up from her desk, facing off with the professor standing farther down the aisle between the classroom desks. She rapid-fire flipped through the binder to a xerograph of a blurry gray image, a circle with an X-shape.

“Sit down, Miss Meredith!” shouted the professor.

Lara ignored him. “This is Photo 51, taken by Rosalind Franklin. Photo 51 is an X-ray diffraction image of a DNA molecule. This x-shaped image resulted from X-rays diffracting off the DNA molecule’s atoms, revealing the helix structure of the molecule. Gaps in the X indicated that a second helix was present, intertwined with the first. *This* is the breakthrough.”

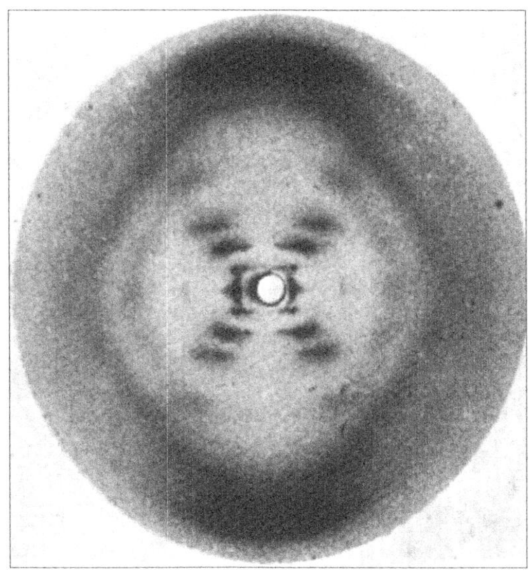

“Sit down this instant, Miss Meredith!”

Lara continued: “Franklin understood the molecule’s double helical structure long before Watson and Crick’s epiphany. Moreover, she knew Watson and Crick were wrong on the orientation of the phosphates and sugars relative to the base pairs in their model. They were weak on chemistry, and they insisted, stubbornly, that hydrophobic material should be exposed, unprotected, on the outside of their model. ‘Hydrophobic’ means it’s sensitive to water.”

"I know what 'hydrophobic' means, now sit down!"

"It was ridiculous! Dr. Franklin knew better"

"Miss Meredith, if you do not take your seat and settle down this instant, you will be suspended from this class!"

"Franklin's colleague Maurice Wilkins," Lara continued, "leaked Franklin's research to Watson and Crick. Even though he had nothing whatsoever to do with the discovery, he shared the Nobel Prize with Watson and Crick as a reward for pirating Franklin's work. And, hang on, listen to what he writes about her in his book, *The Double Helix*..."

Lara reached into her bag and retrieved a copy of *The Double Helix*, pages dog-eared and pocked with paperclips.

"'I suspect that in the beginning Maurice hoped that Rosy would calm down. Yet mere inspection suggested that she would not easily bend. By choice she did not emphasize her feminine qualities. Though her features were strong, she was not unattractive and might have been quite stunning had she taken even a mild interest in clothes. This she did not. There was never lipstick to contrast with her straight black hair, while at the age of thirty-one her dresses showed all the imagination of English blue-stocking adolescents. So it was quite easy to imagine her the product of an unsatisfied mother who unduly stressed the desirability of professional careers that could save bright girls from marriages to dull men.'"

Lara slammed the book shut.

"Watson was describing a brilliant Cambridge Ph.D. scientist from whom he probably hustled the Nobel Prize. Describing Franklin by her dress and makeup was like the Nobel Committee evaluating the scientific merits of Watson's achievement by taking inventory of the mop-like comb over of his receding hairline, bad teeth, bug eyes, and a physique better suited for a praying mantis than a steamy stud muffin male!"

"That's it!" shouted the professor. "You are suspended, Miss Meredith! For your swinish behavior and defamatory work, I will do my dead level best to see that you are expelled from this university!"

Lara was stunned.

What the fuck have I done? she thought.

"Get out!" shouted the professor.

Lara collected her shoulder bag, books, and binder and fled the classroom. In her wake, she heard the professor address the class.

"That, gentlemen, is a textbook example of precisely why women should not pursue careers in science. Their hormone-driven emotions clearly compromise their temperament and objectivity."

• • •

Lara walked dazedly past the 307-foot tall limestone UT Tower. The hot summer sun beat down on the mall. Battle oaks lined the grassy lawn, which rolled downhill like a magnificent carpet all the way to Guadalupe Street, aka "The Drag."

What the fuck have I done? Her mind repeated.

Though her mind drifted in a fog, her feet made a beeline for the Texas Union and the world's largest on-campus bar. She noticed a girl with a transistor radio sitting on a concrete bench. The Mamas and the Papas' "Monday, Monday" played on the radio.

Lara approached the union, a three-story Victorian-Gothic building rendered in a blend of smooth and ashlar fossiliferous limestone. She saw a young couple emerge from the building, holding hands. Lara noticed that the woman, no more than 18, was pregnant—Lara estimated eight months. She wore a beige shift maternity dress with a flowery ribbon around the yoke. Lara noticed how happy the young couple seemed.

Lara heard a loud pop. The percussion echoed off the limestone campus buildings.

A firecracker? She thought.

She watched the young woman fall to the ground. She lay face up on the stone sidewalk. Blood poured from her abdomen.

"Baby!" her boyfriend yelled. As he reached for his girlfriend, another gunshot cracked. The boy's chest exploded as he was knocked onto the pavement. He lay motionless next to his girlfriend.

Lara was immobilized, unable to process the images before her eyes. At that moment, she was knocked forward, breaking her nose as she smacked it on the pavement. As she tried to raise herself off the ground, she felt a screaming pain in her left shoulder blade, shattered by a sniper's bullet. She cried out. Blood pooled beneath her.

Three hundred feet above her, on the observation deck of the University of Texas tower, 25-year-old UT student and former Marine marksman Charles Whitman stared down at his victims on the mall through the scope of his Remington Model 700 rifle. He worked the bolt to chamber another round and fired as the tower clock directly beneath him began chiming the noon hour, the 7000-pound bronze bell's vibrations resonating through his feet.

Unable to move, Lara saw a man wearing a black suit walk past the wounded couple by the union. The young pregnant woman lay flat on her back. She was bleeding, but conscious.

"Help me!" she cried to the man.

Oblivious of the massacre around him, the man mistook the gunshot victims for Vietnam guerilla protesters.

"What are you doing? Get up!" he yelled at the couple as he walked swiftly past.

More shots rang out on the mall. People fell, dead and dying. A physics professor was knocked down midstride as he descended the steps to the lower mall. A police patrolman took cover behind a stone railing. As he peered through a narrow gap between the stone balusters, he instantly fell back, shot in the neck.

Lara lay on the sizzling pavement. She understood she was going to die, but her fear flowed from her with her lifeblood. Her consciousness drifted away as well. She closed her eyes to the world.

University Tower

University of Texas
Austin, TX
August 1, 1966
13:24 hours

Austin police officers Ray Martinez and Houston McCoy rounded the northeast corner of the tower observation deck and fired on Whitman, shooting him to death. On the deck, in addition to Whitman's Universal M1 carbine, they found two additional rifles, a shotgun, three handguns, and over 700 rounds of ammunition. Whitman had also packed canned peaches, coffee, vitamins, Dexedrine, Excedrin, earplugs, jugs of water, matches, lighter fluid, rope, binoculars, a machete, three knives, a transistor radio, toilet paper, a razor, and a bottle of deodorant.

In less than two hours, Whitman had shot and killed 17 people and wounded another 31. At his home, they found the body of his 23-year-old wife, stabbed to death, along with Whitman's suicide note. In the note, Whitman explained his wife's murder:

I don't want her to have to face the embrasssment [sic] my actions would surely cause her....I truly do not consider this world worth living in, and am prepared to die, and I do not want to leave her to suffer alone in it....Similar reasons provoked me to take my mother's life.

Whitman's mother was found dead in her apartment.

Whitman's note attempted to explain his actions that day:

I do not really understand myself these days. I am supposed to be an average reasonable and intelligent young man. However, lately (I cannot recall when it started) I have been a victim of many unusual and irrational thoughts....After one session I never saw the Doctor again, and since then I have been fighting my mental turmoil alone, and seemingly to no avail. After my death I wish that an autopsy would be performed on me to see if there is any visible physical disorder.

Whitman got his dying wish. An autopsy found an astrocytoma tumor in his brain, which was theorized to have pushed against the amygdala, influencing his fight-flight responses.

The university was officially closed on August 2 to clean up the bloodstains left by the 48 dead and wounded. The university opened the next day, August 3, conducting business as usual.

Brackenridge Hospital

Austin, TX
August 3, 1966
09:15 hours

Lara opened her eyes. She lay in bed in a white-walled room lit with sunlight pouring through a gauzy-draped window. A glass bottle hung next to her bed, dripping clear liquid through a tube into her arm. A vase of white carnations rested on a bed stand.

Lara tried to sit up. She felt a shrieking pain in her left shoulder blade. Gasping, she sunk back into the bed. She found her left arm immobilized, wrapped tightly against her chest. She reached toward her face, touching the tip of her bandaged nose. Gauze strips extended from her nose to wrap around her head in the shape of an X.

"Hello?" she called weakly.

A woman with salt-and-pepper hair and a nurse's dress and cap appeared at the door.

"You're back with us, dear," the nurse said.

"Where am I?"

"You're at Brackenridge Hospital," the nurse said. "They brought you here after the...accident."

"I was shot," Lara affirmed, as conscious thoughts began to

coalesce in her groggy mind.

"You are very lucky to be alive," the nurse said.

"Will I be OK?"

"Yes, dear," the nurse said. "You are going to be just fine. We phoned your parents and they're on their way from Waxahachie. You have another visitor who is eager to see you."

"Who?"

"Just a minute," the nurse said, exiting the room.

A minute later, Professor Garfield appeared at the door. He saw the surprise and disappointment on Lara's bandaged face.

"Hello, Miss Meredith," he said. Lara saw the pained expression on his face. "How are you doing?"

Lara ignored the question. "Why are you here?" she asked.

"I heard you had been hurt," he stammered. "I felt badly."

The professor looked down, unable to make eye contact.

"If it were not for me, you would not have left class early that day. I feel responsible…" he drifted off, then summoned himself. "I am very sorry for what I said to you in class. I regret it. You are most welcome to return to my class when you are well."

Lara was quiet, considering the professor's words.

"Thank you for saying that, sir. I appreciate it…

"…but I don't believe I'll be returning to class.

"You see, in the same day—the same hour, even—I got my first F, I was suspended from class, and I was shot and nearly killed. It must have been a woman who shot me. Lord knows a man wouldn't have done something so crazy."

Professor Garfield looked at the floor.

"Anyhow, I'm just thinking maybe someone out yonder in the great beyond may be trying to tell me that the University of Texas may not be the perfect school for me and my hormone-driven emotions."

Columbia University

New York, NY
August 3, 1970
09:15 hours

"You're late."

Lara's boss, Dr. Steven Schramm, caught a glimpse of her as she attempted in vain to sneak past his doorway without being detected. Lara sighed and rolled her eyes as she back stepped to his office door.

"What's the excuse this time?"

"Alien abduction," she said with her Texan twang. "Those anal probes were a bitch."

"Those are the worst," he agreed.

"Anyway, it's not like we do anything here that anyone cares about," Lara said.

"That's not true. I have a very important scientifical assignment for you."

"What's that?"

"You can fetch me some coffee, Dr. Meredith."

Lara raised her eyebrows at Dr. Schramm. Without saying a word, Columbia's youngest associate professor turned and left the office. A few minutes later, she returned with a glass Erlenmeyer chemistry flask full of a steaming dark liquid and set it on his desk.

"What's that?" asked Dr. Schramm.

"Where I come from, we call it coffee," she replied.

"Asshole," he said as he picked up the flask by the neck and gamely drank.

"Pig," Lara retorted. "Will that be all, Dr. Schramm?"

"Just one more thing, Dr. Meredith. There are some army generals waiting for you in your office."

"What?"

"It seems they're interested in your work with two-dimensional chromatography, though I can't for the life of me understand why."

"Maybe they want to sequence DNA," Lara said.

Dr. Schramm laughed. "Remind me, how old are you?"

"Twenty-five."

"Well then, if you eat right and exercise, you might live long enough to see that happen…maybe…probably not."

"How long have they been waiting?" Lara asked.

"From the time you were supposed to be at work until now."

"Jerk," she said. "Enjoy your coffee."

Dr. Schramm grinned and took another swig from his flask.

Lara speed-walked to her office and swung open a door with a black plastic name placard reading "Dr. Lara Meredith" in white letters. The door crashed into a chair containing a large white middle-aged man in an olive-green uniform. The man grunted and scooched his chair forward, allowing Lara to squeeze between the door gap into her tiny office. Three army generals sat squeezed into a space between the desk and the wall that was already tight for one person.

"Howdy," Lara said. The generals watched with curiosity as the skinny young woman, wearing bell-bottom jeans and a black T-shirt emblazoned with the Rolling Stones' tongue and lip logo, squeezed behind her desk. The battle-experienced officers instantly recognized the mushroomed metal pellet hanging from a silver chain around her neck as a spent 6mm sniper's rifle bullet. All three deduced the bullet to be a gruesome memento from the 15-year-old Vietnam War.

"Here," she said as she tugged on her desk, "let me make more room for y'all." She felt the ache in her left shoulder blade that had never fully abated in the four years since the shooting.

"When will Dr. Meredith be joining us?" asked one of the generals, looking at his watch.

"I'm Dr. Meredith," Lara replied.

The generals looked at each other, surprised.

"Doctor," one of the generals began, "do you mind if I ask your age?"

"Not at all," Lara replied. "You're only the second person to ask me that this morning. I'm 25."

The generals looked at each other again. "Are you some kind of genius?" asked another.

"Indeed, I am. What can I do for you gentlemen?"

The generals looked at each other a third time, attempting to resolve telepathically whether they should continue or abort their mission. One finally spoke.

"Doctor, your recent *Nature* article on two-dimensional

chromatography has been reviewed with great interest. We're here to determine whether it might make sense for you to head up a team that is working on a classified project for the Department of Defense."

"What project is that?" asked Lara.

"It's classified," replied the general.

"How can we determine whether or not it makes sense for me to join the project if I don't know what the project is?"

The generals were silent for a few moments, staring at Lara while they collectively pondered the paradox. Lara wondered whether the three men shared a single brain. One finally broke the silence.

"It involves sequencing DNA."

Lara laughed. The generals' flat expressions didn't budge.

"To say that is a monumental undertaking would be the understatement of a lifetime. It's the Holy Grail of genomics."

"We are aware that it's a significant project."

"It's a significant project multiplied by one million," Lara said. "My work on two-dimensional chromatography only begins to lay the foundation that is required to begin to estimate the vaguest contours of the project. It's not impossible, but the time and funding required would be extraordinary."

"What would you estimate the time and money to be?" asked one of the generals.

"My sophisticated, wild-ass guess would be 20 years and a billion dollars."

The generals looked at each other again. Lara was surprised to see that they were nodding their heads with approval.

"When can you start?"

"This is one of Dr. Schramm's sick jokes, right?" asked Lara.

"This is no joke."

"I spend half my precious research time writing grant proposals begging for mere thousands of dollars from the NSF and other agencies. No one drops a billion dollars on a project that's on the edge of science fiction."

The generals continued to stare at Lara. They appeared to be serious.

"Where would I be working?"

"We can't say."

"So, basically, you're saying that, aside from the fact that I'd be given $1 billion and 20 years to sequence DNA, there's nothing else you can tell me about this project," summarized Lara.

"I think that sums it up well, Doctor," replied one of the generals.

Lara was silent for a moment, returning the generals' stares.

"OK," she said.

Groom Lake, NV

August 10, 1970
11:12 hours

Lara felt a jolt and heard the plane's tires yelp as the aircraft touched down. Lara was the sole passenger in the cavernous cargo bay of a C-130 military plane. She sat strapped into a pull-down seat, one of dozens that bordered each side of the bay. Lara shared the bay with pallets of boxes and equipment destined for the same destination she was.

Lara wondered where she was. The bay lacked any windows that would enable Lara to know. She held her bullet pendant with her fingertips as the plane rolled to a stop. Lara heard the plane's giant propeller engines cut off. Silence.

An electric motor whirred on. A sliver of bright sunlight appeared at the rear end of the plane as its cargo bay door and off-ramp descended onto the tarmac. Bright yellow light and a blast of hot dusty wind filled the cargo bay.

Lara unfastened her seatbelt and walked to the ramp. Two men awaited her on the tarmac, a young man in a lab coat and a military policeman.

"Dr. Meredith, welcome!" the young man said, extending his hand as Lara walked down the ramp into oppressive heat and the blinding summer sun. She carried a denim shoulder bag and hauled a large Samsonite suitcase in yellow vinyl.

"I'm Richard Kaminski," he said. "I'll be working with you."

Lara dropped the suitcase, raising one hand to shield her eyes and another to shake Richard's hand. She scanned the strange landscape, a desert salt lakebed surrounded by rocky mountains. Squat buildings and aircraft hangars stood to the west of the runway.

"What country am I in?" asked Lara. "Or, rather, what planet is this?"

"This is planet earth," replied Richard. "Specifically, Groom Lake, Nevada. How was your trip?"

"Unique in my experience."

Richard laughed. "I know exactly what you mean. Mine was unique too. Say, you suppose unique trips are still unique if there are more than one?"

"You and I are going to get along just fine," replied Lara.

"Hop in," Richard said, gesturing to a jeep parked on the tarmac. "We'll take you to the complex."

Lara climbed into the back of the open-cockpit jeep as the MP and Richard boarded the front seats. Lara noticed they were driving onto the desert lakebed, away from the buildings.

"Where are we going?" Lara shouted over the hot wind noise. "It looks like civilization is in the rearview mirror."

"It's called 'Area 51,'" Richard shouted back. "It's run by the CIA. They test spy planes there. We share the same turf, but the Army runs our facility. We don't really talk to each other."

"How far is it?"

"Not far."

In the distance, Lara could see a structure emerge from the horizon. Though its image was distorted by the mirage effect from the lakebed, Lara could see that it was an aircraft hangar. As they drew closer, Lara could see that the hangar was old, with flaking white paint accented with rust.

As they neared the hangar, Lara saw that it was circled by a chain link fence. A small guard shack was parked outside the gate. An MP emerged from the shack and opened the gate, saluting to his fellow MP as he motored by. The hangar doors slowly slid open, and the jeep drove in. The hangar was completely empty, save for two more armed MPs. They saluted the jeep driver and motioned to a charcoal steel platform, 20 feet by 20 feet. A painted yellow circle circumscribed the square. Yellow and black hazard stripes adorned the perimeter.

"This way," said Richard, gesturing to the platform.

The three walked onto the platform. The MP nodded to the other two guards as one worked a control lever, causing the platform to descend.

"Whoa!" said Lara.

Richard grinned.

"What is this place?" asked Lara.

"It's called 'Dreamland.'"

"Like the 'Wildfire' laboratory in *Andromeda Strain*?"

"Not exactly."

The platform descended approximately 100 feet. Utility lights on the wall marked the group's progress as they moved down. The platform came to a stop in a bay with a drab large olive-colored steel freight door. "Level 1" was stenciled on the wall outside the door.

The MP walked to a wall phone next to the door, picked up the receiver, and dialed zero on the rotary dial.

"Today's code word is 'mystic,'" he said.

The door's latches clacked as they unlocked, and the door slid open. Richard gestured Lara past two armed MPs into a reception room. The walls were two-tone cinderblock, white and a drab olive green. The floor was speckled cream linoleum. A hanging ceiling with fluorescent light panels capped the room. Directly in front of Lara was a wooden reception desk. A uniformed woman sat behind it, flanked on either side by two flags, that of the United States and that of the 3rd Army. A bank of four elevators stood on the wall behind the receptionist's desk.

Richard saw disappointment on Lara's face.

"What's wrong?" he asked.

"I was hoping for *Andromeda Strain*," she said.

"It gets better," said Richard.

"Miss Meredith –" began the receptionist.

"Doctor," corrected Lara.

"My apologies, Dr. Meredith, welcome. We've been expecting you. I have your identification tag and the key to your quarters. Please wear your identification tag at all times you are outside your quarters. Orientation is at 14:00 hours in Conference Room A, which is on this level. You can find it on this map."

The receptionist unfolded a roadmap-style pamphlet, pointing to a conference room near the reception room. Other sections of the map revealed other levels of the underground facility.

"Dr. Kaminski will show you to your quarters."

"Actually, I'd like to see the lab now, if that's all right," said Lara.

"Not a problem," said Richard as he gestured to one of the elevators.

The receptionist smiled curtly and gestured toward the elevator bank behind her.

The elevator was cramped, with wood veneer paneling, illuminated with a single fluorescent bulb.

"The Dreamland facility has five levels for administration, labs, living quarters, utilities, and a warehouse for storage," Richard explained as the elevator descended to Level 3.

"How many people are here?" asked Lara.

"About 1,000."

"I think you'll find the science facilities here to be top notch, though the living quarters and food aren't much better than prison."

"Speaking from experience?"

Richard laughed. "No. Just hoping prison food isn't worse than Army MREs."

The elevator doors opened to a cinderblock corridor, painted two-tone white and blue. The floor was green vinyl.

"This is Level 3, where the science happens," said Richard. "Biology, physics, material sciences."

"This place looks ancient," Lara observed. "How old is it?"

"Parts of it date back to 1947," said Richard as he walked to a large set of swinging doors. "The lab was overhauled recently."

"So why all the secrecy for a science project?"

"You'll see."

Richard pushed through the swinging doors into a cavernous room with lab benches and equipment. Unlike the cramped hallways and the reception room, the ceiling in the enormous room was high, 20 feet, with hanging fluorescent lamps, air conditioning and ventilation shafts, and conduits for power and network cables. The lab was a hive of activity, with men and women in white coats working at lab benches.

Lara gasped. The lab was packed with the most sophisticated equipment she had ever seen.

"Those electrophoresis units are state of the art. Is that an SDS PAGE unit?"

Richard nodded, grinning.

"So, you're doing protein analysis here?"

"Yup."

"I'm in a nerd dream. Please don't wake me up."

Lara noticed that the lab benches were unusual in that a computer terminal was parked on each one.

"Are those CDC terminals?"

Richard grinned. "Yup. Connected to the world's fastest supercomputer. All lab instruments and experiments are plugged in. We log every byte of data from every experiment in a 10-gigabyte database."

"I can't believe it," Lara said. "I've begged, borrowed, and stolen to get grant money for a few thousand dollars' worth of equipment. There are millions of dollars' worth of hardware in this room alone."

“There’s another million dollars’ worth in those crates over there,” Richard said, pointing at wooden crates stacked in a corner. “We just haven’t gotten around to cracking them open yet. It’s the first lab I’ve ever seen that’s overfunded.

“There’s more,” Richard added. “I have a welcome gift for you.”

He reached into his lab coat pocket and retrieved an oblong black box out his pocket. It had a numerical keypad, as well as buttons marked “X^y,” “LOG,” “ARC,” “SIN,” “COS,” and more. He flipped a switch, and a red “0” flashed onto an LED display.

“Holy shit! Are you kidding me?” Lara exclaimed.

“I told you it got better,” Richard said, grinning. “This is a prototype of a Hewlett Packard HP 35 scientific calculator. It’s the first handheld device ever to perform logarithmic and trigonometric functions with one keystroke—the world’s first electronic slide rule. They’re not scheduled for production release for a couple of years, but we managed to get five of these jewels for the lab. This one is yours.”

“Oh my God!” Lara exclaimed, her hands shaking as she held the calculator.

“Don’t drop it. These cost us $100,000 a pop.”

At that moment, the lab doors flew open, pushed by a refrigerator-sized wooden crate on a dolly wheeled by a soldier in fatigues. A middle-aged scientist in a wheelchair was in hot pursuit. His hair was a chaotic mess of fluffy salt and pepper. He wore tinted glasses and a lab coat.

“Herr Dr. Strangelove!” Richard called to the man.

“Dr. Strangelove?” Lara asked. “You’re not serious.”

The scientist hooked a sharp left turn in his chair and slid to a stop in front of Richard and Lara. He looked at Richard with a comical grin.

"*Guten Tag*, Richard!" Strangelove said.

Lara burst out laughing.

"I'm so sorry!" she gasped, trying to suppress her laughter. She regained her composure, then squealed again, holding her hands to her mouth. The scientists in the lab covered their mouths and turned away, trying to avoid contagion.

"I'm so sorry," Lara said, wiping tears from her eyes. "It's just that you look exactly like –"

"Dr. Strangelove," the scientist said with a German accent, grin intact. "Yes, yes, that's what they tell me. I've never seen the movie myself. Perhaps we can watch it together sometime."

"Doctor, are you hitting on me?" asked Lara.

"Sure, sure. Why not?" replied Strangelove. "Do you like movies? I like movies. They have movies here."

Lara's mouth hung open. She didn't know what to say to the funny man who looked to be old enough to be her father.

Richard interrupted the awkward pause. "Dr. Lara Meredith, I would like you to meet Dr. Gunther Appel. Dr. Appel, this is Dr. Lara Meredith. Dr. Appel heads up our physics section. Dr. Meredith will be leading our DNA sequencing project."

"Ah, yes," said Strangelove. "I heard you were coming. I read your *Nature* article. Very intriguing."

"What shall I call you?" asked Lara.

"Everybody here calls me 'Strangelove,' so, 'Strangelove' is good.

I like 'Strangelove.' So, do you like movies?"

"What brings you to the bio lab, Herr Doctor?" deflected Richard.

"Ah, they just delivered our new scanning electron microscope. I am excited to see it!"

"How did you come to be here, Doctor?" asked Lara.

"Me? Oh, I came to the States with Herr Dr. von Braun after the war. I was part of his rocketry team. We made the V2 rocket. You've heard of it, perhaps?"

"Of course," said Lara. "It nearly destroyed London."

"Yes, yes, it was a tremendous success. So, we were all rounded up by the Americans and brought to the States so we could build rockets. They called it 'Operation Paperclip.' We weren't prisoners of war, exactly. We were prisoners of peace," Strangelove said, chuckling.

"Anyway, Herr Dr. von Braun got to make moon rockets. They sent me underground. I'll never get to see Bavaria again, but what does Bavaria have that this place doesn't have? With the exception of beautiful mountains…and forests …and lakes and villages and German beer and..."

"So, what do you do here, Doctor?"

"Material science, primarily," said Strangelove. "Quite tedious, actually. I'd rather be building moon rockets with Wernher. That seems like much more fun."

A loud crack echoed across the lab as the soldier began prying the wooden microscope crate apart.

"Ah! I'm off to see our new toy. *Wiedersehen*!" said Strangelove as he spun his chair and wheeled away.

“I’ve a feeling I’m not in Kansas anymore,” said Lara in Strangelove’s wake.

“You have no idea,” replied Richard. “Would you like to see where you’ll be working?”

“Yes, please.”

Richard walked across the lab through a gauntlet of lab benches and scientists to a locked black steel door. An intercom box was next to the door. Richard pressed a button on the box.

“Today’s code word is ‘mystic,’” He said.

The door’s electric lock buzzed, and he pulled the heavy door open, gesturing Lara in.

Lara’s lab looked much like a smaller version of the outer lab, 1,000 square feet, with a similar assortment of lab benches and state-of-the-art equipment.

“This is your lab,” said Richard. “You’ll get to pick your team members. There’s one more thing I need to show you.”

Richard gestured to a large stainless-steel door against the far wall.

“In my wildest dreams, I never thought I’d have the chance to work on a project to sequence human DNA,” Lara said as they walked to the door.

“That’s good, because you won’t be sequencing human DNA,” Richard said.

Lara felt her heart sink.

“Earthworm DNA?” she asked.

“Not exactly.”

Richard opened the steel door. Inside were four human-sized

stainless-steel drawers. Richard pulled one open, sliding out a body covered with a Mylar sheet. He peeled down the Mylar to reveal the Gray's head, with its oversized cranium, black almond eyes, and tiny down-curved mouth.

"Jesus, Mary, and Joseph!" exclaimed Lara.

"Better than earthworms?" asked Richard.

Lara nodded, laughing. "*That* is fucking cool!"

Dreamland Research Facility

Area 51
Groom Lake, NV
October 12, 1970
10:25 hours

Strangelove pushed his wheelchair down a cinderblock corridor on Level 3. He reached a locked double door at the end of the corridor with a black plastic sign marked "Hangar." He reached as high as he could from his wheelchair to reach the button on the intercom box next to the door.

Nothing happened.

Finally, a man's voice crackled from the box: "Code word?"

"Ah, yes, my apologies," replied Strangelove. "Today's code word…let's see…'Ruby'…No, wait a minute. Ruby was yesterday's code word. 'Amethyst.' No, that's not right. 'Baloney,' perhaps?"

Strangelove heard a sigh from the box.

"Doctor, I'm the one who gets in trouble if there's a security breach. Today's code is 'lightning.' Please try to remember it."

"Yes, yes, I will remember," said Strangelove. "I have an excellent memory."

"Mind like a steel trap," the voice said as the door lock buzzed.

"*Danke schön*!" Strangelove said as he pushed through the

double doors. Inside the underground hangar was a yacht-sized, saucer-shaped, charcoal-colored object. Scaffolding surrounded the craft, whose surface was fractured from the explosion that ripped it apart during a lightning storm in 1947. All of its pieces had been found and reassembled like a three-dimensional puzzle. A cardboard tag was taped to each of the fragments, listing its index number.

Aside from the cracks formed by the explosion, the craft had no seams whatsoever. It was featureless—without windows, doors, or apparatus of any kind—a uniform piece of solid carbon. The interior of the craft was identical. It was a round room without equipment, control panels, or seats.

Strangelove had visited the craft countless times over the years. He had carefully examined each and every fragment. Every piece had properties identical to every other. They were all featureless solid chunks of carbon, indestructibly hard yet light as a feather. "Chunk" was the operative word—every one of the spacecraft's fragments was completely solid, without features of any kind. There were no mechanisms, no instruments, no controls. no circuitry, no power source. They were simple blocks of carbon. There was nothing about the fragments, individually or in the aggregate, that could enable the Grays to travel anywhere, much less traverse interplanetary space. It was as though someone had dropped a cheap Hollywood science fiction prop in the middle of the New Mexico desert as a terrible prank.

Twenty-three years after being assigned to the underground bunker facility, Strangelove and his team knew little more about the Grays' spacecraft than they had the day they held the wreckage in their hands for the first time. They had quickly assessed that the material comprising the fragments was some type of carbon allotrope, which had a structure similar to that of its cousins, graphite and diamond. Beyond that, decades and hundreds of millions of dollars of research conducted in America's most secret facility had yielded virtually nothing.

Strangelove rolled his wheelchair closer to the craft and gazed up at it. The ever-present grin on his face belied his frustration. While the Saturn V rocket of his mentor, Wehrner von Braun, had sent Americans to the moon, Strangelove had accomplished nothing in this military dungeon. Each time he visited the strange craft, he hoped for some epiphany that would unlock its puzzle and provide some meaning for a lifetime away from his beloved Bavaria. He was now at his wit's end. The prudence of the scientific method had given way to desperation.

His set his hands on his thighs, made silent by polio when he was a teenager. Back then, growing up in his native Bavaria without the use of his legs, a younger Gunther Appel had relied instead on his imagination to propel him throughout the stars, aided by the works of Jules Verne. Now, he stared at the impossible spacecraft, something light-years beyond anything he or von Braun or Jules Verne could have possibly dreamt up.

"*Bitte schön*," Strangelove said to the ship, "please reveal yourself to me."

The double doors of the hangar burst open. Another scientist, a man in his thirties, appeared in Strangelove's office doorway. The man was out of breath.

"Herr Doctor, you must see this!"

Strangelove looked up. "You have found something, Sherman?"

"Yes, Herr Doctor, come quick, please!"

"Sherman, if you please," said Strangelove, motioning to the handgrips on his wheelchair. Sherman trotted to Strangelove's wheelchair and rolled him rapidly out the door and down the hallway.

"Careful, Sherman—you are going to pop a wheelie!" cautioned Strangelove.

Sherman spoke breathlessly as they hurried down the corridor. "We just installed the new scanning electron microscope. It gives the electrons much higher energy than the previous generations. It enables much deeper penetration into thick samples."

They arrived at a door with a sign marked "Electron Microscopy."

Inside the room, a tall cylinder, a five-foot-tall electron microscope, rose from a long desk. A computer monitor and keyboard rested on the desk next to the microscope. The much shorter wavelength when using electrons as a light source instead of visible light enabled the electron microscope to render detail with over 1,000 times the extent possible with a traditional light microscope.

"We took a second look at one of the fine granular fragments—take a look!" said Sherman.

Strangelove leaned in and stared into the microscope's binocular eyepieces. He pulled back from the microscope.

"*Gott im Himmel*!" he exclaimed.

University Avenue

Palo Alto, CA
April 17, 1985
16:15 hours

Helen Mason honked the horn of her black BMW 735i at the endless line of cars in front of her on University Avenue as they crept toward downtown Palo Alto. The 47-year-old litigator had just hung up her car phone after getting the news from Stanford Hospital that her son had been involved in some kind of accident and rushed to the emergency room.

She honked again. An arm protruded in a U-shape from the driver's side window of the Lexus directly ahead of her. It extended a finger. Helen slapped her steering wheel, lowered her window, and screamed at the finger: "My son is dying, you son of a bitch!"

The Lexus hand signal morphed, gesturing forward at the long line of slow-moving cars before hoisting upward into the international symbol for "what the hell can I do about the cars in front of me?"

Fifteen minutes later, Helen trotted through the ER's sliding glass doors in a pair of slick beige heels. Dressed in a collarless gray silk Armani power jacket, matching knee skirt, beige silk blouse, and pearls, she was instantly out of place against the wave of young men who faced her, clad in red and white jerseys, tight white equestrian pants, and leather riding boots with knee guards. It was the Stanford polo team. Seeing Helen, the team parted and pointed toward a bed where Kyle was sitting up.

"Hi, Mom!" Kyle said.

"You're not dead," Helen said. "Good, because I'm going to kill you."

"I love you too, Mom."

A doctor approached. "Are you this young man's mother?"

"I am."

The doctor slapped an X-ray on a fluorescent light panel next to the bed. "Your son has at least two broken ribs. I say 'at least' because these are the breaks we can see on the X-rays." He pointed to jagged breaks in two ghostly ribs on the film. "Broken ribs don't always show up."

"What can you do about it?" asked Helen.

"Not much," said the doctor. "We can give him something for the pain. Ribs take about six weeks to heal. He'll be sleeping upright for a while. Definitely no polo for at least eight weeks."

"No polo *ever!*" said Helen. "We talked about this. You're in high school. What on Earth are you doing playing polo at Stanford?"

"It's exciting, Mom. I love it! The guys are cool—they taught me how to ride."

"Not well enough, apparently."

"No, it was rad," countered one of the team members. "I've never seen anyone gallop that fast bareback before. Your son is an amazing rider."

"Bareback?" Helen exclaimed.

"Oh shit," the team member said.

Helen shoved a stern finger in the preppy team member's face. "Can you say 'expulsion?' I'll bet you can. Do you have any idea how many lawyers there are on Page Mill Road? I do, because I'm one of them!"

"Yes ma'am," the young man replied. "We didn't mean anything. Kyle really is a great..."

Helen shook her finger to shush the polo player. He stopped talking and turned, ushering his teammates to leave.

Helen turned to Kyle, shaking her head.

"How do you feel?" she asked.

"It only hurts when I laugh," he said. "And breathe…actually, it hurts all the time."

Helen pulled up a chair to sit next to the hospital bed.

"Your father and I aren't trying to keep you from having fun. We're just experienced enough to see around corners that you aren't able to yet."

"Really?" asked Kyle. "You and Dad ride horses?"

"No, and now we understand *why* we don't ride horses."

Helen reached into her purse and retrieved an envelope. The return address read West Point, NY.

"This came for you today," she said, handing Kyle the letter. "Why are you getting mail from West Point?"

Kyle didn't say anything as he opened the envelope and read the letter. He looked up at the ceiling and sighed.

"What is it?" asked his mother.

"I wanted to find a better time to tell you this," Kyle said, looking at his mother. "I've been accepted to West Point."

Helen's jaw dropped. Kyle's parents had always assumed their son would attend an Ivy League school and pursue a career in law or medicine or technology—anything but the military. His grades and pedigree were excellent. Kyle could write his ticket.

"You've never talked about the military before," Helen said, astonished. Up to that moment, she had thought her relationship with her son was a close one. Helen was aware of the process required to get into West Point. The fact that Kyle had kept it a complete secret wounded her.

"Why didn't you say something?"

"I didn't think you would support me," Kyle said, twisting the knife. "Was I wrong, Mom?"

Helen looked at the purse in her lap. "You're lying in a hospital bed. Your bones are broken. All you did was ride a horse."

"Bareback," Kyle added. "Really fast."

"OK, you were riding a horse bareback, really fast," Helen clarified. "But no one was shooting at you, and you still ended up in a hospital. Where will you end up when people start shooting at you?"

Tears welled in her eyes. "I have always wanted to support your choices. But I don't think you have the first clue how much I worry about you."

Kyle was silent, considering his mother's words. It had never before occurred to him that he might be mortal.

Dreamland Research Facility

Area 51
Groom Lake, NV
March 15, 1985
10:25 hours

Lara Meredith burst out of her lab door and stormed down the hallway toward the elevator, clutching a pair of overhead transparency slides in her hand. Her destination was a debriefing to which she had not been invited. She was never invited to meetings where Dreamland's senior science staff briefed the generals about their research findings on the Grays. The reason she was left out was because the generals were no longer interested in her research focus, which was the Grays themselves. The generals were much more concerned about what the spacecraft research team had to report. Over 80 percent of the Dreamland facility's scientific research capacity was now dedicated to analyzing the spacecraft.

Once in the elevator, Lara rapid fire punched the first-floor button.

• • •

Three floors above her, at the briefing meeting Lara was about to crash, three generals were seated on one side of a large black conference table in a cinderblock-walled conference room that resembled a bunker. Though Dreamland was big on science, its creature comforts had not evolved in the 15 years since Lara had arrived. An overhead projector positioned on the conference table lit up a screen erected on the far side of the room. Strangelove sat opposite the generals. The purpose of the meeting was to brief Dreamland's latest commanding officer, Lieutenant General James Buchanan "Buck" Patterson, on the scientists' progress.

"Good morning, gentlemen," Strangelove began. "With your permission, I will begin the briefing."

"Go ahead, Doctor," replied General Patterson.

"For the benefit of General Patterson, who is new to our group, I will begin with a summary of our research and findings. As you know, nearly 40 years ago, the spacecraft wreckage was brought to Groom Lake for triage examination. Eventually, this facility was constructed, and our research has continued here. After the completion of the Dreamland complex, the bodies of the extraterrestrials were transferred here from their temporary home at Wright-Patterson Air Force Base.

"Something that perplexed us from the outset of our work was the lack of features on the spacecraft. The craft appeared to have no means of propulsion, no instrumentation, no controls, no features of any kind. The fragments that broke away from the spacecraft were solid objects. We tried cutting into them to determine if they were hollow and if they contained any mechanisms. Again, they were solid matter—there was nothing inside."

Strangelove asked his assistant to place a transparency on the projector. It was a photograph of one of the fragments, a charcoal-colored object. The image was dated May 17, 1949.

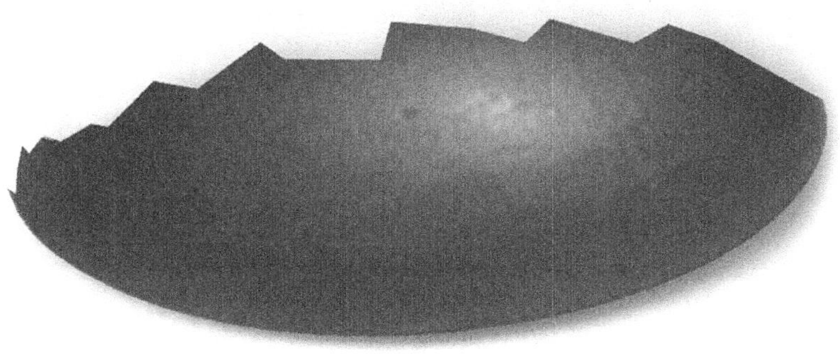

2 3 4 5 6 7

```
Dreamland Research Facility
Flying disc photography
Craft section: 14
Artifact: 72
Photograph: 1148
Date: May 17,1949
```

TOP SECRET
EYES ONLY

"This is one of the fragments," Strangelove said. "It appears to be an ordinary piece of some graphite-type material. However, when we take a closer look, we find something very interesting."

Strangelove asked his assistant to display the next slide. An image showing an intricate lattice network displayed on the screen.

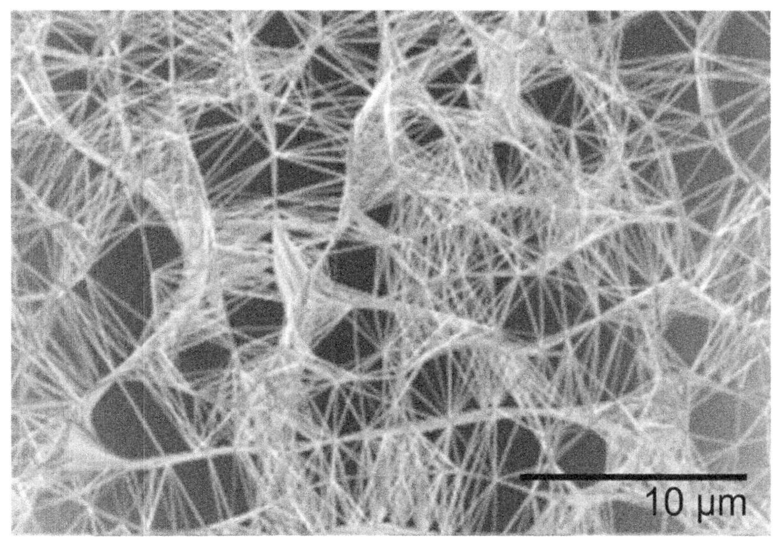

Dreamland Research Facility
Electron microscopy
Craft section: 14
Artifact: 72
Image: 112697
Scan date: May 21,1962

TOP SECRET
EYES ONLY

"This is a small sliver of the object, magnified 2,000 times," said Strangelove. "It reveals an artificial network of some kind. When we took an even closer look at the network, using a scanning electron microscope, this is what we found..."

Strangelove's assistant placed the next transparency on the overhead projector. A fuzzy image of white glowing hexagons resting atop a lattice substrate appeared on the projection screen.

Dreamland Research Facility
Electron microscopy
Craft section: 14
Artifact: 72
Image: 112697
Scan date: May 21,1962

TOP SECRET
EYES ONLY

"This," Strangelove continued, "is an electron microscope scan of a portion of one of the spacecraft fragments. We found that the craft's mechanisms are embedded into the hull at the molecular level."

"What is that—some kind of micro circuitry?" asked General Patterson.

"It is circuitry, but much, much smaller than our current micro circuitry," replied Strangelove. "These circuits are comprised entirely of carbon molecules. Some of these structures are 2,500 times smaller than that of a red blood cell."

"How is that possible?" asked General Patterson.

"We did not fully understand how it was possible until a breakthrough discovery happened this year," Strangelove explained. "Three scientists from Rice University and Sussex University created a new carbon allotrope, or molecule, that has the potential to revolutionize miniature technology. The new molecule also explains the Gray circuitry perfectly."

Strangelove asked his assistant to display an image that looked like several stacked sections of chicken wire. Each section was a lattice of connected hexagonal structures.

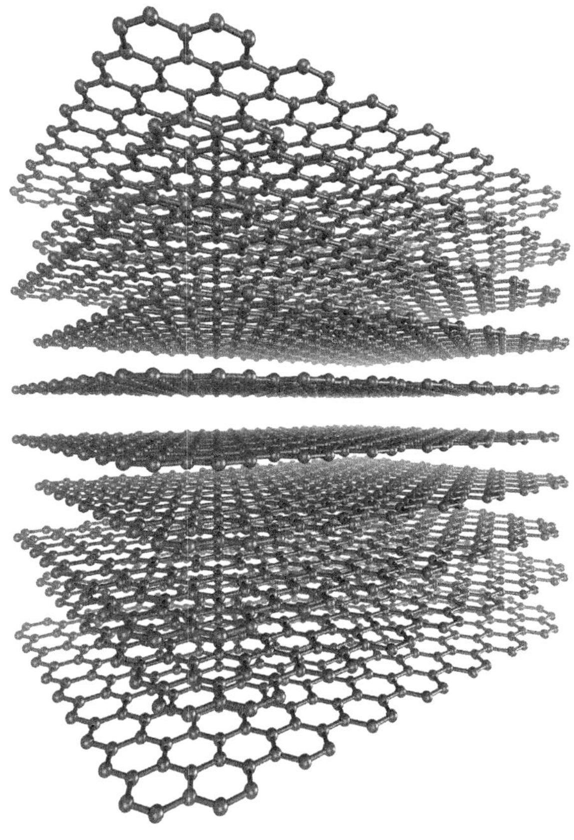

"This is a graphical representation of a graphite molecule, a carbon allotrope. As you can see, each carbon atom is bonded to three other carbon atoms. The exceptions are the edges of the lattices, where the bonds dangle. Carbon and other atoms, like hydrogen, are attracted to those dangling bonds. Because other carbon atoms are attracted, the lattice does not have a fixed number of carbon atoms.

"The Rice and Sussex scientists, Richard Smalley, Harold Kroto, and Robert Curl, inadvertently created a new carbon molecule by firing a laser at a graphite target. The molecule consistently had 60 carbon atoms—no more, no less. Because a traditional carbon molecule structure would not have a fixed number of carbon atoms due to the dangling bonds, they realized that they had created a fundamentally new carbon molecule structure. The only way that it was possible for the molecule to have a fixed number of carbon atoms was if all of the carbon atoms were connected to each other—there could be no dangling bonds. They theorized that the molecule had some form of closed cage structure. The question was, what structure and shape would enable 60 carbon atoms to connect with each other?

"Harold Kroto was reminded of the Buckminster Fuller's geodesic dome that housed the U.S. Pavilion at the Expo 67 World's Fair. He wondered if their mystery molecule might have a geodesic shape.

"The geodesic dome was their inspiration. With some trial and error, they determined that the following shape could array 60 carbon atoms in a closed cage configuration."

Strangelove motioned to his assistant to place a transparency showing a wireframe sphere on the overhead projector.

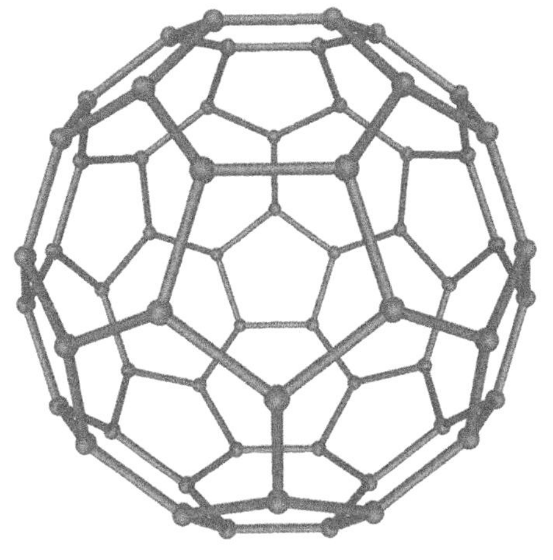

"But that looks like..." began General Patterson.

"A soccer ball, yes," said Strangelove. "It's a soccer ball. A combination of 20 hexagrams and 12 pentagrams connecting 60 carbon atoms."

"The scientists named the new molecule 'Buckminsterfullerene'..."

General Patterson had heard enough. He was convinced that Strangelove was playing some kind of propeller-head joke. "Doctor! Seriously, a new molecule that looks like a soccer ball called 'Buckminsterfullerene'? What kind of fools do you take us for?"

Strangelove put his hand on his chin, pondering the question. "Well, I am not entirely sure how many different varieties of fools exist in the army."

"What in God's name does Buckminsterfullerenes have to do with alien technology!" thundered General Patterson.

"The Gray technology is an adaptation of Buckminsterfullerenes, albeit a very advanced adaptation. Observe," said Strangelove.

His assistant placed another slide on the projector. This slide depicted a diagram of a wireframe tube.

"The Rice and Sussex scientists have shown us that it is possible to create new carbon molecules in a variety of configurations. This is a carbon tube, only one nanometer wide—about the width of two silicon atoms. These 'nanotubes' are quite remarkable in terms of their properties. They are formed into a variety of shapes and sizes, and perform electronic functions, including conducting, insulating, or superconducting electricity. They can be configured to generate intense magnetic fields. They can also be configured into nanomachinery, like motors and gears. These carbon structures are the heart of the Grays' technology.

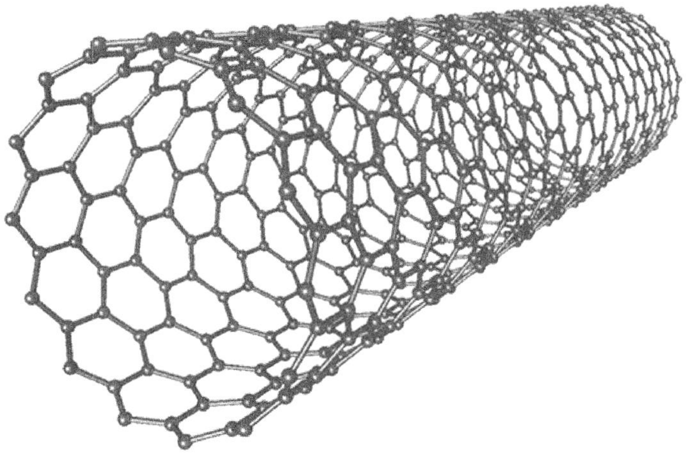

"Trillions of carbon nanostructures are configured throughout the craft's hull to perform a variety of functions, including computing, navigation, power generation, and communications.

"Given the precision with which the nanotube lattices have been integrated into the hull and surfaces of the craft, it is our belief that the craft was not manufactured in the conventional sense. We believe the carbon matter was programmed into this configuration.

"In effect, the Gray's spacecraft wasn't constructed—it was *grown*.

"Our efforts have been focused on reverse-engineering the various functions of the nanomechanisms. This is exceedingly tedious work, as the nanostructures are integrated completely into the craft's hull, and it is extremely difficult to microscopically analyze a section of nanotube lattices without damaging them. We can't slice through part of the hull without damaging or destroying millions of nanotubes. In recent years, we have used X-ray computerized tomography to map the infrastructure. This has been an effective approach, though the mapping process is slow due to limitations of computing bandwidth, even with our Cray supercomputer.

"In the course of our macro-level survey of the craft, we have found what we believe is its power source. The Grays appear to have mastered a way to manufacture antimatter onboard the craft and manage a controlled antimatter reaction."

"Antimatter? Please explain." said General Patterson.

"Antimatter is the opposite of matter," explained Strangelove. "It is comprised of antiparticles. These particles have the same mass as those with which we are more familiar, such as protons, neutrons, and electrons, though their charge and other properties are precisely opposite those of their matter counterparts. For example, an antimatter hydrogen atom is the exact opposite of a matter hydrogen atom. The opposite of an electron is an anti-electron, or positron.

"When an encounter between matter and antimatter occurs, they annihilate each other. The reaction yields a tremendous amount of energy. Antimatter is prohibitively difficult to manufacture and store with our present technology. Additionally, the output of an antimatter reaction would be impossible to contain with current technology."

Strangelove asked his assistant to display a transparency illustrating a matter-antimatter reaction between an electron and a positron.

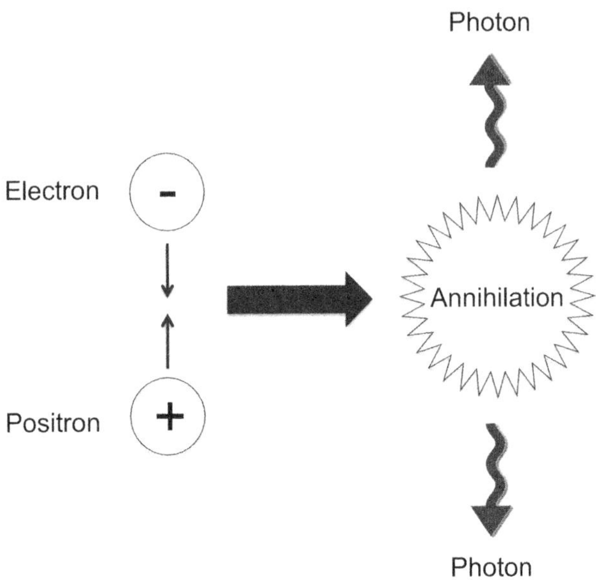

"What would be the yield of an antimatter reaction?" asked General Chaffee.

Strangelove asked his assistant to display another slide. This slide presented Einstein's famous $E = mc^2$ equation indicating the equivalence of mass and energy. Values were substituted for each variable:

$$E = mc^2 = 6.2\text{kg} \times (3 \times 10^8 \text{ m/s})^2 = 5.58 \times 10^{17} \text{ Joules}$$

"It would vary according to the amount of matter and antimatter annihilated," said Strangelove. "Take, for example, the atomic bomb dropped on Hiroshima.

That bomb contained 140 pounds of Uranium 235 and had a blast yield of 15 kilotons, with a perimeter of severe blast damage of 1.1 square miles.

"A bomb with the same amount of antimatter, 140 pounds, would have a perimeter of severe blast damage of over 92,000 square miles...enough to destroy the United Kingdom."

The generals' eyes widened.

"Of course, the output of the Grays' antimatter reactor is considerably greater," said Strangelove.

"How much greater?" asked General Patterson.

"The energy generated from this spacecraft's reactor is approximately one hundred million times that of the Hiroshima atomic bomb."

The generals rocked back in their chairs, aghast.

"What can you tell us about the craft's weapon systems?" asked General Patterson.

"The craft does not appear to have any weapons," replied Strangelove.

"But if it did?" asked the general.

"If it did, this single craft, the size of a yacht, could easily generate sufficient energy to completely destroy the Earth in an instant," replied Strangelove with little more emotion than if he were reading the *Wall Street Journal* aloud. Strangelove was not fearful of the Grays. He was awestruck by them.

Strangelove could see from the generals' faces that their reaction was very different from his. The generals were *very* afraid. Strangelove found their response amusing. He knew there was no possible defense that humans from twentieth-century Earth could muster against such vastly advanced technology. If the Grays wanted them dead, they would be dead. It was as simple as that.

"However, that is not what concerns me at present," Strangelove continued.

"So, if Earth's destruction doesn't rate, what does, Doctor?" snapped General Patterson.

"The absence of any apparent means of propulsion through interstellar space. We do not understand how this spacecraft was able to traverse hundreds or thousands of light years. Approximately 40 percent of the craft's mechanisms appear to be dedicated to manipulating gravity. We have theorized that there is a possibility that the ship is somehow distorting space-time in order to appear to move faster than light," explained Strangelove.

"Translation, Doctor," ordered General Patterson.

"Einstein's general theory of relativity describes the relationship between space and time and gravity. A way to think about space-time is like an elastic fabric," said Strangelove, signaling to his assistant to place a slide displaying a wireframe matrix on the overhead.

"If you place a bowling ball into the fabric," he continued, "it

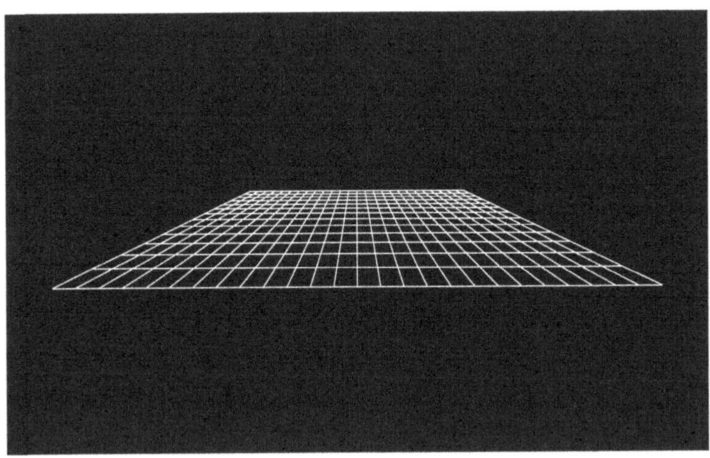

sinks into a well, pulling the fabric around it."

Strangelove asked his assistant to display a diagram illustrating the effect of gravity on space-time. A wireframe of a sphere sinking into a plane appeared on the screen.

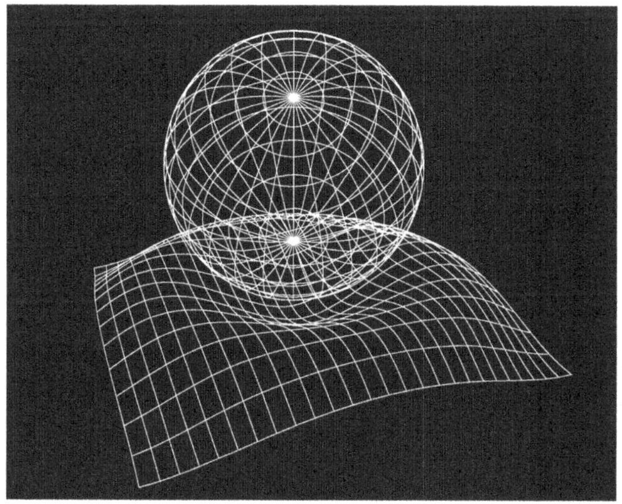

"This is a good way to think about the effect of gravity on space-time. Gravity bends and distorts the fabric of space-time. A simple example of this is the military's GPS system. GPS relies on precise time in order to provide accurate positioning coordinates. However, because GPS satellites are moving rapidly in low gravity, time is measured slightly differently on those satellites than it is for terrestrials on Earth. Without compensating for the difference, GPS wouldn't work," explained Strangelove.

"One theory is that the Grays have developed a way to manipulate gravity in order to bend space-time. Think of a paper map. If you lay the map on the table, the distance between two points on opposite sides of the map might be 100 miles. However, if you fold the map, you can greatly shorten that distance—perhaps to 10 miles. Perhaps less. For great distances, like those involved in interstellar travel, it would appear as though the spacecraft could travel faster than light. This is one of the theorized properties of a black hole, that its gravitational energy can warp space in this manner. If it were possible to traverse a black hole, it is theorized that one could emerge in a different space-time.

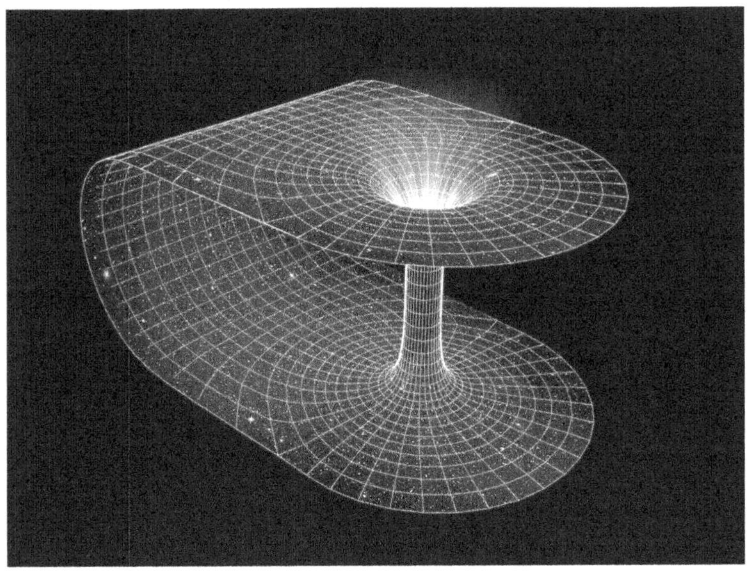

"However," Strangelove continued, "from what we have discerned thus far in our efforts to analyze this gravity engine, I am skeptical that its purpose is interstellar travel. Forty percent of this spacecraft remains a mystery."

At that moment, the conference door burst open. Lara blew into the room with an armed guard in tow.

"Greetings, Lara!" said Strangelove, smiling, genuinely amused at her unexpected appearance.

The generals were angry.

"Miss –" began General Patterson.

"Doctor," corrected Lara.

"...Doctor," continued the general, "this is a closed meeting."

Lara ignored the general. "Strangelove, you know that 40 percent you haven't figured out yet? Well, I know what it does."

Everyone in the room stared at her in stunned silence.

"The Grays aren't from another world. They're from this one. That craft isn't a spaceship. It's a time machine!"

Dreamland Research Facility

Area 51
Groom Lake, NV
March 15, 1985
10:45 hours

The generals burst out laughing. Strangelove's perma-smile evaporated. His expression was one of shock. Lara was astonished at the generals' juvenile reaction. After everything these people had witnessed—the craft, the Grays, the presumption of interstellar travel—why was it such a fantastic stretch to entertain the possibility that these beings might be time travelers?

General Patterson was the first to regain his composure. "Doctor, aren't you a biologist?"

Lara raised one of the transparencies in her hand and shook it. "This is the result of a DNA test we just completed. As you know, mass spectrometric analysis performed on Gray tissue years ago confirmed a DNA signature. That's what led to our project to map Gray DNA. We're still years away from completing that index, but in the meantime, we took advantage of a shortcut.

"Most of our DNA is identical to that of all other humans and, for that matter, of other primates. However, certain areas of DNA exhibit polymorphism, meaning they can take on many different forms. This polymorphism makes each individual's DNA unique. There is a new process, called restriction fragment length polymorphism, or RFLP, which is used to isolate and analyze these areas of human DNA. For the hell of it, I decided to run a RFLP analysis on Gray DNA—primarily to gauge some of the broad stroke differences between Grays and humans.

"I performed RFLP tests between Grays and several dozen human ethnic groups. These are the results of those tests."

Lara held up one of the transparencies, pausing for effect.

"And?" asked General Patterson.

"And the Grays are human," replied Lara.

"More precisely, they're from the Han ethnic group—they're Chinese."

Again, the generals burst into laughter. Strangelove stared straight ahead, grim-faced, saying nothing.

"You've got a bizarre sense of humor, Doctor," said General Patterson.

"This is no joke, general," said Lara through tight lips. "Look!"

Lara slapped the transparency on the overhead.

On the screen, a series of short fuzzy parallel bands appeared, organized in columns and rows. Each column had a heading that corresponded to each test subject. The five subjects, four Grays and one Han Chinese, enabled side-by-side comparison of the placement of the bands. The band placement corresponded to the relative weight of the DNA fragments of each subject. Smaller fragments appeared at the bottom of each column. Larger fragments appeared at the top. Fragments of identical size were located in the same row. In one row, bands aligned for all five subjects.

"The four markers for the Grays line up identically with our Han Chinese test subject. We've repeated the test three times with identical results. The results are conclusive. The Grays are human."

"Well, they don't look very human, do they?" said the general.

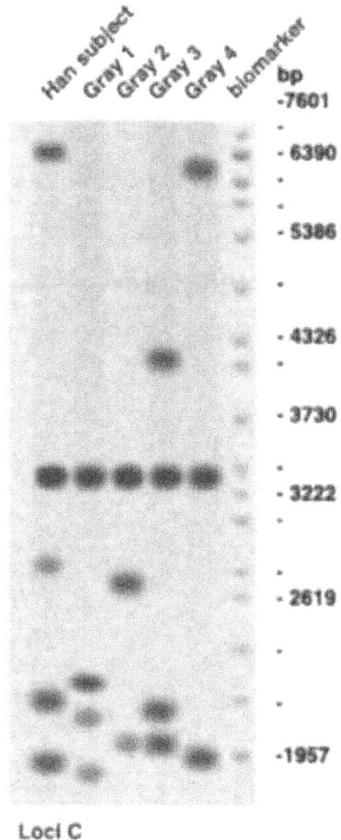

Dreamland Research Facility
RFLP Analysis 12: Han Ethnic Group
Image: 5543772
Date: March 15, 1985

TOP SECRET

"Inside, they actually look very human. That's something I always found uncanny, that life in another star system could independently evolve into something virtually identical to humans. Aside from their heads—larger craniums and brains—and the eyes, they are virtually identical to humans anatomically. Their chromosomes are identical to humans," said Lara, displaying a transparency of a karyotype analysis of one of the Grays. Twenty-three pairs of wormlike squiggles appeared on the giant screen—the chromosomes of a male humanoid.

"Now we know their DNA is human too," explained Lara.

The generals, speechless, looked at each other with confusion. Finally, Strangelove broke the silence.

"She's right!" he said. "My God, she's right."

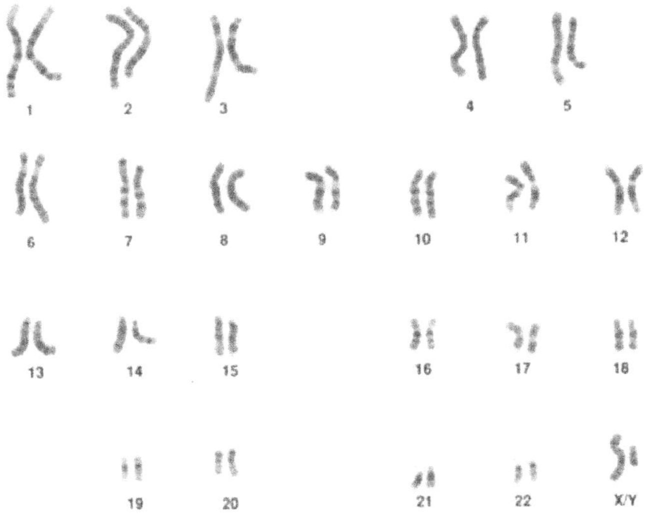

Dreamland Research Facility
Karyotype analysis
Subject: Gray 1
Image: 63519
Date: December 12, 1955

TOP SECRET
EYES ONLY

Strangelove looked directly at Lara. Tears welled up in his eyes, and his smile returned to his face. After working the problem for decades, the gift of a lifetime had dropped into his lap out of nowhere. The generals stared at Strangelove, stunned.

"Strangelove, please explain this," said General Patterson.

"General, as I said previously, while we have never identified any function that would enable the craft to be propelled in interstellar space, we have discovered a mechanism that can manipulate gravity. While we have theorized that it could be used to warp space-time for interstellar travel, it could also fold space-time back upon itself. If what Dr. Meredith says about the Grays' DNA is true, it is absolutely conceivable that the Grays are from our distant future."

The generals sat stunned, mouths agape.

General Patterson turned to Lara. "Holy shit, Doctor."

146-05 32nd Ave

Flushing, NY
September 10, 1991
06:47 hours

Padma Mahajan stared into her vanity mirror. Her father, Vivek, had purchased the vanity for her 10 years earlier when she was a teenager. Its slick white surface, embellished with pink rosettes on its corners, made for an article of furniture that Cinderella would have kept in her Disney castle. Padma half-expected her oval mirror-mirror to begin speaking to her. Instead, the image of a 24-year-old brown-skinned woman with long black hair stared back.

Behind the face in the mirror, Padma saw sketches pinned to the wall. Padma had loved to draw when she was younger. She turned to look at one of the sketches, a charcoal drawing of an autumn leaf floating in a pool of water. She furrowed her brow. She loved art, and she was good at it. But her father forbade her from pursuing it professionally, insisting instead that she become a doctor, a lawyer, or something similarly prestigious. Padma's mother aided and abetted him, parroting the parameters her father had imposed on her life. Padma had chosen investment banking for no other reason than because she was gifted in math, and math would make for a much more lucrative career in banking than would science.

Padma turned back to her vanity. On her right sat a coffee mug, steam rising. Padma took a sip, noticing the mocha ring the mug had left on the surface of the white princess vanity. Padma replaced the mug precisely in the ring's circumference.

On her left stood a small blue ceramic Krishna figurine, merrily playing a golden flute. The miniature deity had been given to Padma when she was a child. Though Padma did not adhere to any faith, her little Krishna had nevertheless accompanied her on all her travels.

Padma had spent little time in her room in her parent's Flushing, Queens house since leaving for school years before. Though she had attended Columbia for her undergraduate degree, she'd managed to convince her parents that the commute to uptown Manhattan was siphoning too much time from her studies. Though the cover story was partly true, the reality was that her parents were driving her crazy. Her less bridled American teenage culture often collided with the rigidity of her parents' imported Indian traditions. Though her parents had succeeded in weaving focused discipline into Padma's DNA, she rejected their ascetic perspective on life, particularly as it applied to boys. Padma had thought her father was joking when he would speculate about the prospective husbands he was considering for her. She had laughed in his face, then froze in mortification when she'd seen that his pained face wasn't laughing with her. She knew then that it was time to leave the nest.

Padma found a cheap apartment uptown with a five-minute subway ride to campus. Her parents' carping didn't cease after her move. In addition to voicing concerns about her safety, they complained that uptown was beneath her station. Padma was well aware that her choice of neighborhoods had scrambled her parents' carefully ordered sense of caste. When she began dating a black schoolmate, the Harlem masala was a bridge too far for her parents. They threatened to stop paying for her apartment. Padma retaliated by landing a part-time job in a neighborhood pizzeria. Mortified that their daughter was performing commoner Sudra work, and fearing that her grades might suffer, they relented and began paying her ransom rent.

When the time came for graduate school, Padma had packed up her Krishna and moved across the country to Palo Alto to attend Stanford.

Now, Padma was temporarily back in her parents' house as she interviewed for jobs on Wall Street, bunking in her old room, staring at her Armani pinstriped reflection in her Cinderella vanity as she prepared for an interview. She shook her head at the absurdity of the scene.

The furniture did nothing to bolster her confidence for her final interview for an associate position at Goldman Sachs. She felt like a toddler wearing her mother's high heels and pearls for the first time. She struggled with the simplest choices.

Pants or skirt? she thought for the umpteenth time.

"Shit!" she shouted in frustration, then clapped both hands to her mouth for fear her mother would hear the obscenity.

"Padma," called her mother, Sarita, from downstairs." Are you all right? Are you ready? You don't want to be late for your interview."

Padma rolled her eyes. It wasn't even 7:00 AM yet. Her interview downtown wasn't until 10. She could wait a full hour and a half to arrive at the 7 line's train stop and still arrive half an hour early.

"Padma, do you hear me speaking to you?" called her mother.

"They can hear you in Brooklyn, Momma!" shouted Padma.

"Do not take that tone with me, young lady..."

Padma buried her face in her hands. She knew by heart the next words her mother would call up the stairwell. She said them aloud with her mother, mocking her lilting Indian accent.

"...Your father and I have worked very hard and sacrificed much in order for you to get an excellent education and obtain a position with a prestigious firm. You will not disappoint us and bring shame and humiliation upon our family. We expect you to be prompt to all of your professional appointments."

Padma closed her eyes and gritted her teeth. "Yes, Momma. I am very sorry. I will not disappoint you or Papa or bring shame and humiliation upon our family."

"This isn't helping," Padma complained to her reflected self.

"I'm scared," she confessed to her mirror-mirror. "I want to tell my mother I'm scared. I want to tell her that I'm going to do my very best, as I always do, but right now I'm scared, and I just need a hug."

Padma sighed. She looked at her reflection. She reminded herself that this person in front of her was a Stanford MBA summa cum laude graduate. She reminded herself that this person had always excelled at everything she had ever attempted to do. She reminded herself that she had every right to feel confident.

She looked closer at the brown skinned woman with long straight black hair.

She reminded herself that she was pretty.

She stood and tilted the vanity mirror, stepping away so she could see most of her 5-foot-10-inch self. She put on her navy suit coat and looked at the skirt-suit ensemble.

“Pants,” she said, unzipping her skirt.

World Trade Center, North Tower

New York, NY
September 10, 1991
11:55 hours

Padma sat on a cement bench in front of the World Trade Center's North Tower. After her interview, she had wandered, dazed, from Goldman Sachs' Broad Street office, somehow ending up on the bench. A Goldman Sachs envelope rested on the bench next to her. Padma stared forward as businesspeople in suits walked to and from the tower. Pigeons congregated around her shiny interview heels, hoping for a handout. She felt her long black hair, warm in the summer sun.

One of the suited businessmen spotted Padma as he walked briskly toward the North Tower's front doors. Rob Reynolds, Cantor Fitzgerald's CFO, instantly sized up the beautiful young woman. It was the season when freshly scrubbed and coiffed young MBAs were interviewing on Wall Street, hoping to land a job on the first rung of a flaming stairway to hell. From this young woman's blanched expression, he could tell her interview had not gone as planned. Recognizing an opportunity, he detoured to her bench.

"I'm sorry," he said.

"What?" Padma asked, waking from her daze. She looked up at

the shadowed corona of a paunchy fifty-something man, silhouetted by bright sunlight. Padma raised her hand as a visor.

"About the interview," Reynolds said. "You look like someone who didn't get the job."

Padma reached for the Goldman Sachs envelope resting next to her on the bench.

"Actually, I did get the job," she said, holding up the envelope.

"Well, then, you are the sorriest looking new Goldman Sachs analyst I've ever seen."

Padma nodded somberly. "Right."

"My name is Rob Reynolds. I'm the CFO of Cantor Fitzgerald. May I sit?"

Padma suppressed an eye roll. Cantor Fitzgerald was a bucket shop, and a second rate one at that. No Ivy League MBA would be caught dead setting foot in the uppermost North Tower floors where the Cantor Fitzgerald investment bankers dwelled.

Padma gestured without a word for Reynolds to sit.

"So, why do you look like someone just ran over your puppy?"

"Post-purchase dissonance," she said.

"You can't have post-purchase dissonance," corrected Reynolds.

"Why not?"

"Because you didn't buy them. They bought you."

"Right," she said. "My whole life, up to this point, has been committed to this moment." She didn't understand why she was opening up to a perfect stranger who was likely trying to hit on her. All she knew was that she couldn't share her feelings with her parents or her few classmate friends.

"Now that I've arrived, I don't think this is what I want."

"Shitty time for an epiphany," Reynolds said.

Padma nodded. "You got that right."

"My parents and classmates would think I'm crazy," she said.

"They'd have good reason to think so," Reynolds said. "Ten thousand MBAs apply to Goldman Sachs every year. A hundred are chosen. You're one of the elite."

"You're an enormous help," Padma said. "Don't you have some CFO-ing to do in that big building?"

Reynolds laughed.

"I was probably just picked to satisfy their diversity program," Padma said.

"Where'd you go to school?"

"Stanford. Summa cum laude," she added offhand.

"Well, I can tell you with complete confidence that Goldman Sachs doesn't pick Stanford summa cum laudes just because of their ethnicity and gender. That was just icing on the cake. They got a twofer with you. They love that."

Padma was silent.

"Do you want an alternative?" asked Reynolds.

"Not from Cantor Fitzgerald," Padma said flatly.

Reynolds was stunned at the young woman's audacity. He laughed again.

"You could at least wait to hear my pitch before you insult me."

"I'm not interested in shoveling bonds in a boiler room sales pit," she said, trotting out her shiny elitism on full display.

"I'm not asking you to," Reynolds said. "But if you're really not interested in what I have to say, I can go back upstairs and C-F-off."

Padma sighed. "I'm sorry. I was rude. Please tell me what you have in mind."

"M&A," Reynolds said. "Mergers and acquisitions for Cantor Fitzgerald. You assess opportunities and work with me to make them happen. You'd be buying companies."

Reynolds had Padma's attention. Padma knew the career track he was proposing was a radically different path than the main-stream cattle chute MBA recruits were normally driven through at the elite investment banks.

"Go on," Padma said.

"You know what a first-year recruit training program looks like at Goldman Sachs," Reynolds said. "You bust your ass in research and analysis writing make-work reports for the managing directors. You'll spend three weeks with no sleep on one of those reports, then it'll get chucked in the trash five minutes after you turn in your homework."

"So, you're saying I'd get to sleep at Cantor Fitzgerald?"

"No, I'm saying you'd have something to show for the sleep deprivation. It's also a fast track to managing director with all the money that comes with that."

"It's the Bolivian army," Padma said.

"Maybe, but you'd be a fucking general in the Bolivian army instead of a corporal in the royals."

Padma was quiet again.

"Are you hitting on me?" she asked.

"Sure...But everything else I said is true too."

Padma was silent for a moment.

"If I tell you I won't sleep with you, do I still get the job?"

Reynolds smiled. He loved the young woman's pluck.

"Yeah," he said. "I'll give you the job. Whether you keep it or not depends entirely on how much money you make for us."

"That won't be a problem," Padma said with ice-cold confidence, rising from the bench and extending her hand to shake Reynolds'.

Reynolds rose and shook Padma's hand.

I am certifiably insane, thought Padma.

World Trade Center, North Tower

New York, NY
September 11, 1991
07:45 hours

Padma Mahajan stood at the foot of the World Trade Center's North Tower, staring up the side of the colossal building. The building disappeared into a cloudbank some 70 floors up. The clouds blocked the sun, casting a cold gray shadow over the city.

Padma took the elevator up to the 105th floor and asked the receptionist for her new boss, Rob Reynolds. As she waited for Reynolds, she gazed out the glass windows of the world's second-tallest building. Her view faced uptown, staring upon the sunny side of the cloudbank. The white fluffiness blanketed the city, obscuring all of its buildings save one. The silver spire of the Empire State Building punctured the clouds, shining brilliantly in the sunlight.

Padma's back faced the southern view of the tower, where the Statue of Liberty and Ellis Island both lay somewhere beneath the clouds. Padma thought about Ellis Island and the millions of immigrants that facility had gatewayed into the United States. Ellis Island had closed long before her parents immigrated to the United States from India, though the experience of being alien in the country had not evolved much since that time. Padma's parents had tried hard to instill the belief in their daughter that she was at least as good as white people, while also pushing her to succeed in order to offset the racism she would face from those same white people. Reconciling the conflicting thoughts was easy: Life was sometimes unfair, but dwelling on life's unfairness was futile.

Padma steeled herself, stuffing her cognitive dissonance in the place where she stored all her inconvenient truths.

Padma's parents had reacted to her news of passing on Goldman Sachs' offer in favor of Cantor Fitzgerald with stunned disbelief. The scope of their daughter's failure was incomprehensible. Decades and hundreds of thousands of dollars spent preparing their daughter for success had instantly evaporated before their eyes. It was as though Padma had come within inches of summiting Mount Everest, then decided to turn back to base camp. Though his daughter had always been rebellious, Vivek Mahajan now wondered whether Padma suffered from some incapacitating mental defect. He insisted that Padma immediately call Goldman Sachs and reverse her decision. Padma tried to communicate the rationale of her choice—what the Cantor Fitzgerald opportunity lacked in prestige, it more than made up in title, money, and excitement.

Her father wasn't listening. He ordered her daughter to take the job at Goldman.

"No," Padma replied.

Padma's mother admonished her daughter: "Indian girls do not disobey their parents' wishes."

"I'm not an Indian girl," Padma replied. "I'm an American woman."

Padma turned from the conflict and ran upstairs to her teenage bedroom. She stuffed clothes and toiletries into a bag. As she opened her door to leave, she turned to take a last look at the room of her childhood. She reached for the sketch of the leaf in the pond. She peeled it off the wall, folded it in half and slid it into her briefcase.

As she descended the carpeted stairs, her mother was waiting for her.

"What are you doing?" she asked.

"I'm leaving."

"Where are you going?"

"To the city. That's where I work now," Padma said as she brushed past her mother, slinging her bag, briefcase, and purse. "I'll find a hotel for tonight."

"No! You cannot go! It's dark. It's dangerous!"

Padma ignored her mother as she sped toward the door. She saw her father sitting in the living room. He did not look at his daughter.

"At least wait until tomorrow, when it's safe!" pleaded her mother.

"Goodbye mother," Padma said as she walked out the front door, slamming it in her wake.

• • •

A woman's heels clicked the polished stone floor as she entered the Cantor Fitzgerald lobby.

"Padma?" asked the woman.

"Yes," Padma said, rising from her seat.

"Hi, I'm Lois Meyer, Mr. Reynolds' assistant. He'll see you now."

"Thank you very much."

Lois led Padma along a phalanx of executive offices into Reynolds' office. When Reynolds saw Padma, he bounded from his desk, reaching his hand to shake Padma's.

"You're here! Welcome aboard! I wasn't sure you'd show."

"Neither was I," replied Padma, shaking Reynolds' hand.

"I'm going to take you to HR and get you squared away, then we can meet and talk about the way forward."

"Sounds good," said Padma.

"We'll stop and meet some of the team members on the way to HR."

They walked down a hallway into an area filled with cubicles. Padma instantly noticed that the floor was a sea of white men. Reynolds approached a man in one of the cubes. He was a short man in his late twenties with prematurely balding black hair. As was the case with all the other men, he wore a white dress shirt and tie with dark suit pants. The sleeves of his shirt were rolled up to the elbow. The man was swearing into the phone. Reynolds turned and smiled to Padma. She smiled politely in return.

Reynolds tapped the man on the shoulder. He acknowledged his boss.

"Gotta go," he said, hanging up the phone.

The man stood up. He was three inches shorter than Padma.

"Padma," said Reynolds, "this is Larry Stein. Larry, Padma is joining the team as of today."

"Good. Glad you're here. Coffee's over there. I take mine with two sugars."

Reynolds and Padma exchanged glances. "Padma is not a secretary."

Larry looked confused. "What's she doing? Mail room?"

"Padma is our new M&A analyst."

Larry's eyes bugged wide. "No shit?"

He looked Padma all the way up and down her 5-foot-10-inch frame.

"Huh," Larry said. "Well, good luck with that."

29°32'41.0"N 46°37'33.0"E

Iraq
Operation Desert Storm
February 25, 1991
22:11 hours

Lieutenant Kyle Mason watched endless miles of dark desert road unfold through the dirty windshield of his Humvee. The sand road, lit by his Humvee's headlamps, disappeared into a sandstorm cloud in the vehicle's rearview mirror. Headlamps from the trailing Humvee convoy pierced the man-made sirocco.

Kyle's desert platoon convoy of five Humvees had covered hundreds of miles of desert roads on a scouting mission. Now they sped toward their base on the Saudi side of the Iraq-Saudi border. The current view of the desert road was identical to that of the previous 500 miles. Fresh out of West Point, the newly minted officer's first command had been equally monotonous. His platoon's desert storm had had the thrill of watching grass grow in Toledo.

Kyle glanced at his driver, Corporal Levi Mackey. Phosphorescent green from the Humvee's dashboard lights lit up the corporal in his desert camo uniform. Corporal Mackey was a 20-year-old Texan from Fort Worth. Kyle's platoon command was even younger than the 39-day-old war. He didn't know the men under his command well. Given how rapidly the war was coming to a close, it was unlikely he would learn much more about them before they were packed up and shipped off to their peacetime assignments.

"This is a lame-ass war, LT," complained Mackey. "We've been in this fucking sandbox nearly two months without a single engagement. Zero action. Not what I signed up for, LT."

"Roger that," shouted Private First Class Albin Cervantes from the Humvee's machine gun turret.

"Careful what you wish for," Kyle cautioned, even though his thoughts echoed his soldiers' view of the actionless war.

"What happened to that 'mother of all battles' that Saddam promised?" asked Mackey.

"It's the fucking grandmother of all battles," replied Cervantes.

"Hey, watch it!" said Mackey. "My grandma could whip your skinny ass, Cervantes."

"I heard your grandma liked whips!" shouted Cervantes.

Light flashed to the right of the Humvee. In the instant before the men turned their heads to look, their Humvee was blown onto its left side. Kyle was thrown onto Mackey, pinning him against the driver's door. Cervantes was thrown from the gun turret out into the desert.

"That enough action for you?" Kyle asked.

"Roger that, LT," replied Mackey, groggily shaking his head.

Kyle pulled himself up and kicked through the windshield. The two men climbed out.

The other Humvees in the column slid to a stop behind Kyle's toppled ride, the men running out to assist. His First Sergeant,

Zion Ford, was the first on the scene. At 35, Ford was the most experienced man in Kyle's platoon and 13 years Kyle's senior.

"What are we into, Sergeant?" shouted Kyle.

Ford pointed to the west at several moonlit tanks. "Four Hajji T-69 tanks, 200 yards out, advancing on our position. They look pissed."

A yellow muzzle flash lit the desert as the lead tank fired at the platoon. The shell overshot the Humvees, exploding behind the men. The blast concussion knocked the men down and pelted them with desert sand. They climbed to their feet.

"Good assessment on the pissed part," said Kyle, shaking off sand.

"Thank you, LT," replied Ford.

"Orders, sir?" asked Ford. "We buggin' out?"

Kyle felt the adrenaline surging through him, a mix of terror and thrill.

"Orders, sir!" Ford shouted.

"I need my radio operator and my javelin gunners!" Kyle shouted.

"Lieutenant! We're outgunned. We still have four good Humvees. We can outrun those tanks. We can't push this bad position!"

"Cervantes is out there somewhere," Kyle shouted. "We're not leaving him."

Ford shook his head and leaned in to whisper to the young lieutenant.

"You'd best not fuck up, LT."

Kyle nodded at Ford. The sergeant turned and began shouting at the men. Three men instantly appeared—one with a radio pack and two who were each hauling what looked like overstuffed bazookas.

"Radio—call in troops in contact. Need Apache air support and medevac dustoff. Javelin gunners, target the lead two tanks. We've only got two javelins, so make sure you don't shoot the same fucking tank!"

"Roger that, LT," the men shouted.

"Ready javelins?"

"Ready!" shouted the men in unison.

"Javelin gunner one, take out that lead tank—fire!"

A plume of brilliant yellow fire erupted from the first javelin gun as its anti-tank missile rocketed toward its target. Moments later, a yellow blast from the lead tank lit the sky.

"Javelin gunner two, take out your target!"

The gunner's missile soared toward its target. Moments later, the tank's turret exploded off the tank, landing directly in the path of the third tank. The two remaining tanks halted.

"Now what, LT?" asked Ford.

"Somebody give me the bullhorn—right the fuck now!" shouted Kyle.

One of the men handed Kyle a bullhorn. Kyle flicked it on.

"*Aistislam 'aw yamut*!" Kyle shouted through the bullhorn. His words echoed across the desert.

"What are you doing, LT?" asked Ford. "We're out of javelins!"

"They don't know that."

"*Aistislam 'aw yamut*!" Kyle repeated through the bullhorn. "Surrender or die!"

The turret hatch on one of the two surviving tanks opened. A rifle barrel rose from inside the turret. A white handkerchief was tied to it. The second tank followed suit.

A roar erupted from Kyle's platoon.

Kyle pointed at the platoon interpreter, handing off the bull-horn. "Order them out of their vehicles—on their knees and hands on their heads," ordered Kyle. "Take prisoners and set charges in the remaining tanks."

"Radio—cancel the Apaches. Keep the medevac. Let's find Cervantes."

Ford shook his head. "You got very lucky tonight, LT."

"Yeah. But I didn't fuck up," Kyle said.

"No. You didn't fuck up."

Forward Operating Base (FOB) Grey

Iraq
Operation Desert Storm
February 26, 1991
07:00 hours

A barrel-chested African American man in his early fifties wearing desert camo fatigues strode out of an arc-roofed Quonset structure toward a waiting Blackhawk helicopter. Aaron Craig wore four stars on his lapel. His army was crushing its Iraqi opponents even faster than his most optimistic projections. He was racing to catch up to the battlefront's leading edge before the war wrapped up.

As he neared the charcoal-colored Blackhawk on the desert sand, he noticed the pilot standing next to his helicopter. She was small—tiny, actually. The young woman wore camo fatigues strapped with a pilot's utility harness, its pockets stuffed with gear and a sidearm. The charcoal-colored aviator's helmet on the bantam-sized Captain Annika Wise's head made her look like Marvin the Martian. As the general neared, she saluted.

"Captain," the general said, returning the salute. "Are you sure you can reach the pedals on this thing?"

"I can, but when I do, I can't see over the dashboard," replied Captain Annika Wise.

The general laughed and climbed aboard the co-pilot's seat, strapping on an aviator helmet with its audio headset.

The cockpit of the Blackhawk was compact. Wraparound windshields met the helicopter's console, with mirrored sets of instruments for each pilot, including a spherical blue-tanned attitude indicator, a compass-like horizontal situation indicator, LED status gauges, and switches. The ceiling was packed with toggle switches and the helicopter's throttle levers for its dual turbo engines.

Annika flipped the switches, bringing the Blackhawk to life. As she switched on its auxiliary power unit, the rising whine of the Blackhawk's turbine engine whistled through the cockpit.

Annika's voice crackled through the intercom headsets: "Ladies and gentlemen, the captain has turned on the Fasten Seat Belt sign. If you haven't already done so, please stow your carry-on luggage underneath the seat in front of you or in an overhead bin. Please take your seat and fasten your seat belt. And also make sure your seat back and folding trays are in their full upright position.

"We remind you that this is a non-smoking flight. Smoking is prohibited on the entire aircraft, including the lavatories. Tampering with, disabling, or destroying the lavatory smoke detectors is prohibited by law.

"If you have any questions about our flight today, please don't hesitate to ask one of our flight attendants. Thank you."

"Has anyone ever told you you're a wise ass?" asked the general.

"You're my first today, sir," replied Annika.

Annika throttled up the Blackhawk and ascended skyward from a cloud of desert dust.

“Grey flight control, Bengal 13. We’re going to Jalibah.”

“We need to make a stop at FOB Cobra on the way,” corrected the general.

“Forward Operating Base Cobra. Roger that,” repeated Annika as she banked the Blackhawk east-northeast toward the new destination.

“So, what’s your story, Captain?” asked the general.

“The short version is that I tried to get into Special Forces, but I was denied because of a birth defect.”

“What’s that?”

“Born without a penis.”

The general nodded. “If it’s any consolation, Captain, we black folks know a thing or two about bias.”

“Yes sir.”

“Since you ask about my fascinating life story...” began the general.

“I didn’t ask about your fascinating life story, sir.”

“I *said*, since you ask about my fascinating life story...”

Behind her darkened helmet shades, Annika rolled her eyes.

“Sir, would you please tell me your fascinating life story?”

“Why yes, I’d be delighted to. I was born in 1945 in Augusta, Georgia, right smack in the middle of the Jim Crow south. I went to high school with Jessye Norman at Lucy C. Laney Senior High. When I was in high school, I worked as a caddie at the Augusta National Golf Club. The club’s founder was a guy named Clifford Roberts. He used to say, ‘As long as I’m alive, all the golfers will be white, and all the caddies will be black.’”

"He sounds like a bona fide asshole," said Annika.

"He was that. Now I'm a life member of the club. The kicker is that I don't even live in Georgia anymore. So, you fly helos to stay close to the action?"

"That's exactly right, sir. What are we doing at Cobra?"

"I want to meet someone," said the general. "Brand new lieutenant, fresh out of West Point. Bluffed an Iraqi tank platoon last night holding nothing but a pair of javelins."

"I heard about that," said Annika, envious. "Pretty badass."

"He's getting a Silver Star," the general continued. "This war's gonna wrap up in a couple days, and I wanted to meet him before we all pack up and go home."

The general watched a newly transformed patch of desert grow as the helicopter approached. Established only two days earlier, Forward Operating Base Cobra was already a hive of activity, with tents, temporary buildings, barracks and offices, fuel tanks, and dozens of helicopters, Humvees, tanks, and trucks. Earthmoving equipment was flattening terrain around the camp, paving the way for expansion.

The Blackhawk descended into a cloud of desert sand and dust, touching down in front of a tan-colored Quonset structure with an arced roof. Two soldiers stood guard outside. As Annika shut down the Blackhawk's turbine engines, General Craig climbed out. The soldiers saluted. The general returned the salute as he went inside.

Annika climbed out of the Blackhawk, removed her helmet and tossed it in her pilot's seat. Annika's black hair was cut in bangs over her forehead, with a ponytail falling onto her back.

She pulled a pair of aviator sunglasses out of one of her utility bags, then unfastened the harness and slid out of it, tossing it into the Blackhawk. She began walking around her helicopter, inspecting it.

As she leaned down to examine her starboard landing gear, she felt a hand on her butt. Annika looked over her shoulder. A young soldier smiled back at her.

Annika glanced at the soldier's collar, noting the corporal's rank. "Oh good, you're not an officer," said Annika. "You know what that means?"

The corporal grinned eagerly as he groped Annika. "No, what?"

Annika grabbed the corporal's wrist and pivoted to face him as she crimped his wrist, crashing him to his knees. The soldier whimpered in pain.

Annika smiled fiendishly at the man on his knees as she held his wrist. "It means I don't get court martialed when I beat the living shit out of you."

Holding the corporal's wrist with one hand, Annika calmly removed her sunglasses and set them on the landing gear tire. She then released the corporal as she swung her leg Billy Jack style in the blink of an eye, striking the man on the side of his head with her boot. He fell to the ground unconscious.

A big man's arms wrapped around Annika from behind. Another man approached from the front. Annika turned her head, pursing her lips to the soldier holding her. "Come closer," she whispered.

The man leaned in over Annika's shoulder. Annika kicked vertically, striking the man in the face. He grabbed his face with his hands, blood spurting from between his fingers. Annika leapt in the air, smacking the approaching man in the chin with a bicycle kick. The man fell backward like a tipped board, hitting the ground with a thud. He lay motionless.

Annika turned to the bleeding man. "Here, let me look at that." The man lowered his hands from his face.

"Oh no," she said, shaking her head as she examined the soldier's bloody face. "That nose is broken. Lemme take care of that for you."

Annika clamped his nose between her fingers. The soldier screamed. Annika thrust her knee between his legs, doubling him over. She leapt in the air and landed on the back of his head with a scissor kick. He crashed to the ground, unconscious.

Annika bent down, wiping the soldier's blood off of her hand and onto the man's fatigue jacket. She picked her sunglasses up from the landing gear, then calmly resumed her inspection of the Blackhawk. Moments later, General Craig emerged from the Quonset. He eyed the three motionless men on the ground by Annika's helicopter, surmising what had happened. He looked at Annika without expression, as though three unconscious men weren't lying on the ground before him.

"Ready to go, sir?" asked Annika cheerfully.

General Craig stepped over one of the men.

"Uh huh."

Back in the air on their way to Jalibah, the general broke the silence.

"So, where'd you learn to fight?"

"In China," replied Annika. "My parents worked for the State Department. My dad was deputy consul to Hong Kong and Macau. My mom is Chinese American and worked as a translator at the consulate. When we landed in Hong Kong in 1972, Bruce Lee was a rock star. I pestered the crap out of my dad to take me to see *Fist of Fury*. I was totally hooked. I started studying Wing Chun—that's the foundation of Bruce Lee's Jeet Kun Do mixed Kung Fu style. I even met Bruce Lee's teacher, Yip Man, before he died that year.

"So," continued Annika, "would you like to hear a fairy tale, sir?"

"I would."

"According to legend, Wing Chun was created by a woman. Her name was Ng Mui. She was a nun at the Henan Shaolin Monastery. Qing soldiers burned her monastery and killed the monks, but Ng Mui escaped, fleeing to the White Crane Temple in the Daliang Mountains. At the temple, she created a new style of martial art, inspired by watching a crane and a fox in combat. Ng Mui taught the new style of fighting to a young woman named Yim Wing-Chun, whom a bandit was forcing into marriage. The core principles of Ng Mui's brand of Kung Fu promoted elegance and speed over brute strength. Ng Mui named her fighting style after her first student…"

The pair heard a loud bang as the Blackhawk's tail was knocked to the left.

The general saw a rocket trail from the ground on the Blackhawk's right side.

"We got clipped by an RPG."

“Fuckers hit the tail rotor,” confirmed Annika.

The Blackhawk shuddered as the tail rotor wobbled on its axis.

“I have to put her down,” said Annika, throttling back the engine and pitching the helicopter forward, making a beeline for a large dune. The pair felt their stomachs rise in the weightlessness of the rapid descent. The helicopter descended rapidly.

“That’s not friendly country down there,” warned the general.

“The alternative to putting this helo down right-the-fuck-now is not good,” said Annika.

Annika called into her radio: “Bengal 13, mayday! Mayday!”

A loud clanking sound came from the tail as the damaged rotor flew off, leaving nothing to push against the torque of the helicopter’s main rotor. Dashboard alarm lights and buzzers went off as the Blackhawk began to spin. The dashboard’s HSI compass spun in sync with the whirling landscape.

“So, that’s not good,” said Annika.

“Have you got this?” asked the general.

“Have you got a plan if I don’t?”

As the spinning landscape whizzed by the windshield, the general resisted his temptation to grab the co-pilot’s joystick between his legs.

“Don’t put the rotor in the ground!” shouted the general.

“I know how to fly what’s left of the fucking aircraft, sir!

“Hard landing,” Annika shouted. “Brace!”

The Blackhawk slammed into the dune and flipped over, its crippled rotors whipping sand into the air.

The cockpit was silent. Smoke wafted into the compartment.

Dim orange sunlight seeped through the sandblasted windows.

Annika opened her eyes. She hung upside down in her seat. She raised her helmet visor and turned to the general. He was motionless in his seat.

"Sir?" Annika asked. "Are you OK?"

The general's helmet moved. He raised his visor.

"I believe I am."

"We'll have company in a minute," said Annika. She unlatched her seat harness and held onto it as she righted herself in the up-ended cockpit, kicking her door open and sliding out. The general knocked his door open and climbed out.

They stood on the high edge of a desert dune. Their Blackhawk lay on its back, a crumpled, smoking wreck. They scanned the landscape. Several miles to the north, the blue Euphrates River pierced the arid desert tan.

Annika turned south. She pointed at an approaching truck, several hundred meters away.

"Republican Guard platoon," she said.

Annika unzipped one of her utility harness bags and retrieved her Beretta M9 pistol, chambering a round. The general placed a hand on her wrist and shook his head.

"Don't," he said.

"You don't strike me as someone who runs from a fight," Annika said.

"I'm old enough to know when to pick them."

The desert camo troop carrier truck stopped at the base of the dune. Six soldiers emptied out of the back of the truck and trained their Kalashnikov rifles on Annika and the general. The truck driver and passenger doors swung open, and two more soldiers emerged. The soldiers shouted in Arabic at Annika and the general, motioning for them to put their hands on their heads and walk down the dune. The pair complied, shuffling down the dune, their boots crunching as they sunk into the sand.

When the pair reached the truck, soldiers grabbed them by their arms and forced them onto their knees. The soldiers took off the pair's helmets and removed Annika's utility harness. Then they ordered the pair to stand with their hands on their heads. Annika observed the soldiers. They were all in their twenties and had dark hair and tan skin. All had mustaches, with the exception of their commander, a captain, who sported a neatly trimmed beard. All of the soldiers wore camouflaged fatigues, and some wore keffiyeh scarves in various colors, wrapped around either their necks or heads. All carried Kalashnikov rifles. One had slung an RPG-7 launcher over his shoulder.

The captain spoke to one of his soldiers. The soldier rapidly frisked the general, then moved to Annika, taking his time as he moved his hands over her body.

"You could at least buy me dinner first," said Annika as she stared forward. The soldier paused his groping to bellow in Arabic in Annika's face.

As the soldier reached Annika's ankle, he found a small knife strapped to her leg. He shouted to his captain, thrusting the prize into the air. The soldier held the knife in front of Annika's face as he shouted. She shrugged.

The captain ordered his soldiers to load the captives into the back of the truck. The troops climbed in. In a few moments, the truck was speeding through the desert, headed toward the Euphrates.

As they neared the river, they approached a grove of palm trees near the ruined mud brick walls of an ancient structure. They stopped and ordered the pair to get out, motioning for them to sit under a tree.

The captain spoke to one of his soldiers. The soldier pulled a canteen from the truck and tossed it to Annika. She caught the canteen, opened it, and drank, then handed it to the general.

"Sir, when is your army going to rescue us? This is getting old."

The general gave Annika a sharp look.

The soldiers sat under the palm trees. The captain sat separately from his men, under a tree directly across from the general and Annika. He leaned his rifle against the tree. As his men rested and munched on snacks, the captain lit up a cigarette. He stared at his captives.

Annika stood up. The soldiers grabbed their rifles.

"It's OK! It's OK!" she said, holding her hands up. She slowly reached for the top button of her camo jacket and unbuttoned it.

"Hot," she said, fanning herself with her hand.

The soldiers watched as she continued to unbutton her jacket and remove it. Under the baggy fatigue was a petite torso clad in a sweaty black tank top.

Annika's dog tags rested against her chest. Annika dropped the fatigue jacket on the ground and sat down. The soldiers put down their rifles and continued eating, drinking, and talking.

Annika looked at the captain. She held two fingers to her mouth, motioning for a cigarette.

"I speak English," the captain replied with a British accent, holding up a red and white pack of Mikados.

Annika got up and walked slowly to the captain. She took a cigarette, then knelt down as the captain flipped open a Zippo lighter. Annika held her cigarette to the flame. The cigarette tip crackled as she inhaled.

"May I sit?"

The captain gestured for her to sit next to him.

"My name is Nasim," said the captain.

"Annika."

"Your English is great," said Annika. "Where did you learn?"

"Cambridge," said Nasim. "I studied electrical engineering. Obviously, I should have stayed there."

"Why didn't you?"

"Qusay Hussein is my cousin. I was compelled to return to defend the homeland from the American invaders. The Husseins can be very persuasive," Nasim added, turning to look at Annika.

He took another drag on his cigarette, gazing past the general at the river.

"Did you know that you are sitting in the cradle of civilization?" asked Nasim. "This is Mesopotamia. We're on the outskirts of Uruk, one of the world's first cities. It was built 7,000 years ago."

Nasim pointed at the broken wall of rough flat mud bricks that tumbled into the Euphrates. "That's Sumerian, from the time of

Gilgamesh, about 2700 BC. The Sumerians invented the wheel. They also invented a base-60 system of mathematics that is still used today to measure time. Hours are divided into 60 minutes. Minutes divided into 60 seconds. Isn't that fascinating? That the way we divide time in the present was divined in the ancient past.

"Do you know the *Epic of Gilgamesh?*" asked Nasim.

Annika shook her head.

"It's considered the earliest surviving great work of literature. The oldest cuneiform clay tablet is over 4,000 years old. One of the tablets tells a story of God warning of a great flood. God instructs Gilgamesh to build a gigantic boat. God gives Gilgamesh the precise dimensions of the boat, then instructs him to load his family and all the animals of the field onto it. It rains for six days and nights and all life on earth is destroyed, except for Gilgamesh's family and the animals onboard. Sound familiar?"

Annika was silent.

In the distance, they could hear U.S. bombs exploding onto Jalibah Airfield. They felt the percussion beat in the sand.

"This is where civilization began," said Nasim. "I think maybe this is where it ends too. These things have been around for thousands of years. Now they're gone. Our archeological sites have been bombed. Our museums have been looted. Artifacts have been smuggled to private collections in the West. They cannot be replaced.

"Neither can the thousands of women and children who have been bombed in your bullshit war. Perhaps it's convenient to think that every bombed building in Baghdad was a military installation filled with soldiers and evil people concocting schemes for America's doom with diabolical weapons of mass destruction.

"People lived in some of those buildings. Just people. Families. Now they're dead. What you would call 'collateral damage.' I knew some of that collateral damage.

"Saddam is a despot. We have no illusions about that. But those dead children would be alive right now had you not come. They would be with their living mothers. They'd be having breakfast, going to school, playing with their friends. Instead of being crushed in the rubble of an apartment building. They're dead. Our history is destroyed.

"I was going to be an engineer.

"America has actually made me appreciate life under Saddam Hussein. I did not think that was possible. Before this war, I did not hate America. Now I do.

"I am not the only one. We weren't scheming before the invasion, but now we are. I think you Americans don't understand that you manufacture terrorists faster than you kill them."

"I don't hate you," said Annika.

"You might," replied Nasim, "if I had killed your family for oil."

"I'm sorry," Annika said, glancing at the general. "We follow orders."

Nasim nodded coldly. "As do we."

Annika extinguished her spent cigarette in the sand. The two were silent.

"May I have another?" asked Annika.

Nasim held up his pack. Annika took a cigarette and put it

to her lips. Nasim flipped open his steel lighter. Annika leaned in, placing the cigarette tip in the flame. The tip crackled and glowed as Annika inhaled. As Nasim snapped the lighter shut, Annika jammed the lit cigarette in his eye. As he screamed, Annika grabbed Nasim's rifle, raised it on one knee, and sprayed the other soldiers with bullets. In seconds, all except Nasim lay dead. Annika stood up and faced the general. The general's eyes were wide. Nasim screamed again. Without taking her eyes off the general, Annika pointed the rifle at Nasim's head and fired one shot. His body dropped to the ground.

"I want to go home now," said Annika.

Fort Campbell

Hopkinsville, KY
May 1, 1991
09:27 hours

"So, I have good news and bad news."

Annika listened to General Craig's voice over the phone in a vacant office at Fort Campbell. A fluorescent light from a drop ceiling illuminated a room with four bare walls, a Steelcase desk, and a chair.

"The good news is that you're getting the Distinguished Service Medal. You're also being promoted. You are now the youngest major in the army."

General Craig waited for Annika to voice gratitude for the enormous honors he had conferred. Annika waited for the bad news.

"The bad news," the general continued, "is that the Pentagon has turned down my request to put you into Delta training. I am sorry, Major. I went to bat. I took a big swing for you. They aren't ready."

"I understand. Thank you, sir."

Annika hung up. She stared forward at the office door, reconciling her thinking and feeling selves. Her thinking-self spoke to her of the extraordinary dual honors of her promotion and the Distinguished Service Medal. Normally reserved for senior officers, only 14 captains had ever been awarded the medal.

Annika's feeling-self screamed back. Only a handful of special ops soldiers could have pulled off her Desert Storm feat—maybe. Had it ever occurred to the brass that it was her femininity that enabled her to get close to Nasim? Though her fighting skills were exceptional, maybe, just maybe, a woman could actually contribute something that went beyond the capabilities of the boys.

Annika rose from the desk and headed for the tarmac. As she approached her Blackhawk, she saw a man standing on the helicopter's service step. He had opened a hatch and was examining the helicopter's engine. Annika could see he was not wearing a maintenance airman's overalls. The stranger was wearing a black suit.

"What the fuck are you doing, and who the fuck told you it was OK to touch my helicopter?"

The man startled, lost his balance, and fell to the tarmac, landing on his back with a thud. He gasped for air. The man was in his early thirties, blond with a beard. Freckles were sprinkled across his nose. He opened his blue eyes to see Annika standing over him, scowling.

"I am so sorry," the man said with a Swedish accent. "I'm an engineer, from Sikorsky. The Pentagon sent me here to assess the latest generation Blackhawk."

Annika looked away from the man, knowing she had overreacted. She reached down to offer a hand up. The man took it.

"Are you OK?" she asked.

"Oh, yes, I believe so."

"Look, I'm sorry," Annika said. "I just got some bad news."

"I understand," said the man. "It's OK."

The two paused awkwardly.

"Maybe you'll let me buy you a drink to make it up to you," Annika suggested.

"That would be lovely," said the man as he extended his hand. "My name is Casper."

"Annika."

World Trade Center, North Tower

New York, NY

February 4, 2001

16:12 hours

Padma Mahajan stood outside the main entrance of the World Trade Center. Wearing a long black wool coat, she clutched her chest with crossed arms in the freezing cold. Snowflakes fell from a dark gray sky and moved fitfully in a shifting breeze. Padma held a black leather gloved hand to her lips, dragging on a lit cigarette. A handful of other smokers stood nearby. None of them knew each other, but they all shared the bond of exile from the non-smoking building.

Padma wore a foul expression as she watched well-bundled businesspeople spin in and out of the North Tower's revolving doors. She hated the cold. Her long coat wasn't warm enough to stand up to New York City's brutal winters. The city somehow amplified the damp cold. Taxi exhaust corrupted white snow into curbside pools of gray-brown slush. The wind howled down avenues and inverted umbrellas. Millions of people huddled anonymously as they brushed past each other under miles of metal-tubed scaffolding that seemed to forever cocoon pedestrian walkways by buildings under construction or repair.

Padma's scowl was further twisted by the hollow victory of her promotion to managing director—three full years after Larry's ascendance. The promotion wasn't the firm's idea; it was the product of Padma's ultimatum. She knew well that her contribution to the bottom line was double that of Larry's. When she threatened to walk to Goldman Sachs, the execs caved. Though she got the title and office she deserved, the promotion was a reminder of the firm's brazenly distinct standards for white men and women of color.

Padma looked at her glowing cigarette. She couldn't remember precisely when she'd started smoking—it had happened sometime in the 11 years since she joined the firm. Though she couldn't remember when she started, she could definitely remember why. Though she could stand up to the burnout hours and intensity of the work, the added strain of double standards and incessant sexual harassment pushed her envelope to its ragged edge. The harassment was the worst—the innuendos, the jokes, the touching. When she went to HR, her complaints were met with a shrug. It was her word against that of her white male coworkers and superiors. HR was not enthusiastic about pressing Padma's complaints and expressed pessimism about her odds of success. The likely outcome was a work environment that was even more difficult than the one she already knew. Moving to a rival company wouldn't help. Harassment was woven into the industry's DNA.

Padma began taking smoke breaks as brief respites, despite the fact that she didn't smoke. As was the case with abuse, smoke breaks were understood and accepted in the firm's culture. Padma began taking the long elevator ride down from the 105th floor and standing outside in the cold with her hands in her coat pockets. One day, she stopped at a green corner bodega to buy her first pack of cigarettes.

"What brand do you like?" she asked the bodega operator.

"No smoke. All the same," the Pakistani man replied impatiently as a line began to form behind Padma. Padma was well aware that NYC bodega choices demanded split-second timing.

She looked at the colorful packs and pointed at a blue box with an image of a Native American in a feather bonnet smoking a peace pipe. The bodega operator handed her the pack of American Spirits.

Padma liked the irony of an East Indian woman smoking a brand with a West Indian logo. Now she was addicted, both to the nicotine and to the fleeting vacations from her caveman masters on the stratospheric floors of the World Trade Center.

Padma's parents were aghast at the changes in their daughter. After two years in exile, their daughter had once again begun visiting their Flushing home. Their disappointment regarding Cantor Fitzgerald was amplified by her physical and behavioral devolution. Lines had formed under her eyes. She never smiled. Her language was mined with F-bombs. Worst of all, she had become a chain smoker. When her parents forbade her from smoking inside their suburban house, Padma welcomed the excuse to terminate her visits. The non-stop criticism served up by her parents wasn't helping. She needed someone to listen to her. She needed someone to at least pretend to care.

Padma took one last drag on her cigarette and threw it on the pavement, grinding out orange sparks under the sole of her boot.

She swirled through the North Tower's revolving door, flashed her Cantor Fitzgerald badge and headed for the elevator bank. When she reached the 105th floor, she navigated the maze of cubicles and people to her office. She found the door open. She could have sworn she had closed it when she left for her break.

She pulled off her coat and hung it on the back of the door. She briefly took in the view of New York Harbor hundreds of feet below. The Statue of Liberty looked like a microbial version of itself from this altitude.

Padma flipped on the dual-screen Bloomberg terminals on her desk to take in the vital market statistics she was tracking. Her blue ceramic Krishna cheerfully blew his golden flute next to the terminal monitors.

She noticed a manila envelope on her desk. She opened it. Inside was a Xerox copy of a man's hairy genitalia.

"Larry, you fucking asshole."

Padma pulled a strip of Scotch tape from a dispenser and taped the photocopy to a glass window panel next to her door, enabling her coworkers to see Larry's man parts. She then grabbed a red marker from her office whiteboard and began writing furiously on the glass panel above the Xerox:

"Have you seen this child?"

She threw the marker against the whiteboard and grabbed her coat. She slammed her office door shut and locked it.

"I'm leaving for the day," she yelled to Lois Meyer, now Padma's assistant.

"It's not even five o'clock," she replied.

Padma gave Meyer a sharp look. She got the message. As Padma turned to leave, Larry, joined by a small band of partners in crime, stood in her way. Larry began to clap. The others joined in. Padma's skin was usually thicker. It was bad enough that Larry pulled this crap. It was worse to let him know he had found the right button to push.

"It's just a joke, Padma," Larry said. "Can't you take a joke? Whatsa' matter with you?"

Padma walked up to Larry. "The joke is that three-inch dick of yours. How do you reach with that little thing?"

"Whoa!" Larry's cohorts roared.

Padma pushed past the men and headed for the elevators. When she reached the ground floor, she spun through the revolving door and started walking uptown.

Café Noir

32 Grand Street
New York, NY
February 4, 2001
17:09 hours

Padma pushed through the door of Café Noir. The interior was something out of Casablanca, with tan-colored French Moroccan arches and tin cutout lanterns that hung down and cast stars against the walls. Small cream, green, and burnt orange tiles covered the floor in mosaic patterns. The placed smelled of lamb kabobs. Cigarette smoke hung from the ceiling.

Padma wasn't in the habit of visiting bars. Time was money, and work was cutthroat competitive. She spent nearly every waking minute at the office. Today, though, Padma needed a stiff drink chased with an epiphany about her future.

It was early, and there were still seats at the bar. Café Noir didn't have a coat check. She dropped her black leather briefcase on the floor next to her barstool, draped her coat and purse over the stool back, and slid into her seat. She tossed her head back and ran her fingers through her long black hair in an attempt to bring order to the windblown chaos. She tugged on her black suit jacket and the collar of her cobalt blue blouse. She checked her neckline, opting to keep her partial buttons as they were. She wasn't looking for company, though she knew offers were coming anyway. Offers were always coming to the gorgeous tall Indian woman. All she wanted was to knock back a drink without saying a word to anyone, save the bartender, then catch a cab to her Upper West Side apartment.

Behind the bar, flanked by shelves of liquor and glasses, was a large red 1930 advertisement for Crüwell Mekka Arab Tobacco. It featured a dark-skinned, bearded Arab man wearing a white *keffiyeh* on his head with white-and-chocolate-striped *thawb* robes. A long, thin pipe was positioned between his teeth. He held a box of Crüwell Mekka in his right hand, and he pulled tobacco from the box with his left.

The bartender was a large white man with dark hair that curled up at the edges. He sported a heavy black mustache, a black shirt, and suspenders. He patted the bar in front of Padma.

"What can I get you?"

"Manhattan on the rocks," Padma said as she lit up a cigarette, setting her American Spirit pack and lighter on the bar.

"Lose the cherry," she added.

The bartender slid Padma a rock glass with ice cubes swimming in tawny-colored whiskey. She took a generous gulp and chased it with a drag on her cigarette, closing her eyes as she exhaled.

Padma opened her eyes. She made the instinctive mistake of scanning the room. Her eyes met those of a man at the end of the bar. She compounded her mistake by holding eye contact a moment too long. He smiled. She turned back to her drink.

Swirling in her drink, her mind's eye saw the image of the man she had captured in the moment of eye contact. He was a soldier—an officer—in his early thirties, wearing camo fatigues. His sandy hair was cut short. His chiseled face ended in a dimpled chin. His eyes were almost jade green. Padma acknowledged that he was handsome. He was *very* handsome.

I'm not here to meet a man, she reminded herself.

The ice in her glass clinked as she finished her drink. She set it on the bar, debating whether to have a second or pack up and head home.

At that moment, a second Manhattan appeared.

"The man at the end of the bar wants to know if he can buy you a drink," the bartender said.

"It looks like he already has," Padma replied.

"It would appear so," the bartender said, patting the bar twice with his hand before turning to wipe a glass with a towel.

Padma sighed, looking at the drink. After a moment, she took it, turned, and hoisted the glass perfunctorily toward the soldier with a curt smile. The soldier rose from his stool and rounded the bar toward Padma. Padma watched him peripherally as he approached. The man was over six feet tall. Even though his fatigues were baggy, she could tell his physique was godlike. The soldier wasn't cute. He was gorgeous.

This is such a fucking mistake, she thought.

"Hi. I'm Kyle," he said, extending a hand.

Padma took his hand in a brief clasp. "Padma," she said, smiling politely. "Please sit."

"You looked like you could use another drink," Kyle said.

"Did I? How kind of you to notice," Padma replied with an irritated edge to her voice.

"How was your day?" Kyle asked.

Padma was momentarily disarmed. It was the question that a caring partner would ask at the end of a day, not that of someone cruising for a hookup. With a simple question, the stranger had flung a lightning rod into her shitty day and career. Padma felt an overstuffed backlog of tears fighting within her to surface.

How did you know I needed you to ask me that?

Padma's brow furrowed. In an instant, she regained her composure.

What the fuck is wrong with me?

"It was not my best day," Padma conceded.

"I'm sorry," Kyle said. "I don't know you, but I suspect you deserve better."

Padma looked at her drink, shaking her head. "You need to stop doing that."

"Doing what?"

"Excuse me."

Kyle turned. A plump man with shaggy hair, a beard, and horn-rimmed glasses was standing next to him. The man pointed at Kyle's shoulder insignia, a sword within a red arrowhead.

"Are you Delta Force?" asked the man.

"Yes...well, part of it, anyway."

"I recognized the insignia," said the man. "This is such a tremendous honor!" said the man, extending his hand to shake Kyle's. "My name is Charles Kolb! I'm so excited to meet you!"

Kyle glanced at Padma. Her eyebrows rose into intrigued arches.

"My name is Kyle. It's a pleasure to meet you," Kyle said, shaking Charles' hand. "Did you serve?"

"Me? Oh no. I just watch the movies. It's just so rare to meet an operator in real life. I've never met one before. Can you talk about your missions?"

"I'm afraid not."

"You could tell me, but you'd have to kill me, right?"

"Something like that."

Charles paused awkwardly, looking at Kyle, unable to find words in his star-struck excitement.

"Well, I'm sorry to interrupt you. It's such a pleasure again to meet you. Thank you for your service."

"It's a privilege to serve," said Kyle.

Charles nodded at Padma, who smiled courteously. He rejoined his friends at a table and pointed excitedly at Kyle.

Kyle turned to Padma.

"Sorry," he said. "That happens sometimes."

"I didn't realize I was in the company of greatness," she said. The interruption had bought her time to stuff her tears back where they belonged.

"You're not," Kyle said smiling.

"What's Delta Force?"

"It's what the movies call the 1st Special Forces Operational Detachment-Delta."

"Delta Force is snappier," observed Padma.

"Hollywood thinks so."

"So, you're in show business?"

"Oh, no," Kyle said. "They make action movies about Special Forces—Delta, Navy Seals, Green Berets."

"Not my cup of tea," said Padma.

"Right."

"You're the real thing," said Padma

"I am."

"How does one become a…what did he call you? An 'operator'?"

"By outlasting everybody else."

Padma laughed. She instantly realized that she had no idea how long it had been since she had last laughed. Within minutes, the stranger had made her laugh and nearly made her cry. She looked intently at Kyle's face. She reminded herself that she was vulnerable at that moment, liable to make bad choices. Her sensibleness clashed with her feeling self, which told her that she deserved to feel good—to laugh or have a long-overdue cry. The man was beautiful. He was an officer in some elite delta thing. He was saying all the right things. How bad could it be?

"So, is this your uniform?" asked Kyle, nodding to Padma's navy Yves Saint Laurent suit.

"It is," said Padma. "I'm a banker. I'm a managing director at Cantor Fitzgerald."

Padma read Kyle's vacant expression. He didn't know her company.

"It's Wall Street stuff."

"So, you're good with numbers?"

"I am. There's research and analysis and some intuition involved too. I buy companies for a living."

Padma paused, swirling her drink.

"It's odd," she said. "We live in such different worlds. Mine is numbers. Yours is...physical."

"I have to think too...occasionally," replied Kyle.

"I don't think that came out right," she said. "I meant that your world is real. Real people."

"Real consequences."

Padma went quiet again, looking at her drink.

"Are you at a crossroad?" asked Kyle.

Padma shook her head and smiled as she looked at her drink.

"How do you do that? What are you? Some kind of interrogator or something?"

"Not really, no, though I can offer some unsolicited advice."

"What's that?"

"Yogi Berra said, 'When you come to a fork in the road, take it.'"

Padma laughed again. Kyle's eyes lit up. He loved her deep laugh.

"That was corny," Kyle said. "You should make me work harder for a laugh."

"I don't remember the last time I laughed," she said.

"That means you either don't laugh enough or you've got a really crap memory."

"I'm pretty sure it's the former. What are you doing in town?" asked Padma.

"Passing through, on my way to Fort Bragg for assignment."

"Assignment where?"

"Can't say."

"Can you at least say whether it's in or out of this country?"

"It's not here."

"How long are you in town?"

"Tonight. I fly out tomorrow morning."

Padma gasped. She looked at Kyle's face. The man was going overseas in the morning. He was going into the real world, into real danger. She felt a pang of fear. It felt like more than concern for the wellbeing of a stranger going into harm's way. What she felt was the hollowness of a sudden loss.

"Padma!"

Padma turned. Larry was standing at the door. Padma turned to Kyle, closed her eyes, and sighed. When she opened her eyes, she saw Kyle's concerned expression.

"Is that your bad day?"

Padma nodded. "My bad day. My bad life."

"Would you like me to kill him for you?"

Padma's head snapped up, her eyes wide. She wasn't sure whether Kyle was kidding. She entertained the fantasy of dead Larry.

"Humiliated, for sure. Torture would be nice," she added, nodding.

Larry walked to the bar and sat down, flanking Padma. He reached in front of her to shake Kyle's hand across the bar. Padma leaned back out of the way of Larry's arm.

"G.I. Joe! Larry Stein. Glad to meet you!"

"Kyle Mason," Kyle said, shaking Larry's hand.

"Fuck! That is some grip!" Larry said. "So, you ever kill anyone, Kyle?"

"For fuck's sake, Larry!" exclaimed Padma.

"What? It's a question. So, Kyle, have you?"

Padma observed Kyle as he looked at Larry. She saw his face change. The easy smile disappeared. He didn't appear angry. He was intently focused on Larry, as though Larry were the object of precision work requiring Kyle's complete attention. Though Kyle was serious, Padma also saw confidence in his face. Padma realized that not only had Kyle killed before, he was also very good at killing. Kyle was assessing his target.

"Not today," Kyle replied. "At least, not yet."

Larry pressed. "No, seriously, have you killed anyone?"

"Yes," Kyle said. "I have."

"No shit?" Larry said. "What's it like?"

Padma interrupted, "We were just leaving, Larry."

"Where you going?"

Padma looked at Kyle. "To my place."

Kyle's focused expression broke. His eyebrows raised. Larry saw the surprise on Kyle's face.

"No shit! So, you like dark meat, Kyle?"

Larry laughed as he saw Kyle's expression change. Larry's epithet had found Kyle's button. Incensed, Kyle began to rise from his barstool. Padma put her hand on his arm.

"Well, Kyle?" she asked matter-of-factly. "Do you like dark meat?"

Kyle plopped back onto his seat, confused. Though courageous in the face of life-and-death battle, he was anxious in answering a question that he feared had no good answer. He settled on the truth.

"I do."

Padma turned to Larry. "Kyle like dark meat."

She turned to Kyle. "Dark meat like Kyle."

She turned back to Larry, shaking her head. "Dark meat no like Larry."

She downed her drink, extinguished her cigarette, and rose from her seat. She threw on her coat, picked up her briefcase, and slung her purse over her shoulder.

"You coming?" she asked Kyle.

Kyle leapt off the barstool. "Roger that."

Larry watched the couple, gobsmacked, as they started toward the door. He noticed how tall the pair seemed compared to everyone else in the bar.

Padma stopped before she reached the door, touching Kyle on the shoulder to pause. As she turned toward Larry, she unbuttoned her uppermost blouse button. She bent down directly in front of the small man on the bar stool, providing Larry with a generous view of the breasts he would never be permitted to touch. She leaned in to whisper in his ear.

"Dark meat fuck Kyle now."

She flashed a fiendish smile at Larry, turned to Kyle, and took his arm as they left the bar.

Larry stared in the couple's wake, realizing Padma had finally bested him. He chuckled and returned to his drink.

• • •

Hours later, Kyle and Padma lay naked in her bed. Padma's head and hand rested on Kyle's chest. The lovers were covered in sweat. Kyle felt Padma's breath on his chest.

"You were right about outlasting everybody else," she said.

Kyle flashed a Cheshire grin. Padma reached to kiss him, then laid her head back on his chest. She thought about the impossible odds of the events that had conspired that day to bring them together. She knew she was already hopelessly lost in him. Up to that day, the notion of losing herself in another would have seemed pitifully weak to her. Now she didn't care. She was content to be completely lost in this man, regardless of what happened the next day. It didn't matter.

Padma instinctively reached for the blue pack of American Spirits on the nightstand. An elephant-shaped brass lighter from India stood dutifully by the cigarettes and a glass ashtray with spent cigarette butts. Before her hand reached the pack, Padma stopped herself and put her hand back on Kyle's chest, suppressing her crave to smoke.

"It's OK if you want to light up," said Kyle.

"That's all right. I don't need it."

They were quiet for a moment. Padma listened to Kyle's heartbeat.

"I hope you are what you appear to be," she said.

"I was just thinking the same about you."

"We need to know. This means you can't die," Padma said, tears welling. Her hand gripped Kyle's chest. "Please don't die."

"I won't."

They went quiet in the moment. Padma broke the silence.

"Kyle?"

"What?"

"What's it like to kill?"

"The first time, elation, then remorse…then rationalization.

"The second time is…less complicated."

Fort Hood, TX

September 11, 2001
07:58 hours

Lieutenant Colonel Annika Wise stared at a black clamshell cell phone resting on a wood veneer desktop in a vacant office at Fort Hood. The fluorescent light fixture in the office's hanging ceiling was switched off. Blades of morning sunlight sliced through half-closed metal window blinds, casting yellow bands against white sheetrock walls.

Annika folded her camo fatigue-clad arms and looked up at the clock on the wall.

7:59 Central Time

She sighed. The decorated army officer, heroic in the face of battle, dreaded the call she was about to make. She knew Casper would be at his desk in the west side of the Pentagon promptly at 09:00 hours Eastern Time. He was always on time.

Annika reached for the phone and keyed in Casper's number. She felt her heartbeat quicken as she listened to the phone's ring tone.

"Casper speaking," he answered in Swedish-accented English.

"Hi. It's Anni."

"Hi, honey," her husband replied.

Annika rolled her eyes. Throughout their seven years of

marriage, she had hated the term of endearment. She doubly disliked being greeted by "honey" at the start of a difficult call.

As was often the case, the couple was physically separated. Assignments moved them to different parts of the world. Annika was presently flying Apache attack helicopters in Texas. Casper was in DC.

While Casper suffered their time apart, Annika relished it. She regretted marrying Casper. She had resisted his proposals for years. He was persistent. He was also very nice, and Annika was lonely. In a weak moment over drinks, she surrendered. Though she instantly knew it was a mistake, she didn't take it back. She saw that her answer had made Casper joyously happy. She knew their jobs would give her plenty of "me" time.

Maybe it will be OK, she had thought.

"Have you heard the news?" Casper asked.

"No. What's up?"

"A plane hit the World Trade Center. It's on the news."

"No. I hadn't heard." Annika took a breath. "Casper, I need to talk to you."

"What's wrong?"

"Casper, you are a wonderful man. You are the kindest man I know." Annika's voice trembled. "And I am awful to you. I treat you horribly."

"That's OK, honey. I don't mind," Casper replied, pleasantly surprised at Annika's rare show of contrition.

Annika shook her head, frustrated. "You don't understand. You never push back. You're just nicer to me when I beat you up. I *punish* you for it. I just treat you like a punching bag."

Casper was silent. The second hand of the wall clock swept 30 seconds past 8:01.

"Why do you tolerate that?"

"I tolerate it because I love you," replied Casper.

"You shouldn't love me," she said. "I'm not someone who deserves your love. You should find someone better."

There was a long silence.

"Are you breaking up with me?"

Annika took another breath.

"I am."

There was silence. The clock rolled past 8:03. Annika heard shouting in the background from Casper's phone.

"Another plane has hit the World Trade Center," Casper said. "We're under attack. I have to go. I love you."

Annika heard silence on the phone as Casper waited for her to respond. Without a word, she shut her phone.

Annika heard commotion in the hallway. The door swung open. A pimple-faced corporal, surprised to see Annika, saluted in the doorway. He was holding a cell phone in his non-saluting hand. Annika surmised he was also looking to make a call in the vacant office.

"Motherfucking hadjis hit us, Ma'am!"

Annika bolted from the desk and ran down a hallway, pushing past soldiers with cursory salutes on her way out of the building. She ran by carbon-copy beige buildings in the fort complex until she reached the officer's mess.

Inside the cafeteria, several dozen men in camo fatigues stood watching a large-screen television tuned to Fox News. Annika gasped when she saw the images of the World Trade Center's Twin Towers, smoke billowing from both buildings.

The only sound in the room was that of the Fox News anchor, repeating that America was under attack by hijackers. The officers watching the TV were silent.

Annika couldn't process the images.

This isn't happening, she thought. *This isn't happening.*

Close-up images showed orange flames of burning jet fuel leaping from the gashes in the sides of the towers. Replays showed the second plane, United 175, crashing into the South Tower.

"Oh my God," the correspondent said. "Oh my God."

There was silence, then the correspondent began speaking again. "There was a crash on the pavement...people are jumping from the tower."

Annika shook her head in horror.

This isn't happening.

At 9:39, Fox News Channel correspondent David Asman cut in. "We...we are hearing...right now that another explosion that...has taken place...at the Pentagon."

Annika gasped. She pulled out her flip phone and hit the redial button.

Annika heard an automated message through the phone: "All circuits are busy. Please try your call again later."

"Motherfucker!" she shouted as she hit the redial button again.

"All circuits are busy. Please try your call again later."

US Airways Flight #2071

Central Virginia
September 11, 2001
09:50 hours

Kyle Mason watched the lush green of Central Virginia pass beneath his gaze on his flight to Charlotte, North Carolina. He was returning from his NYC honeymoon to Fayetteville and Fort Bragg, where he would report for duty for his first Delta assignment.

From his window seat on the left side of the aircraft, Kyle could see the Rivanna River snake around Charlottesville, the former home of Thomas Jefferson. Kyle smiled as he sipped his ice water. Sweet memories of the past 48 hours with his bride in New York drifted through his mind. Padma's beautiful face was imprinted on everything he saw.

The plane suddenly banked sharply to the left. Moments later, the pilot's voice sounded through the plane's PA system.

"Ladies and gentlemen, this is Captain Rogers. I'm afraid I've got some bad news. We're experiencing instrument problems, which means we're going to need to make an unscheduled landing in Richmond."

A collective groan erupted in the passenger cabin.

"There is nothing wrong with the aircraft and no need to be

concerned," continued Captain Rogers. "But the FAA requires us to land immediately in the event of any sort of instrument malfunction. I apologize for the inconvenience. We will do everything we can to get you to your destination as quickly as humanly possible."

Looking out his window, Kyle saw a dozen commercial aircraft circling the airport to land. The congestion seemed unusual for an airport the size of Richmond. There were also a lot of planes on the tarmac. Something was wrong.

Kyle's flight awaited its turn to land. At 10:30, the plane's tires squelched as the plane touched down. Kyle's cell phone rang as the plane taxied to the terminal.

"Hello?" Kyle answered.

"Uh, hello? Is this Kyle?" replied a woman's voice.

"Yes. Who is this?"

"My name is Joan Mann. You don't know me. I have a message from Padma."

"Is she OK?" Kyle asked, alarmed.

He heard the woman take a deep breath.

"What is it? Tell me!" said Kyle.

"She tried to call you," began Joan. "The phones have been crazy. She couldn't leave a voicemail for you. She called random numbers until she got an answer. She wanted me to get a message to you."

"What message? What's going on?" demanded Kyle.

"She's in the tower," Joan said.

"Yes—she works in the World Trade Center. What's wrong?" demanded Kyle.

"Oh my God! You don't know," the stranger said. She began to cry. "The towers are gone."

"What do you mean the towers are gone? Is this a prank? This isn't funny!" Kyle said, raising his voice. He felt a pang of fear. His heart raced.

Kyle noticed that many of the passengers were talking on their cell phones. Their expressions were blanched.

Joan continued to cry as she tried to explain. Her words were incomprehensible to Kyle. How could the towers be 'gone'? It was impossible.

"I'm sorry, I can't talk," Joan said, sobbing. "Padma told me to tell you this...

"...Beloved, I love you."

World Trade Center, North Tower

New York, NY

September 11, 2001

08:45 hours

Kyle ran frantically up the metal steps of the concrete stairwell—the final flights to the top floor of the North Tower. He glanced at his watch—8:45:45. With his knowledge of the future, Kyle understood that Padma was only 45 seconds away from disaster.

He swung open the stairwell door onto the 105th floor. It was empty. He looked around anxiously for Padma. The plane would hit in 30 seconds. Bright morning light filled the floor through the tall windows.

Kyle spotted Padma on the opposite side of the expansive floor, 60 yards away, her back to the floor-to-ceiling windows and the spectacular panoramic north-facing backdrop of Manhattan.

When she saw Kyle, she smiled and waved, excited to see him. Relieved to have found Padma, Kyle waved back and ran toward her. As he crossed the sprawling floor, he saw a shape appear in the windows behind Padma. It was an approaching plane descending over the Hudson River from the north—American Flight 11. The plane banked toward the tower. It was on a collision course!

He shouted at Padma, trying to warn her. Too far away to hear him, Padma beamed her loving smile to Kyle, unaware of the danger. The building shuddered and rocked as the plane hit, somewhere below the floor they were standing on. Kyle was knocked off his feet. He struggled to regain his balance and stand. He had to save Padma! Ceiling light fixtures and tiles began to fall, obstructing his vision. Smoke filled the floor. Through the chaos, he caught glimpses of Padma, still standing on the far side of the floor.

Suddenly, the floor beneath Padma's feet collapsed as half of the tower sheared away. Kyle watched in horror as Padma fell and disappeared into the crashing debris. Kyle walked to the edge of the floor and looked down at the rubble piled into a smoking heap over a thousand feet below.

He felt his body shake violently. He opened his eyes. A man was holding his shoulders, shaking him in pitch darkness.

"Dude, wake up," the man said.

Milawa Base Camp

Tora Bora, Afghanistan
December 12, 2001
1:20 hours

Kyle sat up on a filthy mattress on the floor, his back against a cinderblock wall. He rubbed his eyes in the cold dark.

"Fuck," Kyle said, groggy. "Did I do it again?"

"Yeah," replied the voice in the dark. "Another nightmare."

Kyle recognized the voice. It was Tony Darwin, a member of Kyle's Delta team.

"Sorry," Kyle said. "Try to get some sleep."

"No prob, bro."

Kyle checked his watch: 01:20 hours. He shook his head and sighed.

Though Kyle was exhausted, he fought to keep his eyes from closing. Sleep invited the recurring nightmare vision. Unable to find an exit in his waking mind, Padma visited Kyle in his dreams and died again every night. Unable to accept Padma's death, Kyle crushed that darkness deep inside, where it festered, eating away at him from within. Every replay of Padma's death seemed to etch the lines under Kyle's eyes a little darker. Though Kyle was still a professional operator, his fellow warriors were worried about him. His friend Tony was especially worried. Even Delta soldiers required sleep.

Kyle knew his candle was burning at both ends. He didn't care. They were close, very close, to killing Bin Laden. He only needed to last one, maybe two more days, and it would be over. After that, nothing mattered.

He remained propped up against the wall, eyes open. Moonlight beams through glassless windows revealed the specter shapes of Kyle's fellow Delta soldiers, scattered on the floor of their makeshift base, trying to get back to sleep. In a few hours, they would be back in the Spīn Ghar Mountains and Bin Laden's Tora Bora fortress.

• • •

The simple cinderblock structure his Delta unit had commandeered had been a school before the Taliban took charge of Afghanistan. The Taliban had rapidly filled the power vacuum left in the wake of the Americans' departure after Operation Cyclone had forced the Soviet Union out in 1989. Operation Cyclone, the CIA's largest-ever covert operation, had been a spectacular success. Shoulder-launched Stinger missiles supplied to muhajideen fighters had turned the tide against the Soviets, downing countless Soviet attack planes and helicopters and flipping the expected rout of the Afghan fighters into the Soviets' Vietnam quagmire. The Soviets' last man out of Afghanistan, Lieutenant General Boris V. Gromov, strode across the steel Friendship Bridge to Uzbekistan the morning of February 16, 1989. As he did, he was reminded of something Alexander the Great had said over 2,000 years earlier:

"Afghanistan was easy to march into. Hard to march out of."

Operation Cyclone was the fruit borne of an odd alliance, which included U.S. congressman Charlie Wilson, CIA case officer Gust Avrakotos, and Houston socialite Joanne Herring. Herring was instrumental in ginning up support for military aid to the muhajideen, encouraging Wilson to meet with Pakistani leadership and visit Afghan refugee camps within Pakistan. There, he witnessed firsthand the atrocities committed by the Soviets against Afghan men, women, and children.

Among the muhajideen fighters aided by the Americans was a young, skinny, six-foot-four-inch Saudi named Osama Bin Laden. The son of a billionaire Saudi construction magnate, Bin Laden joined the muhajideen in 1979, outraged at the injustices the Soviets were committing against the Afghan people.

As Operation Cyclone wound down, Charlie Wilson foresaw the rise of militant fundamentalists in Afghanistan and argued for the funding of modern infrastructure and education in Afghanistan. Congress ignored Wilson, America departed Afghanistan, and the Taliban filled the void, providing al Qaeda a safe harbor to construct the launch pad for the planes that blew through the Twin Towers and the Pentagon on 9/11.

As Charlie Wilson said of the aftermath of Operation Cyclone: "...we fucked up the end game."

• • •

Now the Americans had returned to Afghanistan, this time to kill their former ally. When the Delta mission was announced, Kyle moved heaven and earth to land a spot in the unit. There were obstacles in his way. His fitness for duty was questioned, as his bride had been murdered only three months prior by the man he would be tasked with hunting. Also, his unit already had an officer and didn't need a second—particularly on the forward deploy.

Bucking protocol, Kyle took an enormous career risk and reached out to General Craig, the man who had presented him with his Silver Star for valor in Desert Storm. He asked the general for a favor—to get him into the game at Tora Bora. Kyle had gambled that his bride's death in 9/11 might enable his superiors to excuse his end run.

"That's a mighty big ask," General Craig said over the phone.

"I know, sir. I'm sorry."

"You understand that if you pull an end run like this, no one will want you in their command when you come home."

"I understand," Kyle said. "There won't be anything left for me to do when we return."

There was a pause on the phone.

"OK, Major," the general said. "You've just burned the only favor you get. Now you owe me."

"I understand, sir. Thank you, sir."

Kyle was shipped off to Afghanistan, with the condition that he was to stay out of the way of his commanding officer, as well as his unit's master sergeant.

They were tantalizing close to Bin Laden. Only days prior to the Deltas' arrival, a CIA operative had picked a radio off the body of a dead al Qaeda fighter. The radio was tuned to the enemy's frequency. Delta could now eavesdrop on al Qaeda to learn their condition and movements. The screams of the al Qaeda fighters over the airwaves in response to bomb drops called in by Delta enabled the commandos to gauge the accuracy of their airstrikes and fine-tune as needed.

The Americans' relentless bombing had pulverized the ancient Tora Bora fortress. Bin Laden's al Qaeda forces were shredded. SIGINT told Kyle's unit that they had advanced to within 100 meters of Bin Laden's position the previous day. Kyle and his fellow operators smelled blood. Today was going to be the day he avenged Padma's death. He fully intended to ignore the "capture" part of his unit's "capture or kill" orders. In a few hours, Bin Laden would die.

Milawa Base Camp

Tora Bora, Afghanistan
December 12, 2001
05:00 hours

It was pitch dark and very cold on the rugged mountain ridge. From the rocky perch that had been Osama Bin Laden's home only hours earlier, Kyle Mason and his fellow Delta operators surveyed the glowing phosphorescent green landscape through night-vision goggles. Bin Laden's Milawa Base Camp now lay shattered after days of ceaseless bombing by U.S. air forces. Now, Kyle's two dozen-man Delta mission support unit had actually set foot on the terrorist's doorstep, an entrance to a vast cave complex thousands of feet above sea level on the border of Pakistan. SIGINT told them they were close—within a hundred meters of Bin Laden.

Kyle tugged the brown wool blanket wrapped around him a bit tighter to keep warm. In order to blend with the locals, he and his fellow soldiers had abandoned their winter Army wear in favor of traditional muhajideen dress, known as *shalwar kameez*—baggy drawstring pants, knee-length, long-sleeved shirts, and a floppy wool hat called a *pakul*. They had also grown their hair and beards. While other special forces units maintained stricter military dress code, Delta was special. The objective was the mission. Whatever increased their odds of success was embraced, including wearing baggy pajama pants into battle. Some members of Delta even carried the AK-47 assault rifles favored by the muhajideen, but Kyle preferred his trusty M4 rifle, as well as his M1911 sidearm. What the soldiers lacked in Gore-Tex in the cold mountain air, they made up for in armament. In addition to their precision firearms, their web vests were packed with explosive charges, ammo, and infrared targeting pointers to guide bomb drops.

The fact that the Delta soldiers had advanced so deep into al Qaeda's mountain stronghold was near miraculous, given the obstacles placed squarely in their path by their own government. Washington had refused to commit large numbers of American troops to the hunt for the mastermind of 9/11. Instead, their unit commander had been ordered to cut deals with two rival Afghan warlords, effectively buying Mujh mercenaries with shrink-wrapped bricks of cash served up by the CIA. The two warlords, General Hazret Ali and Haji Zaman, jockeyed for the position of top dog in Nangarhar Province. Neither had any particular interest in the Americans' mission to kill Bin Laden. Indeed, Bin Laden had become a revered figure in the region, in no small part thanks to the money he dispersed to locals from his personal fortune. Ali and Zaman's interests were purely financial—how much money could they siphon off the Americans, and how much political influence would it buy them in their efforts to topple each other.

Ali and Zaman's ragged mercenary armies numbered some 2,500 men. The CIA estimated that between 1,500 and 3,000 al Qaeda fighters and allies were holed up in the mountain caves of Tora Bora.

For the Delta operators, working with the muhajideen had been maddening. They had found the Mujh to be little more than bands of lawless thugs for hire to the highest bidder. To the exasperation of the Deltas, the Mujh fighters would advance on the enemy by day, then quit and go home at night, giving up the territory they had won during a day's fighting. In the absence of a passionate cause to fight for—like ousting the Soviets from their homeland—they didn't see the point of overnighting in harm's way on the frigid mountains. The morning after the previous day's fight, the muhajideen would clock in and pay for the same bloodied real estate over and over again.

From Bin Laden's former mountain aerie, the soldiers witnessed a glint of brilliant yellow sun cresting the horizon. Towering angled shapes slowly emerged from the pitch dark as daylight fell on the spectacular snowcapped Spīn Ghar Mountains to the south. On the other side of the white peaks, mountain trails led from Tora Bora to bordering Pakistan.

Both the Deltas and the CIA feared that when the Americans turned up the heat at Tora Bora, Bin Laden would simply walk out the backdoor to Pakistan via those mountain trails to the south. They knew that Bin Laden had become intimately familiar with the trails over his decades spent in the region. Kyle's Delta commanding officer had sent repeated urgent requests to CENTCOM to guard the Pakistani mountain trails. His first request was to deploy seven hundred Army Rangers to guard the backdoor trails. The request was denied. His second request was to mine the trails in order to halt an escape and enable sensors to track mine detonations to acquire al Qaeda targets. Again, request denied. Finally, exasperated, the CO proposed an audacious plan for his Delta unit to scale the towering White Mountains with bottled oxygen in order to guard the Pakistani passes themselves. Request denied. Kyle was astonished—mission critical requests from Delta unit commanders were not made lightly, and he had never before heard of one being refused.

Though all soldiers were accustomed to idiotic orders from Washington, to Kyle this course was pure insanity. Bin Laden was here. Why didn't Washington commit thousands of professional American soldiers to kill the man that murdered thousands of innocent Americans in cold blood? Why instead deploy only a couple dozen special ops operators and a band of untrained cutthroat mercenaries against an impregnable mountain fortress guarded by thousands of fanatics, committed to die for their "Father"? Why were America's leaders refusing to guard Bin Laden's backdoor exit to Pakistan? It was madness!

Approximately 100 meters down the ridge, the Delta operators could make out nearly 100 muhajideen fighters—Haji Zaman's men. Kyle's unit carefully made their way along the rocky ridge to link up with them and press forward with the hunt for Bin Laden. The fighters were a motley crew, an assortment of ages ranging from teenagers to old men. All wore beards and the traditional baggy *shalwar kameez* with floppy *pakul* hats. Some wore vests, some coats. Most were wrapped in blankets to stave off the mountain cold. Their AK-47 assault rifles, the weapon of choice of peasant armies around the world, were carelessly handled. An acrid smell wafted from joints smoked by several of the younger fighters.

The Mujh commander, a thirty-something man with a dark beard, sat on a rock, smoking a cigarette. His AK-47 was propped against the rock. He watched the Americans warily as they approached.

The master sergeant of Kyle's mission support unit motioned for his unit to halt. He walked toward the Mujh commander with his interpreter to discuss the day's plan to pursue Bin Laden. Kyle tagged along, remaining within earshot. The unit's master sergeant was a bruiser, code-named "Hammer." Kyle considered Hammer to be the archetypal Special Forces master sergeant—big, muscular, and very tough, with endurance that could outlast any operator. The Mujh commander took another drag on his cigarette from his rock seat as he watched the trio approach.

Hammer pulled a black walkie-talkie from his vest and switched it on. A CIA operative had picked the radio off the body of a dead al Qaeda fighter several days before.

Osama Bin Laden's distinctive manicured voice crackled through the radio, exhorting his troops, "…the time is now, arm your women and children against the infidel."

The Mujh fighters gasped. "Father!" several said with reverence.

Hammer nodded to his interpreter. "I guess we know whose back these assholes really have."

"Here's the deal," Hammer said to the Mujh commander. "When Bin Laden talks on his radio, our SIGINT triangulates his position, and we drop a bomb on him. We listen to how loud his fighters scream. The louder they scream, the closer we are to the target. We bomb. They scream. We fine tune our targeting and repeat.

"Today, we're not bombing. The reason is that SIGINT has Bin Laden's position at only 100 meters in that direction." Hammer pointed toward the mountain pass in front of them. "That's about one football field away from where we're standing.

"So, today, our mission is simple. We're going to walk down that trail, shoot Bin Laden and go home."

The Mujh commander stared at Hammer, mute. After several awkward moments, he took another draw on his cigarette and looked away. As he exhaled, he began to speak.

"No one will be shooting the Sheikh today," he said calmly through the interpreter.

"I beg your fucking pardon?" exclaimed Hammer.

"Our leader, Haji Zaman, has negotiated al Qaeda's surrender. Shooting the Sheikh would be…rude."

Hammer's jaw dropped. "With all due respect, Commander, you are full of piping-hot shit."

The Mujh commander laughed at the translation.

"Regardless of what I'm full of, no one will be shooting the Sheik today."

"That's fine, we'll go without you," said Hammer.

The Mujh commander raised two fingers, casually motioning toward Hammer. His fighters trained their guns on the Delta soldiers.

"You are fucking kidding me," Hammer said.

The Mujh commander grinned. "You are not going anywhere."

A sergeant in Hammer's unit approached, holding a radio.

"Master Sergeant, I'm sorry to interrupt this perfect shit storm, but the major wants a SITREP."

Hammer sighed. "Of course he does."

"I need a second opinion, Sergeant," said Hammer. "How would you assess our situation?"

"I'd say it's pretty fucked up, Master Sergeant."

"You have a keen eye."

"Thank you, Master Sergeant."

"Please excuse me," Hammer said to the commander as he turned and snatched the radio.

"Redfly, this is Hammer. Do you read? Over."

"Reading you 5-by-5," said Redfly, Hammer's commanding officer. "What is your situation?"

"Our situation is fucked, sir," said Hammer. "We are 100 meters away from OBL, and four dozen of our good friends from Haji Zaman's army have their weapons pointed at us."

"Motherfuckers," said Redfly.

"Their commander is giving us a bullshit story about Zaman negotiating a surrender with OBL."

"That turd bucket is on CNN at the press camp right now announcing the surrender," said Redfly. "CENTCOM is going nuts."

"So, when can we expect Bin Laden to walk out of his cave with his hands on his head?"

"Zaman says he's negotiating the details of the surrender and that they'll close the deal by 17:00."

"Seventeen hundred gives OBL nearly 12 hours to walk right out of here into Pakistan. Recommend that we take him while he's on this side of the border. We'll take good care of our Mujh friends standing in the way."

"Negative. We've been ordered to stand down until 17:00. I've told CENTCOM Bin Laden's going to get away. This has gone all the way up the chain to Washington. Our nation's leaders are busy at work cluster fucking the entire op as we speak. If Bin Laden doesn't show by 17:00, we start our bomb runs again."

"He'll be long gone by then," said Hammer. "There won't be anything left to bomb."

There was a pause.

"Preaching to the choir, Sergeant. The situation is FUBAR," the major said. "We have our orders. Stand down until 17:00. Firefly out."

"Un-fucking-believable," said Hammer, shaking his head.

"That's it?" asked Kyle. "We're not going to get Bin Laden?"

"That's it, Major," said Hammer.

Kyle was stunned. They were minutes away from killing his wife's murderer.

Kyle scanned the Mujh fighters, calculating the odds. The Delta operators were outnumbered four to one by poorly trained and equipped muhajideen. Those weren't bad odds for the world's most elite warriors.

"We can take them," said Kyle.

"It doesn't matter if we can take them or not," Hammer said. "We have our orders."

"Fuck orders," Kyle said. "Court martial me."

Kyle began to walk toward the Mujh fighters, raising his weapon.

"Exactly what-the-fuck do you think you're doing, Major?" asked Hammer.

The Mujh fighters, anxious, trained their weapons on Kyle. The Deltas snapped up their rifles at the muhajideen.

"Stand down, Major!" shouted Hammer.

Kyle continued walking toward the fighters. He aimed his weapon at their commander. The commander lowered his cigarette to his side. A surprised look replaced his smug expression. He hadn't expected the outnumbered Americans to challenge his fighters. Frightened, he yelled at his troops to prepare to open fire.

Hammer raised his assault rifle at Kyle's back.

"Major, take one more step, and I will shoot you myself!" Hammer shouted.

Kyle halted. He closed his eyes. It was over. Bin Laden was going to get away.

He turned to Hammer, his face was twisted with anguish.

"We all want what you want," said Hammer. "We'll try to get you your shot. Don't do that again."

Kyle walked past Hammer to rejoin the unit. Hammer slapped him on the shoulder as he passed.

"Make yourselves comfortable gentlemen," said Hammer. "We're going to be here awhile."

Kyle glared at the Mujh commander, who grinned at the helpless Americans while enjoying his smoke on his rock perch.

Kyle found his own rock to lean against, took off his pack, and sat down on the ground. He pulled a knife from his belt sheath and began carving ruts in the dirt.

At 17:00, 12 hours after the commandos' arrival at Milawa Base Camp, Master Sergeant Hammer looked at his watch. Al Qaeda had not surrendered.

"Time!" he said. "Ruck up!"

The Delta operators shouldered their packs and began to move out. Hammer stared at the chain-smoking Mujh commander.

"Don't raise your weapons at us," Hammer warned the commander.

The grin disappeared from the Mujh commander's face. He could plainly see that Hammer's patience had run out. The world's best soldiers were ready for a fight—maybe even looking for an excuse to kill every one of the Mujh who had denied them their target. Their commander tried to raise Zaman on the radio for instructions as the Delta operators walked out of sight. He heard only static in response. Zaman was nowhere to be found.

• • •

At 17:02, the mountain shuddered as the first American warplane dropped its payload. The Mujh rapidly retreated from their Milawa Camp position. The warplanes were hot, as were the Americans' tempers. The Mujh, realizing their allies might be less cautious about friendly fire than normal, decided to exercise the better part of valor and retreat from the battlefield.

Over the next few days, bombs rained destruction on the few remaining al Qaeda targets, though Kyle and his Delta comrades knew it was too late. With a wide-open backdoor to Pakistan and a full day to walk through it, Osama Bin Laden was long gone.

Five days later, on December 17, Haji Zaman and General Ali declared victory in the battle for Tora Bora. A few days later, Kyle and his fellow Delta commandos' mission formally ended, and they headed back to Bagram Airbase to await their next orders.

The U.S. government put the best possible spin on the outcome: The Taliban and al Qaeda had been routed in Afghanistan. Hundreds, perhaps thousands, of al Qaeda fighters had been killed. Though the precise whereabouts of Osama Bin Laden were unknown, he may well have been killed in the relentless bombing. Al Qaeda had been hurt—badly.

Al Qaeda's pain did not console Kyle's. They didn't get Bin Laden. There was no doubt in Kyle's mind that Osama Bin Laden had walked out of Afghanistan on December 13, when a corrupt warlord shielded his escape. What mystified Kyle was why CENTCOM had refused their requests to block the exits to Pakistan. There was zero doubt that Bin Laden was at Tora Bora. The Deltas and the CIA believed the odds were high that they could have captured or killed Bin Laden right then and there.

"Why did they let Bin Laden escape?"

Kyle couldn't shake the question. It cycled endlessly in his mind, intertwining with the suppressed reality of Padma's death. The growing blight in his head fought to break into the daylight of his consciousness, like a raging monster locked behind an aged wooden door. Kyle denied it with the same tenacity that he had battled al Qaeda. Weakened by sleep deprivation, cracks began to form in the armor that blocked Padma's memory. She forced herself into Kyle's consciousness, overwhelming him.

In the officer's mess at Bagram, he sat down at a table, alone with his lunch tray. He looked at the empty seat across from his.

His mind broke.

Tears began to stream down his cheeks. Panicking, he tried to wipe away the tears before anyone saw the grown man crying. He began to shake. The tears flowed. He cried uncontrollably. A nurse appeared and put her hand on his back. Gently, she stood him up and guided him out of the mess hall to the infirmary.

Despite the military's attempts to help Kyle with counseling and medication, he spiraled into a cavernous depression. He didn't eat, didn't bathe, and didn't leave his quarters. The decorated war hero became unrecognizable to his colleagues and friends. They worried for his life. He was no longer fit for duty. He wasn't fit for anything.

Early in 2002, Tony Darwin helped Kyle submit his request to resign his commission and be released from active duty. Within a few months, Kyle Mason, former elite soldier and war hero, was a civilian for the first time in his adult life.

7 West 75th Street

New York, NY
July 23, 2008
11:48 hours

Slivers of daylight peeked around the edges of Padma's bedroom window shade, casting dim light onto her unmade bed. A white duvet was pulled aside. A slept-in pillow with a strand of long black hair sat at the bed's black wrought-iron headboard. On an onyx wooden nightstand, a brass elephant-shaped lighter stood watch over a single cigarette, extinguished seven years earlier, resting in a glass ashtray.

A layer of dust coated the elephant and the nightstand. Padma's clothes hung in her bedroom closet, untouched since she had left for work for the last time seven years earlier.

Outside the bedroom door, a wooden board had been nailed into the corner between the door and its jam, sealing the room shut. In the kitchen, dozens of plastic plates from microwave meals littered the table and counters. More plates lay on the floor of the living room, where a blanket and pillow were tossed on the sofa. A couple pairs of jeans, shirts, underwear, and socks were scattered across the living room floor.

In the bathroom, Padma's toothbrush sat in a glass on the right side of the sink. In the shower, her shampoo and conditioner rested on the tub's ledge. A box of tampons was under the sink. Kyle rarely bathed, and he entered the bathroom as infrequently as possible. Every time he did, he cycled the same question about Padma's toiletries:

Should I do something with these?

The answer was always the same.

I don't know.

For years, the daily question would bring tears. In 2005, Kyle noticed that he had run out of tears. His depression had not abated. He simply had no more tears. The Padma toiletry Q&A cycle was a fixed part of his daily Sisyphean routine.

In the living room, a wadded blue blanket lay on a distressed brown leather sofa. On the wall hung a lonely framed sketch—Padma's teenage drawing of a leaf resting on a pool of water.

For weeks after returning from Afghanistan, Kyle scarcely moved from Padma's sofa. Though Padma's tony neighbors in the three-floor brownstone walk-up encouraged their landlord, Mrs. Dana, to evict the eye-and-nose-sore from the premises, the elderly woman instead tried to care for the broken man. Mrs. Dana lived on the first floor of the brownstone, directly beneath Padma's apartment. She checked on Kyle from time to time, hired a cleaning woman to straighten up once a week, and occasionally brought Kyle a home-cooked dinner. Money wasn't a problem. The combination of Padma's nest egg, life insurance, and Cantor Fitzgerald survivor benefits were enough to set Kyle up for life. Kyle had handed Mrs. Dana a checkbook, not caring whether or not she could be trusted with the money.

When the cleaning woman tried to work, Kyle would lay motionless on the sofa, eyes open, unnerving the woman. He remained catatonic during her visits up until the moment the woman attempted to open Padma's bedroom door. Kyle summoned his former reflexes, leaping from the sofa down the hall to the door, which he pulled shut in the woman's face.

"Don't," he said. "Ever."

Kyle returned to the sofa and threw his blanket over his head. Later that day, he ventured out of the apartment to buy a hammer and nails and a section of 2x4 to seal the bedroom door shut.

When the woman threatened to quit, Mrs. Dana encouraged Kyle to begin visiting Padma, adding the tint of guilt that it was his responsibility to do so. It worked. Kyle began making daily sorties on the A train to the 9/11 site, enabling the woman to do her job without the looming presence of a half-dead crazy man on the couch.

Six miles south of Padma's apartment, Kyle viewed the construction zone where the Twin Towers had once stood. A chaos of vehicles and gantries were partially voided by two perfect square excavations—the graves of the north and south tower buildings. Within the squares was dark brown earth. In the footprints of the Twin Towers, the 9/11 Memorial would be built—two enormous square fountains that would pour water from their perimeters into the dark shadows below.

Adjacent to the twin squares was the foundation of a new building. Nearly seven years after 9/11, after mourning, infighting, and lawsuits, construction was finally underway on Freedom Tower, eventually destined to become the world's fourth tallest building. The new skyscraper had yet to clear street level. Nearly 8,000 miles away, the world's tallest building, the Burj Khalifa, had been completed in Dubai in less time than it took New York City to break ground on Freedom Tower.

Kyle stared into the hole of the North Tower. His wife was in there, somewhere. How did she die? Was she vaporized with hundreds of others when the tower collapsed? Did she die of smoke inhalation from the burning jet fuel from American 11? Or, when faced with being burned alive, was she one of the 200 that chose to jump to their deaths? Which was the less horrible way to die? Kyle cycled the question. One couple was seen holding hands for the 10 seconds it took to fall to their deaths 1,350 feet below the 105th floor.

Kyle longed to hold his wife's hand in her final 10 seconds.

A sprinkling rain began to fall from the gray sky. Kyle stood in it for a minute. He looked up, forcing his eyes open as the raindrops hit his face. He turned to leave. He would visit Padma again the next day...and the day after that.

Kyle took the A train uptown. Riders stayed clear of the man who looked and smelled like one of Manhattan's homeless on his worst day. His hair was long and shaggy, as was his beard. A stained T-shirt and jeans hung from a skinny frame, 75 pounds lighter than his former fighting self. He wore flip-flops on his feet, exposing overgrown toenails. Weighted by his depression, the simplest tasks required enormous effort, including getting out of bed, eating, bathing, and lacing his shoes.

Kyle noticed a *New York Times* left on the subway seat next to him. A front-page article speculated about the whereabouts of General Aaron Craig.

WHERE IN THE WORLD IS GENERAL AARON CRAIG?

Neil Feinman | July 23, 2008

Four-Star General and Bush Nominee for Secretary of Defense MIA for Six Years

After turning down President Bush's offer to become secretary of defense six years earlier, the four-star general had vanished without a trace. There was no record of a transfer, retirement, or move to the private sector. No one seemed to know what had happened to him. It was as though he had left for coffee one day and never returned.

Kyle climbed the stairs of the 72nd Street stop to street level, next to the Dakota. The great German Renaissance-style building was home to Yoko Ono, whose own spouse had been murdered there decades earlier. Across the street from her home, near the entrance to Central Park, was a tribute to John Lennon called "Strawberry Fields." The park was flush with green on the summer day.

Kyle reached his 75th Street brownstone and climbed the stairs.

He unlocked the black enamel-painted door to apartment 2. As the door swung open, he was startled to see a barrel-chested African-American man in a full army general's dark green dress uniform standing in his living room. The man was examining Padma's framed sketch of a leaf floating on a pool. His arms were folded behind his back. He turned to face Kyle. Though the man had been MIA for years, Kyle instantly recognized General Aaron Craig.

7 West 75th Street

New York, NY

July 23, 2008

12:15 hours

"Hello, Major," said the general.

Kyle instinctively raised his hand to salute and then dropped it feebly, remembering that he wasn't in the Army anymore.

"How have you been, son?" the general asked in a fatherly manner, conveying genuine concern.

Kyle looked at the floor, aware of his deteriorated state, "I guess I've seen better days, sir."

General Craig nodded, "I know you have."

The general paused, looking at Kyle, "Have a seat," he said, motioning toward the blanket-covered sofa. Kyle sat, and the general pulled up a chair across from him.

"You must be wondering why I'm here," said General Craig.

Kyle nodded. "Yes sir."

"Major, I have a question for you. It's a simple question, but an important one, and I don't ask it lightly. I want you to think about it before you answer."

"Yes sir. Of course, sir," replied Kyle.

"Major, what if you could change everything? What would you

give if you could make everything right again?"

Kyle's face crunched into confused pain. Tears welled in his eyes. He didn't understand why this Army legend, missing for years, had suddenly appeared in his home, asking such a ridiculous question. Was this a psych test? What was going on?

Kyle's brain was exhausted. He had no capacity to outfox a test. All he had left was the truth.

"I would give anything," replied Kyle.

General Craig looked closely at Kyle, pausing before speaking.

"That was the right answer, son," he said.

Kyle felt a childlike pride akin to that of winning a father's approval.

"Major, I'm here because I'm on a recruiting mission," said General Craig. "I can't tell you what I'm recruiting for, only that it has the real potential to fix a lot of things that are broken today. One of those broken things belongs to you.

"You may not believe this," General Craig continued, "but you are on a very short list of people I believe has the greatest chance of success. I can't tell you much of anything about the mission, except that the risk is great, and the potential reward is much, much greater."

Kyle's head was swirling. Nothing about this scene seemed real—the full general sitting in his derelict living room, the absurd idea that Kyle was qualified to do anything important—it was insane.

"Sir, are you sure you've got the right guy?" Kyle asked. "You know some of my marbles have gone missing."

General Craig laughed. "I told you, you wouldn't believe me. I can share some, but not all of the reasons you're on the list. They include your skillset and experience, of course, your demonstrated valor and ability to keep a clear head in a crisis, but there's one more thing."

"What's that?" asked Kyle.

"You've got nothing to lose," replied the general, giving Kyle a hard look.

Kyle nodded. "Well, sir, you sure got that part right."

Kyle sat silent for a few moments.

"Is there anything else you can tell me, sir?" asked Kyle.

"Only this: If you agree, we leave now, go to an airport, and fly to a facility where you will be fully briefed. You will be reinstated in the Army with the rank of Lieutenant Colonel. I cannot tell you when you will return. You will not need to pack or deal with your landlord. Everything will be taken care of. If you do not agree, I will leave, you will likely never see me again, and you will forget that this meeting ever happened."

"It's like the blue pill and the red pill," said Kyle.

"Sorry?" said the general.

"In the movie *The Matrix*, Morpheus offers Neo the choice between the blue pill to remain asleep in the Matrix and the red pill to see how deep the rabbit hole goes," explained Kyle.

"Ah, I see," said the general with a broad smile. "Son, you have no idea how right you are."

Kyle was quiet for a minute.

"I choose the rabbit hole," he said.

The general smiled. "Good for you." He reached into his pocket and pulled out a small walkie-talkie.

"We're leaving," he said.

"Roger, sir," crackled the reply.

The general rose and walked toward the door. Kyle began to follow, then hesitated. He scanned Padma's living room. The realization that he might never see her home again hurled a bolt of sadness through him.

"Just a second, please, sir," Kyle said as he walked to the sketch of the leaf on the wall. He removed it from the wall and pulled off the back of the frame. He took the sketch, folded it in quarter and shoved it in his hip pocket.

In the minute it took the two to emerge from the brownstone, a black Chevy Suburban SUV had pulled up. The windows were dark. A uniformed driver leapt from the car to open the rear passenger door. A uniformed guard stepped out of the passenger side, carrying an MP7 submachine gun. He scanned the street for trouble. As Kyle climbed in the back seat with the general, he noticed Mrs. Dana peeking from behind her first-floor window shade. Kyle raised his hand into a scarce wave. He knew the gesture was a wholly inadequate "thank you" for her kindness over the years. Mrs. Dana lifted her hand in reply, confused and worried about Kyle.

The driver turned on a siren and flashing blue and red grill lights. The SUV flew along 72nd Street through Central Park, the east side, and onto FDR Drive, headed downtown. Minutes later, they pulled up at the Downtown Manhattan Heliport, located at Pier 6 on the East River near Battery Park at the southern tip of Manhattan. The heliport pier jutted out into the East River in an

L-shape. Several white circles with crosshairs were painted on the dark tarmac—landing targets for the helicopters that normally ferried Wall Street executives to and from meetings and airports. Light rain began to fall from the gray sky, and chop from the East River lapped against the pier. At the farthest end of the pier sat a Blackhawk helicopter, engine running, with two Army Rangers in full combat gear standing guard with M4 assault rifles. Two additional Rangers stood at the pier entrance, blocking business commuters' passage onto the heliport. The SUV drove onto the pier. The guards saluted as it passed.

Several Wall Street businessmen, whose flights had been delayed because of the general, watched in confusion and awe as the general and a mystery man exited the SUV and walked to the Blackhawk. The hulking Blackhawk was an intimidating contrast to the executives' comparatively lightweight business helicopters.

One young exec made the mistake of walking up to one of the Rangers, a master sergeant, to complain about his delayed commute. The thirty-something businessman had prematurely receding, combed-back black hair, and he wore navy pinstripes and French cuffs with gold cufflinks. A perfect blue and gold Hermès tie thrust from a white contrast collar cresting a blue dress shirt.

"Step back, sir," the sergeant told the exec firmly.

"Look, I'm going to miss my flight at JFK. Who do I talk to about this?" demanded the exec.

The sergeant glared at the man, took a step toward him, and jutted his face forward, until their noses were almost touching.

"Who do you talk to, motherfucker?" the sergeant shouted point blank into the executive's face. "You talk to me and my mother-fucking M4 machine gun, that's who you talk to! Now, I asked you respectfully to step back, and what did you do?"

"I, I," the executive stammered.

"I, I," the sergeant mocked. "'I…*disrespected* you.' That's what you say. Now you try it."

"I disrespected you," repeated the exec, terrified.

"That's right. That's what you did. Now what do you say to a man with a machine gun who might blow a hole in your sorry ass when you disrespect him?"

"I'm sorry. I am truly sorry, sir."

"Excellent choice of words," replied the sergeant. "I accept your apology. Step back, now."

The exec trembled, unable to move. One of his colleagues took him by the arm and guided him back several steps. As the Blackhawk's rotors revved, the sergeant and the other soldiers backed toward the helicopter. The men turned and leapt into the Blackhawk as its wheels left the ground. As it ascended into the gray sky and sped away, the executives on the ground watched, dumbstruck.

Moments later, Kyle, the general, and the guards were ascending in the Blackhawk. The crew compartment interior was bare bones, standard-issue military gray, with two facing rows of folding seats.

Through the Blackhawk's large side windows, streaked with rain, Kyle watched the great city beneath him. He saw the Twin Tower construction zone where he had stood only an hour earlier.

"Goodbye, beloved," he whispered.

Within the hour, the Blackhawk slowed as it approached

McGuire Air Force Base in New Jersey. Among the assorted military aircraft on the tarmac, one stood out—a white unmarked Boeing 727 with no passenger windows.

"That's our ride," said General Craig through his headphone mike.

The Blackhawk touched down within 100 feet of the white plane. The door of the helicopter was pulled open by ground crew, and General Craig and Kyle strode to the 727. The engines were already warm. Within minutes, the plane lifted off.

The windowless 727 was originally designed to be a cargo plane for companies like FedEx, though this one had been configured for passengers who did not need to know where they were going. The interior was spartan, but there was standard commercial airline seating, as well as small conference tables.

"I take it that I'm not supposed to know where I'm going," said Kyle.

"I'll tell you where you're going…after you get there," replied General Craig, smiling. "Flight time is about four and a half hours. Get some rest or something to eat. We have sandwiches."

Several hours later, the pilots of the white plane spotted a craggy brown mountain with a white spot at its base. As they approached, the spot grew and mellowed into a cream color. It was a desert lakebed.

The 727 approached to land. Kyle could feel the plane's decent and hear the landing gear drop as they prepared for landing. He felt the bump as the aircraft touched down. The aircraft taxied for a few minutes, then came to a halt. The engines shut down, and a crewman opened the main hatch. General Craig rose from his seat and motioned for Kyle to follow.

"C'mon," General Craig said. "It's time to see the rabbit hole."

The two men walked out of the 727 hatch and stood atop the air stairs, gazing at the desert lakebed and the hive of buildings before them. Kyle was blinded by the brilliant sun reflecting off the desert lakebed.

"Welcome to Area 51," said General Craig with a broad smile.

Area 51, NV

July 23, 2008
13:15 hours

"So now you're going to show me the little green men?" asked Kyle sarcastically.

"They're not green," replied General Craig, grinning like a schoolboy.

Kyle whipped his head to look at the general, his eyes wide. He couldn't tell whether or not the general was joking. The general continued to stare ahead.

"And the spaceship?" Kyle fished.

"It's not a spaceship."

Kyle waited for the general to let him in on the joke.

"Holy shit!" said Kyle. "You're serious!"

The general laughed. They walked down the air stairs and climbed into a desert camouflaged Humvee parked on the tarmac. The Humvee sped north across the lakebed, away from the Area 51 complex. As they approached the northern edge of the lakebed, a building began to emerge through the mirage distortion off the desert. It was a solitary hangar.

"Is that where you keep it?" Kyle asked, excited as a kid on Christmas morning.

"Settle down, soldier, all your questions will be answered soon," replied the general.

As the Humvee approached, the hangar doors opened. Kyle was disappointed to see that the hangar was empty. No spaceship. The Humvee entered the hangar, and the doors closed behind. The hangar was big—big enough to house the 727 they had just left on the tarmac. Kyle noticed a large yellow circle painted on the hangar floor—approximately 40 feet in diameter. The driver drove the Humvee to the center of the circle. He turned and handed a digital pad to General Craig.

"Code in," said General Craig.

"Code in," replied a computerized voice from the pad.

"General Aaron Craig, Code 149, alpha, alpha, epsilon, 982, confirm," said the general.

"General Craig, confirmed," replied the voice.

The floor beneath them began to descend. They were on an elevator.

"That's a neat trick," said Kyle.

"Trust me, you ain't seen nothin' yet."

Kyle watched the unpainted gray concrete walls of the enormous freight elevator move past them as the pad descended. Blue lights spaced at three-foot intervals enabled Kyle to approximate their depth. At approximately 100 feet, the exterior walls changed to painted red. "Level 1" was painted on the wall in giant white letters. Recessed LED lighting illuminated the room. On one wall was an enormous steel vault door, approximately 20 feet by 20 feet, with two giant hinges on the left. An area of the floor in front of the door, also 20 feet by 20 feet, was painted with yellow and black hazard stripes. A series of blue strobe lights hugged the door's perimeter. Smoked plexiglass bubbles housing security cameras protruded from all four walls. As the elevator descended into the bay, two armed soldiers on either side of the vault door leveled their M4 automatic rifles at the Humvee.

"Time to go," said General Craig.

The two men exited the Humvee and walked to the vault door. To the right of the door, on the wall, was a console with a black glass panel, a speaker, and a keypad. The soldiers' guns remained trained on General Craig and Kyle as General Craig looked directly at the black panel, adjusting it to his height.

"Authorize," said General Craig.

"Authorize," replied the console.

"General Aaron Craig, Epsilon, Three, Two, Five, Seven, Four, Andromeda, Authorize," he said.

The black panel lit up, scanning the general's face and eyes.

"Authorized," replied the console.

A loud klaxon sounded, and the door's blue perimeter lights began to strobe brightly. The soldiers shouldered their weapons and saluted. As the vault door slowly swung toward them, Kyle could see that it was thick—five feet. When the door cleared its frame, Kyle gasped at what he saw inside. General Craig extended his hand for Kyle to enter.

Inside the entryway, two more armed guards bearing assault rifles saluted the general and stood aside to allow Kyle and him to pass. They were standing on the edge of a polished 40-foot-wide mezzanine, which curved gradually to close a donut circle approximately 300 yards in diameter. The ceiling was some 20 feet above them. The mezzanine floor was a cream color. Kyle walked to the railed edge of the mezzanine. In the center was an enormous atrium, nearly 300 yards across, with a depth of nearly 100 feet. Kyle could see two floors beneath them, each with subtly different pastel color schemes. At the base of the atrium was a park, with a forest, ponds, and streams with bridge crossings. At the center of the atrium ceiling, a waterfall poured into a pond 100 feet below. The ceiling appeared to be a glass skylight, but the bright sunlight pouring into the complex from the ceiling was artificially generated. Kyle could see children swimming in the pond, playing in the waterfall.

Kyle noticed an insignia on the wall—two blue triangles forming an hourglass against a black circular background.

"General, what is this place?" Kyle asked, overwhelmed.

"It used to be called 'Dreamland,' but it was renamed when I took command and renovated the place. Officially, this is now known as the Temporal Displacement Complex, which hosts the Temporal Displacement System, or TDS. However, so many people began referring to the TDS as "titties" that we all just started calling it the 'Time Tunnel.'"

"Time Tunnel as in *time travel*?"

"Right," said the general.

"You are fucking kidding me…sir, sorry sir," exclaimed Kyle.

"No, actually, this is very real…or, at least, we think it is. No one has gone anywhere yet with it… or, rather, any*when*.

"You have a million questions," the general continued. "You're going to get a full briefing, but first, you're going to get cleaned up. You need a haircut, a shave, change of clothes. And frankly, Colonel, you stink—start with a shower."

The general turned and motioned to an attractive young woman with fair, freckled skin and blond hair who was standing behind them out of earshot. She was dressed in business casual khaki slacks and a pink polo shirt. Kyle noticed that most people in the complex were not wearing uniforms.

"This is Julia. She will show you to your quarters and give you the express tour. The complex is way too big for you to see it all in a couple of hours, which is how much time you have to get cleaned up and to meet me in mission control. Julia will take you where you need to go," directed the general.

Julia extended her hand toward an electric cart parked next to the wall. Kyle took a few steps, then turned back to the general.

"Sir, is this real?" he asked, bewildered.

"We're going to find out—together," replied the general.

• • •

General Craig watched Julia and Kyle drive away in the cart. With Kyle's arrival, the general had moved his last game piece into place. Beneath his fatherly veneer, the mechanics of a strategic mind were in overdrive. General Craig had never revealed his reason for choosing command of Dreamland over the much more prestigious position of secretary of state. The choice seemed like lunacy to the general's colleagues, the press, and the president.

The general's associates and superiors were unaware that he had made command of Dreamland his top priority from the very first time he had visited the complex in 2000 as vice chief of staff. He had instantly seized on the facility's potential—something that was lost on the other generals, who viewed the crazy notion of a time machine as nothing more than a harebrained scientific exercise. Even if it could be made to work, they saw no useful military application, as it could not be weaponized. While the possibility of witnessing the nineteenth-century battle of the Alamo firsthand might be thrilling for a historian, there was no benefit to present-day battlefields. The generals were much more interested in harnessing the unbelievable power of the Grays' antimatter reactor, which had the potential to annihilate entire countries without the downside of nuclear radiation. The generals thought it amusing that, in an era of green consciousness, they were developing the world's first clean doomsday weapon.

General Craig knew there was much more to the Grays' technology than the capacity to blow things up. In an age of terrorism, traditional warfare between countries with borders drawn on a map was as much of an anachronism as Civil War generals' use of eighteenth-century Napoleonic tactics against cannon and long rifles. Those generals routinely marched infantry regiments packed shoulder to shoulder into slaughter against the enemies' artillery and Springfield rifled muskets with effective ranges as great as 400 yards. A devout student of military history, General Craig had learned its single most important lesson: Victory belonged to the general whose strategy and tactics were as current as his weapons technology. The general knew that, with the introduction of time travel, the scope of the battlefield was no longer limited to three dimensions. There was now a fourth.

General Craig focused on Dreamland with singular purpose, waiting for his opportunity to barter for the command of a lifetime. When that opportunity arrived two years later in 2002, he snapped it up without hesitation. After wresting control of the complex, the general made his presence known from day one, when he fired the complex's entire senior military staff. He replaced them with a relatively small number of handpicked people—people he could trust. He upended the complex, reorganizing key civilian positions and personnel and accelerating the tempo of development. He changed the name of the facility from "Dreamland" to the "Time Displacement Complex," in order to focus the facility's staff on its new mission. He increased the size of the complex by a factor of 100, completely overhauling it from a drab underground bunker into a utopia.

In the course of overhauling the complex's operations, the general ratcheted up the facility's secrecy to a new level. He leveraged his position and status to squeeze off access and communications to and from the complex. The general was now the sole gateway controlling the flow of people, materials, and communication in and out of the facility. The only civilian the general permitted to inquire about the complex was the president, who still knew the facility by its former "Dreamland" moniker. Members of congress and others not authorized to know about the complex rapidly found themselves at the business end of a military investigation if they as much as speculated about the complex's existence. Post-9/11 America was a paranoid place, and General Craig took full advantage of the climate of fear to become lord and master of the Time Tunnel. Now, six years after assuming control, his agenda was about to be realized.

Time Tunnel Complex

Area 51, NV
July 23, 2008
14:30 hours

Julia drove Kyle along the curved mezzanine to a freight elevator. She clicked a button on the dashboard, the elevator doors opened, and they drove in. The elevator began to descend.

"How would you prefer to be addressed, Colonel?" asked Julia.

"'Kyle' is fine," replied Kyle, embarrassed about the deferential treatment he was receiving.

"It is a pleasure to meet you, Kyle," Julia said, smiling. "Please call me Julia."

"It's very nice to meet you as well, Julia." Kyle returned her smile. It had been years since he had been in the company of a pretty woman, and he suddenly felt self-conscious about his scruffy appearance.

"So, I'm going to be giving you a lot of information in a hurry, since I have strict orders to get you cleaned up and delivered to mission control by 16:30 hours. Because we live in a Time Tunnel, we tend to be preoccupied with deadlines around here," Julia said, giggling.

"So, the general wasn't kidding about that?" asked Kyle.

"No, he wasn't," replied Julia, her expression becoming more serious. "I can't give you details…the general and senior staff will do that in your briefing."

The doors opened on Level 3, and Julia drove out onto the tinted yellow mezzanine.

"This is Level 3, the living level," explained Julia. "This level includes staff quarters, food, restaurants, shopping, recreation, movie theaters, schools, churches, medical facilities, our park, and more. I'm going to take you to your quarters now so you can tidy up."

"How many people work here?" asked Kyle.

"Approximately 10,000 people live here, though not all of them work here," replied Julia. "Some are children."

"Ten thousand! How big is this place?"

They turned into a corridor, one of several spokes leading away from the main mezzanine circle. Julia took the turn a little too fast, causing the cart's tires to squeal.

"Sorry," Julia said, "I've got a lead foot."

The corridor was very wide—more of a road than a hallway, with high-speed moving walkways for pedestrians and lanes for electric carts and Segways. Bright yellow doors to living quarters dotted the corridor. People and carts buzzed through the thoroughfare, along with rolling droids delivering groceries and goods purchased from local shops. An occasional dog was walked on a leash, headed to or from the park at the center of the living level.

"Approximately 20 million square feet—about ten Empire State Buildings. There are an additional three levels below this one. Level 1 is administration, which includes offices and meeting rooms.

Level 2 is science, which includes labs, offices, and more. Level 3 is living. Level 4 is food processing, where we grow and process all our food. Level 5 is engineering, which includes power generation, utilities infrastructure, water, waste processing, manufacturing, and various shops for repairs. Level 6 is the Time Tunnel and mission control. That will be covered in the briefing," explained Julia.

They took a turn down another corridor. Though Kyle had only seen portions of two corridors, the complex already seemed endless.

"This is a city!" exclaimed Kyle.

"It *is* a city," replied Julia. "It's a completely self-contained city. We don't require anything from the outside. We grow all our own food, generate our power, recycle our waste, and manufacture everything we need."

"Why are there kids here? That seems strange," said Kyle.

"The Time Tunnel is designed to be a multi-generational facility, so there are families here," explained Julia. "As to the reasons why it's multi-generational, I think I should leave that for your briefing."

Julia pulled the cart to a stop at Q99—Kyle's domicile.

"Here we are," said Julia. "I'll give you a quick tour of your new home, but first I have to get you registered."

She took a digital pad from the dashboard and typed on it. The pad responded:

Lieutenant Kyle B. Mason

Biometric entry 1: R. Thumbprint

"Please put your right thumb on the pad," said Julia.

Kyle did as requested. The pad chimed and displayed "Complete."

Kyle removed his thumb. A green image of his right thumbprint displayed on the pad.

Julia tapped the pad again. The display changed:

Lieutenant Kyle B. Mason

Biometric entry 1: Right Retina

"Now hold the pad and look into it with your right eye."

Kyle followed Julia's instructions. The pad chimed again, this time displaying the blood vessels of Kyle's inner eye.

Julia tapped the pad again.

"Last thing," said Julia. "You get a password. I need you to tap this button on the pad. You'll have 60 seconds to memorize it before it deletes."

Kyle tapped the button and read the password.

"Do I need all three challenges to get into my apartment?"

Julia laughed. "No. You only need your thumbprint to enter your apartment. All three challenges are only needed for secure areas. Your thumbprint can also be used to buy whatever you need at shops and restaurants. Money doesn't mean a lot here—you can get whatever you need, but the administrative people like to keep track of things anyway because that's their nature.

"C'mon," Julia said. "I'll give you a tour of your new home."

They climbed out of the cart.

"Go ahead and touch the sensor by the door," Julia said. "It's coded to you."

Kyle placed his thumb on a black square sensor next to the door. The latch made an electronic growling sound and opened.

Kyle was amazed. He was expecting bare-essentials military barracks. What he got instead was a luxurious split-level townhouse with a spacious living room, kitchen, and a view of… the ocean?

"You're probably wondering about the view," smiled Julia.

"I was, actually," replied Kyle, marveling.

"We're deep underground, and we're going to be here for a long time," explained Julia. "The designers were concerned about the effects of bottling up thousands of people in a closed space for years. This was one of the ideas they thought up to minimize cabin fever. It's a super high-resolution display that looks like the view from a window. You have them on several walls in your apartment. You've got a choice of exterior views. I like this one—it's the west-facing view from the island of Moorea. If you like, you can listen to the surf. It puts me right to sleep after a long day. The sunset is gorgeous, by the way."

Kyle wondered what Julia's definition of "long time" was.

The townhouse was spacious—Kyle estimated 3,000 square feet. The walls were taupe with white trim, and the floors were hardwood, with occasional Persian-style rugs placed in strategic locations. The furnishings were arts-and-crafts wood and leather.

"The rest of the apartment is pretty straightforward," continued Julia. "Your bedroom and master bath are upstairs. We've taken the liberty of stocking your closet with several changes of clothes. You can get whatever else you need on the promenade. There are food and drinks in the kitchen. There's a big screen TV and stereo as well. You're lucky—only senior staff get apartments this big."

Kyle's head was swimming. This morning, he had woken up in a cluttered Upper West Side one-bedroom brownstone. Now he was standing in his luxury townhouse in a Time Tunnel over 200 feet underground.

"I'm going to leave you for a bit and pick you up a little later for your appointment with the barber. Don't worry about the shave—they'll take care of that. You can also get a mani-pedi if you like," Julia said with a wink.

"I'll be back at 15:30 to pick you up—OK?" Julia asked.

"Sure—thank you," Kyle said, feeling dizzy.

"Don't worry," Julia said. "It's a lot to take in at once. It'll get easier. If you've gotta live in a cave, this is definitely the way to do it."

Kyle took a long hot shower and changed into khaki slacks and a long-sleeved black V-neck shirt. He noticed the feel of the fabric was unusual. When Julia picked him up, she explained that the clothes were made from a mix of recycled paper and cloth—like dollar bills, but with a higher cloth-to-paper ratio. At the Time Tunnel, they didn't launder clothes; they recycled them.

Julia drove Kyle to the arcade and gave him a speed tour of some of the shops and restaurants. In addition to restaurants that were unique to the Time Tunnel, there were familiar chains, such as McDonalds and Starbucks, though those chains were managed and staffed by Time Tunnel personnel. The Time Tunnel's cheerful feel was anything but standard Army issue. It was all part of the designers' vision to create a world where humans in captivity would be content, even happy.

Time Tunnel Complex

July 23, 2008
16:30 hours

Julia drove Kyle to a freight elevator at the end of a corridor on Level 3. Once inside, she pressed her thumb to a sensor on the elevator console and looked into a panel that scanned her retina.

"Julia Rothschild, Code 777, Charlie, echo, bravo, 987, confirm," said Julia. "Level 6 is secure access. You have clearance."

The elevator descended. Kyle could feel the pressure build on his ears.

The elevator doors slid open on Level 6, revealing an anteroom with a steel vault door and an armed guard. Another authentication panel, identical to that found at the complex main vault door, was placed next to this door. Julia authenticated in with her triple authentication. The big door unlatched and began to swing open, with bright blue LED strobes flashing on the door's perimeter.

"This is where I get off," said Julia. "Go right in. They're waiting for you."

Julia turned and left. Kyle walked through the vault door entryway into a mission control room. The room was configured amphitheater-style, measuring approximately 150 feet wide and deep, curving toward six mezzanine levels of workstations in a concave shape. A theater-sized array of giant screens mirrored the concave mezzanines in a reflecting curve. The walls and furnishings were graphite gray. The wall coverings were made of a gray corduroy-style carpet material. The room was quiet, absorbing echoes. Blue-tinged bright white LED lighting illuminated the room.

Each workstation included its own computer consoles and displays. Small signs identified group functions, including "Temporal Core," "Temporal Navigation," "Reactor," "Timeline Analysis," and "Biometrics."

Some workstation groups were configured in semi-circles—Kyle assumed these were for use by team members who needed to collaborate with one another. Kyle noticed that the hive of workstations clustered around the "Timeline Analysis" sign also included a large rose-colored translucent light cube with the letters "TVA" on four sides. In the center of the Tier-3 mezzanine was an isolated workstation under the sign "Mission Director."

The giant curved LCD panels at the front of the room were dark, with the exception of the blue hourglass graphic, the date, time, and a status message: "TDS Offline."

At the base of the room, in the large convex well left between the giant displays and the front row of workstations, was a large black oval conference table. A dozen people sat at the table, including the general, who waved to Kyle.

"Over here, Colonel."

Kyle walked down the mezzanine steps to the group. The general had changed out of his uniform into khaki pants and a long-sleeved black business shirt. He sat at the center of the large conference table, his back to the giant screen. He and the others seated rose to greet Kyle, with two exceptions—an old man with wispy white cotton-candy hair seated in a wheelchair and a petite woman in her thirties with brunette bangs and a ponytail. While the other members of the group smiled as Kyle approached, the tiny woman glared at him with palpable contempt.

Kyle shook hands and exchanged names before taking a seat at one end of the oval table. When Kyle extended his hand to the woman, she ignored it. She turned to the general.

"General," she began. "With due respect—is this a fucking joke? Because this is a fucking joke. Look at him, for Chrissakes!"

"Colonel Wise," General Craig snapped back to Annika Wise, "I'm going to clue you in on a little secret: You know my rank of full general? That didn't happen because of pure dumb luck. There are times when I really do know what I'm doing."

"Yes sir. Sorry, sir," replied Annika. "Sorry," she tossed offhandedly to Kyle.

"Have a seat, Colonel Mason. Everyone, you know why the colonel is here, even though he doesn't yet," began General Craig. "Let's start by going around the room—please state your name and title."

A middle-aged woman with white-streaked blond hair and a lab coat said, "I'm Lara Meredith, chief of life sciences."

The old man with fluffy white hair in the wheelchair and tinted glasses spoke next. "My name is Gunther Appel. I am chief of physics." He smiled. "They call me 'Strangelove.' It is okeydokey if you do too."

Lara was seated close to Strangelove and looked at him

affectionately as he spoke. They appeared to be a couple.

A pale man in his fifties, sporting a full brown and gray beard and a checkered shirt, said, "Roger Summit. Chief historian."

A young Asian woman next to Roger said, "Aysha Voong. I'm also on the history team."

A Cuban-American man in his forties said, "Gus Ferrer. Mission director." He bore a square jaw, a flattop haircut with white-striped temples, and a very serious expression. His polo shirt was a little too small, accentuating his pecs and powerful tanned biceps. To Kyle, the combination of Gus' chiseled body, striped hair, and mean expression gave him the appearance of a superhero.

The next man to speak was the Chief Technical Officer: "John Kaomea."

The last to introduce herself was the woman who had gotten the meeting off to such a bad start. "Colonel Annika Wise. I'm your team mate..."

"*...unfortunately*," Kyle read the thought bubble over the scowling woman's head.

General Craig turned to the historian. "Roger, start us off. Can you please give us an overview of the early history of this project?"

"Certainly," Roger began. "In 1947, a flying disc crashed outside of Roswell, New Mexico. There were two debris fields. The best known is that on the Foster Ranch near Corona, where pieces of a craft made of an unusual material were recovered. The fragments were extremely strong and lightweight—nothing that existed on this planet at the time."

The old 1947 map of the crash sites appeared on the big screen.

"A second, much larger debris field was found some 70 miles to the east. Though there had clearly been some kind of catastrophic event that caused extensive damage, it was evident from the debris that the remains were from some kind of craft. The fragments at site two were very unusual, not only because they were very strong and light like at site one, but also because they were featureless. There was no discernable machinery in the conventional sense, no instruments, no power source—nothing."

Roger paused, taking a breath.

"There's more," he continued. "Four bodies were recovered at site two. They were not human in appearance. They were short in stature, less than five feet in height, with abnormally large heads, atrophied limbs, very large, almond-shaped black eyes, and gray skin. They did not appear to be from this world."

General Craig turned to Kyle. "You OK so far?"

Kyle felt his pulse quickening, "Yes sir—it's a lot to take in."

"Please continue, Roger," said the general.

"The Army issued a cover story that the debris was really from a weather balloon. The press was misdirected to a briefing at Fort Worth Army Air Field. The distraction enabled the Army to collect and relocate the debris and bodies to a secure location—an abandoned World War II Army airfield on Groom Lake, Nevada.

"A temporary facility to store and analyze the craft wreckage was erected, but it was decided that a more secure facility was needed. So, they went underground. The initial Dreamland Research Facility was modest compared to this one—a couple hundred thousand square feet. Over time, obviously, the facility has expanded considerably. Its primary mission has also changed from analysis of the remains to something very different as a result of some remarkable findings by Drs. Meredith and Strangelove. Strangelove, perhaps this is a good place for you to pick up the story?"

"The analysis of the craft wreckage began very slowly," Strangelove began, "and, quite frankly, was very frustrating. As Roger said, the craft fragments revealed no discernable mechanisms—no propulsion, power source, instrumentation, etc. The objects appeared to be solid. We tried cutting into the fragments to see if they contained anything on the inside. Again, they were solid matter—there was nothing inside."

Strangelove clicked a remote and pointed to the giant screen. An image of the curved charcoal-colored fragment Strangelove had shown to the generals over 20 years earlier displayed on the screen.

"This is one of the fragments," Strangelove said. "It appears to be an ordinary piece of some graphite-type material. Using spectroscopy, we were able to quickly determine that the craft fragments were comprised of carbon. When we take a closer look, we find something very interesting."

Strangelove clicked a remote. The image of the graphite fragment zoomed in thousands of times, revealing an intricate lattice network that resembled a crystalline spiderweb.

"This is a small portion of the object, magnified 2,000 times," said Strangelove. "It reveals an artificial network of some kind. When we took an even closer look at the network, using an electron microscope, this is what we found..."

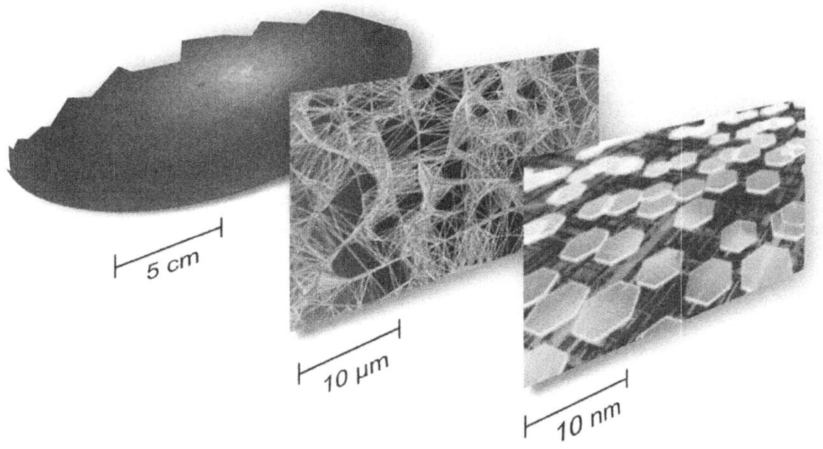

Strangelove clicked the remote, displaying a series of images on the screen. The images were of geometric shapes, some connected by tiny tubes. The geometric shapes glowed with an eerie phosphorescence.

"These are carbon nanomechanisms, comprised primarily of carbon nanotubes," Strangelove said. "Some are as small as one nanometer in diameter. To give you an idea of the size of one nanometer, it is 2,500 times smaller than the width of a red blood cell. These nanotubes have been configured into circuitry, and even machinery with moving parts. There are trillions of them throughout the hull of the craft. This infrastructure provides all of the craft's functionality.

"Once we made this breakthrough, we could begin the painstaking process of reverse-engineering the nano-infrastructure to determine its purpose. This was very difficult, in part because of the practical difficulty of scanning the fragments without damaging the nanotubes. A compounding challenge was the fact that we could not observe the nanostructure in action. We were forced to theorize its functionality and test our assumptions—sometimes using replicas of the nanotechnology built from current-generation materials. In some cases, once we were able to determine a mechanism's function, we were able to reactivate it.

"It was an exceedingly difficult process, but over decades, we were able to determine many of the craft's basic functions. We were able to determine that antimatter reactions powered the craft, and we have speculated that an accident with their antimatter reactor may have been the cause of the catastrophic event that destroyed the craft. An antimatter explosion could have easily destroyed the entire planet, so we are fortunate that this craft had the capacity to shield the reaction.

"Though we made significant progress in reverse-engineering the craft's functions, we could not identify any obvious means of propulsion. We could not determine how the craft could possibly be capable of interstellar travel. One clue we found was in the craft's ability to manipulate gravity. We theorized that the Grays were warping space-time, which could conceivably be used as a means to rapidly cross vast distances. It was at this time that Dr. Meredith had the final breakthrough that solved the puzzle. Lara, would you like to continue?"

Lara clicked a remote. A ghastly image of one of the Gray cadavers appeared on the big screen, with its oversized cranium, almond eyes, and gaping mouth. It looked as though it was terrified at the moment it died. Kyle squelched a gasp at the sight of the dead creature.

"Necroscopy performed on the Grays found them to be remarkably human-like anatomically," said Lara. "Though their heads and craniums are larger than ours, their eyes appear to be different, and their limbs are atrophied compared with humans, the Grays are otherwise identical to us. Mass spectrometric analysis on Gray tissue confirmed the presence of DNA. Gray cells were karyotyped, revealing that they contained 23 pairs of chromosomes—the same as humans."

Lara clicked the remote to display the karyotype test she had shown the Army generals over two decades earlier.

"In the early seventies," she continued, "the possibility of sequencing DNA began to evolve from science fiction into something that might be plausible. Sequencing is the process of determining the precise order of nucleotides within a DNA molecule. I was hired to run the DNA sequencing project here at the complex. At the time, the objective of sequencing Gray DNA was to identify weaknesses in their biology that could be exploited for the purpose of developing bioweapon defenses. We began sequencing Gray DNA in the 1970s, but with the limited computing bandwidth of the time, we projected that it would take 20 years to complete an index of Gray DNA.

"In 1985, we had a breakthrough. A new process became available to profile and compare DNA from different subjects. It was called restriction fragment length polymorphism, or RFLP analysis. RFLP was originally developed as a tool for crime investigation and to resolve paternity cases. Since the eighties, more sophisticated tools for DNA profiling have become available. RFLP was not a

DNA sequencing method. It was a way to isolate and compare areas of DNA that exhibit polymorphism—these are the areas of DNA that make individuals unique.

"In 1985, for the hell of it, I decided to run a RFLP test on Gray tissue and compare it against human DNA sampled from various human ethnic groups. Ostensibly, the goal was to note the high-level similarities and differences between Gray and human DNA, though in reality, the reason I ran the test was because we were running out of things to do on the Grays. They had been dissected, spectra-analyzed, karyotyped, and our DNA sequencing was a rote routine that was going to take years to complete. I had to get creative to keep the research moving forward."

Lara clicked the remote to display the results of the 1985 RFLP test.

"I didn't really expect to find much of anything of interest when I ran the RFLP test. So, imagine my surprise when the results came back with an exact match against the Han ethnic group. As it turned out, our Grays were Chinese—two males and two females. The Grays are not from another world—they're from this one. Their craft is not a spacecraft, it's a time machine."

The room was silent. All eyes were on Kyle as his mind overloaded.

"Holy shit!" he said.

"That's what the other Army guys said twenty-something years ago when I dropped this on them," said Lara.

"We went ahead and completed the DNA sequencing in the nineties, though the goal of the exercise had changed, obviously.

It didn't make much sense to concoct bioweapons to kill the Grays, as there is no shortage of such weapons that will kill humans. Now we're mostly just curious to find the Gray's great-great-great-great-great-great-grandparents—who presumably live somewhere in China."

"But what about their physical appearance?" asked Kyle. "They don't appear to be human."

"We can explain much of it through studies conducted on astronauts after prolonged periods in outer space," answered Lara. "Head swelling and atrophied limbs are common side-effects of space travel. A distinct possibility is that the appearance of our descendants will change over many generations living in space. Perhaps they are explorers. Perhaps the Earth is no longer inhabitable in the future. Whatever their reason for living in space, it is unlikely that their bodies could withstand Earth's gravity for long periods of time. It would be like a modern-day human trying to swim several thousand feet below sea level.

"As far as the Gray's black eyes are concerned, we found that their eyes were covered by an artificial material—kind of like a permanent contact lens, but these lenses are embedded with more nanotechnology. It gives the Grays superpower vision—optical enhancements to see along the entire EM spectrum, along with various sensors to analyze things they see. They also have an enhanced pattern-recognition capability. They can match up patterns in a database—useful for instantly identifying objects or life forms. It could also come in handy if you forget someone's name at a party.

"The last item of interest is the Gray's brains. We found several specks of artificial material embedded in their brains. They were tiny—as small as grains of sand. In the early necroscopies performed on the Grays in the forties, the specks were lost—they probably went unnoticed, or were dismissed as terrestrial contamination. Fortunately, only two of the four Grays were dissected back then. When we took another look in the seventies, we found the same specks in both remaining subjects. When we turned them over to Strangelove's team for examination, the specks turned out to be more nanotechnology. The Grays integrate artificial technology into their brains. The tech enhances brain functions, as well as integrating knowledge bases. Strangelove's group is working on downloading and decoding those knowledge sets. It will be very exciting to know what these people knew."

Lara turned to Strangelove. "Would you like to finish the story?"

Strangelove smiled at Lara, "From Lara's epiphany, many pieces rapidly fell into place. We determined that the craft's gravity engine was used to manipulate space-time to fold it back upon itself. If you think of space-time as a pliable flat plane, that plane is distorted by gravity."

Strangelove typed on his keyboard, displaying the same space-time wireframe images he had previously shown the generals years before.

"Stars and planets distort space-time in their gravity wells like objects of various weights placed onto the plane. The Grays found a way to use their gravity engine to further distort space-time, actually folding it back upon itself. This is what enables the craft to move through time."

Strangelove displayed an image of a wireframe of space-time curling back upon itself like cosmic origami.

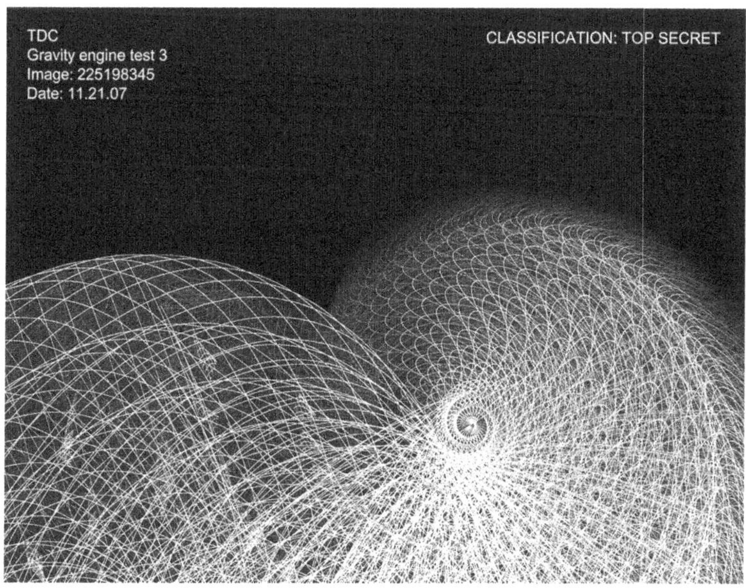

"From that point in 1985, we made the decision to focus on reverse-engineering the gravity engine and its antimatter power source. After General Craig's arrival, this complex was re-tasked to the purpose of developing a practical means of time displacement. The result of our work is the Temporal Displacement System, or what we call the 'Time Tunnel.' We believe it is now fully functional."

"Meaning, you can send someone through time," said Kyle.

"He is quite astute, as you said, General," Strangelove said playfully, with his characteristic smile. He shared a look with Lara, who smiled and touched his sleeve.

"Which brings us to why you're here," said the general.

Not sure I like what's about to come next, thought Kyle.

"Now that we've built the thing, we've been struggling with what to do with it—or whether we should use it at all," said the general. "We can study time. We can change time, though as you can imagine, there are many implications associated with that. And the implications are not limited to history—we'll get to that. When we began construction of the Time Tunnel, we set up a taskforce to focus on history—past and future. Go, Roger."

Roger nodded and continued the explanation. "The primary purpose of my taskforce was to identify key 'inflection points' in history, where altering the outcome of an event could cause a significant change in the timeline. Our focus was on the inflection points that most impacted America. We are in agreement that there is one that has had a profoundly negative impact on the United States and rapidly accelerated its decline."

The general looked Kyle in the eyes. "9/11."

"Though it is impossible to calculate the full impact of 9/11," Roger continued, "there is much that we can quantify. Had the terrorist attacks of 9/11 not occurred, the United States would probably not have gone to war in Afghanistan and Iraq. The total projected costs of those wars alone, including ongoing medical benefits and interest payments on the debt used to finance the war, will likely top $6 trillion. The total direct and indirect costs to the economy, including ripple effects, are estimated at $10 trillion. Coincidentally, the country's current national debt in 2008 is about $10 trillion. Of course, in addition to the severe economic impact, the lives of thousands of Americans would have been spared—both those who perished on 9/11, as well as those who died in battle in Afghanistan and Iraq. Additionally, as many as 500,000 Iraqis died in the Iraq war.

"The part that is most difficult to quantify may also be the most impactful. America's reaction to the attack was different than it was after previous national crises. Though Americans certainly had fearful reactions to other major crises, like the Great Depression, Pearl Harbor, and Sputnik, in each of those events, America leveraged the crisis with bold advances that propelled the country forward. Nietzsche famously said, 'What does not kill us makes us stronger.' Though each of these crises inflicted damage on America, each time America emerged as a more advanced, more powerful country.

"For example, a key response to the Great Depression was the Works Progress Administration, or WPA, a colossal public works program that produced the most modern infrastructure the world had ever seen. The WPA literally laid the foundation for the post-war economic boom that lasted a quarter century. Seventy years later, we still rely on those roads, bridges, dams, and electrical infrastructure. Pearl Harbor galvanized this country's industrial capability. By the end of World War II, the U.S. produced half of the world's industrial output. The G.I. Bill produced the world's best-educated workforce. That workforce reacted to the Sputnik scare with huge advances in American aerospace, computing, and communications technologies.

"By contrast, our reaction to 9/11 was markedly different. Instead of transmuting the crisis into the kinds of bold progress we've seen historically, America regressed. A national depression pervaded our society. Politicians exploited polar divisions in the population. That attitude had an outsized effect on priorities—security was prioritized over infrastructure, education, and research. The nation's security apparatus was ratcheted way up. While our focus has been on the Middle East and security, we've allowed our infrastructure and educational system to deteriorate. Meanwhile, China has made enormous investments in modern infrastructure and has made science and math education a top priority. Chinese students are ranked first in the world in science and math. U.S. students rank 23rd and 30th in science and math, respectively. China is expected to become the world's second largest economy in 2010, and it is projected to overtake the U.S. by 2030.

"Obviously, this is not to suggest that America's reactions to foreign attacks throughout history have always been constructive. America's internment of Japanese Americans during World War II was abhorrent, but racism was not the sole defining aspect of the country's response to Pearl Harbor. Our country had many remarkably positive achievements during this time that thrust it forward and made it the world's preeminent economic, scientific, and military superpower.

"Not so with 9/11. If 9/11 did not happen, we can project the probability that a number of material changes would occur in the timeline. Of course, there are many more that we cannot project. As discussed, we project that the Afghanistan and Iraq wars would not have happened. Though there are those in the current administration who advocated war in Iraq independent of 9/11, we do not believe it would have been possible to muster sufficient support in Congress without 9/11. We do not believe President Bush would have been elected to a second term. It is difficult to forecast a Kerry presidency, but we believe it is unlikely that we would be seeking out foreign military engagements. It is, however, likely that the housing crash and subsequent recession would still have happened, which may well have made Kerry a one-term president. The good news is that the country would have much more economic dry powder to combat the recession than it does in the present timeline. Finally, it is impossible to know what contributions that the thousands who died on and after 9/11 would have made. Just one example is Daniel Lewin, the co-founder of Akamai. The algorithms he wrote had a profound impact on Internet performance. He was only 31.

"Regardless of whether or not these individuals would have changed the world, if nothing else, they are sorely missed by their loved ones."

Kyle felt a bolt of pain as Padma's face flashed through his mind.

"What we know for certain is that 9/11 inflicted a deep economic and psychological wound on this country and irrevocably changed its path for the worse. While we don't believe preventing 9/11 would make things all better, we are convinced that, at worse, it would greatly slow America's decline—perhaps giving it the opportunity to make the choices that would reverse that trend line."

There was silence in the room.

"You want to send someone back to stop 9/11," said Kyle.

"Again, very astute," said Strangelove, smiling.

"We want to send *you* back to stop 9/11," said General Craig.

Time Tunnel Complex

Mission Control
July 23, 2008
17:15 hours

"More precisely, we want to send you and Colonel Wise back," said the general.

"Why only two people?" asked Kyle. "Why not send an army?"

"Power," replied Strangelove. "The Time Displacement System requires enormous power. With our current capability, two is the most we can send, with a minimal complement of weapons."

"What weapons?" asked Kyle.

General Craig held up a credit card. "This weapon." He slid it across the table to Kyle, who picked it up. The name on the card was "Robert Small."

"So, this some James Bond gadget?" asked Kyle, examining the card.

"James Bond. That is good. Very clever," said Strangelove, chuckling.

"No, actually, it's an ordinary debit card," replied General Craig. "We don't have the power to send firearms back with you—pretty much just the clothes on your back, identification, debit cards, a universal key card to open the hijackers' hotel rooms, and one other gadget, which we'll get to in a minute."

Gus Ferrer stepped in to explain. "We have complete historical financial records, as well as historical records of individuals. We found two wealthy people who died in late August 2001, whose bank accounts and credit cards were not locked up until after 9/11. You'll have almost unlimited funds to get cash or buy whatever you need to complete your mission. You'll have the requisite ID in case someone wants to check to make sure you're really who you claim to be."

"We can place the terrorists at certain locations and times," Roger continued. "Some spend extended periods in hotel rooms. Some take flying lessons. Some use ATM machines at specific times. Some visit strip clubs. We will drill you on the terrorists' identities and the times and places they appear."

"Your job is to show up at the appointed times and places and take them out," said General Craig.

"I see," said Kyle, overwhelmed.

"There is an issue," said General Craig.

"Only one?" asked Strangelove.

The general ignored Strangelove. "Your attacks must be tightly coordinated, as the ripple effect from one attack could disturb the timeline and affect the times and places in which other terrorists appear. For example, if one of the terrorists misses a meeting or a phone call, how does it affect the actions of the others? Killing one terrorist may result in losing the rest."

"Also, you're going to need to improvise a bit," said the general. "Strangelove?"

"There is a random effect to this process," Strangelove explained. "This is due to the Heisenberg uncertainty principle, which says that particles do not behave in a completely predictable way. There is a probability of possible outcomes."

"Translation, Strangelove," said General Craig.

"We cannot insert you into a specific time and place with complete precision," said Strangelove. "We can chart a range of likely probabilities for your space-time arrival coordinates."

Strangelove clicked the remote. A 3D scatter chart appeared on the big screen, charting a series of points along three axes: longitude, latitude, and time. The greatest concentration of points clustered in the center of the chart, around a longitude of W 74° 36' 41.4061" and latitude of N 40° 19' 10.5961", with a date of August 23, 2001.

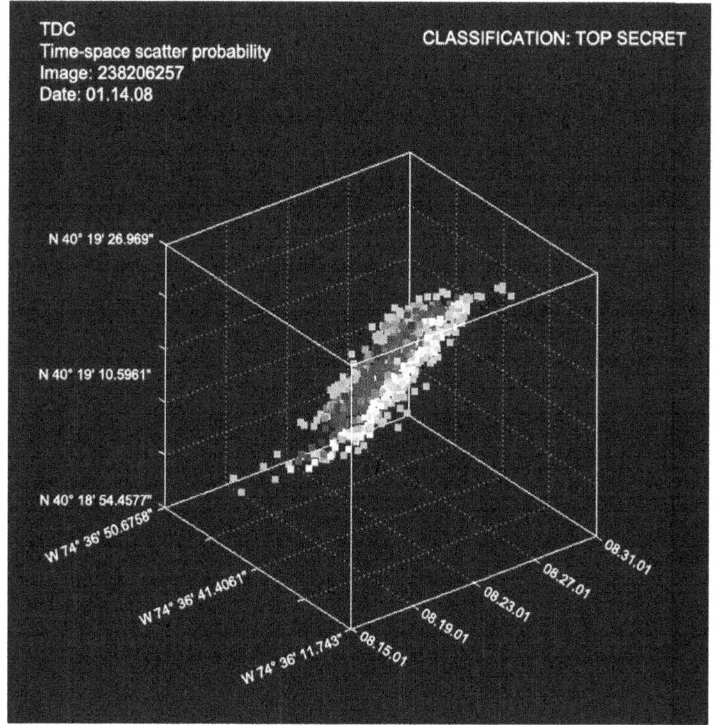

"The time range we will insert you into is a two-week period between August 15 and September 1, 2001," Strangelove said. "This should give you sufficient time to complete your mission. You will need to adjust the details of your mission depending on the date you arrive. Regarding the place, we have found a location range that is unlikely to be populated, though it will be sufficiently close to civilization to enable you to get in the game. Obviously, it would be undesirable for the two of you to appear out of thin air during rush hour in Times Square."

"It is important to be aware that your 2001 counterparts will be where they were at that time," added General Craig. "Obviously, you must not have contact with them or anyone who knows them. We anticipated the remote possibility that you might encounter someone you knew in 2001. One of the reasons you were selected is because of your ability to pass as your former selves with minimal cosmetic work."

Kyle glanced down at his chest, recalling his 2001 Adonis physique. "I don't think I would pass as my 2001 self, sir."

"You'll get it back, soldier," said General Craig. "We'll make sure of that."

"How do *we* get back, sir?" asked Kyle. "Or *do* we come back?"

"You come back," replied the general. "Strangelove?"

"You will take a device with you," Strangelove said, holding up a small metal box the size of a cigarette pack. "This is a temporal transponder. It will enable us to pinpoint your space-time coordinates and return you to our time."

"How does this actually work? What is the actual apparatus and process?" asked Kyle.

"From the perspective of the temponauts, it is actually quite simple..." began Strangelove.

"The 'what-o-nauts'?" interrupted Kyle.

"Temponauts. That's what we call you time travelers," explained Strangelove. He clicked the remote. A wireframe diagram of a sphere surrounded by a donut-shaped ring flashed onto the screen. The wireframe sphere contained figures of two humans.

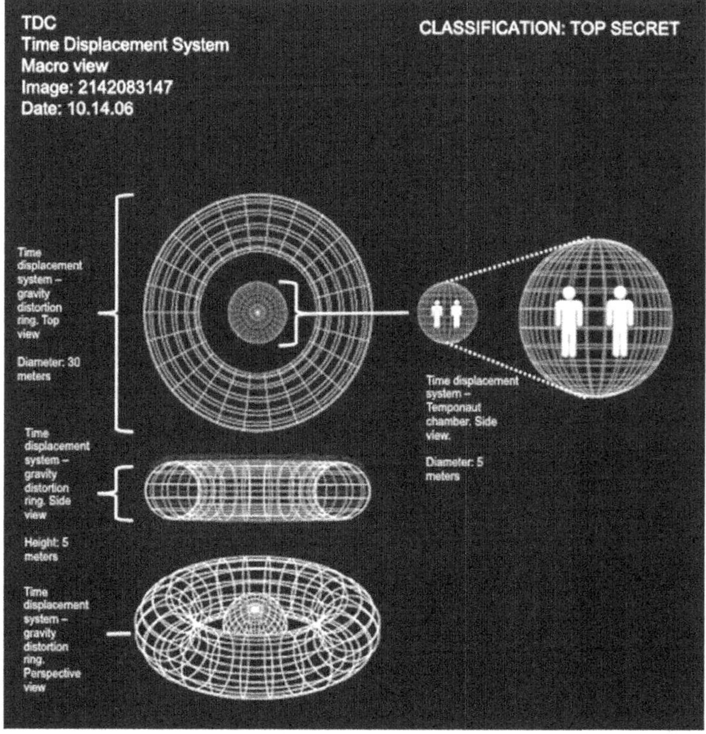

"The visible apparatus is a spherical glass chamber that hosts the temponauts, explained Strangelove. "The sphere is surrounded by a large carbon ring that resembles a giant donut. The ring is the focal point of the apparatus, which warps gravity in order to fold time."

"In other words, it's the sharp end of the Time Tunnel stick," added the general.

"The sphere is your portal through time," said Strangelove. "It is the doorway through which you depart into the past. It is also the doorway through which you return. At the conclusion of your mission, when you activate your transponder, the Time Tunnel will locate your time-space coordinates, lock on, and return you to the sphere.

Strangelove pushed a button on the remote. An animation of two temponauts in the spherical glass Time Tunnel chamber appeared on the screen.

A brilliant bright light preceded the sudden disappearance of the animated temponauts. Moments later, the light flashed again, and the temponauts reappeared in the chamber.

"The relative perceptions of time between the temponauts and those of us in the complex will be very different. Even though you and Colonel Wise will spend several weeks in 2001, from the perspective of those of us in the complex, you will only be gone an augenblick."

"A what?" asked Kyle.

"It means a 'blink of an eye,'" said Lara. "For those of us in the tunnel, you'll only be gone a moment."

"Obviously," Strangelove continued, "it is critical that you do not lose or damage the transponder. We will have no possible way to return you without it. You will be lost in time."

"Questions?" asked the general.

All heads turned to face Kyle. Asking him whether he had questions about a briefing on time travel was like asking a dog whether he had questions about his first chess lesson. In less than 12 hours, he had fallen through the earth's crust, straight down the rabbit hole into Wonderland. He struggled to construct a question that would give the appearance that he was much smarter than he felt.

"What can you tell me about the actual time travel experience?" asked Kyle.

"No human has ever used the Time Tunnel, so our knowledge is limited," said Strangelove. "What we can tell you is this: First, as we have transported and retrieved animals without apparent ill effects or trauma, we believe the process is safe. We can tell you what we have witnessed as observers, which is that you will experience a humming and an intense vibration. An extremely bright light will precede the actual time displacement. After that point, we don't know what you will experience. Obviously, we will be very keen to hear your report when you return."

"Am I assuming correctly that the process of time travel is not entirely risk-free?" asked Kyle.

"That's a fair assumption," replied General Craig.

The chief technical officer, John Kaomea, stepped in. "We have constructed our version of the gravity engine to the precise specifications used by the Grays. In our tests, the Time Displacement System has performed flawlessly."

"How did you test it?" asked Kyle.

John seemed annoyed by the question. "Because we do not wish to risk interrupting the current timeline in advance of the mission, we have sent both inanimate objects and animals into the future and then retrieved them. We send them to remote areas of the planet, where the odds of their encountering humans are virtually zero."

"So, you've never tested this by sending anything into the past?" Kyle asked.

"There is no known reason why the process should work differently in the past," replied John.

"So, that's a 'no'?" pressed Kyle.

"We're quite confident of our work. I think it might be best if you focused on your part of the mission."

"So, that's a 'no,'" repeated Kyle.

"You afraid?" snapped Annika.

"Colonel, I haven't been afraid of much of anything for six years, ten months, and ten days, not counting today." Kyle returned Annika's glare. "My question wasn't about my personal safety. It was about the odds of a successful mission."

"Dial it back, all of you," commanded General Craig. "The mission is not risk-free. No special ops missions are."

An awkward pause occupied the room.

"What's TVA?" asked Kyle, changing the subject as he pointed to the TVA light cube.

Roger glanced at the general. The general nodded his approval to proceed.

"TVA stands for 'Temporal Variance Alert,'" Roger said. "Using this temporal technology, we are able to establish a nexus between the history of this timeline and the new one you will create. Our historical databases will be synced to those in the new timeline. When our computers detect a variance in the historical record, it triggers the TVA alert. This lets us know that time has changed and will prompt my team to begin analyzing how it has changed."

"I'm confused," said Kyle. "If time changes, don't the people in the complex change? Don't their experiences and memories change? Does the Time Tunnel even exist in the new timeline?"

The general nodded to Strangelove.

"That is an essential aspect of the mission," explained Strangelove. "You see, you and Colonel Wise are not the only ones who will be displaced in time."

Time Tunnel Complex

Mission Control
July 23, 2008
17:35 hours

"You are precisely right, Colonel Mason," said Strangelove. "Assuming your mission succeeds, unless we somehow counteract the new timeline, everything about this complex will change the very moment you and Colonel Wise jump back in time.

"In that timeline, 9/11 will not have happened. The people who inhabit the complex will have different experiences than we do. Perhaps there will be less urgency to make that Time Tunnel operational. Perhaps the staffing of the complex will be different. Perhaps there will be no Time Tunnel at all—it may well be the case that the people who run the complex focus on weaponizing the Grays' antimatter reactor instead of time travel. In any case, even if the Time Tunnel exists in that timeline, no one will remember sending you back in time, and there will be no way for you to return home."

"So, how do you counteract the timeline?" asked Kyle.

"At the precise moment you and Colonel Wise make your time jump, we will use the Time Tunnel to move this entire facility outside time," answered Strangelove.

"Hang on! What do you mean 'outside time'?" asked Kyle.

"The Time Tunnel will shield the complex from the change in the timeline. Think of it as a temporal 'bubble' that surrounds the complex, enabling time to flow around it. This will block changes to our timeline, including changes to the facility and its inhabitants. That is how we retain our memories, our capacity to bring you home, as well as the ability to monitor changes in the timeline you will change," explained Strangelove.

"So that other Time Tunnel, the one that happens in a world without 9/11, that won't exist?" asked Kyle.

"That Time Tunnel may or may not exist," said Strangelove. "The people in that timeline may or may not choose to build it. If they do, it may occupy precisely the same physical space as the one we will. It will simply exist in a different time—the time in which you and Colonel Wise will reside for a few weeks until you complete your mission. It is the same time we all share today. However, from the moment you kill the first hijacker, the time we inhabit today will change forever. When you force that detour in the timeline, this facility will not turn onto that road. It will remain in this time, separate from the new one you create."

Kyle felt like his head was going to explode.

"I'm very confused," said Kyle.

"That is understandable," said Strangelove.

"So, does this mean our complex will reside in the world where 9/11 happened?" asked Kyle.

"No," answered Strangelove uncomfortably. Strangelove looked at the general for permission to continue. The general nodded.

"The complex will not reside in that world," said Strangelove.

"You and Colonel Wise are ending that time and that world. The complex will not reside in any world."

Kyle rocked back in his chair, stunned.

"Using the Time Tunnel, we will, in effect, create a parallel universe. However, while the conventional universe is 150 billion light years in diameter, our universe will only be about a kilometer in diameter. It will end at the vault door to the complex," said Strangelove. "There will be nothing beyond that door."

"What do you mean, 'nothing'?" asked Kyle.

"I mean absolutely nothing," replied Strangelove. "It is the same 'nothing' that exists outside the conventional universe.

"That's why the complex is 100 percent self-contained," said the general. "It's also why it was designed to be a multi-generational facility. This is where we will spend the rest of our lives. It's where our descendants will live out their lives as well."

The team members seated around the conference table stared at Kyle as he absorbed the colossal scope of the revelation. They understood what Kyle was feeling. They had all experienced the very same jolt, as the shockwave of an incomprehensible reality hit them squarely in the face. Kyle looked at their faces, dead serious, realizing that each and every one of them had made the choice to spend the rest of their lives in a universe that measured only a mile in diameter. They would never swim in the ocean or feel the warmth of the sun again. A meal at their favorite neighborhood restaurant, a simple pleasure taken for granted by millions in the real world, would be completely beyond their reach.

Kyle dwelled on his feelings as they morphed from shock to

regret and sadness. He noticed the general studying him. Kyle's face betrayed his emotions. He sensed that the general had observed the same progression of feelings countless times before.

"You understand the greater good here, right?" asked the general.

Padma's face flashed in Kyle's mind. Every person at the complex had a reason for being there. At last, Kyle understood why the general had recruited him for the mission.

"Yes sir. I do," Kyle replied.

Time Tunnel Complex

Level 3

August 20, 2008

09:10 hours

Kyle walked along the gently curved hallway of Level 3 toward the sports complex. He was late for his sparring practice session with Annika. It was not his first time to be tardy for a mission training session.

Kyle had struggled to engage the training regimen. His thinking mind shouted all the valid reasons why he should commit fully to the mission and why he should be thrilled about this extraordinary opportunity.

I am going to go back in time! I am going to fix everything!

But even though his thinking mind kept repeating the mantra over and over, he still couldn't fully engage. Something was stuck in his head. The passion required to be a special ops warrior was missing. Without it, Kyle drifted spiritlessly through preparation as if living a dull dream in washed-out colors. Kyle didn't understand. He was frustrated. The fire he'd had as a young Delta operator had been extinguished. For the first time in his life, the overachiever was a C student, disengaged, plodding forward without purpose.

His training sessions with Annika had been tortuous. Both of the temponauts were not only required to be in supreme physical condition, they needed to know every detail of the hijackers' whereabouts and movements over the two months leading up to 9/11—hotels where they slept, restaurants where they dined, ATM machines they withdrew money from, prostitutes they engaged. As mission commanding officer, Annika was in charge of the training. Until the moment he began training with Annika, Kyle had thought Delta Force was the toughest mental, physical, and emotional training regimen on the planet. He was wrong. Annika Wise was a whole new breed of sadist.

Training began with a run at 06:00 hours and continued in the gym and classroom until late at night. No quarter was offered for mistakes, tardiness, or poor performance. It seemed to Kyle that the goal was not to train him, but instead to break him. In his foggy emotional state, he could not engage or keep up. He fell further behind. Though Annika's shock tactics woke him up temporarily, his increasing reaction to her brutal approach was to simply shut down.

Kyle knew that Annika had tried repeatedly to get him kicked off the mission. He didn't blame her for trying. He knew that the mission demanded excellence and that he was a burnout. The stakes were high and the team did not have the luxury of coddling a PTSD case in the hope that he might recover and become the soldier he once was. Why the general had rejected Annika's sensible requests was a mystery. Kyle knew he was a great soldier—once—but that soldier was long gone. This useless shell was all that remained.

Today, Annika had changed up the daily routine by summoning Kyle to sparring practice. Kyle surmised that the hope was that changing up his daily training routine might produce signs of life from the total zombie of a warrior he had become.

Kyle reached the large glass door of the sports complex. The door slid open to reveal a lobby with a smiling blond-haired woman in her twenties sitting behind a charcoal-colored counter.

"Hello, Colonel Mason," greeted the woman. "Colonel Wise is waiting for you in Studio 6."

Of course she is, Kyle thought.

Kyle walked down one of the sports complex's many corridors toward Studio 6. Along the way, he passed several of the complex's arenas and spas. The complex was no neighborhood gym with a workout room, showers, and sauna—it was a vast facility with accommodations for most sports. There was even a playing field with a cavernous ceiling with an LED blue sky for football, baseball, and soccer. As was the case with everything at the Time Tunnel, the sports complex was conceived to support the mission of keeping the tunnel's denizens happy and able to perform at peak efficiency for decades—possibly even centuries. The tour added some unexpected color and wonderment to Kyle's otherwise dreary dreamscape.

Kyle opened the glass door to the studio to find Annika waiting for him. The room was approximately 100 by 100 feet in size, with a 20-foot ceiling. The walls were a subtle cadet blue. The floor was made of firm black rubber matting. Bright blue-white tinged LED lighting illuminated the room.

To the side of the studio, Annika was standing on one leg with the other propped on a balance bar. She was wearing sweatpants and a sports bra top and was already gleaming with sweat from her warm-up workout.

"Morning," she said, glancing at the clock on the wall.

"Morning," Kyle replied. He was surprised that Annika had not reprimanded him for his tardiness.

"Ready for a spar?" Annika asked.

"Sure—why not?" Kyle replied perfunctorily. Unlike Annika, his muscles were cold and stiff, but he was not feeling motivated to warm up. Besides, she didn't look all that tough to him.

They both walked to a shelf with bright red hand-and-ankle sparring gloves and began strapping them on.

"Ready?" Annika asked.

"Good to go," answered Kyle.

They walked to the center of the studio and assumed sparring positions with raised fists and locked eyes.

"Go," said Annika.

Kyle threw a half-hearted punch at Annika's face, which she easily deflected. He followed up with a lackadaisical roundhouse kick. Annika pushed it away with both hands. She looked frustrated.

"Stop," she said.

She stepped toward him, smiling. "You're pulling your punches because I'm a girl—or maybe because you're sleepwalking—whatever. Let me help you with that."

Annika punched Kyle hard in the nose. He could feel the crunch of his nose cartilage and a sudden explosion of pain. Before he could react, Annika followed up with a crisp sidekick to his gut, doubling him over. She leapt in the air and landed a flying kick to the back of the head, sending Kyle crashing to the floor like an old tree.

"Jesus!" he shouted, his nose dripping blood on the floor.

Kyle pulled himself off the mat. Kyle looked at her with a rush of feelings. His surprise and rage at being bushwhacked were charged with a jolt of awareness and purpose, as though Annika had electroshocked him out of a coma. His murky existence instantly crystallized into sharp relief—everything in the room seemed brighter, more colorful, more crisply defined.

Annika saw the instant change in Kyle's face and body. His eyes were wide, clear, and laser-focused on his target. She didn't recognize the man standing in front of her. Startled at Kyle's transformation, she paused for an instant.

Kyle exploited Annika's lapse, spinning clockwise and connecting a kick to Annika's cheek, knocking her off her feet. She slapped the mat in frustration.

Incensed, Annika threw a flurry of punches to Kyle's face and gut. Each time she hit his broken nose, an electric pain fired through his face and the back of his neck. Annika spun into a crescent kick, smacking Kyle on the side of the face, knocking him to the mat. Kyle pulled himself off the mat and launched into a flying front kick. Annika dove under Kyle, rolling on the mat to her feet and unloading a side kick into the base of his spine, knocking him onto the floor. When he pulled himself up, she didn't wait for him to raise his hands before she pummeled him with punches to the face. Blood from his nose spattered the two fighters.

Kyle was completely out of his league with Annika. He had never seen anyone throw punches as fast as hers—they landed before he saw her launch them. He fell to the mat again and again. Annika appeared to savor every moment of the beating she was giving the big Delta operator.

As Kyle began to get off the mat, he swept a roundhouse kick to the back of Annika's legs, knocking her off her feet. She growled her frustration as she leapt to her feet, only to be knocked back to the floor with a side kick to her chest.

Enraged, she jumped to her feet. Before Kyle could land another kick, she flipped backward, smacking him on the jaw with her foot as her legs cartwheeled over. Annika followed up with a sequence of rapid-fire kicks and punches, overwhelming Kyle and landing him to the mat again. The match turned in Annika's favor. Kyle rose to his feet more slowly. Annika spun like a tornado, smacking him on the temple with her foot and disorienting him. He fell to the mat again. As he rose, Annika punched him in the side of the face, causing blood to splatter and sending him down again.

"Had enough?" Annika asked cheerfully, dancing on her feet while Kyle lay bleeding on the mat.

Kyle slowly pulled himself off the mat and raised his hands. Again, Annika smacked him to the floor. Again, Kyle crawled up from the floor. He could scarcely see through his swollen eyes. He was too exhausted to throw a serious punch or kick. Annika knocked him down again. Kyle staggered to his feet.

"Want some more?" Annika asked. "No problem. Here you go."

Annika whacked Kyle on the side of the head with a roundhouse kick, sending him to the mat. Again, Kyle pulled himself off the floor.

"You're beat! Give up!" screamed Annika.

Kyle shook his head and raised his hands to fight.

Annika cracked Kyle in the face with a flying sidekick, felling him again. Annika knew it was a reckless, potentially lethal kick. She didn't care. Kyle was going to submit—no matter what the cost.

Yet again, Kyle climbed off the mat, stood up, and raised his hands.

"Give up!" screamed Annika. "I'll kill you! *I'll kill you!*"

Annika shook with rage. To her astonishment, she noticed that tears were streaming down her cheeks. Why was she crying? She covered her face with her gloved hands and began to sob. The only way she could beat this man would be to kill him. She finally realized why the general had selected this mess of a soldier for the mission. No man could punch through her armor. He had instead stripped it from her. She was the superior fighter, but Kyle had defeated her—the first man to ever do so.

Annika could not stop the dark wellspring erupting from deep inside. Years of hurt packed inside her now rushed to the surface. She fell to her knees, crying. She cried out her bitterness about an Army that had stolen her childhood dreams. She cried out the guilt she had buried with her dead husband. She didn't know whether or not she loved him, but she knew he was a really good man who didn't deserve to die. He hadn't done anything wrong. It was unfair. What they did was *unfair!*

Kyle witnessed Annika's breakdown, not knowing what to do. Until that moment, he hadn't believed Annika was actually human, much less someone he could feel sorry for. He realized that they had one thing in common—they were both wounded warriors, trying to maintain some semblance of sanity in a completely insane situation. Their mission was impossible. Their lives were impossible. Even if the mission succeeded, their best-case scenario was one in which another Kyle and another Annika lived happily ever after with their resurrected spouses. This Kyle and this Annika would never have that life. If they survived the mission, their world, the rest of their days would be spent in this artificial city—cocooned, not only from the world, but also from time itself.

Kyle lowered his hands from his fighting stance and began to trudge toward Annika, not knowing what he would do when he reached her. She began to compose herself, rising to her feet as he approached. Her face was red, her eyes swollen. She looked at the bloody pulp of a man barely standing before her. She nodded approvingly, patted her gloved hand on his chest, and then walked out of the gym.

Kyle watched Annika walk away. She discarded her gloves on the mat on her way out the door, not caring that, for once in her life, she did not put something back in the precise place it belonged. She did not turn around to face him as she exited.

Kyle stood alone in the quiet gym, trying to wrap his mind around what had happened. An hour earlier, he had arrived for a simple sparring practice. He had not expected a transcendental reawakening and his partner's emotional breakdown. He shook his head. The Time Tunnel was a truly crazy place.

Kyle made the long walk back to his apartment, passing on the opportunities to use moving walkways or Segways to get home. People in the corridors gasped when they saw the battered and bleeding temponaut. They offered him assistance. He waved them on with a pained smile.

When he reached his apartment, Kyle went straight to his upstairs bathroom to survey the damage to his person. He splashed water on his face. Bloody water swirled down the sink's metal drain. He looked in the mirror—his nose was broken and still dripping blood, and his eyes were swelling badly. He laughed—he looked like shit, but he hadn't felt this good in years.

Kyle stripped and turned on the shower.

His doorbell rang. He threw a towel around his waist and went downstairs.

He opened the door. It was Annika, still sweating in her sports bra and pants. Her eyes and face were red and puffy from her big cry. Kyle didn't say anything, looking at her quizzically.

"Kyle?" Annika asked in an unfamiliar forlorn voice.

He grabbed her wrist and pulled her into the apartment. Annika began kissing Kyle hard, bloodying her face as she ripped off his towel. Before he could pull at her top, she had peeled off her clothes and was on top of him on his living room floor.

Time Tunnel Complex

Level 3
September 15, 2008
14:30 hours

Kyle sat at an "outdoor" table at the Starbucks next to the Level 3 park. He was dressed casually, in jeans and a black T-shirt. From his black wrought-iron table under a tree, Kyle studied his mission book while sipping a coffee. Names, faces, places, times—he was committing to memory every known action of the terrorists between July and September 11, 2001. He knew the minute when Hani Hanjour and Majed Moqed had used an ATM at the First Union National Bank in Laurel, Maryland, on September 5. He knew when prostitutes had visited Abdul Aziz al Omari and Satam al Suqami in their room at Boston's Park Inn on September 7. He knew when Mohamed Atta and al Omari had been having dinner in a Pizza Hut in South Portland, Maine, on September 10. Kyle also knew the identities and locations of shadow gun dealers from whom he could quickly and easily acquire weapons. He couldn't take a computer through the tunnel, and his ability to instantly recall each and every one of these moments was a fulcrum point of the mission's success or failure.

Next to Kyle's mission book was a copy of the *Wall Street*

Journal. Newspapers weren't delivered to the complex, but the Time Tunnel's own media service republished the major outlets. The Time Tunnel's version of the *Journal,* reprinted twice a day, based on the latest online news, was actually more current than the traditional hardcopy version. The headline of the afternoon issue was "AIG, Lehman Shock Hits World Markets." Lehman Brothers had filed for Chapter 11 bankruptcy protection that morning. The largest bankruptcy in U.S. history had sent the stock market into a death spiral and world markets into full panic.

Across the walkway from the coffee shop, Kyle could hear that there was a waterfall in the park. Birds flew through the enormous atrium. It occurred to Kyle that one thing he could not hear was an echo. Normally, atriums with artificial nature ricocheted sounds off their surfaces. This park seemed almost real. Yet, as was the case with everything within the Time Tunnel complex, it had a Disneyesque feel to it.

Three months had passed since Kyle had arrived at the Time Tunnel, and he was finally getting into the groove. His physical reconditioning was progressing well, and he was the most fit that he had been in years. A few nip tucks from the complex's surgical staff had fixed his broken nose and turned back the clock on his face. When Kyle looked in the mirror, his 33-year-old self was reflected back.

With the aid of his counselor, his emotional reconditioning was going well too. The first month had been tough. For years, he had been terrified of facing the loss of his wife. Festering in his mind and body, the pain had exacted a terrible toll. General Craig made a bet that Kyle could be brought back from the terrible place where he seemed stuck. The bet was paying off. Kyle was on a good path.

"May I join you?" asked General Craig. The general was wearing his trademark khaki pants and a forest green polo shirt.

Kyle looked up, startled. "General! How did you creep up on me?"

"By being a sneaky bastard," the general replied with a broad smile.

"Please, sit." Kyle motioned to a vacant wrought-iron chair.

The general sat down. "How are you doing, son?" he asked.

"Pretty good," Kyle nodded with a smile. "I'm actually starting to feel a bit like my old self."

"It's a good feeling, isn't it?"

"Yes sir, it is," replied Kyle. "I was gone a long time."

A Starbucks barista with gorgeous long red curls approached. "Can I get you anything, General?"

"Black coffee, please," replied the general.

The general looked around. "You've found one of my favorite spots," he said.

"Yes sir. I like this place. I'm productive and peaceful at the same time," said Kyle.

"How are you and Colonel Wise getting on?"

"Better," answered Kyle. "I think she may actually have a pulse after all."

They laughed. Kyle did not let on that they had been sleeping together for the past month, though it would not have surprised him if the general already knew.

The two men paused, looking at each other.

"You look like a man with a question," said the general.

"I am, sir," replied Kyle, smiling at the general's insight. "Sir, there are no elected officials in the Time Tunnel Complex, correct?"

"Correct."

"No president, vice president, cabinet, congress, etcetera, right?"

"That's right."

"Will they be joining us before the jump?" asked Kyle.

"No, they won't," replied the general.

"So, their timeline will change," said Kyle.

"Yes."

"Sir, they don't know about this place, do they?"

The general paused, looking at Kyle.

"No, they don't," answered the general.

Kyle nodded. Both men sat silently. The barista broke the silence with the general's coffee.

"Here you go, sir," she said.

"Thank you very much," replied the general with a big smile.

After the barista was out of earshot, Kyle leaned forward. "Sir, how can they not know? This place cost trillions to build."

"It's not nearly as big of a lump to hide under the carpet as you might think," the general explained. "We take a piece of the Area 51 budget. There aren't a lot of line items. There's no "Time Tunnel" line item. Keep in mind we've been building this place for over half a century, so there haven't been any big spending spikes that would attract attention. We also get money from other sources. America's lead in microprocessors and composite materials wasn't purely the result of having all the smartest guys in the room. We were able to quietly monetize some of our reverse-engineering research on the

Grays by licensing it out. It's a win-win—America's got a competitive edge in high tech, and we make bank. Unlike the government, the Time Tunnel runs an impressive surplus.

"We toss a bone to the president from time to time about the marginal progress we're making in our Gray research," the general continued. "His eyes glaze over a couple minutes after we start talking about carbon nanotubes."

"But sir, if we're changing the country and leaving our government out of the loop, isn't this sort of...this is sort of a temporal coup, isn't it?" asked Kyle.

The general mused over the question. "Well, Colonel, that's a strong way to put it, but there's no denying that we're changing things, and they aren't invited to the party."

Kyle nodded and went silent, processing.

The general leaned forward and tapped on the *Wall Street Journal*'s Lehman crash headline. "Colonel, do you believe we could possibly do a worse job than they are?"

Kyle shook his head. "No sir, I don't believe we could."

"I'm glad you're here, Colonel," said the general as he rose from his seat and extended his hand.

Kyle stood up and grabbed the general's hand firmly. "I am grateful to be here, sir. Thank you for bringing me along."

The general smiled, picked up his coffee, and strode off.

Time Tunnel Complex

Mission Control
September 15, 2008
11:21 hours

"Your turn, Colonel Wise."

Historian Roger Summit punched a button at his TVA console in the mission control amphitheater. The overhead lights were dimmed in the colossal room. From their seats, Kyle, Annika, and General Craig saw the image of a grinning young man wearing a suit and wire rim spectacles flash onto the giant mission control screen. He'd been number 18 of the 19 9/11 terrorists.

"Name?" quizzed Roger.

"Ziad Jarrah," replied Annika, reciting from memory. "Jarrah piloted United Airlines 93. The other hijackers on UA 93 were Saeed al Ghamdi, Ahmed Ibrahim al Haznawi, and Ahmed Abdullah al Nami. Their target was the White House, but the hijackers were defeated by the passengers, and the plane crashed in Shanksville, Pennsylvania.

"Jarrah was Lebanese. He attended Christian schools as a child—because of his family's wealth, not religious preference. He moves to Germany in 1996 to attend school at the University of Greifswald. Spends more time at discos and beach parties than his mosque. Meets Aysel Şengün, a German-born woman of Turkish ancestry. They date off and on for the rest of his life and live together for a while.

"Jarrah moves to the Hamburg University of Applied Sciences to study aerospace engineering. That's where he meets Mohamed Atta, Marwan al Shehhi, and Ramzi bin al Shibh. They form the Hamburg cell in 1998. In 1999, they travel to Afghanistan, where they meet Osama Bin Laden and are recruited into the 'Planes Operation.'

"As Jarrah's religious attitudes shift right, he is increasingly critical of Aysel's Western behavior and dress. They fight. They make up. They fight again.

"Jarrah moves to the U.S. in June 2000. He enrolls in flight school in Venice, Florida, and trains until January 2001. He constructs a replica of a commercial airline cockpit in his apartment using cardboard boxes.

"On September 10, 2001, Jarrah writes Aysel a four-page letter. He thanks her and apologizes to her for the 'very wonderful, hard five years' she had spent with him. He promises her 'a very beautiful eternal life' when they meet again, which will be spent 'in castles of gold and silver.'

Denke an was Du bist und wer könnte Dich verdienen.

Ich umarme Dich und ich küsse Dich auf den Händen und auf den Kopf. Und ich bedanke mich bei Dir und mich entschuldige für die ganz schöne, harte fünf Jahren, die Du mit mir verbracht. Deine Geduld hat einen Präze, die Genat inschaAllah...

Ich bin deinen Prinz und ich werde Dich Abholen

Aufwiedersehen !!

Deinen mann für immer

Ziad Jarrah
10-9-2001

"The morning of September 11, Jarrah calls her from a payphone at Newark airport, tells her he loves her, then boards UA 93 with al Ghamdi, al Haznawi, and al Nami. He sits in seat 1B in first class, closest to the cockpit. The plane is late. It takes off at 08:41. At 09:28, the hijackers take control of the aircraft. Around 10:00 hours, the passengers storm the cockpit and attempt to retake the plane. They use a food cart as a battering ram against the cockpit door. Jarrah rolls and pitches the aircraft to try to throw the passengers off balance. When they fail to defeat the passengers, Jarrah pitches the aircraft forward. UA 93 crashes in a field outside Shanksville at 10:03, killing all onboard."

"Where did Jarrah spend the night on August 28?" asked Roger.

"The Pin-Del Motel, in Laurel, Maryland. Room 105. He checks in on August 27 and checks out on September 7."

"Where does he go after that?"

"Newark," replied Annika. "He checks into the Marriott Newark Airport Hotel on the 7th and stays there until the morning of the attack. Jarrah is in room 466. His companion, Al Haznawi, is next door in 468. By the way, Al Haznawi was able to recite the entire Qur'an from memory, leading him to be given the revered title of 'Hafiz.'"

"Now you're just showing off," said Kyle.

Annika ignored him.

"On what dates did Jarrah attend the Masjid Rahmah Mosque in Newark?" asked Roger.

Annika knew it was a trick question. "Never," she said. "There is no known record of any of the hijackers ever attending a mosque while in the United States. However, they did spend plenty of time in bars, strip clubs, casinos, and adult books stores.

"On the 4th of July, Hamza Alghamdi and Marwan al Shehhi spend $252 on porn videos and sex toys at Video Outlet in Deerfield Beach, Florida. They spend another $183 there on July 27. Jarrah was a regular at Wacko's Strip Club in Jacksonville, Florida, from February 25 through March 4.

"Escorts serviced Waleed al Shehri and Wail al Shehri at the Park Hotel once on September 7 and twice on September 9. Mohamed Atta and others spent $200 to $300 each on lap dances in the Pink Pony Strip Club in Daytona, Florida. Majed Moqed visited the Adult Lingerie Center in Beltsville, Maryland, late night before 9/11. And don't get me started about their time in Vegas. These devout Muslim boys partied their fucking brains out.

"To be fair though, it's important to note that they weren't completely godless. Apparently, some of them performed Muslim ablution rituals before they left for the airport on the morning of 9/11. They shaved their body hair and bathed. They left quite a mess for the hotel maids to clean up."

"Your turn, Colonel Mason," said Roger.

Kyle took a sip of three-hour-old cold coffee from a paper cup as the image of another terrorist flashed onto the screen. The clean-shaven young man had short, coarse black hair that had been brushed back. His lips were thin, pulled tight with contempt. His eyes, sunk into naturally dark shadows in his face, chilled the amphitheater from the grave.

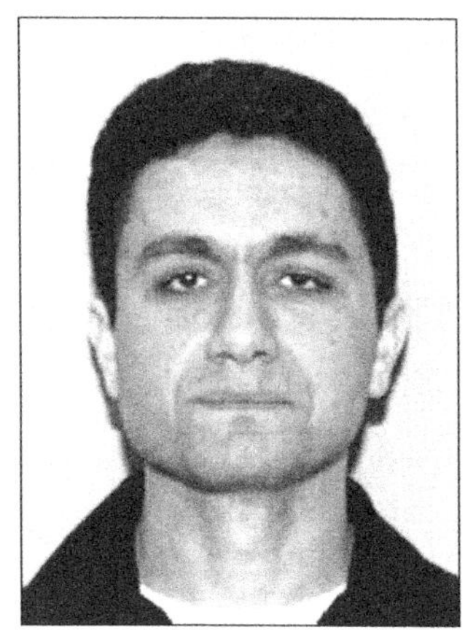

"Mohamed Atta," replied Kyle. "Atta is the ringleader of what Osama Bin Laden called the 'Planes Operation.' He was born September 1, 1968, in Kafr el-Sheikh, Egypt. Atta was the son of a lawyer, trained in both secular and Sharia law. His mother, also educated, was from a wealthy family. Atta's father isolated his family, didn't allow Atta to play with other kids. He focused on his homework and excelled at school.

"Atta graduates from the University of Cairo with a degree in architecture in 1990, then moves to Germany, where he studies urban planning at the Technical University of Hamburg. As Colonel Wise said, Atta meets Jarrah, al Shehhi, and al Shibh, and they form the Hamburg cell.

"In late 1999, Atta and the other members of the Hamburg cell travel to Afghanistan and meet Bin Laden. Before the four showed up, Bin Laden was about to scrap his 'Planes Operation' because he lacked the convincing Western-educated Muslim operators necessary. Atta and the other members of the Hamburg cell pledge themselves to Bin Laden, and the plan is green-lighted.

"Atta trains in Afghanistan in early 2000. In July 2000, Atta begins his flight training in the U.S. By September 2000, he earns his private pilot's license. Only three months later, Atta earns his commercial pilot's license from the FAA."

"Where was Atta on August 27?" asked Roger.

"Valencia Motel. Laurel, Maryland. Room 343. Atta has a final planning meeting with the American Airlines 77 hijack team. American 77 is the plane that hits the Pentagon."

Kyle glanced at Annika. She did not meet his eyes. She continued to stare at Atta's face on the giant screen.

"How about the evening of September 8?" asked Roger.

"Atta treated several of his fellow terrorists to dinner at their favorite local restaurant, the Food Factory in College Park, Maryland."

"You're up, Colonel Wise," said Roger. "Which terrorist is this?"

The image of another young man appeared on the screen. He had a baby face and curly black hair. He wore fatigues and carried an automatic rifle. Annika knew it was another trick question.

"This isn't a terrorist," said Annika. "It's Daniel Lewin. He was the co-founder of Akamai. It's one of the dot-bomb success stories. He was a Ph.D. candidate at MIT and wrote a set of algorithms that boosted Internet performance.

"Prior to Akamai, Lewin was a Captain in the Sayeret Matkal, an elite counter-terrorist special forces unit of the Israel Defense Force. He was the first person to die on 9/11 when he tried to defeat the hijackers on American 11. He was 31."

"Let's talk about the plan," General Craig interjected. "Colonel Wise, what is your thinking?"

"The challenge is logistics," Annika replied. "We need to be able to hit all 19 targets at approximately the same time. If there's too much of a time gap between hits, it raises the odds that one of the targets will attempt to communicate with another and get spooked when they can't make contact. If they deviate from the timeline we know, we'll lose them for good."

Annika signaled to Roger to pull up an aerial map. It appeared on the screen with four hotels highlighted.

"I like the evening of September 7 for the hits. The targets are concentrated in four hotels in two cities, Boston, Mass, and Laurel, Maryland.

"I'm thinking I take the Boston targets, and Colonel Mason takes Maryland. All of the Boston terrorists order an escort that evening. According to her driver, the escort starts at the Park Inn, then proceeds to the Days Hotel later that evening.

"I can take al Suqami, Abdulaziz al Omari, and the al Shehri brothers in the afternoon and cap the al Ghamdi brothers that evening."

She took a breath before continuing. "I'll be the escort."

Kyle and the general looked at Annika, incredulous, eyebrows raised. They couldn't imagine the makeup-less warrior in camo fatigues in such a role.

"What?" asked Annika.

Kyle and General Craig exchanged awkward glances, each hoping the other would speak first.

"You can't pass," Kyle finally said flat out.

"I'll take that as a compliment and go fuck yourself," snapped Annika.

"You might want to consider shaving your armpits for the part."

"Handy tip. Thanks," she said. Her poker face masked the realization that shaving her armpits had not occurred to her. Neither had shaving her legs. She tried to remember the last time she had shaved. The warrior who could fly an assault helicopter into battle or assemble a 50-caliber machine gun blindfolded suddenly realized she was completely out of her depth when it came to feminine charm.

Time Tunnel Complex

Promenade
September 15, 2008
15:30 hours

Annika walked along the Time Tunnel's shiny promenade, eyeing the women's apparel shops while pretending not to. In all her years in the Time Tunnel complex, this was the first time she had set foot in its mall. She was painfully aware of how out-of-place she appeared, wearing her standard issue camo fatigues, boots, and black tank top in the tunnel's fashion district.

Annika avoided eye contact with her fellow shoppers as they spotted one of the tunnel's two celebrity temponauts. When there was a window in the pedestrian traffic, she darted into a Victoria's Secret.

The shop attendant, an attractive middle-aged blond-haired woman in a lemon-colored Chanel suit, looked up from the magazine she was reading. Annika saw the woman's surprise upon seeing her. Annika was visibly embarrassed.

"Colonel Wise, welcome! What can I do for you?"

"I need your help with something," Annika said. "It's a matter of national security."

Time Tunnel Complex

Level 3—Kyle Mason's apartment
September 15, 2008
18:20 hours

Kyle entered his townhouse and bounded the stairs to the master bath. The door was shut. He tried the knob. The door was locked.

"Occupied," came Annika's voice from within.

"Sorry," Kyle said. He was confused. He and Annika didn't normally close the bathroom door behind them, much less lock it. He sat on the bed.

The door opened. Kyle's jaw dropped.

Annika emerged from the bathroom wearing tight low-rise black leather pants and a tiny black bandeau tube top that barely covered her breasts. Her eyes were lined and shaded with blue shadow transitioning to magenta. She wore rouge on her cheeks. Her dark hair, professionally styled and liberated from its ponytail, fell onto her bare shoulders.

Kyle gasped. He had never before seen Annika wear makeup or clothes other than military issue. He found Annika attractive, but he'd never imagined she could be the irresistible siren standing before him.

Confused and awestruck, Kyle searched for words. He could only summon "Wow."

Annika did not react. Her face was emotionless. Her newly minted bedroom eyes were fixed on him.

"Am I passing, Kyle?" she asked.

"I have a really bad feeling there isn't a right answer to that question," Kyle said.

Annika stared at Kyle impassively, then pulled off the bandeau top, kicked off her ankle boots, and shucked her pants. Kyle saw that Annika's normally ungroomed petite body was thoroughly shaved and waxed. Her finger and toenails were painted deep cobalt blue.

"Am I passing?" Annika repeated. "Do you want your whore?"

Kyle stood and approached Annika. Before he could touch her, she brushed past him and walked to the bed.

"How do you want me?" she asked.

She climbed onto the bed on all fours with her butt facing him.

"Do you want me like this?"

Kyle's head was spinning. This submissive person was the polar opposite of the Annika he knew. He didn't understand what was happening. He also didn't care.

"Fuck it. Yes. I want you," he said. "Like that."

Kyle's clothes flew off. Annika stared forward as he grabbed her hips and pushed inside her. She reached back with one hand to stroke him.

"That's it, baby," she said softly as she felt him build inside her.

She felt Kyle shudder as he climaxed, digging his fingernails into Annika's thighs.

Annika lunged forward, reaching under a pillow. She pulled a Glock pistol, and spun onto her back to face Kyle. Kyle winced as she pulled the trigger.

The gun hammer clicked against the empty chamber. Kyle stared at the naked assassin laying on the bed, her gun pointed at Kyle's face.

"Am I passing, Kyle?"

• • •

Later that evening, the couple lay in bed in an awkward silence, back to back. Kyle waited patiently for Annika to speak.

"Is that what you want, Kyle?" she finally asked.

Kyle thought for a moment, choosing his words with caution.

"It's what I want to fuck," he said. "It's not what I want to love."

"You men are fucked up."

Padma's face flashed through Kyle's mind. He couldn't stop himself from comparing.

Sex was fun with Padma, he thought. *Sex wasn't complicated.*

"You're disappointed with me," Kyle said.

"I don't know," Annika said. "Maybe. You're all weak."

"I don't take my armor to bed with you," replied Kyle.

"Maybe you should," Annika snapped.

"What were you doing?" Kyle asked. "Were you testing me? Did you want me to fail? All you needed for the mission was to look the part."

Annika was silent.

"Unless you plan to..."

"Fuck them?" Annika asked. "No, I don't plan to fuck them. Anyway, I've only ever found one Arab man attractive."

"How did that work out?"

Annika got out of bed and began getting dressed.

"I shot him in the head."

"You were right about wearing armor to bed."

"Fuck you!" she screamed. "You know why you didn't avenge your wife? It's because you were weak! All you men are weak—doing whatever your fucking dicks tell you to do! I'm sleeping at my place tonight."

Kyle glared at Annika, incensed. "Don't let the screen door hit your butt on the way out!"

She grabbed a remote and tossed it at Kyle as she walked out.

"There's porn on TV. Have fun."

Time Tunnel Complex

Level 3—Kyle Mason's apartment
September 16, 2008
07:20 hours

Kyle stirred in bed. The smell of fresh croissants and coffee filled the room. He opened his eyes. Annika was sitting on the edge of the bed, holding a cardboard box from one of the Time Tunnel's bakeries in one hand and a tall paper cup of coffee in the other.

Kyle sat up, brushing his hands across his face and back against his hair. He was surprised to see that Annika wasn't wearing her signature outfit of camo pants and a tank top. She wore a slim-fitting long sleeved black sweater tucked into jeans. A pair of ankle boots completed the ensemble. Her hair was pulled back into its ponytail, but a small gold cuff held her hair in place instead of the usual elastic. She wore petite gold hoop earrings and light makeup.

"I got breakfast," she said, detouring around the elephant in the room. She handed Kyle the coffee and a croissant wrapped in paper. The croissant shed flakes onto the bed. Annika wiped them off.

"Sorry," she said.

"This is nice," Kyle said.

Annika looked nervously from side to side. Kyle could see she was mustering herself to say something. He waited patiently, sipping his coffee.

"What you said last night. About me wanting you to fail. That might be right."

She took a breath.

"Part of me wants to trust you. Part of me needs to fuck it up."

Kyle was quiet, listening.

"Since I was a child, I've never told anyone that I was afraid of anything. It's tough enough to be a woman in a man's world. It's tougher to be a woman in the Army. I've never been able to admit fear.

"I'm afraid, of course. I'm afraid of lots of things. I'm afraid of crashing in a helicopter. I'm afraid of snakes.

"I'm afraid to have feelings for you. I'm afraid to trust you with my feelings.

"I know it doesn't matter whether I'm afraid or not. The helicopter still crashes."

Kyle took Annika's hand. "I hope you know by now that you can trust me with your life."

"I do know that," she said, nodding. "I know trusting you with my life should be enough. It just doesn't feel right for some reason. I don't know why. I'm not sure why I'm afraid. It's strange, just telling you I'm afraid feels so weird, but it also feels good."

Tears began to stream down her cheeks. She clutched herself. "Look at me, I'm shaking."

Kyle set the coffee and croissant on the nightstand, moved close, and hugged Annika. Annika rested her head against Kyle's shoulder and began to cry.

"I wonder if what I need is to trust you with *your* life instead of mine. I think maybe I need to trust *you* not to die."

"Is this about Casper?"

Annika nodded. "I think maybe it is. All I had to do was not call him on 9/11, and he would have lived his last minutes in bliss. It's stuck in my head. I would give anything to take it back."

"You get a second chance. You can save his life."

Annika nodded again. "I want that. I'm sorry this is in the way of us," she said. "I do have feelings for you, whether I'm afraid of them or not. You need to know it's a big fucking deal for me to tell you this."

"I know that," Kyle said. "I have feelings for you too."

"Really?"

Kyle nodded.

"That makes me happy," she said through her tears. She wiped her cheeks. "I feel badly about last night. I was a jerk. What can I do to make it up to you?"

Kyle saw Annika's tiny bandeau lying on the floor. He picked it up and handed it to her.

"Asshole," she said, snatching the bandeau. "I was kinda hot, though, wasn't I?"

"You still are."

Annika wrapped her arms around Kyle's neck, kissing him.

Time Tunnel Complex

Mission Control

October 1, 2008

10:05 hours

The general glanced at his watch. John Kaomea was five minutes late to the mission update meeting. He shot Gus Ferrer an irritated look. Gus got the message and reached for a phone on the conference table.

"This is Gus Ferrer. Please page Director Kaomea to mission control."

Moments later, a woman's voice was heard over the PA system: "Director Kaomea, please call mission control."

"Perhaps you should send the MPs to collect him," said Gus.

Strangelove hid a chuckle beneath his hand.

"Remind again why you picked Mr. Kaomea, Gus," said the general.

Gus shook his head. "John was not my first choice, as you know, General. My first two picks from DARPA turned down the offer of CTO. I was able to recruit him from a particle beam weapons project."

"As I recall, that was your only project that came over the line overbudget and behind schedule," replied the general.

Gus scowled. “Yes, General, John broke my perfect record. That’s why he’s being micromanaged on this project.”

“How’s that working out?”

“It’s unpleasant—for both of us.”

“Are you able to apply any skills from your sugar plantation days?”

Gus laughed. “I was a kid in Cuba when my dad ran the family sugar cane business. I didn’t really have firsthand experience into his personnel management techniques.”

“I never asked you how you ended up in the States.”

“My dad backed the losing side in the 26th of July Movement coup,” Gus replied. “Castro overthrew the Batista dictatorship. My parents and two little sisters escaped from Havana to Miami on a private boat. It was 1:00 AM on New Year’s Day, 1959. We were wealthy the day before, but we ended up in America without much more than the shirts on our backs.”

“That must have been rough.”

“Yes,” Gus said. “My dad ended up going to work for a liquor distillery. I bussed tables in a Cuban restaurant. I learned to cook, eventually.”

“Really?”

“Yeah, in addition to managing the development of spacefaring orbital test vehicles and satellite-killing, high-energy, liquid-laser-area defense systems, I also make a mean *rabo encendido*.”

“Renaissance man.”

Gus smiled.

The general looked at his watch, shook his head, and picked up the phone.

"This is General Craig. I want two MPs to find John Kaomea and bring him to mission control on the double."

At that moment, the mission control vault door opened, and John Kaomea entered. He was accompanied by an Asian woman in her mid-thirties. The woman, Zhang Li, was Kaomea's lieutenant, a Ph.D. in electrical engineering from MIT. Zhang Li had been Kaomea's righthand woman at DARPA. There were some who believed she was the real brains behind Kaomea, keeping him propped up. If so, she never revealed the emperor's naked state. Zhang rarely spoke unless spoken to, and her icy expression never betrayed what she was thinking.

Kaomea descended the steps to the conference room table at a leisurely pace. Zhang measured her steps to match Kaomea's.

When the two engineers reached the table, Kaomea casually tossed a notebook onto it before taking a seat. His expression was smug. Zhang's expression was blank.

The general turned to Strangelove. "Doctor, am I correct in understanding that the time displacement system demands a very high degree of precision in order to function properly?"

"That is an understatement," replied Strangelove. "The tolerances required of all aspects of the system are exceptionally narrow and unforgiving. An infinitesimal fraction of variance from the specification in any of the subsystems could well result in a catastrophic event."

"That concerns me," the general said, turning to Kaomea. "I wonder if imprecision in one's work habits might reflect imprecision in their work product."

Kaomea laughed. “Sorry I’m late, General.”

The general glared at Kaomea. “Do you think this is funny? Because I can demonstrate just how un-funny it is, if you’d like.”

Kaomea understood the general’s threat, but he needed to balance the demands of his expansive ego against the unlikely possibility that the general would toss him in the Time Tunnel’s stockade. The general needed him, and they both knew it.

Kaomea adjusted his tenor to the minimum threshold required to avoid escalating the situation.

“My apologies, General,” he said. “Shall we begin?”

“We shall,” replied the general. “Gus, get us started.”

Gus clicked a remote on the table. Numbers flashed up on the giant screen—the results of recent Time Tunnel tests. The numbers were aligned into three columns: “Specification,” “Actual,” and “Delta.” The delta column highlighted the difference between the specification numbers and the actual numbers. If the actual numbers were within system specifications, they appeared in green, preceded by a “+” sign. Numbers outside specifications were presented in red, preceded by a “-” sign. Nearly half of the delta numbers were red.

“These are the results from the last system test,” said Gus. “As you can see, we are outside specification on about half of the subsystem tests.” Though the permanent scowl on Gus’ face was not a direct reaction to the second-rate test results, the results deeply embarrassed him nonetheless. The project was Gus’ responsibility, as was Kaomea.

“Strangelove, what are the implications of these numbers?” asked the general.

"The implications are ominous," replied Strangelove. "As discussed, the system demands the most precise tolerances. Operating a space-time warp engine outside those specifications is potentially disastrous. At best, it expands the range of space-time coordinates where the temponauts would land. They could land decades off target in the middle of the Atlantic Ocean. At worst, if the antimatter reactor goes critical, we blow up the Earth."

Kaomea smiled. "I think you're overstating the potential downside. We're within spec on the majority of metrics. The majority of negative variances are negligible."

"And I think you are playing fast and loose with the lives of everyone on this planet!" shouted Strangelove.

The general and Gus looked at Strangelove. This was the first time they had witnessed heated words from the usually affable scientist.

Kaomea laughed. "I think somebody needs a nap," he said.

The general short-circuited his instinct to lunge across the table at Kaomea. Before he could open his mouth to respond, Gus beat him to the punch.

"Shut up John!" snapped Gus. "Right now, Strangelove has a helluva lot more credibility at this table than you do. These specs are not flexible. Neither am I. At the outset of this project, you committed to meeting or exceeding each and every spec. We're less than 30 days away from the jump date. We never should have been having this conversation so close to D-day. You've put the mission at risk. You've put lives at risk. This is a reprehensible, pathetic excuse for the deliverables you promised to this team!"

The smile on Kaomea's face was replaced by stunned indignation. Zhang's poker face didn't waver.

"I only have one question for you at this time," said Gus. "Can you complete this project within specifications prior to the jump date?"

Kaomea paused before speaking. In his career, he had grown accustomed to fawning and accolades from colleagues. No one had ever spoken to him with anything remotely resembling the white-hot contempt Gus had shown him. Humiliation and rage churned inside him.

"Yes," Kaomea finally uttered. After an awkward silence, he said, "Will there be anything else?"

"No. You're dismissed," replied the general.

Kaomea collected his notebook and beat a hasty retreat from the meeting with Zhang in tow.

Gus turned to the general. "General, I am sorry. I've let you down. You have my word that I will turn this around."

"I know you will," replied the general.

Strangelove was silent. The smile that normally lit his face had collapsed into a worried frown. He looked as though he had aged in the course of the short meeting.

"You're worried," the general said to Strangelove.

"Yes, General, I'm worried."

Until the moment of the exchange with Kaomea, Strangelove had been immersed in the most fascinating of intellectual exercises, transforming theoretical physics into the actual possibility of sending people through time. In a matter of minutes, the Time Tunnel had morphed from theory to titanic reality. The belated epiphany chilled Strangelove's bones as he now realized the red numbers on the big screen were not engineering power and gravity wave variances.

The numbers were body counts.

Time Tunnel Complex

Level 3—Kyle Mason's apartment
October 26, 2008
23:00 hours

Annika rested her head on Kyle's chest in bed. His arm wrapped around her bare back. In 10 hours, they would either be sent back in time, or into oblivion.

During their time together, Kyle had discovered a completely different Annika—one with vivid dreams and a child's playfulness and mischievousness. He liked this Annika a lot.

Annika liked this Annika too.

Annika liked being able to trust Kyle. She was not accustomed to lowering her shields around people. It was, at once, uncomfortable and exhilarating for her to be vulnerable around him. The more vulnerable she allowed herself to be, the happier she became. Her face lit up when she saw him. Though they had kept their relationship discreet for its first few weeks, it wasn't long before the general outed them. He couldn't help but notice that Annika was treating Kyle with much less contempt than everyone else in the complex. He reminded her that life was much too short not to seize every waking moment.

"Carpe diem," the general advised Annika.

The general laughed as, for once, Annika was caught speechless. She didn't know how to feel about her life in this strange place. Her rigid discipline, which had enabled her to compete with the big boys throughout her military career, seemed to be unraveling into chaos. She didn't entirely trust chaos, though she secretly kind of liked it.

Annika righted her head, resting her chin on Kyle's chest.

"Kyle?" she asked.

"Hmm?"

"Should we talk about the future?"

"Uh oh. Incoming," Kyle joked.

"Seriously, what are we? Are we a couple? Are we friends with benefits?"

"Whoa, back up," Kyle said. "When did we become friends?"

Annika slugged him in the shoulder.

"Fine!" she said in a huff, rolling off his chest onto her side of the bed, her back to him.

Kyle put his arm around her small shoulders.

"Let me try this on," Kyle said. "How about, I love you."

She spun to face him, her face beaming. She kissed him.

"Then, I say, I love you too," Annika replied, allowing a rare giggle.

They embraced, happy in each other's arms. For Kyle, his love for Annika was a different one than the head-over-heels kind he had known with Padma. His relationship with Annika had been forged, like beating two molten alien metals into a single indestructible alloy. Through hardship and circumstance—even physical pain—the two had become inseparably close. Cracks in the walls they had erected to block out pain had enabled them to enter and fill each other's empty spaces. For the first time in years, Kyle and Annika looked forward to the future, once they concluded their business in the past.

Time Tunnel Complex

Level 6—Time Tunnel Chamber
October 27, 2008
08:00 hours

Annika and Kyle stood in a small charcoal-gray anteroom facing a heavy steel door. In a few moments, technicians on the other side would unlock the door to the Time Tunnel chamber. The temponauts were wearing casual attire, not the "astronaut coveralls" Kyle had originally envisioned when he was told he would be sent back in time. Kyle wore jeans and a taupe dress shirt. Annika also wore jeans, a long-sleeved black T, and ankle boots. There were no cameras in this room. Kyle and Annika knew this would be their last private moment before they crossed time. Their eyes met. They embraced and then shared a long final kiss.

They heard a loud "clack" as the big gray metal door unlatched. The door swung open and two technicians, wearing white cleanroom overalls, hoods, and booties ushered them in. They entered a square black room, about 100 feet by 100 feet, with a ceiling the height of a college basketball arena. In the center of the room was a glass sphere, approximately 15 feet in diameter. The sphere was suspended five feet off the floor by a black metal pedestal. Stairs from the floor led to an open hatch on the side of the sphere.

Surrounding the sphere was a donut-shaped black carbon ring, 75 feet in diameter with a width of 20 feet. The ring was suspended from the ceiling using cables. Cameras were positioned on the walls of the chamber to allow operators in mission control to view the two temponauts.

The technicians assisted Annika and Kyle up the steps and into the chamber and pointed them to yellow targets painted on the floor of the sphere, where they were told to position their feet. They stood side by side. The technicians latched the glass door to the chamber and then removed the steps from the room before exiting.

The heavy vault door to the Time Tunnel slammed shut with a metallic "clank" that echoed through the chamber. Kyle and Annika stood alone, facing forward, their feet squarely within the circular yellow targets. The chamber was completely silent—so much so that Kyle could hear Annika's breathing. He could sense the rise and fall of her chest with each breath. He wondered if he would ever be with her again.

Mission control buzzed in preparation for the time jump. The room swelled with over one hundred staff as they performed final system checks. Staff members darted about the room, congregating for brief conversations with colleagues before settling at their workstations. Dozens of workstation display screens were alive with numbers, graphs, and tables, as well as images of system components. On the center of the giant screen at the front of mission control was the live image of the Time Tunnel chamber, with Kyle and Annika in the glass sphere. Key system performance metrics and status indicators flanked the video feed of the temponauts.

Gus Ferrer stood at his mid-tier mezzanine station, surveying the room and the staff members. The room was electric with anticipation. One mezzanine below, John Kaomea's team was huddled at the engineering workstation hive, reviewing last-minute system readout numbers. Strangelove sat nearby in his wheelchair. He tried to eavesdrop on the engineers' conversation, though they largely ignored him. John's confidence in himself and his team of engineers was supreme. He did not require assistance from the aging physicist.

Roger Summit and Aysha Voong sat with their history hive, huddled around the rose-colored TVA light cube. If all went according to plan, the TVA cube would light up the moment the temponauts disappeared, signaling that the timeline had changed.

Lara Meredith stood at the side of the room near the vault door, wearing her lab coat. Her arms were folded across her chest. She had little to contribute to the time jump beyond monitoring Kyle's and Annika's vital signs up to the moment of the jump. She had copied her workstation's readouts of heartbeats, temperature, respiration, and blood pressure to a thumbnail tile on the giant screen so she could monitor them from a distance.

Gus looked at the clock readout on the giant screen and clicked a switch attached to his belt to broadcast a message throughout the complex. He spoke into his wireless headset microphone.

"All staff, this is mission control. Countdown is T-minus 10 minutes and counting. Prepare for final system check at T-minus five minutes. Repeat: final system check at T-minus five."

The bright blue strobes on the mission control vault door began to flash. The door swung open, and General Craig entered the room. His attire was uncharacteristically formal, a crisp green full general's uniform. Four brass stars gleamed on his epaulettes. Lara went to the general and kissed him on the cheek.

"You look positively dashing!" she said, smiling.

General Craig returned her smile. "I thought I would dress for the occasion. It's not every day that I get to send off time travelers."

"Well, you're certainly sending them off in style," Lara replied.

The general nodded toward the big screen and the readout of the temponauts' vital statistics. "How are our time travelers faring?"

"You're asking me about their current condition?" asked Lara.

"Yes," answered the general.

"Based on all available medical data?"

"Yes."

"In my professional opinion, I'd say they're scared shitless," said Lara.

"Thank you for that scholarly assessment, Doctor," replied the general, shooting Lara a sharp look.

"Anytime, General," replied Lara with a wink.

The general excused himself and walked to Gus. They shook hands.

"General," Gus said in acknowledgement.

"Are we good to go?" asked the general.

"Yes sir, I believe we are. Final systems check in three minutes. Did you bring your hardware, General?" asked Gus.

"I did," replied the general. He reached for the back of his neck and tugged a black lanyard worn beneath his uniform, revealing a large red anodized metal key. The shiny red key was rectangular, with square edges and punched square holes. The Time Tunnel hourglass logo was cut out of the key handle. The general hung the key by its lanyard, allowing it to rest on his chest next to his Time Tunnel card key.

Gus removed his key. It was similar to the general's, but with a blue tint instead of the general's red. The keys would need to be inserted and turned simultaneously in order to enable the jump.

The general noticed that John Kaomea was having a serious conversation with Zhang Li. The two grew increasingly animated—the conversation was building to an argument. The general had never seen Zhang lose her composure before. The general nudged Gus. Gus turned to the engineering team.

"Is there a problem?" he asked.

John turned to Gus. "No Gus, there is no problem. I apologize for the disturbance."

John glared at Zhang, who turned and walked to her workstation without saying another word.

Gus and the general exchanged looks. Gus clicked his microphone switch to address the Time Tunnel staff throughout the complex.

"All staff," he announced, "time is T-minus five minutes. We are at final system check. Respond when called. Reactor."

"Reactor go," replied an engineer. "Power at 30 percent. Go for throttle up."

"Temporal engine," said Gus.

"Temporal engine go," replied another engineer.

"Navigation."

"Navigation go."

"Bio."

"Bio go."

"Transponder."

"Transponder go."

System		Status
Reactor		Green
Temporal engine		Green
Navigation		Green
Bio		Green
Transponder		Green

"All systems, all staff, punch your status buttons now," said Gus.

At that moment, each of the hundreds of people throughout the complex who were tied to the operation of the Time Tunnel pushed one of two buttons—green or red. A single red button would abort the time jump. Gus watched the board for the results.

Percentage of respondents: 100%

Percentage green: 100%

Percentage red: 0%

System wide status		Status green	Status red
Percentage respondants reporting:		100%	0%

"Throttle power to 60 percent," ordered Gus. "Retract tunnel moorings."

Gus and the general watched the live video feed of the Time Tunnel chamber on the giant screen. The cables supporting the donut ring detached and retracted into the ceiling. The platform that supported the sphere retracted into the floor. The ring and sphere, supported with magnetic repulsion, floated in space like a man-made Saturn.

Inside the chamber, Kyle and Annika could see their sphere ascend some 20 feet, to half the height of the room. The carbon donut rose with the sphere. The silence in the sphere was replaced by a deep hum, bringing with it a vibration that trembled gently through their bodies. It was time.

"Any last words?" asked Kyle.

"I'm scared," replied Annika.

"Me too."

Kyle reached for her hand. She grasped his tightly and closed her eyes.

The hum increased in intensity, accompanied by a bright white light. The light did not appear to have a source—it was simply as though the brightness of the room's lighting had been turned up to an uncomfortable level.

Inside mission control, Gus turned to the general. "General, we are ready to proceed on your order."

"Proceed," the general replied.

"General, please insert your key into the panel. Wait for my mark before you turn the key," said Gus.

Both men removed their lanyards and inserted the keys into the panel in front of them.

Gus said, “Turn on my mark—three—two—one—mark!”

Both men turned their keys. The status lamp next to the “Armed” indicator turned from green to red. A red “Armed” indicator flashed on all monitor displays in mission control and throughout the Time Tunnel complex. A klaxon alarm sounded. A large button on Gus’ panel marked “Commit” flashed on.

“Reactor—throttle power to 100 percent,” said Gus.

“Throttle to 100—roger that,” came the reply.

The command to throttle up power threw the Time Tunnel’s energy reactor into overdrive. In the chamber beneath which Kyle and Annika stood, matter and antimatter were injected in equal parts, annihilating with monstrous energy.

Inside the Time Tunnel’s glass bubble, Kyle and Annika felt the vibration increase dramatically, accompanied by an increase in brightness. Even through their tightly shut eyelids, the light strained their eyes. The vibration shook them forcefully, but they did not lose their balance. Kyle realized that it was not the chamber that was vibrating—it was their bodies. The very atoms that comprised them were shaking like vibrating grains of sand.

Gus reached for the “Commit” button. He looked at the general. The general nodded. Gus pressed the button.

The giant monitor beamed a blinding white light from the chamber video feed, forcing the mission control staff to turn away. Moments later, the light faded as system power levels dropped to zero. The monitor flickered back to life. The Time Tunnel chamber was empty. Kyle and Annika were gone.

Place: unknown

Date: unknown

Time: unknown

Kyle witnessed a blinding flash of light, then complete darkness. He felt an intense electric shock through his entire body, as if every molecule had been electrocuted from within. Though his body wanted to cry out, it was frozen—completely immobilized by the tunnel effect.

He felt something pressing on his hands in the darkness—something soft. He felt pressure on his knees. He realized that he was no longer standing; instead, his hands and knees were resting on—carpet? The darkness began to fade. He was disoriented and struggled to regain his faculties. From his all-fours position, he began to take in his surroundings. Beneath his hands was a bland beige-colored carpeted floor. Directly in front of his head was a sheet of polished wood—the footboard of a bed. He looked to his right and saw a large window with a gauzy covering. Behind him was a wooden credenza with a large television resting on top. To his left was part of a wall with vertical white and gold stripes. This was not the "isolated area" the scientists had targeted. Something had gone very wrong.

He had to get to his feet. He reached up and grabbed the top of the footboard and pulled himself up. He gasped at what he saw.

Annika was sitting upright on the bed, her back against the headboard and her hands resting neatly at her sides. She stared directly at him with her brown eyes.

"Are you all right?" Kyle asked.

Annika did not respond. Her stare was fixed on him.

"Annika?"

Kyle moved around the bed to her side. Annika's stare did not follow him.

"Oh no!" he cried.

He put his fingers on her neck to feel her pulse. There was none.

"No no *no!*" he cried as he pulled her off the bed onto the floor. He clutched her head, angled it back, and breathed into her mouth—no response. He began pressing rhythmically on her chest to administer CPR. There was nothing but her cold stare.

"No!" he cried as he realized he had now lost two loves to 9/11.

Kyle hit Annika's chest hard with his fist and began CPR again. Her body shuddered under the impact. At that moment he heard a familiar electronic chirp at the door. He was in a hotel room!

He leapt to the door, sliding behind it just as it opened. He saw a man's arm reach in the doorway, clad in a crisp white business shirt topped with a navy blazer. His hand was holding the card key to the room. He dropped the key when he saw Annika on the floor beside his bed.

"What the fuck?" the man gasped.

As the man turned to flee, Kyle grabbed his arm and yanked

him into the room and onto the floor. The man fell and rolled against Annika. Kyle closed the door swiftly but quietly, then grabbed the man by the throat as he was beginning to rise from the floor. Kyle slammed the man back onto the floor, pinning him by the throat. His captive was a white man, in his thirties, with short sandy hair and terrified blue eyes.

"Take all my money. Please don't kill me," uttered the man.

"I don't want your money," Kyle replied. "If you cooperate fully with me, I won't hurt you. If you don't cooperate, I will kill you. Do you understand?"

The man nodded. "Yes! Yes! I'll do whatever you want."

"I'm going to ask you some questions," Kyle said. "The questions will seem strange to you. You will answer them truthfully. Do you understand?"

"I understand," replied the man.

"Where are we?" asked Kyle.

Confusion blended with terror in the man's eyes. "We're at the Sheraton," he replied.

"Which Sheraton—what city?" demanded Kyle.

"Weehawken."

"Weehawken? Weehawken, New Jersey?" asked Kyle.

"Yes. Yes," replied the man.

"What is your name?"

"Steve...Steve Miller."

"Like the musician?" asked Kyle.

"Yeah. I get that a lot," replied Steve, attempting a grimaced smile.

"Steve, I have weird question for you, but I need you to answer it truthfully for me. Will you do that?"

"Yes. Yes. Anything," replied Steve.

"Steve, what is today's date?"

Steve began to sob as he realized that the man holding him by the neck was insane.

"Steve, what is today's date? Don't make me repeat the question again!" said Kyle firmly, closing his grip on Steve's throat.

"September 10!" Steve replied, crying.

Steve saw Kyle's face go white. Kyle released him.

"September 10—what year?" demanded Kyle.

"2001," replied Steve, praying it was the right answer.

Kyle grabbed Steve's wrist to look at his watch. It was 07:00. Kyle stood up, bringing his hands to his head in shocked disbelief. *Those smug fucking techs!* he thought, *they got* ***everything*** *wron*g. If he ever made it back to 2008, he swore he would toss John Kaomea into the tunnel—maybe send him to the year 3000 where, with his primitive millennium-old knowledge, he might make for an excellent zoo exhibit or child's pet.

Kyle's head swam, a pounding mass of overwhelming feelings and impossible problems. Annika was dead—Annika was *dead!* He had lost his lover and mission partner. He was alone. Even with Annika's help and a week's lead-time, his task was already impossible. Now, in 24 hours, he had to single-handedly save America, while doing something about Annika and his unwelcome guest. Should he abort the mission?

Kyle walked to the windows of the corner room and pulled open the drapes. Across the Hudson River, the Twin Towers stood over Manhattan in the morning light. He couldn't believe it—he was really here.

Kyle moved into the tight space between Annika and Steve, turned to Steve, and said, "Move."

Steve scooched sideways away from Kyle, moving toward the door. As Kyle knelt beside Annika, Steve glanced at the hotel room door, only a scant 10-foot dash away.

"Don't even think about it, Steve," said Kyle, never taking his eyes off Annika.

Kyle stared into Annika's brown eyes, anguished. *I can't believe you're gone,* he thought. *I can't believe you're not here. I need you to be here with me. I need to know what to do.*

Annika's return stare was clear and determined. He could almost hear her say, "Buck up, soldier! Get the fucking job done!"

As he had done in the Time Tunnel, only minutes before, he took her hand and closed his eyes. Her hand was still warm. When he opened his eyes, a few moments later, his face had changed. His pain was replaced by the steely look he had taken into battle years before—the same look he'd summoned after Annika had smashed his nose in their sparring match. He could not grieve his lost love, or even fully acknowledge her death. He didn't have time. As he had done the last time he'd been in the year 2001, he needed to bury his pain and postpone it—for 24 hours.

He shoved his hand into Annika's jeans pocket, retrieving the transponder, along with her IDs, debit card, and universal key card. He glanced at the transponder, then shoved everything into his pocket.

Kyle then got up and walked to the room door, stepping over Steve's legs along the way. He swung the door open and placed the "Do not disturb sign" on the doorknob, noting the room number. He then walked to the phone and dialed the front desk.

"Front desk," the attendant said.

"Hello, this is Steve Miller in room 417, I think my assistant may have made a mistake when booking this room. Can you tell me when I'm scheduled to check out?" said Kyle.

"Just a minute Mr. Miller, I'm checking…you are scheduled to check out tomorrow, Tuesday."

"Ok, that's a relief. Thank you for your help."

Kyle hung up the phone and walked to Steve. Steve backed against the wall anxiously.

"Give me your wallet, Steve," said Kyle.

Steve fished out his wallet and handed it to Kyle. Kyle removed his driver's license and company card key.

Kyle then fished his own Delta ID out of his pocket and held it out for Steve to see. Kyle shielded his name on his ID with his index finger.

"OK, Steve, here's the deal. I'm an officer with Delta Force," said Kyle.

"That's for real? I thought Delta Force was only in the movies," exclaimed Steve, his eyes wide.

"For the purpose of this conversation, we do only exist in the movies, which means I'm not here and she's not here," replied Kyle. "Do you understand?"

"Yes. I understand," replied Steve.

"I need to know why you're here, where you're from, where you're supposed to be today, and who's going to miss you when you don't show up," said Kyle. "And time is not on my side, so make it quick."

"I'm a regional account manager for Akamai Technologies. I'm here for a company meeting."

"Akamai! Daniel Lewins' company?"

"Yes. You know Akamai? We're not really a household name. Danny's here at the conference."

"He's flying to LA tomorrow morning," Kyle said, his voice drifting off.

"How do you know that?" asked Steve.

Kyle shook his head. "It doesn't matter. What are your responsibilities at the conference? Who are you meeting? Who will miss you if you don't show?"

Dread streaked across Steve's face. "Why wouldn't I show?"

"Answer the question!"

"OK, OK! I'm supposed to attend company presentations today. Those are big meetings, and I probably wouldn't be missed, but I have smaller breakout sessions tomorrow. I'd be missed from those."

Kyle thought for a few moments.

"Steve, I have no intention of hurting you, but we weren't supposed to meet, so you're going to need to disappear for about 12 hours until I do what I need to do. After that, you can tell everyone you were abducted, which, technically, will be true."

"Abduction doesn't sound good," said Steve.

"It sounds better than homicide."

Steve nodded slowly, "That sounds about right."

Kyle called housekeeping to request a large duffle bag, the kind they used for laundry. It was an unusual request, but he managed to talk his way through his excuse with the staff member on the other end of the phone. Kyle then called maintenance to request a roll of duct tape. Finally, he called the bell desk to request that a luggage trolley be brought to the room.

A housekeeper and maintenance man showed up at the front door with the items Kyle had requested. Kyle tipped them generously from Steve's wallet.

"I'll pay you back," Kyle told Steve.

"Thanks," replied Steve, "though I'll be happy to get out of this alive."

Me too, Kyle thought.

The bell captain showed up with the trolley and offered to help with the luggage, citing hotel policies prohibiting luggage trolleys from being unaccompanied by bell people. Kyle charmed the trolley away from the persistent bellman, all the while thinking of the incomprehensible gap between their priorities—reconciling the bellman's trolley separation anxiety with Kyle's mission to save the country.

Kyle took the large canvas duffle bag and gave it a shake to open it.

"Hold this open," Kyle told Steve.

Steve did as ordered, standing and holding the mouth of the duffle open. Kyle knelt by Annika and gently lifted her off the floor, cradling her shoulders and thighs. Her head hung as it left the carpeted floor. Kyle gasped softly, still not fully accepting Annika's death.

Kyle awkwardly folded Annika at her waist into a fetal position, then slid her butt-first into the duffle. He drew the drawstring tight and stuffed a towel into the opening to plug the gap. He stuffed the roll of duct tape into the top of the bag.

"Now we go," said Kyle. "Here's how this is going to work: we're walking out of this hotel to your car. You're going to stay next to me the entire way. If you shout or run, it will create a problem for me, but I'll kill you before I start running. The odds are good that I'll escape, and you'll be dead. If you cooperate fully, you'll be back this evening, unharmed, in time for dinner. Are we clear?"

"Yes. Clear," replied Steve.

Kyle lifted the duffel onto the cart. He tossed Steve's roller luggage on the cart as well, along with a hanging suit bag. They exited the room and walked down the hallway to the elevator bank. An elderly man was waiting for an elevator when they arrived. When the elevator doors opened, the man waved to invite Kyle and Steve to join him.

"It's a tight squeeze, but I think we can make it," he said.

"Are you sure?" Kyle said, smiling.

"Sure, c'mon in," the man said.

"Do you know what the weather is supposed to be today?" Kyle asked the man.

"Muggy," the man said. "They say it's supposed to rain this evening."

Steve looked at Kyle wide-eyed.

The door opened, and the man held it open to allow Kyle and

Steve to exit with the trolley. As they exited the front door, another bellman intercepted them, insisting to help with their luggage. Again, Kyle managed to dismiss the bellman with thanks, promising to return his trolley.

"The best service I ever got from a bellman was when I was toting a dead body," Kyle remarked as he pushed the trolley across the asphalt pavement of the parking lot. "Good to know for the future."

Steve shot Kyle a look, "I'm not sure whether or not I'm supposed to laugh."

Kyle was silent.

They reached Steve's rental car, a red 2001 Ford Escort. Kyle clicked the key remote to pop the trunk. He loaded Annika gently inside.

"Get in," he ordered Steve as he clicked open the car doors with a chirp.

They drove northwest. Kyle was looking for some privacy. After driving for 15 minutes, he pulled off the NJ-3 West onto a dirt service road that shadowed a muddy creek. He stopped the car.

"Get out," Kyle ordered Steve.

Steve looked at the desolate scene. Dread flashed across his face.

"No! No! You said you weren't going to kill me!" cried Steve. "Please don't kill me!"

"I'm not going to kill you. I'm putting you in the trunk," Kyle said.

"In the trunk, with the dead person? Are you fucking kidding me?"

Kyle turned to face Steve, "Steve, there are two choices on the menu: one dead body and one live body in the trunk, or two dead bodies in the trunk. Which do you prefer?"

"One live body. One dead body," Steve said, looking ill.

"Good choice," said Kyle.

They got out of the car. Kyle popped the trunk and fished the duct tape out of the duffel.

"Hands behind your back," Kyle said.

Steve complied. Kyle wrapped Steve's wrists a dozen times and then taped Steve's mouth. Kyle helped Steve into the trunk, where he was cuddled with Annika's duffle. Kyle taped his ankles.

"Do I need to remind you to keep quiet?" Kyle asked.

Steve shook his head.

"Good," Kyle said, slamming the trunk shut.

Kyle was back in the car, this time heading east to Manhattan.

Café Noir

32 Grand Street
New York, NY
September 10, 2001
09:15 hours

Kyle drove his car into downtown Manhattan, watching the orderly matrix of right-angle streets and avenues of Midtown devolve into confusion south of 14th Street. He parked the car at the intersection of Thompson and Grand in front of Café Noir, the place where he and Padma had first met. He got out and walked to a bodega on West Broadway, where he bought coffee and a bagel. As he sipped his coffee, he kept watch on the building across the street.

Any minute now, he thought.

The coffee cup quivered in his hand. He was too nervous to eat. The anticipation of what was about to come next was almost unbearable. In all his years of combat experience, he had never been rattled like this before.

At 09:20, the door of the Soho Grand opened, and Padma strode out. Kyle gasped at the sight of her. He could not believe his eyes.

Padma reached into her bag and pulled out a carton of cigarettes, quickly lighting one up as though she had been deprived of oxygen. She gave a satisfied exhale and then started walking toward Grand Street with long, confident strides.

Of all the strange things Kyle had experienced in his Time Tunnel odyssey, the experience of being a voyeur to a scene that had played out more than seven years earlier was the most bizarre and unsettling. It was as though he were watching a movie re-run from a different camera angle. He knew the story, but he had never actually witnessed the part that had happened outside his Soho Grand Hotel room.

Kyle watched Padma as she walked away. He had crossed 2,000 miles and seven years to be here again, with her. Now the gap between them had been closed to within seconds and a few hundred feet. It would be so easy to run after her and touch her again, after all these years.

A few hundred feet might as well be a few hundred years, he thought bitterly. He wasn't here to save Padma for himself. He was here to save Padma for a different Kyle, a Kyle he was beginning to resent terribly.

Kyle walked into the hotel and went to the front desk.

"Good morning, may I help you?" asked the attendant, a tall, thin man in his twenties with short blond hair and a brown suit.

"Good morning, my name is Kyle Mason. I'm in room 1612, and I'm afraid I've misplaced my key," Kyle replied.

Kyle showed him his government ID, picked up the key and headed upstairs in the elevator. He arrived at the room and took a deep breath.

"Here we go," he said, exhaling.

Kyle 2008 entered the room.

"What'd you forget, hon?" shouted a voice from the bathroom.

Kyle 2008 stepped into the bathroom doorway. Kyle 2001 was bent over the sink, wrapped in a towel, splashing water on his face. He grabbed a towel to dry off, and then saw Kyle '08 in the mirror

"FUCK!" yelled Kyle '01.

He wheeled around to face his mirror image.

"What the fuck are you?" Kyle '01 yelled.

"Major Mason, I realize this is going to be very tough to take in, but I you need to listen carefully to me," said Kyle '08. "My name is Colonel Kyle Mason. I'm you. I'm from our future—2008 to be precise. I'm here because thousands of people will die tomorrow unless you help me accomplish my mission. Padma is one of those in danger."

Kyle '01 raised his hands to his face in disbelief. Moments earlier, his life had been perfect—*perfect*. Now he was in a nightmare. He had completely lost his mind. Had he lost consciousness? Had he experienced a stroke? This seemed real—an identical copy of himself was standing in his hotel room, talking to him.

"I get that this is crazy," Kyle '08 said.

Kyle '01 was stunned silent.

"As I said, we don't have much time," said Kyle '08, looking at his watch. "Padma will return from her smoke break in 18 minutes."

"How do you know that?" Kyle '01 asked.

"Because I'm you," Kyle '08 replied. "I was here, with her, on our honeymoon. We were married yesterday at City Hall. I spent everything I had to buy her ring and this room. I know everything that you know, plus a lot that you don't."

Kyle '08 rolled up his right sleeve. On his inside forearm was his Sanskrit tattoo of "Padma." The tattoo was not as crisp and black as the fresh one Kyle '01 wore on his arm, but the symbols carved into his arm were unquestionably the same.

Kyle '01 stared at the tattoo. Other than Kyle, Padma, and the artist who'd inscribed it the day before, no one else knew about it.

"I cannot believe this," said Kyle '01. "I cannot believe this. I've lost my mind!"

"Kyle, listen to me," said Kyle '08. "You just ordered wheat toast, fruit, and coffee for Padma. You want breakfast to be here when she returns from her smoke break. She told you she wanted Starbucks instead of room service coffee. You told her she preferred American Spirits. Yes, there are two choices: You are either completely insane, or what I am telling you is true.

"Look, I will debrief you, but not here. When Padma returns, tell her you've been recalled—matter of national security. She'll be disappointed, but many lives depend on it. You'll understand why soon. I'll tell you everything.

"Last thing," Kyle '08 said as he turned toward the door, "under no circumstances can Padma go to work tomorrow. You can't tell her why. You need to hear her swear to you that she will stay home tomorrow. Her life may depend on it."

"What's going to happen?" asked Kyle '01.

"If you and I are successful, absolutely nothing," replied Kyle '08.

Corner of Thompson Street and Grand Street

New York, NY

September 10, 2001

10:00 hours

Kyle '08 sat in the Ford Escort in front of Café Noir. He watched the other Kyle approach the car and get in the passenger side. He was wearing jeans and a long-sleeved black V-neck. He was carrying a bag with his things.

"OK. I'm here," said Kyle '01.

"How did Padma take the news?" Kyle '08 asked.

"She was very disappointed. So am I. Start talking, *Sir*," Kyle '01 said mockingly to his senior-ranked self.

Kyle '08 began: "Tomorrow at 08:46 hours, the first of three hijacked commercial aircraft will hit their targets in New York City and Washington, DC. A fourth plane will not reach its target in DC because its hijackers will crash the plane in a field in Pennsylvania during an attempt by the passengers to retake the aircraft. The two NYC targets are the Twin Towers. The burning jet fuel compromises the towers' infrastructure. They collapse. Both towers are total losses. In total, 2,606 people die in the World Trade Center, including Padma.

"The DC plane hits the Pentagon, killing 125 people," Kyle continued. "The hijackers were Muslim extremist members of al Qaeda. The attack was ordered by Osama Bin Laden.

"The attack has a profound ripple effect, ultimately resulting in the loss of hundreds of thousands of lives in Middle Eastern wars and trillions of dollars from the American economy. The effect on the country is devastating, and it accelerates the decline of the United States as the preeminent world superpower.

"I was involved in one of those wars. My Delta unit was deployed in the Tora Bora region in Afghanistan after the 9/11 attacks. Our mission was to kill or capture Osama Bin Laden. We could have gotten him, but CENTCOM refused to deploy Rangers to guard the mountain trails to the south. Bin Laden ultimately walked out of Tora Bora into Pakistan. After that, the trail went cold.

"Do you remember General Craig?" Kyle '08 asked.

"Of course," Kyle '01 answered. "He gave me my Silver Star."

"Right," Kyle '08 continued. "General Craig approached me several months ago. I was a total burn out. I never recovered from Padma's death. If you can imagine today what it might be like to lose Padma tomorrow…"

"I can't," said Kyle '01.

Kyle '08 nodded. "General Craig recruited me for a mission—to stop 9/11. '9/11' is what Americans call it. He took me to Area 51. They have an underground complex there—something you wouldn't believe."

"I still don't believe in *you*," said Kyle '01.

"Right," said Kyle '08. "Remember the stories about Roswell?"

"Sure," said Kyle '01. "The aliens. Are you telling me they're for real?"

"Yes, though, as it turns out they're not from another planet. They're from this one. They're from the future. Their spacecraft isn't a spacecraft at all. It's a time machine."

"You're fucking kidding me," said Kyle '01.

"That's what I said," said Kyle '08. "I trained with a partner for months. We were supposed to arrive several weeks ago, but something went wrong. We arrived at 07:00 today."

"Where is your partner?" asked Kyle '01.

"In the trunk," replied Kyle '08.

"Why is your partner in the trunk?" asked Kyle '01.

"Because she's dead."

"OK, so let me get this straight, you're me from the year 2008. You came back in time using a time machine from the Roswell aliens..."

"They're not aliens..." Kyle '08 interrupted.

"What-the-fuck-ever they are...you came back in time to stop a major terrorist attack, and you've got a dead body in the trunk of your Ford Escort."

"Got a live one back there too," said Kyle '08.

Kyle '01 turned to look at Kyle '08.

"His name's Steve," said Kyle '08. "Wrong place. Wrong time. My partner and I were supposed to arrive in an isolated area. Instead, we landed in a hotel room in Weehawken—Steve's room. I showed up alive. My partner was DOA. That pretty much brings us up to now."

"You say you're from 2008," Kyle '01 said.

"That's right," Kyle '08 said.

"But you look just like me," Kyle '01 said. "Damn, I age well!"

Kyle '08 rolled his eyes. "So I've had some work done, OK? We weren't supposed to meet, but I needed to be able to pass as you just in case I came in contact with anyone we know."

Kyle '01 sat silent.

"OK. I'm convinced," he said.

"Seriously? That was easy," said Kyle '08.

"There are only two possibilities," said Kyle '01. "Either I'm talking to myself, which means I'm crazy, or I'm talking to my future self who time traveled to Steve's hotel room in Weehawken and has his dead partner's body in the trunk of his Ford Escort, which means the story is too crazy to make up. Given two sucky choices, I'm gonna go with the one where I'm not crazy.

"So," he asked, "what's the plan, Colonel?"

"One of us goes north to kill bad guys. The other goes south," replied Kyle '08.

"Why the hits? Why not just alert the FBI?" asked Kyle '01.

"We worked that option," answered Kyle '08. "The bottom line is that we concluded that there was a low probability of success. There were multiple attempts to warn both the FBI and the president that the attack was coming. They were all dismissed. The FBI's Minneapolis office tried repeatedly to warn Washington that a co-conspirator named Zacarias Moussaoui was going to hijack a plane. One of the Minneapolis agents actually warned HQ that Moussaoui might fly a plane into the World Trade Center. The

Minneapolis agents' efforts to get a search warrant for Moussaoui's laptop and belongings were all refused. Had they obtained the warrant in time, they may have been able to prevent the attack.

"Warnings came from other sources," Kyle '08 continued. "Richard Clarke, a special advisor on the National Security Council, repeatedly tried to warn the White House that an al Qaeda attack was imminent. His position of national coordinator for counterterrorism was downgraded by National Security Advisor Condoleezza Rice, which meant that his memos would no longer go to the president without first being vetted up the chain in the NSA. All of his memos were bounced back by Rice and her deputy. The CIA repeatedly tried to warn the president in a series of briefings. In May, he was told that an al Qaeda group was in the U.S., planning a terrorist operation. In late June, the CIA warned the president that an attack was imminent and that it would cause major casualties. The White House ignored the warnings. The top guys at the CIA's Counterterrorism Center were so frustrated that one suggested that the staff request transfers so they wouldn't be held responsible when the attack happened.

"So," concluded Kyle '08, "if warnings from the FBI, the CIA, and the NSC special advisor were all ignored, we agreed that an anonymous tip from a pay phone would have next to zero effect."

"You're painting a dismal picture of our government," said Kyle '01.

Kyle '08's younger self reminded him of how optimistic he had been on September 10, 2001. He'd been on the very top of the world, a newly minted Delta operator married to the hottest woman on the planet. Kyle '08's rosy world had imploded less than

24 hours later, though there was a chance that Kyle '01's world could still be saved.

"Those are the facts," said Kyle '08. "The attacks could have been prevented. I wish they had been. I'm here to do the job that our nation's leaders couldn't do.

"Last detail," he added. "We need weapons."

"Don't you have weapons from the future?" asked Kyle '01.

"I'm from 2008. We don't have ray guns. We have iPhones," replied Kyle '08.

"What-phones?"

The two Kyles sketched out a plan. Killing the hijackers as they slept the night of September 10 offered the greatest odds of success, particularly as Kyle '01 did not know what the hijackers looked like. Kyle '08 knew the hotels and room numbers where each of the terrorists would be sleeping that night. Nineteen hijackers would be scattered across seven hotels in four cities—Boston, Massachusetts; South Portland, Maine; Newark, New Jersey; and Herndon, Virginia. The Kyles agreed that they would split up. Kyle '01 would go north and take out the Boston and South Portland targets, while '08 would take Newark and Herndon. From his training, Kyle '08 recalled a shadow dealer in Wilton, Connecticut, where they could obtain weapons. Along the way to Wilton, '08 would rent a car that '01 would drive to Massachusetts and Maine. While in Connecticut, they would also find a spot to dispose of Annika's body. After taking care of Annika, the two assassins would part ways to pursue their respective targets.

Kyle '08 wrote down the names of '01's targets, as well as the names, addresses, and phone numbers of the hotels where the hijackers would be staying that night. '08 also gave '01 the hijackers' mobile phone numbers. While '08 could not imagine a scenario in which '01 might need them, he thought it best for '01 to be fully prepared in case he needed to improvise.

The last item '08 provided '01 was information to leave at the assassination scenes in the form of a "calling card"—bits of key information that would tie the various terrorists into the greater conspiracy and Osama Bin Laden. The one downside of leaving the card was that information about their existence would invariably leak out through the investigating local authorities. It would be crack cocaine for conspiracy theorists, smoking gun proof of U.S. government involvement.

They will be right about U.S. government involvement, thought Kyle '08, *only wrong about which U.S. government.*

Kyle '08 gave Kyle '01 Annika's debit card and universal hotel key card. Though '01 would not be able to use the debit card for over-the-counter purchases, he could still get cash from ATMs.

The Kyles stopped first in Stamford, Connecticut, where Kyle '08 rented a car for '01. They then stopped at a sporting goods store, where they bought an anchor to weigh down the duffle, backpacks for their weapons and gear, Leatherman knives, ski masks, gloves, lithium grease for their gun suppressors, and a few odds and ends.

The next stop was the shadow gun dealer in Wilton, where they bought handguns with threaded barrels and suppressors using Kyle '08's fake ID. Kyle's ID kit included a permit to carry handguns in Connecticut, registered under his alias name, Robert Small. Kyle bought two Glock 17 handguns with threaded barrels, suppressors, four extra magazines, and 500 hundred rounds of 9mm Luger ammo. The 9mm rounds were small compared with the .45 caliber ammo both Kyles were accustomed to, though they would be slightly less noisy when fired through the suppressors. Stealth was prioritized over firepower.

In their separate cars, the two Kyles drove north to New Milford, stopping on a narrow bridge over the Housatonic River in Lover's Leap Park. Kyle '08 popped the trunk on his Escort while '01 kept a lookout for cars. Kyle '08 pulled the anchor out of the back seat. In the trunk, Steve still lay, bound in duct tape, nestling the duffle containing Annika's remains.

"You OK?" Kyle '08 asked Steve.

Steve nodded.

Lush silver maple trees lined the river gorge below. A few hundred feet to the south was a lovely red wrought-iron pedestrian bridge named for the lovers' leap.

Kyle '01 looked at the river below, "Padma and I love this place."

Kyle '08 nodded, "Padma and I *loved* this place."

"I'm sorry," Kyle '01 said.

"You remember the legend?" asked Kyle '01.

"Of course," said Kyle '08, looking at the river and trees. "Padma told me the story about the Pootatuck Indian Princess Lillinonah. Sometime in the early eighteenth century, she nursed a young Englishman back to health. The two became lovers against tradition and her father's wishes.

"Her father was chief of the tribe. He tried to sabotage their marriage plans. Lillinonah and her lover could not bear to be apart. They went to the head of the falls, embraced, then threw themselves over the edge.

Kyle '08 pointed downstream.

"Legend has it that when the lovers' bodies were recovered from the rocks below the falls, they were still in each other's arms.

"Chief Waramaug was heartbroken. Against tradition, he ordered that the lovers be buried together. When the old chief passed in 1735, he was buried alongside the couple."

Kyle '08 thought about Lillinonah and how she had restored her lover to health.

Kyle '08 tied off the anchor to the duffle and pulled it from the trunk, carrying it to the edge of the bridge. He paused for a moment, looking at the beautiful dark water and the lush maple trees.

"Goodbye Annika. I love you. Thank you for bringing me back," he said.

Kyle '08 picked up the duffle and dropped it off the side of the bridge. It fell some 40 feet, making a huge splash in the deep water below. He watched the duffle disappear.

She deserved better than this, he thought.

Kyle '08 walked to Kyle '01 and extended his hand. "This is where we part ways," said Kyle '08. "I don't think I'll see you again. Thank you for what you're doing."

Kyle '01 took Kyle '08's hand in a tight clasp. "Good hunting, Colonel," he said.

"Good hunting, Major," replied Kyle '08 with a smile.

The two Kyles got into their cars and drove away.

Sheraton Lincoln Harbor Hotel

Weehawken, NJ
September 10, 2001
16:45 hours

Kyle '08 drove Steve's Ford Escort into the same Sheraton parking lot where he had begun his journey hours earlier. On the return trip to the Sheraton, Kyle '08 stopped for gas and fast food and pulled off on an isolated rural road to give Steve a chance to eat, drink, and stretch his legs. '08 then re-taped Steve, stuffed him back in the trunk, and headed on to Weehawken.

From the parking lot, '08 could see the Twin Towers against a beautiful rose-colored sunset. He carefully wiped the surfaces of the car he had touched with a towel he'd bought at the sporting goods store. He then popped the lid on the trunk and cut off Steve's duct tape. '08 stuffed the tape into his backpack.

"OK, you can get out," Kyle '08 told Steve.

Aching and stiff, Steve climbed out of the trunk. He looked around to see that he was where he had started.

"Here's the deal, Steve," said Kyle '08. "You're free to go. You can tell anyone you care to one of two things. One, that you were abducted for the day by someone you found in your room with a dead woman, and your abductor inexplicably released you unharmed at the end of the day. Or two, assuming you were missed at all today, you can tell everyone that you fell deathly ill, but that you're feeling much better now.

"If you go for option one," Kyle '08 continued, "here's your evidence: You have a handful of hotel staff who might be able to describe me. You might have a grainy lobby video that shows us walking out the front door together. That's pretty much it. If they were to ever identify me, they would find that I have an airtight alibi. I was in Soho when you thought I was in your hotel room."

"But what about the dead woman?" asked Steve.

"Right, the dead woman," Kyle '08 said. He handed Steve a slip of paper. "This is the dead woman's name and phone number. Her name is Major Annika Wise. If the authorities contact her, they'll find out that she's very much alive. There's no one missing who matches the description of the person you think you saw. Major Wise and I have never met, so a description of me isn't going to help, though you're more than welcome to give it a try."

"I'm very confused," Steve said, shaking his head.

"That is completely understandable," said Kyle '08. "So, the choice is either sick day, or looking like a crazy person to your colleagues. Oh, one more thing, when making your decision it's probably also worth factoring this into the equation..."

Kyle '08 unzipped the backpack enough for Steve to see the Glock pistol and silencer.

"'You don't want to be on my short list of people who've pissed me off,'" said Kyle '08.

Kyle '08 zipped up his backpack and slung it over his shoulder.

He took the keys to the Escort out of his pocket and wiped them off with a handkerchief, then handed them to Steve.

"I am truly sorry to inconvenience you, Steve," Kyle '08 said, turning to leave. "Have a good conference."

Steve stood stupefied as he watched Kyle '08 walk away.

Marriott Hotel, Newark International Airport

Room 466
Newark, NJ
September 10, 2001
23:59 hours

Kyle '08 sat on a twin bed in a dark hotel room, facing the window. In the distance, he could see the Twin Towers rising above the New York skyline.

It's easy to destroy. It's hard to create, Kyle '08 thought as he watched the towers.

One of Kyle '08's high school math teachers had told him that once. Gazing at the towers, Kyle '08 realized that the sorry likes of Osama Bin Laden and Mohamed Atta could never build anything remotely close to the World Trade Center. The very best that Bin Laden had ever accomplished was widening out some caves in Tora Bora with a bulldozer. Bin Laden regarded the destruction of the Twin Towers as his crowning achievement.

You destroy things you are incapable of building, thought Kyle '08.

• • •

Construction of the Twin Towers had begun some 33 years earlier, in August 1968. In December of that year, Astronaut

William Anders snapped the iconic "Earthrise" photo as the Earth cleared the moon's horizon during Apollo 8's voyage. Less than eight months later, Americans would set foot on the moon for the first time. Three months after Neil Armstrong took his "giant leap for mankind," UCLA student programmer Charles Kline sent the first computer-to-computer message on what would become the Internet.

The Twin Towers were glittering monuments to that great period in American history, when America was at its zenith; seemingly capable of doing anything it chose to do.

• • •

Kyle '08 had plenty of time to prepare before his first targets' arrival. He took a cab from Weehawken to a mall in Newark, where he bought clothes, a black TAG Heuer chronograph watch, and some toiletries. He was wearing black jeans, black lace boots, and a black commando-style sweater. His black full-hood ski mask rested bunched on the crown of his head. His backpack was strapped on for a quick getaway.

He got a room at the Marriott, checking in around 21:00 hours using Robert Small's credit card and ID. He showered, ordered room service, and rested. At 23:00, he used his universal key card to enter rooms 466 and 468—Ziad Samir Jarrah's and Ahmed al Haznawi's rooms.

Kyle '08 entered room 468 first and unlocked the adjoining door to room 466. He then moved to 466 and opened its door to 468. He checked his weapon and loaded all three magazines. As a final touch, he applied some lithium grease to his gun suppressor to further dampen the gunshot. Contrary to Hollywood depictions, silenced guns still made a racket, but if '08 was lucky, the guests at the Marriott might still sleep through the ruckus that was to come.

The hotel room layout was typical—the bathroom was adjacent to the room's entryway on the left, creating a short hallway before the bedroom. Two double beds were in the bedroom, across from a wood-veneered chest of drawers. A large television set sat atop the chest. The space between the closest bed and the bathroom wall created the perfect sniper's nest for Kyle '08 to surprise his target as he walked from the hallway into the bedroom.

By Delta standards, the close range of this engagement would be a turkey shoot. Delta recruits were required to achieve 100 percent accuracy at 600 yards with a rifle, and 90 percent accuracy at 1,000 yards—over half a mile. Still, close encounters often yielded unanticipated variables. A target at 1,000 yards can't take a swing or throw a weapon at their assassin.

Kyle '08 glanced at the clock on the nightstand. the dim burnt orange of the clock face illuminated the time: 12:01. It was now September 11.

Kyle '08 waited, watching the Twin Towers.

At 00:15, he heard footsteps in the hallway. He stood up and moved between the bed and the adjoining wall. He could not be seen from the entrance to the room. He pulled his mask over his face. He heard the chirp of the door lock. He raised his weapon, took a breath and quietly exhaled as the door opened. Through the wall, he heard the door to room 468 open as well.

A room light came on and Ziad Jarrah walked past him, carrying a black duffle. The small Lebanese man was wearing jeans, an olive polo shirt, and wireframe glasses. In the millisecond that Jarrah turned in terrified reaction to Kyle '08's black hooded figure, '08 fired one shot into his head and two into his heart. Jarrah crashed into the chest of drawers across from the bed, knocking the television set onto the floor. Before the TV hit the ground, Kyle '08 kicked open the adjoining door to 468. At the sight of the black ninja in his hotel room, al Haznawi, forgetting that he was already scheduled to die that day, screamed and ran for the door. '08 fired two rounds into his back, then one in the head as al Haznawi slumped against the door. Blood trailed down the door, leading to his crumpled body on the floor.

Kyle '08 rifled through al Haznawi's pocket and retrieved a mobile phone. He ran back into 466 and pulled a phone from Jarrah's pants. Before exiting, '08 dropped a calling card, a scribbled note, on Jarrah's body:

"PDB: Bin Laden Determined to Strike in US.

United Airlines 93 hijackers.

Target: White House"

PDB: BIN LADEN DETERMINED
TO STRIKE IN U.S.

PDB: BIN LADEN DETERMINED
TO STRIKE IN U.S.

UNITED AIRLINES 93 HIJACKERS

TARGET: WHITE HOUSE

The note referenced the title of the infamous August 6, 2001, President's Daily Briefing, or PDB, prepared for President Bush by the CIA. Though the eventual leak of the PDB in 2002 had an incendiary effect on public opinion, the CIA had delivered even more alarming briefings to the president in the preceding weeks. Though '08's calling card was cryptic, when combined with calling cards from the other assassination scenes, it would weave together the disconnected and dismissed intelligence from the FBI, CIA, and National Security Council. The reference to the President's Daily Briefing, which had been classified as of September 11 in '08's timeline, would send an unmistakable message that these men were terrorists tied to a single audacious plot. The goal of the calling cards was to increase the vigilance of the nation's security apparatus in the absence of the catastrophic effects of 9/11.

Kyle '08 moved to the door, opened it, and peeked out. The coast was clear. He ran to the nearest stairwell and down the four flights of stairs to the parking lot exit. On the way down, he stuffed his weapon into his backpack. Exiting into the hotel parking lot, he walked into the shadows before removing his mask. He then set out for Newark Airport, only a few hundred yards away.

When he reached Terminal B, Kyle '08 got into a cab.

"Days Inn, please," said Kyle '08.

"Days Inn Airport?" asked the driver.

"Right," replied Kyle '08.

The requisite yellow crown air freshener was perched atop the cab's dashboard. A wooden beaded cover insulated the driver from his seat. Kyle '08 noticed the driver's name, Jameel, on his dashboard ID. The Pakistani driver was wearing a cell phone earbud and carrying on a phone conversation in Urdu on their way to the hotel. Kyle '08 could pick up snippets of the conversation.

"His wife had a baby? Is it a boy or a girl? A boy? Perfect! Now he has a boy and a girl. What? He wants five kids? Has he lost his mind? How is he going to support a wife and five kids..."

When the cab arrived at the Days Inn, Kyle '08 directed Jameel to park the cab in a darkened section of the parking lot and wait for him. Jameel didn't miss a beat of his call as Kyle '08 strode off toward a side stairwell entrance.

"...It's too much responsibility for the father and eldest son. They must work and support the wife and other kids. It's too much. I think he's putting his wishes ahead of what's best for the family. They have to work, and they must worry about making sure the sisters get married..."

Jameel didn't notice six bright muzzle flashes in rapid succession through the drapes in one of the third-floor hotel rooms.

"...and he's not thinking about his family at home. I send money to my father from here for the family. That is the responsible thing to do. With a wife and five children, there will be nothing left for his family at home. The youngest son will be spoiled, and there will be nothing left..."

Kyle '08 opened the back door of the cab and climbed in. The remaining United Flight 93 hijackers, Ahmed al Nami and Saeed al Ghamdi, were dead.

"Newark Penn Station, please," Kyle told the driver.

Park Inn

Newton, MA

September 11, 2001

01:05 hours

"Hello?" said a sleepy woman's voice in the dark.

"I'm sorry to wake you," said Kyle '01 into his mobile phone.

"I'm not," replied Padma, groggy.

"Honey, I've gotta work late again tonight," said Kyle '01.

"What's the excuse this time," replied Padma, sharpening up.

"Gotta save the world."

"There's always something," said Padma sarcastically.

There was a pause.

"Come to my bed," said Padma.

Kyle '01 closed his eyes and sighed. "You're killing me."

"Hey, I'm not the one who has to go save the world," Padma retorted.

"Right about now, I'm thinking your bed is worth a court martial," said Kyle '01.

"My bed's worth a firing squad," said Padma.

"You are making me crazy."

"Good," said Padma. "Then quit the Army and come home."

"You know there is no place else I want to be," said Kyle '01.

There was a pause.

"Are you being careful?" asked Padma.

"I am," replied Kyle '01.

"That's good," Padma said, "because I really don't think I can live without you."

"I wouldn't live without you," Kyle '01 said. The thought brought a bolt of fear. The Kyle from the future lived in a world without Padma. Kyle '01 couldn't imagine that dark world.

The contrast between Kyle '01's cold killing assignment and Padma's warm, loving bed could not be starker. Why wasn't he in Padma's bed? What he was doing was insane. His doppelganger had shown up out of the blue and handed him a list of people to go kill in the middle of the night. How was that different than the serial murderer Son of Sam receiving his instructions from a talking dog? Kyle '01 didn't feel crazy, but then again, David Berkowitz probably felt perfectly fine too during his murder spree in the seventies.

"I have to go, love," said Kyle '01.

"Please be safe. I love you," said Padma.

"I love you," said Kyle '01.

Kyle '01 snapped his phone shut and shoved it into his pocket. He sat in his rental car in a dark corner of the parking lot behind the Park Inn. The Park Inn was the last stop of his Boston assignments. Within the next few minutes, '01 would kill two American 11 hijackers, Wail and Waleed al Sherhi, as they slept. After dispatching the al Sherhi brothers, '01 had one final destination, the Comfort Inn in South Portland, Maine, where he would kill

American 11 hijacker Mohamed Atta along with his companion, Abdul Aziz al Omari.

Kyle '01's previous hits had gone like clockwork. He caught the al Ghamdi brothers, Hamza and Ahmed, sound asleep in their room at Boston's Days Inn. After '01 had shot Hamza in his bed, Ahmed, semi-conscious, realized that he had awoken into a nightmare and made a dazed attempt to leap out of his bed through the window. Kyle '01 shot him mid-lunge before he made it out of bed, leaving his underwear-clad body slumped halfway off the bed.

At his second hit, Kyle '01 had shot and killed the remaining three United 175 hijackers, Marwan al Shehhi, Mohand al Shehri, and Fayez Banihammad, crammed into room 408 at the Milner Hotel in Boston's theater district. Street noise from the active nightlife had helped mask the "crack" of Kyle '01's silenced Glock. After he dispatched the hijackers, Kyle '01 left the agreed-upon calling card in the room and a "Do not disturb" sign on the door.

There was only one problem with the Milner hit: One man was missing. Satam al Suqami, one of the American 11 hijackers, wasn't in the room. As long as he could take down his remaining four targets in Boston and South Portland, Kyle '01 knew the mission would still succeed. Al Suqami was "muscle" on the American 11 hijack team, and he could not pilot a plane. Moreover, when his cohorts failed to show up, it was unlikely he would try anything on his own.

Kyle '01 checked his weapon and stuffed it back into the bag. He got out of the car and walked across the dark parking lot to a stairwell entrance. He climbed the three flights of stairs to the fourth floor and walked to room 433. He retrieved his weapon from his backpack, and then pulled his mask over his face. He took a breath, exhaled slowly, and slid the keycard. The latch chirped open and he entered the room, turning on the lights and leveling his weapon at the closest bed.

It was empty. Both beds were neatly made. Kyle '01 searched the room. The room was vacant and had been cleaned. Was he in the wrong room?

Kyle '01 flipped open his mobile phone and called the front desk.

"Good evening, Park Inn," a woman answered.

"Hello, do you have a Mr. al Shehri staying at your hotel?" Kyle '01 asked. "That's "A-L-S-H-E-H-R-I."

"Let me check," replied the desk attendant. "No, I'm sorry, Mr. al Shehri checked out this evening."

Kyle '01 thanked the attendant and hung up.

I'm fucked, he thought.

All five of the American 11 flight hijackers were still at large. Kyle '01 did not know where they were or what they looked like. He could go to South Portland and hope that some of the hijackers had joined up with Mohamed Atta and Abdul Aziz al Omari, but those odds were very long. He didn't know whether the hijackers had been tipped off and fled, or had simply found a different place to stay.

A chill shot up Kyle '01's spine with the realization that there was now only one possible way he could complete his mission and take out the remaining hijackers. In a few hours, he was going to be on American Flight 11.

Boston Logan International Airport

Boston, MA

September 11, 2001

06:45 hours

A gigantic eagle, over 20 feet above the ground, blazed its blue-white neon light from its perch over Boston Logan Airport's Terminal B hallway. The classic 1945 American Airlines mascot was bookended by two oversized uppercase 'A's that glowed neon red. The eagle was beautiful and fierce, crafted at the end of World War II, when America had left the battlefields of Europe and the Pacific in triumphant and noble victory. American wars had never been the same since.

From his seat near gate B33, Kyle '01 peered over the top of a *Boston Globe* newspaper, taking intermittent sips from the paper cup of black coffee balanced on his armrest. From his vantage, he had a clear view down the hallway corridor of approaching passengers who passed beneath the neon eagle's aerie. He sat in the spacious hallway terminus, where the low ceiling of a comparatively confined corridor vaulted 30 feet high, bordered by a half moon of glass walls. Gray vinyl seats with black armrests were bolted onto burgundy carpeted floors. Kyle wore jeans and a white dress shirt, with sleeves rolled to the elbow. He appeared relaxed, enjoying his morning paper and coffee.

Dawn had broken through the windows behind Kyle '01 some 20 minutes earlier, flooding the terminus with brilliant golden light. Passengers approaching the gate winced and shielded their eyes. Kyle '01 was a dark silhouette against the morning sun.

Kyle '01 had arrived early for the flight to Los Angeles, scheduled to depart at 07:45 hours. Not knowing what the hijackers looked like, he wanted to try to ID possible candidates prior to boarding. Kyle had breezed through the security checkpoint at B5 without incident—this despite the fact that he carried a Leatherman utility knife in his pocket. Two burgundy-vested female employees of Global Aviation Services, the private contractor hired by American Airlines to perform passenger screening, gossiped and joked with each other, scarcely glancing at their monitors as luggage rolled through the X-ray conveyor.

Kyle '01 shook his head at the impotent security procedure. *I should have packed my gun,* he thought.

• • •

In 2001, airlines were charged with the responsibility of making sure passengers didn't bring weapons onto planes. Airline carriers, conscious of cost, outsourced security to companies like Global Aviation Services, which often hired relatively unskilled minimum-wage workers to ensure the nation's friendly skies. Though advocates for greater air travel security repeatedly warned the industry and members of congress that lax procedures would result in disaster, they were generally dismissed. The rationale was that because a disaster hadn't happened, the current process must be good enough. The airline carriers' calculus was that catastrophes were less expensive than the cost of adequate security.

Security holes were not restricted to contract security workers—the system was riddled with vulnerabilities. Magnetometers were calibrated to detect the metal in a small gun—they would not reveal small knives or non-metallic weapons. Passengers were permitted to carry certain kinds of small knives onto planes. The early-generation Computer-Assisted Passenger Prescreening System (CAPPS) identified high-risk individuals for additional screening, but that screening was limited to the passengers' luggage—no wanding or pat-downs were conducted on the travelers themselves. It was not unusual for security staff to ignore CAPPS altogether and skip additional luggage inspection.

• • •

Kyle '01 watched the sunlit passengers as they entered the gate area. While he knew he was looking for young Middle Eastern men, he didn't know much else. He had repeatedly tried to call Kyle '08 to get more intel, but he got voicemail instead. The Kyles had agreed not to call unless something went seriously wrong with the mission. Though this situation qualified as "seriously wrong," Kyle '08's phone was probably switched off—they kept their phones off during hits to avoid a ring or buzz while they were in stealth mode. Kyle '08 was either working his targets or had forgotten to turn his phone back on. Kyle '01 knew that the hijackers were seated in the first- and business-class compartments. Kyle '01 had purchased one of the 11 remaining business-class seats toward the rear of the compartment. That position would enable him to approach from the rear and surprise one or two of the hijackers, improving his current five-to-one odds.

In addition to his Leatherman knife, Kyle was armed with one useful piece of intel—Mohamed Atta's mobile phone number. The number that Kyle '08 had shared "just in case" would be put to good use now.

The passengers of American 11 and other flights began to arrive in the gate area. Kyle '01's perfect vantage down the corridor gave him ample opportunity to observe them from hundreds of feet away. Men and women approached, most dressed casually, some in suits, many holding coffee cups. Kyle '01 scanned each one carefully. No candidates.

Kyle '01's eyes locked onto two young men, walking together. They were Middle Eastern in appearance, clean-shaven with short black hair. One was wearing a blue dress shirt with black pants and carrying a black shoulder bag. The other was wearing a short-sleeved cream-colored dress shirt and khaki pants. Unlike most of the other passengers, Kyle '01 noticed that these two were wide awake. Undistracted by their surroundings, they had focused, purposeful, forward-looking stares. Kyle '01 slipped his phone out of his pocket and keyed a speed dial code for the phone number 305 496 2443.

Kyle '01 watched the two men as they continued to approach, now 100 feet away. Kyle '01 saw the man in the blue shirt reach into his pocket and pull out a mobile phone.

"Allo," Kyle '01 heard Mohamed Atta's voice.

"¿Cómo estás?" Kyle asked in Spanish, holding the phone behind his paper.

Kyle '01 saw Atta hang up, annoyed.

Gotcha, Kyle thought.

As Atta and his companion approached, Kyle '01 was able to make out more detail. Atta was short and slight, with thin, tight lips and menacing eyes.

Unbeknownst to Kyle '01, his companion was Abdul Aziz al Omari. Al Omari had a boyish face and was slightly taller than Atta. As the two men entered the gate area, they scouted out an unpopulated row of seats in which to sit. The two sat side by side and didn't speak.

Minutes later, Kyle '01 noticed the approach of three more young men who fit the profile. Two of the men walked ahead of the third. Kyle '01 continued to look at his newspaper as he monitored the men's' approach. All three men were small—Kyle '01 estimated their height at only five and a half feet. All were clean-shaven with short black hair. They all wore jeans. The two in front wore dress shirts—one blue, one white. The third man bringing up the rear wore a beige polo shirt with a gold chain around his neck. The two men in front were Wail and Waleed al Shehri, the brothers who had failed to appear as scheduled for assassination at Boston's Park Inn a few hours earlier.

Kyle watched to see where the trio would sit. They saw Atta and al Omari and sat in the row of seats facing them. They did not speak to each other, but Kyle '01 noticed Atta nod his head slightly, acknowledging his fellow hijackers. This was the team—five young men, convinced that the lives of thousands of innocent men and women would buy them tickets to paradise, where 72 virgins would service them for eternity.

At 07:25, the gate attendant called for first-class passengers to board the plane. The al Shehri brothers glanced at each other and then rose to follow a handful of other passengers onto the plane.

Several minutes later, the gate attendant called for business-class passengers to board the plane. Atta and al Omari nodded at each other and got in the boarding line. Al Suqami followed them in line.

Though Kyle '01 held a business-class boarding pass, he waited to board until the gate attendant called for coach passengers. He wanted the hijackers settled in their seats so he could scope the landscape as he entered the plane. Kyle '01 stood in a line with the rest of the passengers in the narrow metal jet bridge corridor to the Boeing 767 plane. As he entered the cabin, he was directed to his seat, 10D, in business class. The business-class interior was standard white plastic walls and overhead compartments, with wide blue leather seats. There were three columns of two-seat rows, with blue-carpeted aisles on the left and right dividing them.

Kyle '01's seat, 10D was in the center column of seats in the next-to-last row. The seat to his right, 10G, was vacant. To his left, across the aisle, Satam al Suqami sat in 10B. 10B was slightly to the rear of Kyle '01's seat, requiring him to peer to his left shoulder to see al Suqami.

Not great, Kyle '01 thought, but al Suqami would be moving forward toward the cockpit, enabling him to get a drop on the hijacker from behind.

Kyle '01 got up from his seat and walked to the forward lavatory in first class, located off the left aisle. Flight attendants were busy hanging suit coats and offering beverages to first and business-class passengers while the remaining coach passengers boarded and settled.

After a minute, Kyle '01 exited the lavatory. The al Shehri brothers were directly in front of him on the first row of first class. They stared directly ahead, avoiding eye contact with Kyle '01 as he walked past them on their right.

As Kyle '01 reentered the business-class section, he spotted Mohamed Atta and al Omari in the second center row, seats 8D and 8G. Atta was next to the left aisle, al Omari on the right. Kyle '01 returned to his seat and buckled in.

The flight attendants provided the requisite safety demonstrations, including operation of seatbelts, oxygen masks, and life vests. Kyle '01's heart was pounding. He focused on his breathing as he began to visualize his plan.

The al Shehri brothers' primary task was likely to overpower the flight attendants and gain access to the cockpit, allowing Atta and al Omari access. Al Suqami was likely positioned as a rear guard in case of trouble. Kyle '01 would need to take out al Suqami first, then Atta. By terminating their pilot and leader, his odds of success would greatly increase. The others could cause trouble in the cockpit, but they couldn't fly the plane. Taking out the last three hijackers would be the challenge. There were too many variables to sketch out a precise plan. He would be forced to improvise.

Though outnumbered five to one, Kyle '01 knew he had two things going for him. The first was that the narrow aisles largely negated the hijackers' superior numbers advantage. They could only engage Kyle '01 one at a time. He also knew his superior conditioning and training gave him an edge.

At 07:46, the plane pushed back from the gate and began to taxi toward the runway. He slipped his Leatherman out of his right pocket and unfolded the blade, setting it on the seat next to his right thigh under his newspaper. Kyle '01 didn't plan to use the knife—it would likely get in the way during the engagement. The knife was a contingency.

At 07:59, the 767 throttled up and accelerated down the runway for takeoff, gently lifting into the air moments later.

As the plane climbed into the clear blue sky, Kyle '01 focused on his breathing and visualizing the coming scenario. He hated the anticipation he'd felt before the fight, and he forced himself to shove those feelings out of his mind. He was a professional soldier. He was on a mission. He needed to be present.

At 08:14, the plane's upward pitch diminished to a more subtle climb angle. In the forward galley, the flight attendants began to prepare for the beverage service. Kyle '01 unbuckled his seatbelt.

Moments later, he saw the al Shehri brothers rise from their seats in first class. Atta and al Omari leapt from their seats and moved forward up the left aisle. There was yelling and screaming in first class. A large man, dressed in a black dress shirt and jeans in the left aisle of business class, one row ahead of Kyle '01's, got out of his seat and started to move forward to assist. Al Suqami sprang from his seat with a box cutter in his right hand. He reached for the black-shirted man's throat with his knife.

Kyle '01 leapt from his seat and side kicked al Suqami with the blade of his foot in the back of his right knee, simultaneously grabbing his right wrist. Al Suqami screamed in pain and surprise as his leg buckled, and Kyle '01 knocked him to the floor. With a single punch to al Suqami's throat, Kyle '01 crushed his windpipe.

The man in black wheeled around to see the commotion behind him.

"Get down!" Kyle '01 shouted.

Behind the man in black, al Omari was running toward him, wielding a box cutter in his right hand. The man in black ducked as Kyle '01, crouched on the floor, grabbed the Leatherman in his seat and hurled it at al Omari's face.

Kyle '01 knew the Leatherman wasn't a balanced throwing knife. Though he didn't expect to do serious damage with the throw, even if the knife hit al Omari's face with the blunt end, it could buy a split second for Kyle '01 to position for the kill.

To Kyle '01's surprise, the Leatherman blade hit al Omari squarely in his left eye. The metal handle protruded from his eye socket. Al Omari screamed, joined by the screams and shouts from passengers in business class as they began to scramble out of their seats. The man in black seemed more awestruck than shocked. He grabbed the flailing, screaming al Omari from behind and broke his neck with a crisp twist. Al Omari fell to the aisle floor, limp.

"Nice throw," the man in black said. "I owe you."

"My pleasure," Kyle '01 said. "Special Forces?"

"Danny Lewin," the man replied. "Sayeret Matkal."

"No shit?" Kyle '01 said. "Kyle Mason, Delta Force."

Kyle '01 couldn't believe his crazy good luck. He knew the Sayeret Matkal, an elite counter-terrorist special forces unit of the Israel Defense Force. Kyle '01 could not have asked for a more perfect warrior companion.

Danny pulled the knife from al Omari's face and handed it to Kyle '01. Al-Omari's dead body shuddered.

"I believe this is yours," Danny said.

Kyle '01 took the knife, wiping the blade on his jeans. "Let's go," he said, motioning for Danny to move forward up the left aisle while Kyle '01 slipped to the right. In front of the cockpit door, Wail al Shehri held a box cutter in his left hand and a mace can in the right. At the sight of the two commandos, he began to scream in Arabic and swing his box cutter wildly. Danny grabbed a pot of hot coffee from the galley and splashed it in al Shehri's face. As an encore, he gave the hijacker a stiff whack on his scalded face with the pot, breaking his nose. Al Shehri screamed and cursed, flailing his knife wildly in the air and spraying mace. Kyle '01 moved to grab the wrist of the hijacker's knife hand. At that moment, the plane tilted to the left, throwing all three men off balance. Kyle '01 missed al Shehri's wrist. He felt the hijacker's knife accidentally cut his neck as he crashed into the plane's main cabin door. Blood began to pulse from the wound.

Danny regained his balance and unloaded a side kick to al

Shehri's gut, doubling him over. He followed up with a flying front kick that connected with the hijacker's chin, snapping his head back against the cockpit door. Al Shehri crumpled to the floor, unconscious. Danny looked at Kyle '01. Kyle '01's hand was pressed against his neck. Danny could see from the blood pouring from between Kyle '01's fingers that he was in trouble.

"Danny, we don't have much time," Kyle '01 said. "Get some help and I'll brief you."

Kyle '01 felt his legs begin to buckle beneath him. He slumped against the main cabin door and slid to the floor, pressing his fingers against his neck wound.

Danny called for help. In moments, Danny, the flight attendants, and several passengers were huddled around him.

One of the flight attendants knelt beside Kyle '01 and applied a damp towel to his neck wound.

"My name is Betty. I'll take care of you," she said with a kind smile.

Kyle '01 reached into his pant pocket with his blood-soaked hand and retrieved his military ID to show to the dozen people gathered around him.

"My name is Kyle Mason," he said. "I'm a major with the Army 1st Special Forces Operational Detachment-Delta."

"Delta Force," Danny echoed.

"Danny here is with Sayeret Matkal, Israeli special forces. Here's our situation. Hijackers have taken control of the plane. We've taken out three. Two remain in the cockpit. They are flying the plane. They are on a suicide mission to crash this plane into the World Trade Center's North Tower. You cannot negotiate with them. You must retake control of the plane or everyone on this plane and a thousand more people in the tower will die. Do you understand?"

Danny, the flight attendants, and the passengers nodded and softly voiced, "Yes."

"They may claim to have a bomb," Kyle '01 continued, "but they don't. They have knives and mace. Nothing else. What time is it?"

Danny looked at his watch. "8:22," he said.

"You've got about 20 minutes," Kyle '01 said. "Betty, you've got keys to the cockpit?"

"Yes," she said.

"Give them to Danny," Kyle '01 said.

Kyle '01 looked at the group. "What are your names?" he asked.

"I'm Chris."

"I'm Phil."

"I'm Amy."

"I'm John."

"Dianne."

"Barbara."

"Karleton."

"Peter."

"Carol."

"David."

"Renee."

"Jeff."

"Sara."

"Jean."

"Karen."

“It is a privilege to meet you,” Kyle ’01 said, smiling. The passengers and crew returned his smile.

“I don’t know what you did for a living yesterday, but today, you are heroes,” said Kyle ’01. “There are only two of them against many of you. They don’t stand a chance. Danny will make the plan. He knows what he’s doing. Listen to him.”

“Now, go get your plane back,” said Kyle ’01.

The team nodded. “Yes!”

The team withdrew to make their plan. Kyle ’01 closed his eyes and sighed, slumping against the door. He felt weight on his back as the plane banked to the left. The hijackers were following the Hudson River south to Manhattan and the towers.

“Thank you, Betty,” Kyle ’01 said.

“I’ve got you,” Betty said. “Just take it easy and hang on.”

Boston Air Route Traffic Control Center

Nashua, NH

September 11, 2001

08:20 hours

In a darkened room, Air Traffic Control Specialist Pete Zalewski sat in front of his console watching an array of lines and characters on his display. Clusters of glowing green characters on his screen, known as "targets," represented vital information for the aircraft he was charged with managing in his airspace—identification, altitude, and airspeed. The targets moved along vector lines on the display, representing each aircraft's direction.

The information displayed in the target clusters was signaled to air traffic control by transponders on the aircraft. The detailed altitude, speed, and direction data supplied by these transponders enabled controllers to manage a multitude of aircraft simultaneously with precision.

Along with dozens of colleagues, Zalewski was charged with managing air traffic over one of the busiest airspaces in the country. Millions of planes, carrying tens of millions of passengers, were directed by the Boston Traffic Control Center each year. Pete's job, like that of his colleagues, was to make sure that these planes stayed out of each other's way.

One of the targets on Pete's screen had him worried. After issuing a routine set of instructions to the pilot of American Flight 11, the pilot had failed to acknowledge his order to climb to an altitude of "350"—35,000 feet. In the six minutes since American 11 went dark, Pete had tried to raise the flight a dozen times, varying radio frequencies, even using the emergency channel. One of his colleagues, Tom Roberts, asked another American flight in the area to contact American 11 on American's company channel—no good. American 11 was "NORDO"—no radio contact.

Suddenly, the target on Pete's screen changed direction, veering to the right. It was off course, headed for Albany, New York. Moments later, the transponder data disappeared from Pete's screen. American 11 had turned its transponder off. Pete and his fellow controllers were flying blind.

Pete and his fellow controllers scrambled to create a safe zone, clearing the airspace in front of American 11. While the controllers could still determine the plane's location and direction from ground radar data, without the transponder's altitude data, the controllers were forced to move planes from a huge swath of airspace—from the ground all the way up to 35,000 feet.

Minutes later, Pete watched American 11 make another unauthorized turn—this time to the south. Seconds later, a voice sounded on American 11's frequency.

"We have some planes. Just stay quiet and you'll be OK. We are returning to the airport," said Mohamed Atta.

Atta thought he was communicating to the passengers via the plane's PA system. He was unaware that American 11's captain,

John Ogonowski, had discreetly held down the push-to-talk button on his steering yoke, enabling Boston Air Traffic Control to hear Atta's commands to the passengers and crew.

Seconds later, Pete heard Atta's voice again. "Nobody move. Everything will be OK. If you try to make any moves, you'll endanger yourselves and the airplane. Just stay quiet."

Horrified, Pete shouted for his supervisor, John Shippani. "John! Get over here *right now!*"

American Airlines Flight 11

Southeast New York

September 11, 2001

08:35 hours

Kyle '01's face was pale. His white dress shirt was drenched crimson with blood. He had seen enough people bleed out on the battlefield to know that he didn't have much time. Assuming Danny's assault team succeeded in retaking the plane, assuming the pilots put the plane down at JFK, and assuming emergency personnel were waiting at the tarmac, Kyle '01's heart would still stop beating about five minutes before the main door opened.

Betty sat next to Kyle '01 on the floor, holding a blood-soaked towel against the right side of his neck. Kyle saw that Betty was trying hard to mask her distress for him.

Kyle '01 reached into his pocket with a bloody hand to retrieve his phone.

"I have to make a call," Kyle '01 said.

"You're not serious," Betty said.

Kyle '01 turned his head slightly to look at Betty, "I have to say goodbye."

Betty began to protest, then stopped.

"Can I help you?" she asked.

"No—thank you—I've got it," Kyle '01 replied.

He keyed the speed dial on his phone. It rang.

"Hello?" Padma answered.

"Are you at home?" Kyle '01 asked.

"Yes, I'm exactly where you told me to be," Padma replied cheerfully. "I miss you. When am I going to see you again?"

Tears began to run down Kyle '01's face. Though he was coming to terms with his death, he couldn't bear to give Padma this terrible news. He paused, struggling to find words.

Kyle? What's wrong?"

"I'm not coming home."

"Oh God! *No*," she gasped. "No! No! *No!*"

Though Padma knew the possibility of Kyle '01's untimely death was a risk that came with their marriage, she'd assumed she would have more than 48 hours of married life with him before she was widowed.

Kyle '01 listened to Padma sob on the phone.

"I am so sorry," Kyle '01 said. "I wanted to live with you. You don't know how much I wanted to live with you."

"I do know," said Padma, crying.

Padma tried to pull herself together. "I need to be strong for you," she said, still crying. "What can I do for you? Tell me what you need."

"I was supposed to be the one to protect you," said Kyle '01.

"I know that you already have," said Padma.

Betty continued to press the blood-soaked towel against Kyle '01's neck. Tears rolled down her cheeks.

"Beloved," Kyle '01 said, "know that if there is any way I can be with you, I will. I promise I will. There is no other place I want to be."

"I am selfish, but I don't want you to rest. I want you to haunt me forever," she said.

"I will be your ghost. I feel sorry for the next guy who tries to date you."

Padma laughed through the tears. Kyle '01 loved her deep laugh.

"I don't," she said. "I want to see the look on his face when you rattle your chains."

Danny appeared in the galley space in front of Kyle '01. He looked at Kyle '01. It was time.

"I am so sorry, love. I have to go now," said Kyle '01.

Padma sobbed.

"Goodbye my love," he said.

"Goodbye, beloved," Padma cried. "Please take my love with you."

"I will, love. Always."

Kyle '01 heard Padma crying as he closed his phone and set it on the floor. He wiped tears from his face. Kyle '01 heard the engines throttle back and felt the plane descend—rapidly. They didn't have much time. He looked up at Danny.

"You good to go?" Kyle '01 asked Danny.

"We're set," Danny replied.

"All right then, rock and roll," Kyle '01 said.

Danny nodded to the others in the aisle. A phalanx of passengers and crew huddled behind him. Karen Martin, a flight attendant, pushed past Danny to take her position at the cockpit door, key in hand. Chris Mello, a strapping football and rugby star, stood to the right of the cockpit door, armed with a fire extinguisher. Karleton Fyfe, a financial analyst, stood behind him as backup. Flight attendants Jeff Collman and Sara Low took up positions in the galley, ready to hand off pots of boiling water and fire extinguishers to the assault team. Behind the assault team, every crewmember and passenger were queued up in both aisles, ready to back up the first wave team in case they failed. The plane was descending rapidly, flying erratically. The passengers and crew steadied themselves as best they could by holding seats and bulkheads.

Kyle '01, too fragile to move, remained propped against the main cabin door. Betty huddled with him.

"GO!" said Danny.

Karen turned the key and door latch. Danny kicked the door hard. Waleed al Shehri was caught flat-footed, watching the view out the cockpit windshield, his back leaning against the cockpit door. The door knocked him forward, his face crashing on the cockpit's center console. He screamed as Danny grabbed him by the collar and belt and tossed him out of the cockpit and onto his back on the floor. Chris smacked al Shehri hard in the face with the fire extinguisher. He screamed as his nose and skull cracked. Jeff and Sara dumped boiling water on his face for good measure as the passengers began pummeling the life out of the hijacker.

Danny rushed the cockpit, followed by Chris. At the base of a brilliant blue sky, northern Manhattan was coming into view through the panoramic cockpit windshield. Atta was seated in the co-pilot's seat on the right, with Captain John Ogonowski still seated, slumped over, in the pilot's seat. First Officer Tom McGuinness was strapped into the jump seat behind the captain. He was injured but alive. Hearing the commotion behind him, Atta whipped his head around to see Danny and Chris.

"Don't make any stupid moves!" screamed Atta.

"They've got a bomb!" yelled Tom McGuinness, pointing at a device on the cockpit floor, a piece of clay with wires and a circuit board.

Danny grabbed the fake bomb and ripped out the wires.

"They've got Play-Doh," said Danny, dropping the contraption and reaching for Atta's head.

Atta turned the aircraft yoke sharply, rolling the plane to its right. Danny and Chris were thrown against the cockpit wall. Atta rolled the plane to the left, and the assault team crashed against the opposite wall. Screams erupted from the main cabin. Chris fell across Tom McGuinness' knees, as Tom unstrapped himself from the jump seat to assist.

Atta continued to roll to the left, inverting the plane. Danny, the passengers, and the crew were tossed onto the plane's ceiling. Atta throttled the plane's engines to 100 percent. The engines roared in response as the plane hurtled toward the city.

The plane magically began to right itself. Danny saw that Captain Ogonowski had gripped his yoke and was fighting Atta for control of the plane. Though badly injured, the former Air Force pilot was still more than a match for the puny hijacker.

Atta screamed and cursed as he fought the captain for control. The plane was over the city. The Twin Towers were directly ahead.

Danny lunged for Atta, holding one of the hijackers' box cutters in his right hand. He grabbed Atta by the hair.

"Time to disembark," Danny said, slashing Atta's throat with the razor knife. Atta sputtered blood and air, clutching his throat. Danny and Chris pulled Atta out of the seat and dumped him on the cockpit floor as First Officer McGuinness leapt into the co-pilot's chair. Danny strapped into the jump seat. With its South Tower shadow, North Tower was dead ahead, seconds from impact.

"I'm gonna take it on the right," shouted Captain Ogonowski.

"Roger that, I'm with you," replied First Officer McGuinness.

The 767 was hurtling toward the tower at nearly 600 miles per hour, shaking as it streaked through the heavy low-altitude air. The plane shuddered as Ogonowski and McGuinness wrestled with their controls, fighting to overcome the plane's fierce inertia. The 767, shaking violently, began to bank right. The tower grew larger in the windshield. The vertical silver bars of its exoskeleton crystallized into sharp relief. Tom McGuinness whispered the Lord's Prayer.

"C'mon!" Captain Ogonowski shouted, gritting his teeth as the plane veered right. He knew they weren't going to make it. His left wing was going to hit the tower.

Suddenly, Captain Ogonowski threw the yoke to the right, rolling the plane on its right side. The belly of the 767 faced the tower's east side as it roared past with a few yards to spare. The thick windows of the tower rattled madly as shocked workers inside watched the plane rocket past, flying over the Statue of Liberty as it leveled out and began to climb above the Upper Bay.

"Sierra Hotel, Cap'n!" exclaimed Tom McGuinness, using fighter-pilot code for "Hot Shit." A deeply religious man, Tom was not in the habit of cursing, but he hoped the Lord might give him a pass this one time.

"Never simulated that one before," replied Captain Ogonowski. "Can you hit the transponder, Tom?"

Tom switched on the plane's transponder. Forty miles away, in Islip, New York, the controllers monitoring American 11 at New York Air Traffic Control Center instantly saw AA11's target flash on their displays.

Captain Ogonowski keyed the radio. "New York approach this is American 11, squawking code 4361. Position, 20 miles south of JFK declaring an emergency. Requesting ILS for JFK runway 4Left."

"Roger American 11, state the nature of your emergency please," replied air traffic control.

"The aircraft was hijacked. We have restrained the hijackers. We are not subject to interference now. Repeat, we are not at 7500," replied Captain Ogonowski—"7500" was the transponder code used by pilots to discretely communicate to air traffic control that their plane had been hijacked.

Unbeknownst to the captain, two F-15 fighter jets had already been scrambled from Otis Air National Guard Base in Massachusetts, with orders to intercept the 767.

"American 11. New York, be advised, we have injured onboard. Please have emergency medical personnel standing by to meet the aircraft."

"American 11, roger, scrambling EMT personnel to meet you."

Captain Ogonowski then keyed the plane's PA system. "This is Captain Ogonowski. The hijackers have been defeated. We have control of the aircraft."

The cockpit crew could hear the cheers and shouts from the cabin, drawing smiles from Captain Ogonowski and First Officer McGuinness.

"We're going to need to cut the celebration short, as we're preparing to land at JFK," the captain continued. "The aircraft is in good condition and we expect a normal landing. Please take your seats at this time and fasten your seatbelts. Flight attendants, please prepare for landing."

Passengers who had been strewn about the cabin during the plane's convulsions were guided back to their seats by the flight attendants. Some had sustained minor injuries as they had been tossed about.

Danny unstrapped from the jump seat and ran out of the cockpit to check on Kyle '01. He found him lying on the dark bloodstained carpeted floor in front of the main door. Betty was kneeling beside him. She looked up at Danny and shook her head. Kyle '01's cold eyes were open, staring at the ceiling. At that moment, flight attendant Amy Sweeny approached from the rear of the aircraft, holding a blue blanket. She draped it over Kyle '01, covering his face.

Minutes later, American 11 touched down on runway 4L of John F. Kennedy Airport in a textbook landing.

Times Square

New York, NY

September 11, 2001

10:28 hours

Kyle '08 snapped his phone shut. He had tried again to call Kyle '01 without success. '08's mission to Virginia had been routine. A few hours earlier, he'd killed all five American Flight 77 hijackers as they slept at the Residence Inn in Herndon, Virginia. He then checked in his rental car and caught the train to New York. He didn't want to return to his time until he was able to debrief with '01. He exited Penn Station and strolled up Seventh Avenue to Times Square. It was the last time he would see the world outside the Time Tunnel complex bubble. It was a gorgeous day—a good day to spend his last day on real earth.

The good news was that the towers were standing, and things seemed to be normal in the Big Apple. Times Square was its usual bustling self, with native New Yorkers hurrying to get where they were going, competing for sidewalk space with tourists who gawked at the dazzling marquees.

Against all odds, Kyle '08 had accomplished his mission, with the help of his younger self. The enormity of what he had done had not completely sunk in. Kyle '08 observed the people in Times

Square—thousands of people on the sidewalk—hurrying to appointments, arguing with bodega operators, or simply taking in the view. They had no idea what their alternate selves had experienced in another time, where they were frozen in horror as the North Tower was collapsing at that very moment. Here, in this time, things were precisely the way they were meant to be. Ignorance was truly bliss, even if the food stand operator had forgotten to put the cream in his customer's coffee.

Kyle '08 glanced at a jumbo Times Square marquee display and stopped dead in his tracks. On a news board over 50 feet in the air, Kyle's face was brilliantly displayed. His name and Army rank of major appeared beneath his picture. Other news marquees displayed images of an airplane at JFK surrounded by emergency vehicles with flashing lights—it was American 11! Kyle's face appeared on other marquees, along with pictures of the pilots and a man named Daniel Lewin.

Kyle '08 read the flashing news tickers to try to understand what had happened.

"Holy shit!" he said.

Kyle '01 was dead. The Army Special Forces major was being hailed as a hero, along with Daniel Lewin and the crew and passengers of American Flight 11, who had fought valiantly to retake their plane from a handful of radical Islamist hijackers intending to crash the plane into the World Trade Center. This marked the second time that radical Islamic terrorists from the Middle East had tried to destroy the WTC. It was the second time they had failed. The best of the best of the fanatics had been beaten by a handful of passengers and flight attendants. America was indestructible.

Kyle '08 was stunned, but he didn't have time to contemplate what had gone south with the mission. He was standing in one of the busiest places on the planet, with his face screaming from giant marquee façades on multiple Times Square buildings. He would be recognized in seconds. He reached for the temporal transponder in his pocket. He slid open the cover on the device and keyed in the code that deactivated the safety. A small LCD screen on the device read "ARMED." The red transponder activation button blinked red. The device was armed and ready, waiting for him to press the blinking button.

Time Tunnel

Mission Control
October 27, 2008
08:15 hours

"All staff, time is T-minus five minutes. We are at final system check," said Gus. "Respond when called."

"Reactor," Gus said.

"Reactor go," replied an engineer. "Power at 30 percent. Go for throttle up."

"Temporal engine," said Gus.

"Temporal engine go," replied another engineer.

"Navigation."

"Temporal navigation go."

"Bio."

"Bio go."

"Transponder."

"Transponder go."

"All systems, all staff, punch your status buttons now," said Gus.

At that moment, the hundreds of people throughout the complex tied to the operation of the Time Tunnel pushed one of two buttons—green or red. A single red button would abort the time jump. Gus watched the board for results:

Percentage of respondents: 100%

Percentage green: 100%

Percentage red: 0%

"Throttle power to 60 percent," ordered Gus. "Retract tunnel moorings."

Gus and the general watched the live video feed of the Time Tunnel chamber on the giant screen. The cables supporting the donut ring detached and retracted into the ceiling. The platform that supported the sphere retracted into the floor. The ring and sphere, supported with magnetic repulsion, floated in space like a man-made Saturn.

Inside the chamber, Kyle and Annika could see their sphere ascend some 20 feet, to half the height of the room. The carbon donut rose with the sphere. The silence in the sphere was replaced by a deep hum, bringing with it a vibration that trembled gently through their bodies. It was time.

"Any last words?" asked Kyle.

"I'm scared," replied Annika.

He reached for her hand. She grasped his tightly and closed her eyes.

The hum increased in intensity, accompanied by a bright white light. The light did not appear to have a source—it was simply as though the brightness of the room's lighting had been turned up to an uncomfortable level.

Inside mission control, Gus turned to the general. "General, we are ready to proceed on your order."

"Proceed," the general replied.

"General, please insert your key into the panel. Wait for my mark before you turn the key," said Gus.

Both men removed their lanyards and inserted the keys into the panel in front of them.

Gus said, "Turn on my mark—three—two—one—mark!"

Both men turned their keys. The status lamp next to the "Armed" indicator turned from green to red. A red "Armed" indicator flashed on all monitor displays in mission control and throughout the Time Tunnel complex . A klaxon alarm sounded. A large button on Gus' panel marked "Commit" flashed on.

"Reactor—throttle power to 100 percent," said Gus.

"Throttle to 100—roger that," came the reply.

The command to throttle up power threw the Time Tunnel's energy reactor into overdrive. In the chamber beneath which Kyle and Annika stood, matter and antimatter were injected in equal parts, annihilating with monstrous energy.

Inside the Time Tunnel's glass bubble, Kyle and Annika felt the vibration increase dramatically, accompanied by an increase in lighting brightness. Even through their tightly shut eyelids, the light strained their eyes. The vibration shook them forcefully, but they did not lose their balance. Kyle realized that it was not the chamber that was vibrating—it was their bodies. The very atoms that comprised them were shaking like vibrating grains of sand.

Gus reached for the "Commit" button. He looked at the general. The general nodded. Gus pressed the button.

The giant monitor beamed a blinding white light from the chamber video feed, forcing the mission control staff to turn away.

Moments later, the light faded as system power levels dropped to zero. The monitor flickered back to life. The Time Tunnel chamber was empty. Kyle and Annika were gone.

Strangelove was the first to speak. "They're gone, and we're still here…so far, so good."

It was the understatement of all time. The fact that the Time Tunnel team was alive and aware of what had transpired not only meant that Kyle and Annika had been sent through time—it also meant that the Time Tunnel complex had been moved outside of time. October 27, 2008 was the genesis of an entirely new timeline, in a parallel universe that spanned only 20 million square feet, with a population of 10,000 humans. It was completely self-contained, totally independent of their former world.

"Status check. How does the temporal bubble look?" asked Gus.

"All indicators are green," replied John Kaomea. After a pause, he said, "We did it."

The Temporal Variance Alert cube lit up, and a companion alarm sounded. The letters "TVA" were displayed on the big screen in blinking red letters.

Roger Summit and his team pounced on their workstations, identifying variances in the timeline. Impatient for news, the general interrupted after a few moments.

"Roger? Anything?" he asked.

Roger's face morphed from anxiety to a wide smile. The general looked over his shoulder to view the image on his display.

"Punch it up on the big screen," the general said. "Punch it up on all the screens in the complex."

Cheers erupted throughout the complex, and people began to sob and hug each other as they watched a live video feed from a weather channel. Taken from Hoboken, New Jersey, the Twin Towers stood, gleaming on a beautiful sunny day. Sunlight flickered off the Hudson as a sailboat lazily trekked along the river. The general was unable to fight back the fount of emotion. He wiped tears from his face. Lara Meredith put a comforting hand on the old man's back. He turned and embraced her.

As the others celebrated, Gus alternated his gaze between his console and the video feed of the Time Tunnel chamber. Both were completely quiet. Gus knew the temponauts should have reappeared in the chamber almost instantly after they departed.

"General," Gus said, concerned.

"What is it, Gus?" said the general, his face still beaming.

"General, we haven't received a transponder signal," said Gus. "Colonel Mason and Colonel Wise should have signaled and returned to the Time Tunnel chamber by now."

The smile evaporated from the general's face.

At the history hive, Roger's team continued working through the celebration, taking rapid inventory of how time had changed.

"Roger, you need to look at this," shouted Aysha Voong over the noise of the celebration. She hit a button on her keyboard and dispatched a short summary of news headlines to Roger's workstation. Other members of his team followed with their own urgent findings in rapid-fire succession, dispatching news and information excerpts to Roger's workstation.

"Oh no," Roger exclaimed, terrified. "Oh my God, *no!*"

He looked at his team members' faces around the history cluster. They mirrored his expression of horror.

The general glanced at them. He could not hear what they were saying, but he could tell something was very wrong.

The general walked over to Roger's workstation. "What's wrong?" he asked.

Roger, overwhelmed, could barely speak. He began to hyperventilate.

"Roger, breathe," the general said, "and tell me what the hell is going on."

"General, Colonel Mason is dead," said Roger.

The general took a step back, as though he had been sucker-punched.

"Something went wrong. He was on American 11 and was killed retaking the plane from the hijackers," explained Roger.

The general shot a glance at the video feed of the Time Tunnel chamber—it was still empty. Annika had not returned.

"What about Colonel Wise?" asked the general.

"There's nothing in the historical record about Colonel Wise. She should have returned," said Roger. "General, there's something else..."

"What?"

"General, someone is showing up in the timeline who never existed before 9/11," Roger gasped. "His name is Anderson Wild. He appears out of nowhere. He owns huge chunks of major companies—tech companies, aerospace companies, more. He took outsized positions in credit default swaps in 2007 and made hundreds of billions of dollars. He's worth more than the Fortune 100 – *combined!*

"He's a recluse, very secretive," continued Roger. "We've only been able to find one picture of him. The quality is very poor, but..."

Roger pivoted his computer display to the general. The general's expression went to shock.

"General," Roger said, "there's more. There's *much* more..."

At that moment, another alarm sounded. It was the klaxon of the Time Tunnel vault door on Level 1. The noise of the celebration faded to silence.

Strangelove was the first to speak. "No! That is not possible."

"Who's coming through the door?" asked the general. "Give me a view of the door cameras."

Gus punched up the cameras—they showed only static.

"General, you don't understand..." said Strangelove.

"Show me the Level 1 cameras," shouted the general.

Again—static.

"General!" shouted Strangelove. "You don't understand! The complex is outside time. There is nothing outside. The only way into the complex is through the Time Tunnel chamber."

The general again looked at the empty chamber—nothing.

"General! There is nothing outside the door!" Strangelove shouted.

The brilliant blue strobes of the Time Tunnel vault door began to flash as the great locks unlatched, and the door began to swing open. A man was standing in the doorway. Backlit against the anteroom lighting, it was difficult to make out his features. He took a step out of the shadows into mission control. The man was dressed in an expensive solid black suit over a sleek black V-neck T-shirt. He had aged nearly a decade in the few minutes since the general had last seen him.

It was Kyle Mason.

— END OF BOOK 1 —

Kyle Mason will return.

THE AUTHOR gratefully acknowledges the generous assistance of Andrea Meredith, Ph.D., who performed RFLP analysis on the Grays.

The author also gratefully acknowledges the generous assistance of Captain John Powell for his expert consultation regarding air traffic control communication.

ABOUT THE AUTHOR

RICHARD TODD is an entrepreneur, author, and inventor. As a contributor to the *Huffington Post* and the *San Francisco Chronicle*, he has written on a variety of subjects, including climate change, science education, and economics.

His interview subjects include astrophysicist Neil deGrasse Tyson, Virgin Group founder and chairman Sir Richard Branson, economist and EU advisor Jeremy Rifkin, astrophysicist Brian Greene, Apple co-founder Steve Wozniak, Pulitzer Prize-winning author Jane Smiley, IBM "Watson" supercomputer team leader David Ferrucci, and *Who Killed the Electric Car*'s Chelsea Sexton.

Richard Todd holds four patents in the field of information technology.

He lives on a ranch in Carmel Valley with his wife, Laura, and the many rescue animals under their care.

Made in the USA
Coppell, TX
30 August 2020

35830217R00226